Highest Praise for
John Lutz

"John Lutz knows how to make you shiver."
—Harlan Coben

"Lutz offers up a heart-pounding roller coaster of a
tale."
—Jeffery Deaver

"John Lutz is one of the masters of the police novel."
—Ridley Pearson

"John Lutz is a major talent."
—John Lescroart

"I've been a fan for years."
—T. Jefferson Parker

"John Lutz just keeps getting better and better."
—Tony Hillerman

"Lutz ranks with such vintage masters of big-city
murder
as Lawrence Block and Ed McBain."
—*St. Louis Post-Dispatch*

"Lutz is among the best."
—*San Diego Union*

"Lutz knows how to seize and hold the
reader's imagination."
—*Cleveland Plain Dealer*

"It's easy to see

—

ALSO BY JOHN LUTZ

*featuring Frank Quinn

Available from Kensington Publishing Corp. and
Pinnacle Books

JOHN
LUTZ

PULSE

Mrs. Martine Parker
PO Box 3769
Wenatchee, WA 98807-3769

PINNACLE BOOKS
Kensington Publishing Corp.
www.kensingtonbooks.com

PINNACLE BOOKS are published by

Kensington Publishing Corp.
119 West 40th Street
New York, NY 10018

All Kensington titles, imprints, and distributed lines are available at special quantity discounts for bulk purchases for sales promotions, premiums, fund-raising, educational, or institutional use.

Special book excerpts or customized printings can also be created to fit specific needs. For details, write or phone the office of the Kensington special sales manager: Kensington Publishing Corp., 119 West 40th Street, New York, NY 10018, attn: Special Sales Department; phone 1-800-221-2647.

This book is a work of fiction. Names, characters, businesses, organizations, places, events, and incidents either are the product of the author's imagination or are used fictitiously. Any resemblance to actual persons, living or dead, events, or locales is entirely coincidental.

ISBN-13: 978-0-7860-2028-7
ISBN-10: 0-7860-2028-8

First printing: July 2012

10 9 8 7 6 5 4 3 2 1

Printed in the United States of America

For Jane Ellen Jones
Beautiful soul

PART ONE

There is a panther caged within my breast,
But what his name, there is no breast
   shall know,
Save mine, nor what it is that drives him so
Backward and forward, in relentless quest.

     —JOHN HALL WHEELOCK,
      "The Black Panther"

1

It gave Garvey the creeps, transferring somebody like Daniel Danielle. The sick bastard had been convicted of killing three women, but some estimates had his total at more than a hundred.

They were the women who lived alone and let their guards down because the sicko could be a charmer as a man or a woman. Single women who disappeared and were missed by no one. Those were the kinds of women Daniel Danielle sought and tortured and destroyed.

Nicholson was seated next to Garvey. Like Garvey, he was a big man in a brown uniform. Their job was to transfer Daniel Danielle to a new, and so far secret, maximum-security state prison near Belle Glade, on the other side of the state from Sarasota. It was in Sarasota where Danielle Daniel (he had been dressed as a woman then) had been arrested while crouched over the body of one of his victims, and later convicted. The evidence was overwhelming. As a "calling card" and a taunt, he had put his previous victim's panties on his present victim, panties he had apparently worn to the murder. He was damned by his DNA.

Daniel was all the more dangerous because he was smart as hell. Degrees from Vassar and Harvard, and a fellowship at Oxford. Getting away with murder should have been a piece of cake, like the rest of his life. But it hadn't been. When his appeals were exhausted, he would be executed.

No one was visible on State Highway 72. This part of Florida was flat and undeveloped, mostly green vistas streaked with brown. Cattle country, though cattle were seldom glimpsed from the road except off in the distance. Wind and dust country for sure. Dust devils could be seen taking shape and dissipating on both sides of the road. Miles away, larger wannabe tornados threatened and whirled but didn't quite take form.

The latest weather report said the jet stream had shifted. Hurricane Sophia, closing in on Florida's east coast, now had a predicted path to the south, though not as far south as the dusty white van rocketing along the highway. Taking time to replace a broken fan belt ten miles beyond Arcadia had slowed them down. They were still okay, if the hurricane stayed north. If it didn't, they might be driving right into it.

Now and then a car passed going the other way, with a Doppler change of pitch as the boxy van rocked in the vehicle's wake. Off to the east there were more dust devils, more swirling cloud formations. The insistent internal voice Garvey often heard when some part of his mind knew something bad was about to happen wouldn't shut up.

Suddenly it began to rain. Hard. Garvey switched on the headlights. Hail the size of marbles started smacking and bouncing off the van's windshield and stubby hood.

"Maybe we oughta go back," Nicholson said. "See if we can outrun whatever's headed our way."

"Orders are to deliver the prisoners." Garvey drove faster. The hail slammed harder against the windshield, as if hurled by a giant hand.

The prisoner chained in the back of the van with Daniel Danielle was a young man with lots of muscles and tattoos under his orange prison jumpsuit. He was scarred with old acne and had a face like chipped stone, with a crooked nose and narrow, mean eyes. He was easy to take for a hardened ex-con, but he was actually an undercover cop named Chad Bingham, there for insurance if something weird happened and Daniel Danielle made trouble.

Bingham would rather have been someplace else. He had a wife and two kids. And a job.

The easy part of the job was just sitting there sulking and pretending he was someone else. But the way things were going, he was afraid the hard part was on its way.

The hail kept coming. Nicholson was on the edge of being downright scared. Even if it didn't make landfall nearby, Sophia might spawn tornados. Hurricanes also sometimes unexpectedly changed course. He reached out and turned on the radio, but got nothing but static this far out in the flatlands, away from most civilization.

Garvey could see his partner was getting antsy so he tried to raise Sarasota on the police band. The result was more static. He tried Belle Glade and got the same response.

"Storm's interfering with reception," he said, looking into Nicholson's wide blue eyes. He had never seen the man this rattled.

"Try your cell phone," Nicholson said in a tight voice.

"You kidding?"

Nicholson tried his own cell phone but didn't get a signal.

Both men jumped as a violent thumping began under the van.

"We ran over a branch or something that blew onto the road," Garvey said.

"Pull over and let's drag it out."

"Not in this weather," Garvey said. "That hail will beat us to death."

"What the hell was that?" Nicholson asked, as a huge, many-armed form crossed the road ahead of them, like an image in a dream.

"Looked like a tree," Garvey said.

"There aren't many trees around here."

"It's not around here anymore," Garvey said, as the wind rocked the van.

The van suddenly became easy to steer. Garvey realized that was because he was no longer steering it. The wind had lifted it off the road.

They were sideways now, plowing up dirt and grass. Then the van bounced and they were airborne again.

"What the shit are you doing?" Nicholson screamed.

"Sitting here just like you."

The van leaned left, leaned right, and Garvey knew they were going to turn over.

"Hold tight," he yelled, checking to make sure both of them had their seat belts fastened.

The wind howled. Steel screamed. They were upside down. Garvey could hear Nicholson shouting beside him, but couldn't make out what he was saying because of the din.

The van skidded a long way on its roof and then began

to spin. Garvey felt his head bouncing against the side window.

Bulletproof glass came off in sharp-edged, milky strips, and he was staring at the ground. With a violent lurch, the van was upright again, then back on its roof. Garvey realized that as addled as his brain had become, his right foot was still jammed hard against the brake pedal.

The van stopped. Hanging upside down, Garvey looked out the glassless window and saw that they were wedged against one of the rare trees Nicholson had mentioned. He looked over and saw that Nicholson was dazed and wild-eyed. And beyond Nicholson, out the window . . .

"Looks like a kind of low ridge over there," he shouted at Nicholson. "We gotta get outta the van, see if we can burrow down outta the wind."

"Everywhere!" Nicholson yelled. "Wind's everywhere!"

Garvey unhitched both safety belts, causing the weight of his body to compress onto his internal injuries. Ignoring the pain, he leaned hard to his right, against Nicholson, and kicked at the bent and battered door. It opened a few inches. The next time it opened, the wind helped it by wrenching it off one of its hinges and flattening it against the side of the van.

"Wind's dying down a little," he lied to Nicholson, and then was astounded to notice that it was true. The roaring had gone from sounding like a freight train to sounding like a thousand lonely and desperate wolves. A hurricane-spawned tornado, Garvey guessed. Moving away, he hoped.

He wormed and wriggled out of the van. The hail had stopped, but rain was still driven sideways by the wind. Garvey was sore all over. Later he'd have to take inventory to see if he was badly injured. With great effort he could stand, leaning into the wind. Nicholson was near him, on hands and knees, his head bowed to Sophia's ferocity.

The overturned van's rear doors were still closed, though the roof was crushed and the wire-reinforced glass was gone from the back windows. A pair of orange-clad legs and black prison shoes extended from one of the windows, and a voice was screaming.

Inside the back of the van, Chad Bingham was cut and bleeding from the long shard of glass in Daniel Danielle's hand. Daniel was bleeding himself, from cuts made by sharp glass or metal. Bingham's scalp was laid open and his face was covered with blood. In the wild tumble of the van, Daniel Danielle had managed to wrench the .25-caliber handgun from where it was taped to Bingham's ankle. Bingham, with his outside-the-walls complexion, hadn't fooled Daniel for a second.

Daniel held the small handgun against Bingham's throat. Bingham's legs were twisted backward, under him. The steel rail both men had been cuffed to had broken at the weld. They were free, though their wrists were still cuffed.

It was Daniel's legs protruding from the van's window. Both men knew the gun had hollow-point bullets and would kill easily and messily at close range. Daniel dropped the shard of glass, then used the hand without the gun and rubbed some of Bingham's blood over his own face and into his hair. Both men had prison haircuts. Bloodied up as they were, they could be mistaken for each other. Daniel needed only a moment of mistaken identity, and he would act.

He dug the gun's barrel into Bingham's throat. "Yell that I'm dead, and you want outta here. Do it if you want to live," he said to Bingham. "Don't do as I say, and bullets start slamming around your insides."

Bingham's eyes rolled with fear. He knew Daniel's reputation, and knew the killer had earned it.

"It's me!" he yelled. "It's Bingham. Daniel's dead. Get me the hell outta here!"

All the time he was yelling, Daniel was kicking with his free lower legs.

It seemed a lot of time passed. He jabbed again into Bingham's neck with the gun barrel. "Hey!" Bingham yelled, "Help!" While Daniel kicked.

Finally Daniel felt strong hands encircle his ankles, exert pressure. Pulling, pulling. As his body began to slide out of the van he stared into Bingham's eyes and kept the gun pointed directly at his testicles. Bingham didn't make a sound.

And then Daniel was free—like a cork out of a bottle.

"Thanks!" he kept repeating, as he faced into the wind and gained his feet.

"You guys okay?"

"We're—"

Garvey shut up when he realized the mistake they'd made.

Daniel stepped close and shot him in the forehead.

Nicholson wheeled to run and Daniel shot him twice in the back of the neck. He fell and the wind rolled him a few feet and then lost interest. Daniel bent low into the wind and made his way back to the van. Bingham was still inside, curled up and playing dead. Daniel shot him in the testicles and Bingham began to wail. Daniel knew no one would hear even if they were nearby.

Still cuffed, he began his search for keys.

Five minutes later Bingham watched through the van's distorted rear window as a limping Daniel Danielle disappeared into the rain and wind.

Within minutes the hurricane sweeping across the state hit the area in earnest.

Chad Bingham would later testify in his hospital bed that Daniel almost certainly died from his wounds or from Hurricane Sophia. There was no way he could have survived out in the open as he'd been, without any nearby shelter.

It was Bingham who died from his wounds.

2

He couldn't fly close to New York City, for security reasons. But the pilot, Chancellor Linden R. Schueller of Waycliffe College, made a slight detour so he could have a look from a distance.

His plane was a small twin-engine Beechcraft that, besides the pilot, could carry five passengers and their light luggage. It could range most of the northeastern states. But this was a short flight from Albany, which was where the chancellor had made the connection via rail, and a cab to the airport, where he'd left the plane. It was complicated but safer that way, using small airports and different modes of conveyance. It meant a less traceable course. But it also meant the chancellor had to take more care about what was in his luggage. You never knew what kind of security checks you'd run into these days, even with a private aircraft, a small airport, and a flight plan that kept him well away from New York City

Perilous times, Chancellor Schueller thought, and smiled. Absently, he ran his fingertips over the cover of his flight logbook. It was the softest of leathers. He didn't really need the book now, considering his expertise on the computer, but he enjoyed touching it.

He pressed his forehead against the oblong Plexiglas window for a better view, then sat back in his seat.

Some city down there. How many people now? He wasn't sure, and the figure kept changing depending on whom you asked, or which set of statistics someone wanted to choose.

Millions, millions . . .

There they were below, layered in tall buildings, moving in every direction above and below ground, in and out of vehicles. They represented every age, size, ethnicity, sexual orientation, religious and political slant. . . . The possibilities were limitless.

Out the window and behind the plane now was a blue and hazy horizon. The city was falling away like memories of yesterday.

Minutes and miles passed. The green earth was rising.

The chancellor forgot about the view and sat straighter in his seat. It was time to change his frame of mind, like slipping from being one person to another.

He throttled back and put the plane into a shallow bank, careful to keep the nose up. The sun caught the twin props and turned them to liquid light.

The plane dipped a wing as if saying hello to the earth, now much closer, then began a low, sweeping descent toward the green field below and off to the southwest.

Gravity asserted a heavier hand. Scraggly lines became roads. Glittering jewels became cars and houses. Water glistened in the sun like molten silver.

A narrow grass runway was visible now, a slightly different shade of green bisecting the field. Bordering the south side of the field was an arrangement of similar red-brick buildings connected by walkways lined with mature green trees. The buildings' roofs were identical shades of gray slate. Chancellor Schueller thought it all looked like pieces of a child's toy train setting. Everything but the train.

He would be a part of it shortly.

He would be home. Settled and sated.

For a while.

3

New York, the present

Macy Collins jerked awake. Unable to breathe in, to breathe out. That was because a rectangle of gray duct tape was fixed tightly across her mouth. The man straddling her had her nose pinched between his thumb and forefinger.

She panicked, screaming almost silently, thrashing her legs about so she could feel her heels digging into the grass and hard earth. He was seated on her chest, leaning forward so his weight was over her upper body and his legs kept her arms pinned to her sides. The heavy hardness of his knees had made her arms go numb.

He smiled down at her, then released her nose so she could suck in precious oxygen.

Her head cleared and she suddenly remembered everything and wished she was still unconscious, that she could die. She craned her neck and stared down at the red, raw flesh where her right breast had been, then up into his eyes that were as human as black pearls. When she looked away she noticed that he had an erection. Even after last night . . .

He was so charming. Then he must have slipped something into her drink. Something that made her compliant enough to agree to a walk in Central Park at dusk.

It was well past dusk now, but there was a bright moon in a black sky beyond the shadows of the copse of trees where he had lured her. She would be able to see everything she so feared and dreaded.

He held up a boning knife with a long, lean blade streaked with blood. "I thought you'd want to be conscious for this," he said. "The first one was so much fun."

Macy began thrashing again with her legs as he slowly and deliberately lowered the knife toward her remaining breast. The fear, the pain, sickened her, made her feel faint. She felt herself sliding again into a fearful darkness, yet she welcomed the black void as an escape from this horror. And she *might* escape from it, because it couldn't be real. It couldn't actually be happening.

Or if it was happening, it was to someone else. In another world, not hers. A world she was dreaming . . .

None of this is real. Not the pain. Not the fear.

She was drifting, falling. . . .

He pinched her nose again. Her stopped breath caught in her throat and she was fully conscious again, fully aware.

Again.

It was real.

He was real.

The knife was real.

Later, when he was almost finished with her, he removed his pants all the way. He'd previously only unzipped them. He was wearing pale blue panties, which he quickly removed, pausing only to appreciate their silky softness.

He found the victim's black thong that he'd earlier taken off and tossed to the side, and slipped it on. He then carefully lifted her legs and put the blue panties on her. She wasn't quite dead, and unconsciously helped him by bending her knees or pointing her toes.

He then put his pants back on, and on top of them baggier, triple-pleated pants he'd brought in his attaché case. They were a harsher material, not pleasant to the touch.

Keeping away from the blood, he knelt next to her and whispered, "Are you still here?"

But she didn't hear him. She was in deep shock and on her way to death. He watched her avidly. Watched her eyes.

Are you still here?

When the moment arrived, he was ready.

The last thing he did before leaving was unfold a page from the morning paper and rest it crease-up over her face, like a tent. It was a Macy's department store sale ad proclaiming EVERYTHING SLASHED.

Nobody, he thought, had a sense of humor like God.

4

Frank Quinn lay sprawled in bed in his brownstone on New York's Upper West Side. He wasn't quite all the way awake, listening to the slow rhythm of Pearl's breathing. She was on her side, one bare leg thrown over him, her forehead burrowed into his chest. The morning wasn't yet hot. The window air conditioner was silent because Quinn had gotten up at 3:30 to relieve his bladder, and the room was cool. Half awake, he'd switched off the laboring window unit as he tottered back to bed.

It was getting warm again, as the sun rose beyond the stone and brick buildings and the struggling trees on West Seventy-fifth Street. The morning noises of the city had begun—a distant clanging of trash containers, a growing rush of traffic punctuated by the rumbling and growling of trucks and buses, a faraway police siren, a brief shouted exchange down on the sidewalk. Quinn felt pretty good, there in the dawn of wakefulness, his flesh pressed to Pearl's, his city shaking off the night and coming to life around him.

The phone by the bed jangled, making him jump. It was an old landline phone that Quinn had owned for years. He kept it because its jarring ring would rouse him from the soundest sleep. And because . . . well, it was familiar, well used, and reliable. And it looked like a phone.

Pearl stirred and said, "Time isht?"

"Six-thirtyish," Quinn said, gazing at the glowing digital clock near the phone. The clock actually read 4:37, but that was so early in the morning that Quinn didn't feel like being precise.

The phone jangled again. Persistent pest.

"Let it ring," Pearl said.

"We're cops," Quinn said. "We don't let phones ring. We answer them."

"We're private cops."

"That's no different," Quinn said, as he stretched out an arm and lifted the heavy receiver from its cradle.

Pearl muttered something he didn't understand, but it sounded snarky.

"Quinn," he said into the cool, hard plastic jammed against the side of his face.

"I know it is. I'm the guy who called you."

Harley Renz. Exactly the last person Quinn wanted to talk to.

Renz was New York City's police commissioner, and he didn't intend to retire from that office. He had bigger plans. He and Quinn had been adversaries for the same positions within the NYPD years ago. Quinn had stayed honest and away from office jobs and unnecessary contact with the higher-ups in the department. Renz was enthusiastically corrupt and ambitious, an unabashed schmoozer and climber. His every move was designed to edge him upward or forward. Quinn was sure he hadn't called to say howdy.

He was right.

"Wanna see a dead body?" Renz asked.

Quinn couldn't help glancing down at the nude Pearl,

who was awake now and listening to his end of the conversation.

He took a couple of deep breaths to make sure he was all the way awake. "A homicide victim, I presume."

"When you see it you'll know it's not just a presumption. I'm looking at it right now."

"A woman?"

"Was."

"You know I've seen dead women before," Quinn said, "so there must be something special about this one."

"Oh, there is. Come over here and you'll see why. You'll also see why the city is going to hire you and your agency."

This wouldn't be the first time Quinn had done work for hire for the city. Renz, the most popular police commissioner in New York's history, could arrange that with no trouble. He had before. The sleazeball did know how to work the levers of power.

And he knew not to work them too often, so this murder must be special.

"You think the killer's going to be a repeater?" Quinn asked. That was why he often became employed by the city even though he was out of the NYPD. He'd gained a reputation as a unique talent when it came to tracking serial killers. And of course Quinn and Associates, or Q&A, had solved other politically sensitive homicides. In a city as large as New York, there was little downtime between investigations.

"I think we've got a serial killer operating in this town," Renz said. "We both know that's usually why I call you. But this time there's something more to it than that."

"Where are you?" Quinn asked.

"In Central Park, but not very far in. Where Seventy-second Street runs into it, but a little north. Walk up Central Park West and look into the park, over the low stone wall. Where there's this clump of trees, you'll see some police cars and a lot of yellow crime scene tape. You can't miss us."

"It's still dark out, Harley. And don't tell me you've got lights. The city's been doing nighttime work in the park. I'm just as likely to be walking toward a midnight-shift maintenance crew."

"Okay. I'll meet you right outside the Beymore Arms, opposite the park, and walk you in."

"So where exactly is the Beymore Arms?"

Renz gave him a Central Park West address. "Look for a gray stone building with a green awning out front. It's down the block from a coffee shop."

"Isn't everything?"

"Yeah. Even dead people beyond the rejuvenating power of lattes."

"I'm on my way."

"Bring Pearl. I know she's there. I can hear her grinding her teeth."

Renz knew Pearl didn't like him. Nobody really *liked* Renz except the citizens, who knew only the Renz facade and not Renz.

"Should we see the victim before or after we eat breakfast?" Quinn asked.

"Before, I would say. Though on the other hand, she isn't going anywhere real soon. And when you learn more about the situation, you'll see why this one will interest Pearl, too."

"I'll check with Pearl," Quinn said. "But she might wanna sleep in."

"It would behoove her to be here."

"What exactly does that mean, *behoove*?" Quinn asked. "It sounds like something a blacksmith might do to a horse."

"You wanna discuss blacksmithing and word roots,"

Renz asked, "or do you wanna be introduced to the late Miss Macy Collins?"

"You make it sound like social networking," Quinn said.

"In a way it is. You'll definitely wanna know people who knew the victim. One person in particular."

"Now you're making it sound like a quiz show."

"Yeah. Well, it isn't that. I guarantee you Pearl won't think so, either."

"Okay," Quinn said. "I'll wake her up."

"I'm awake," she said, from somewhere beneath Quinn's unshaven jaw.

"Renz wants—"

"I heard him," Pearl interrupted. "Tell him to go fu—"

Quinn moved the receiver away as far as he could, then turned his head so he could speak to Renz. "She says she's on her way."

"I thought I heard her talking. She got a message for me?"

"That was it," Quinn said. "More or less."

5

Quinn and Pearl found the Beymore Arms with no trouble. Renz was waiting for them beneath the green canopy. He was wearing a well-tailored blue suit, a white shirt, and a red and black striped tie. He looked ready to broadcast the evening news, but the clothes didn't disguise the fact that he'd put on even more weight since becoming police commissioner.

The three of them waited for a break in traffic that was already starting to build on Park Avenue West, and then fast-walked across the street. Fat as he was, Renz moved quickly and gracefully. They climbed over the low, age-darkened stone wall that bordered the park. Quinn was curious to see if Renz would go over the wall that way, which involved not much more than boosting up the body, then sitting, and swiveling. Renz clambered over the low wall with impressive nimbleness. Didn't do his tailored suit much good.

They walked across dew-damp grass toward a cluster of trees that emitted a faint white glow. Then Quinn saw the crime scene tape, and that the glow was coming from a white tent that was eight or ten feet square. Shadow movement on the taut white material indicated a lot of activity inside.

A tall, poker-faced uniform posted outside the flap entrance to the tent seemed not to pay them any attention. Renz stood to the side of the flap and motioned with an arm for them to enter, but he stayed outside in the interest of giving people in the tent more room to move.

What was going on inside the tent was nothing like social networking, even with the Napoleonic and twisted little medical examiner, Dr. Julius Nift, smiling from where he stood over the body and saying, "Miss Macy Collins, may I present Frank Quinn and Pearl Kasner." He made a motion with his hand, palm up. "Pearl, Quinn, this is—"

"Just shut up," Pearl said.

The tent had no floor and was illuminated by brilliant lights on flimsy-looking metal stands. Quinn had to duck his head slightly, but Pearl could stand up straight. Where there was room to move, two CSU guys were using it, carefully tweezering up possible evidence and placing it in plastic evidence bags. They were dressed in white and wearing white gloves and looked as if they'd arrived in a box with the tent.

What was left of the victim lay on bent and blood-stained grass. A rectangular flag of gray duct tape clung by a corner to her lower lip. Her bulging brown eyes bespoke horror.

She was on her back with her arms taped to her sides, her legs together, toes turned down as if frozen that way by painful spasms. Her body was arranged with a symmetry and neatness suggesting she'd been posed after death. She was wearing only blue panties. Both of her breasts had been removed.

"Her breasts—" Quinn began.

"Haven't found them," Nift said. "Judging by the removal circumference, she must have had quite a rack."

Quinn was aware of Pearl stiffening beside him. "Sick necrophiliac," she said under her breath.

Nift heard her and smiled. He enjoyed getting under people's skin, and Pearl was a favorite target.

"There's a mathematical formula for everything," Nift said.

"Like for how much longer you'll live with that mouth of yours," Pearl said.

Nift seemed not to have heard her.

The CSU techs said they'd done all they could until the body was removed, and left the tent.

Quinn nodded toward the victim. "Notice anything about the panties? The way they're rolled up at the waistband in back?"

"She didn't put them on," Pearl said. "Somebody else did, after she was dead, and while she was lying on her back the way she is now. The panties dragged and rolled in back and didn't go all the way up."

"I was wondering when one of you would notice that," Nift said. "Very good, Quinn. Now, another question: do you recognize the M.O.?"

Any cop who'd been involved in a serial killer case, anyone at all interested in serial killers, would recognize the M.O.

So like the Daniel Danielle murders.

Quinn nodded. Beside him, Pearl said, "Daniel Wentworth, aka Daniel Danielle."

"Or Danielle Daniel," Nift said. "Depending on which sex he wanted to be at the moment."

"There's not a lot of blood on the scene, either," Pearl said, "considering what was done to her. Daniel Danielle was good at managing blood flow. Got a guess as to the actual cause of death?"

Nift grinned at her. "I'd estimate that she was alive when all or most of the butchering was done. He wanted to share that with her. If she was lucky, she died of shock at some point before the abdominal wound." Nift's grin widened. "You look down where you're used to seeing what musta been a huge rack of tits and see your insides instead, it's probably quite a shock."

A cop near the door flap was giving Nift a fish-eyed look. Not much expression. Probably he knew Nift. Almost everyone who dealt with the city's lower forms of life knew Nift, at least by reputation.

Pearl moved over to see the newspaper page lying on the floor near Nift's black leather medical case. There were bloodstains on it, but it was readable. The EVERY-THING SLASHED Macy's sale with its play on the victim's name.

"I saw it," Quinn said, before she pointed it out. "Sick sense of humor."

"Oh, I don't know," Nift said.

"That's for damn sure," Pearl told him. "You don't have the slightest idea."

Nift merely continued grinning at her. "I love getting under your skin," he said. "No pun intended."

Quinn gave him a look, letting him know he'd gone far enough. Knowing dangerous ground when it started to shift on him, Nift stopped grinning.

"Any sexual interference?" Quinn asked.

"I'll have to do the postmortem to know for sure." Nift was all business now, tired of verbally poking at Pearl. "I can call you later with the details."

"Got an estimate as to how long she's been dead?"

"Not more than a few hours. But that's an approximation. We can be more precise later."

Quinn looked over at the cop with the scarred eye. "You catch the squeal?"

"Yeah, but not alone. They directed two radio cars over here. No nine-eleven call. An anonymous call direct to the precinct house. They took it serious."

"He must have left here shortly after the murder and made the call," Quinn said.

"He might've wanted there to be a show for us when we got here," Pearl said. "Might've even watched us arrive. A shared experience. That's how these sickos think. Ask Nift."

"Set a sicko to catch a sicko," Nift said, not bothering to glance over at her. "Pearl's right. The killer might be standing across the street right now, taking it all in. Maybe waiting for the body to be removed."

Quinn knew that what Nift said was true in some cases, but this killer was different. Always had been.

If it was the same killer.

Nift did a quick visual study of the corpse, head to toe, as if trying to fix everything in his memory. He flashed his nasty little smile. "Just like in the textbook chapter on the Daniel Danielle murders."

Quinn nodded. "What do you think? The methodology the same all the way through?"

"Close enough. Would I swear this is a Daniel Danielle murder? No. I couldn't call it that close. I never actually saw one of his—or her—victims." He shrugged without seeming to have moved any part of his hefty little body. "And of course it couldn't be a Daniel Danielle murder, Daniel Danielle being dead. Killed in a hurricane. Body never recovered."

"Tornado," Quinn said.

"What's the difference?"

"Smaller."

"Copycat killer?"

"Well, there's that same lively sense of humor. Most of that didn't get into the media. But I couldn't rule out a copycat. They're most likely to be inspired by infamous killers."

"That would give the killer a motive," Pearl said.

"Which is?" Nift asked.

"He's nuts. Like you are."

Nift chewed on his tongue and seemed to consider that. "No, not like I am." He leered at Pearl. "Well, maybe a little." He nodded toward the body. "One thing's for sure—the killer's got Daniel Danielle's taste in women. Macy would have had the second best rack in the room."

Pearl took a step toward Nift. "You asshole."

Quinn raised a plate-sized hand as a signal for her to stop, which she did. They had more important things to consider than Nift's bad manners.

"Take a look at the vic," Quinn told her. "Imagine her with her hair brushed back off her forehead."

"I don't have to look," Pearl said. "The resemblance struck me when I walked in the room."

In one way or another, the Daniel Danielle victims had all resembled Pearl. Quinn hadn't liked that ten years ago, during the killer's rampage of death, even though Daniel had never taken a victim in New York. He didn't like it now.

Nift stooped, then snapped his rubber gloves and peeled them off. He began arranging his instruments in his bag, preparing to leave. "When you're done with the beautiful Macy, you can have her removed. She and I have a date for later."

When Nift straightened up and moved toward the tent flap, Quinn stood in the way with his arms crossed.

"Something more?" Nift asked.

"The missing breasts . . ."

"I rolled her over and looked under her, looked all over the place. The CSU had uniforms search the surrounding grounds. They will again tomorrow. But we both know the killer must have taken them with him. Like Daniel Danielle."

"Souvenirs," Pearl said.

"Or maybe *more* souvenirs," Nift said, and strode around Quinn and out of the room.

That was when Renz entered.

His suit had taken the night's strenuous activity pretty well and still looked as if he'd just put it on. The brilliant lights in the tent glittered off his gold accoutrements. Renz looked like what he was—a corrupt politician. Quinn wondered if, when people got older, they began to look more and more like what they were. Renz's over-stuffed features were beginning to resemble a rodent's.

"So Nift introduced you to Macy Maria Collins," he said.

Pearl made a note of the victim's full name.

Renz waited with feigned politeness until she'd finished writing. "College girl living in the Big City, maybe looking for a summer job."

"Where'd she go to school?" Quinn asked.

"Someplace upstate. Wycliffe . . . Waycliffe. Kinda place where you have to be either rich or smart to get in."

"Or both," Pearl said.

"Jealous?"

"Not of Macy Collins. If you look close enough you might notice she's dead."

Renz grinned and looked at Quinn. "She's still got the mouth, huh?"

Quinn shrugged.

Renz flashed a gold cuff link and glanced at his watch. It looked like a gold Rolex. "Gotta run. Late for a meeting."

"At this time of night—morning?"

"Uh-huh. We all sit around with cards and chips. I interrupted the game to come over here. Thought you should see the crime scene. I knew you'd understand why."

Quinn did.

"I'll call you later," Renz said.

"No doubt."

Ignoring Pearl altogether, Renz nodded to Quinn as he turned, ducked his head into the folds of fat beneath his chin, and left the tent.

Quinn and Pearl followed Renz and breathed in fresh morning air.

The CSU guy in charge was still standing outside the tent, smoking a cigarette. Quinn almost said something to him about fouling a crime scene and then saw that it was one of those battery-operated cigarettes that look like the real thing.

He was a short man, built like a miniature bull, with a thick neck and sloping shoulders. Quinn had worked with him before. His name was Bronsky. He waited with patient brown eyes for what Quinn had to say.

"What've we got so far?" Quinn asked, thinking that after Renz it would be a pleasure talking with somebody like Bronsky. Crime Scene Unit types were almost always all business and no bullshit.

"Looks like the killer wore rubber gloves, so we might as well forget about fingerprints," Bronsky said. "So far, he didn't leave much if anything behind. We might pick up more on him from the victim herself, try for some of his DNA." He pulled a cell phone from his pocket and held it up for Quinn to see. "I just got off this," he said. "We got her address from her purse, and we're going through her apartment."

"Great," Quinn said, wondering again why Renz wanted this one in the worst way.

"There are signs of the killer washing up some in the bathroom, but still with the gloves on. Plenty of smudgy prints here and there throughout the apartment, some bloody. He musta gone there after the murder."

"He was letting us know that," Quinn said.

"We did lift other prints from the apartment, but they're probably what you'd expect—the victim's, neighbors', former tenants', the super's . . ."

Quinn waited until Bronsky finished with the list. All the prints would have to be matched with the people who'd made them. The prints that couldn't be matched would be placed in a separate file, in the faint hope that someday they'd help to convict the killer. Tedious work, but necessary.

"The bloody prints. Could you say if they were a man's or a woman's?"

"No way to tell. Because of the gloves."

Quinn sighed. "So maybe the lab will come up with something."

"Maybe. We'll get the usual hair samples from the carpet. A few nail clippings from the bedroom. But my guess is they probably won't amount to anything useful." He rotated his head on his thick neck. "Not as much blood here, or in her apartment, as you'd think."

"M.E. said she probably went into deep shock when she saw what he'd done to her. Her heart must have stopped shortly after that."

Bronsky pulled a face that made him resemble Edward G. Robinson in an old tough-guy movie. "Jesus! Not a nice man."

"The M.E. or the killer?"

"Killer. I already know the M.E. is a prick. You going

in now to look over the apartment?" The question sounded almost like a warning about what was waiting inside.

"I was about to," Quinn said.

Bronsky took a drag on his cigarette that meant nothing. "Two bedrooms with two twin beds in each. I heard somebody say the victim shared the place with three other students. The roommates all went home for the summer. What if they'd been here, though? All four girls?"

"Richard Speck," Quinn said.

"That's what I was thinking. Would this creep have killed all of them?"

"Why not?" Quinn said.

"Those other girls should know that," Bronsky said. "Realize how lucky they are to be young and still alive. They might be more careful the rest of their lives. More appreciative."

"It'll give them something to talk about," Quinn said. "Then in a few days or a few weeks they'll go back to being themselves."

Bronsky made his Edward G. Robinson face again. "Why do you figure that is?"

"We're all who we are," Quinn said.

"Yeah, I guess we have to live with that."

"And die with it," Quinn said.

He left Bronsky, who continued puffing on his faux cigarette, blowing faux smoke. Six feet away from the dead woman who was real.

6

Central Florida, 2002

It was barely audible but growing louder. Something was striking metal, over and over. It was like a steel drumbeat, and he walked to it.

Daniel Danielle kept his head down and his eyes squinted almost closed as he trudged west. The wind blasting from behind him was fierce, and the heavy rain obscured his vision.

The joy of escape filled his mind. He would make it all the way, he *knew*. Fate was on his side. Destiny belonged to him.

The ground couldn't absorb the rainfall, and half the time he was splashing through pooled water. A few times the howling wind knocked him off his feet, but he always struggled to a hunched standing position and continued his trek west, away from the wrecked prison van and the dead guards. He was armed now, with the small-caliber gun that had been taped to the ankle of the one who'd pretended to be a fellow con, and with a nine-millimeter Glock handgun from the holster of one of the dead guards. He'd managed to find the right key on the cluster of keys dangling from a dead guard's belt, and he was no longer handcuffed. He was still wearing the prison's orange jumpsuit, and that could be a problem.

The metallic banging sound was ahead of him now. Much closer. Curious, he altered course slightly and moved toward it.

An angular dark shape loomed ahead in the driving rain. As he drew near, he saw that it was what was left of a house. Most of the roof had come down, and part of what remained was flapping violently in the wind against what looked like a section of steel ductwork. The mad drumbeat got louder as Daniel approached.

The central part of the house hadn't collapsed. A man appeared from the wreckage, bent forward against the wind, and motioned with his arm for Daniel to come to him. He was a tall, rangy guy with a hawk nose and gray hair. His shirt was torn half off him and flapping like a flag.

As Daniel got closer, he saw the man's gaze fix on the orange jumpsuit.

"You here to rescue us?" he called, cupping his hands around his mouth so Daniel could hear. Daniel could see the dread knowledge and doubt in the man's eyes. Rescue workers didn't wear that kind of uniform.

"Sure am," Daniel said. "From everything."

He used the Glock to shoot the man in the chest. He went down hard on his back. A blast of wind rolled him to rest against part of the wrecked roof that was jammed up against the base of the house.

In the wind, the bark of the Glock had been barely audible.

Daniel smiled. . . . *Rescue us? Dumb cracker!*

He picked his way through the wreckage to the central core of the house, what used to be the bathroom.

His luck held. A woman was there, huddled tightly beneath a white porcelain washbasin. It was somewhat quieter in the enclosure, and the wind was partially blocked.

The woman was in her fifties, overweight, and frightened as hell. Through a curtain of rain-plastered hair, she studied Daniel with wide blue eyes. Had those eyes seen what happened outside in the wreckage?

Daniel smiled. "I killed your husband."

The woman said nothing. Didn't even change expression. In shock, Daniel decided. His fault? Or the hurricane's?

He left her and made his way to what used to be the kitchen, rooted through the wreckage until he located the right cabinet and found the drawer where the knives were kept. He chose the largest one, testing the blade's edge with his finger to make sure it was sharp.

He returned to the makeshift shelter and found that the woman hadn't moved. He squatted down next to her and began to cut away her clothes with the knife. She put up no resistance. The maelstrom of storm and events had stolen any sense of reality. She was having a bad dream that would eventually end. This man was here to save her; he was a doctor, cutting away her clothes so he could treat her injuries. There was no other explanation. None that she wanted to explore, anyway.

She couldn't hear him over the wind, but could see that he was laughing. He twisted her around so she was on her stomach and skillfully sliced the tendons behind her knees. She wasn't going anywhere.

Then he began having fun.

An hour later, the wind had died down. At least it was no longer yowling. It was still coming out of the east, and was hard enough to drive curtains of rain when it gusted.

Daniel left the woman and found in the house's wreckage what used to be a bedroom. It was easy to locate some of the husband's clothes.

He stood naked in the searing rain for a while and let it wash most of the woman's blood from him. Then he put on the farmer's clothes. The guy had been well over six feet, so Daniel had to roll up the pants cuffs. The short-sleeved shirts were a little baggy but fit okay. The orange jumpsuit he wadded and shoved into what was left of a dresser drawer.

These people couldn't have lived in this isolated ranch house or farmhouse or whatever it was without some kind of transportation. He walked the perimeter of the house and saw what might have once been a garage. There was a vehicle near it, lying on its side.

Daniel walked over and saw that the wind-tossed vehicle was an old Dodge pickup truck. He considered trying to shove it upright, but he found that he couldn't budge it.

That was when he noticed chrome grillwork peeking out from under the wreckage of the garage. He walked over and saw that it was the front end of a late-model Ford SUV. Suffused with a new strength, he began throwing wreckage this way and that, digging the vehicle out.

When he was finished, and the SUV had a path out to where the gravel driveway was clear, he went to the dead man and found keys in his pocket. One of them was a car key. Good. That meant there'd be no need to hot-wire the ignition.

He then pulled a wallet from the corpse's pants pocket. Eighty-seven dollars.

Daniel smiled. He rummaged through the wallet for more, but there was none. He did discover that he'd killed Flora and Nathan Amberson. *Nice to have met you folks.*

He returned to the SUV, climbed in, and inserted the key in the ignition switch.

The vehicle started on the first try. Daniel studied the dashboard. Half a tank of gas. *Good enough.*

He returned to the woman and dragged her out so she lay on a flattened and shattered window. Then he set to work beating her body with a length of two-by-four from the house's studwork. When he was finished, he threw some of the house's wreckage over her.

Daniel didn't like it, but he left her with her breasts still attached.

He carried his two-by-four to the husband and beat him in similar fashion. It would take at least a while for the bodies to be found, and longer before they'd be identified as murder victims rather than victims of the hurricane or one of its tornados that had destroyed their home.

Meanwhile, Daniel Danielle would be driving.

He poked around the wreckage for a few more minutes, looking for anything useful. There was an old shotgun, but it wasn't loaded, and Daniel didn't have time to search for ammunition, so he left it.

He considered siphoning gas from the overturned pickup truck's tank, but found that almost all of it had run out.

Regretting again that he had to leave the woman with her breasts, he got in the four-wheel-drive SUV and maneuvered it onto the long driveway, then to the road that was cluttered with debris. He headed west. He liked trailing the worst of the weather. Its violence helped to divert attention from his violence.

As he drove, his clothes dried and his heartbeat slowed. If he could make it to Interstate 75 and get south to the heavy population around Fort Myers, he could lie low someplace while time passed. Daniel was resourceful; he'd think of something. Right now, everyone was concerned with what the hurricane was leaving in its wake. If he was a greater danger, the hurricane was a wider one. He was going to be all right. Being captured now wasn't part of his destiny. How else had he been able to escape?

The world held more for him. He was special. If that weren't so, he'd be lying back there with those dead cops. He wouldn't have found Nathan and Flora.

Flora . . .

He drove on, trailing the hurricane-like something spawned by its dark winds.

He let himself relax as much as he dared, thinking about Flora Amberson, how she'd tried to become mentally detached, waiting and praying for it to be over. But he'd seen that trick too often and knew how to deny Flora that final escape, how to delay it. How much longer had that hour they shared seemed to her than to him?

Somebody in the SUV laughed. Must have been the driver.

7

"**Y**ou sure you need all that mentholated goop under your nose?" Sal Vitali asked his partner, Harold Mishkin.

Sal and Harold worked for Quinn, but they'd been partners in the NYPD. That partnership more or less continued, as Quinn usually used them as a team. Harold had always smeared mentholated cream on his brushy, graying mustache so the fumes would keep his head clear and his stomach from getting upset by the various odors of homicide scenes.

But this wasn't actually a homicide scene. Macy Collins had been murdered and butchered in the park.

"The killer only spent a short time here after he killed her," Sal reminded his partner. He knew Mishkin had a delicate constitution, and over the years he'd become protective of him, often in sly and subtle ways. At the same time, Harold could get on Sal's nerves.

No, that wasn't fair. Harold could drive Sal crazy.

"Place still smells bad," Harold said. "Blood and death smell the same. The odor hangs around."

Sal thought maybe Harold had something there. He didn't much like the air in the stifling apartment himself.

They were a Mutt and Jeff team, Harold being average height but a beanpole, and with the bush of a mustache that seemed large enough that it bent him slightly forward. Sal was short, stocky, and animated. He waved his arms around a lot when he spoke. Harold was in most matters oversensitive—especially in regard to his stomach, which was delicate enough that he couldn't stay long at violent crime scenes. Sal pretty much took things as they came. Harold spoke softly, while Sal had a voice like gravel rolling around inside a bucket.

The CSU techs were gone. Since this wasn't the actual crime scene there was a limit to what they could achieve. They had pretty much left things as they'd found them, only with smudges here and there from fingerprint powder or luminol spray.

As instructed, the two detectives began to look the apartment over, starting with the living room. The furniture there was mismatched and inexpensive. On a bookshelf there were stacks of magazines, which Sal examined and found to be mostly fashion and food publications, along with the weekly *Times* review of books. There were a few dog-eared mystery novels by writers like Sara Paretsky, Sue Grafton, and Joanne Fluke. There was a book by Stephen Hawking about . . . well, Sal couldn't understand it. What the hell was a quark? He figured at least one of the roommates for the intellectual type. Maybe the victim.

Near a window was a tiny wooden desk, its top bare except for a banker's lamp with a green shade. Next to the lamp was a chipped white mug stuffed with pens and pencils. The shallow top drawer was full of mostly unpaid bills, some of them weeks overdue. The rest of the drawers contained nothing of interest—scissors, a box of yellow file folders, some blank paper and envelopes, a flash-light that didn't work, colored pencils and a blank sketch pad, an unused or brand-new paperback dictionary, rub-ber bands, a stapler without staples. . . . Sal saw it as the desk of a procrastinator, not the intellectual roommate's desk. He moved on.

Harold switched on the TV to see what channel the victim had last been watching. A free movie channel—no clue there. A *TV Guide* sat on top of the TV. Harold leafed through it to see what movies had been playing on that channel the previous night: *They Drive by Night*, starring Humphrey Bogart. If victim and killer had been here dur-ing that time, had the movie been the victim's choice, or the killer's? Or had the TV been switched off before the killer entered the apartment? Or had it been on mute and used as a night-light while love was being made? Or something like love.

Harold joined Sal in the kitchen. The refrigerator held some basic foods like milk, a head of lettuce, a white foam box containing some tired-looking pasta. No meat. Had the victim been a vegetarian?

All in all, it was the kind of apartment you'd picture four young women sharing. A comfortably sloppy, tem-porary kind of place. A stopover on the road to the good life.

The bathroom was a mess. Bloody towels were on the floor and in the bathtub. The faucets were smeared with blood. Here must be where the killer had seriously cleaned up after the murder in the park.

"No point in both of us going in there," Sal said. "Why don't you start on the bedrooms?"

Harold nodded and moved on down the hall. He was holding his hand cupped over his nose.

Sal left the bathroom as they'd found it. Maybe Macy had fought back, and some of this blood was the killer's.

It might be enough to establish his DNA profile. Even if his DNA wasn't in any of the data banks and couldn't identify him, it could be matched with a sample from the suspect himself—if they could find him.

Sal went into the first bedroom he came to after leaving the bathroom. Harold was in there. Sal noticed that Harold held a hand on his stomach as they examined the bedroom. There was blood smeared here and there, too, as if deliberately. Nothing like the bathroom. Sal hoped Harold wasn't going to be sick or make some kind of fuss.

"Why don't you look around the other rooms some more?" Sal growled. "I'll check out the drawers and closets in here."

"I'll be okay," Harold said, swallowing hard and crossing the room to open a closet door.

Harold, Harold, Sal thought.

"These clothes," Harold said, with his head still in the closet, muffling his words, "they're pretty good-sized. And here's something, Sal. She wore a lift in one shoe."

"That's her roommate's closet," Sal said.

"Ah!"

"You notice something's missing?" Sal asked.

"The lift in the other shoe?"

"No, Harold. A computer. How many people do you know who don't own a computer? Especially if they're the victim's age."

"I could count them on one thumb," Harold said. Then he thought. "Maybe CSU took it."

"It wasn't on the list," Sal said, though he hadn't seen any list. It was just that Harold was beginning to irk him.

"Ah," Harold said.

They finally left the apartment with some sense of who the victim had been—which was part of their purpose. They also hadn't discovered anything in the nature of a clue that Quinn, Pearl, and Q&A's fifth associate, Larry Fedderman, might have overlooked during a previous visit. No surprise there. They were an effective trio; even the lanky, potbellied Fedderman, who dressed like a bewildered refugee in a suit he had found, had a mental gear for every problem.

Now for the main purpose of their visit to the building: interviewing the dead woman's neighbors.

That could be a waste of time, but not always.

As Harold was fond of saying, it was surprising what they didn't know they knew.

8

Daniel was finishing topping off the SUV's tank at the gas pump he'd managed to get working at the storm-damaged service station. The few people who drove past glanced at him but saw nothing unusual in what he was doing. The station obviously wasn't open, but this wasn't an ordinary time. People did what they must in order to survive.

"Have you seen a brown and white dog?" a female voice asked, causing Daniel to jump.

"Didn't mean to scare you, mister."

Daniel finished replacing the nozzle and turned around to see a thin girl about fourteen standing around ten feet from him. She was wearing a thin white T-shirt with MARLINS lettered on it, cut-off Levi's, and brown leather sandals. The T-shirt was wet and her nipples were visible as dark nubs pressing out against the fabric.

"You didn't scare me, sweetheart," Daniel said. "Just startled me, is all. What's wrong, you lost your dog?"

"Candy. I haven't seen her since . . ." Her eyes teared

up and her breath caught in her throat. ". . . since me and my mom got under the bed at home."

"Where is your mom?"

"She wasn't moving when I left her. I'm sure she's—"

"That's okay, sweetheart." Daniel went to her and hugged her. "And now you're looking for Candy."

"I saw her run away when the hurricane hit."

"How far away did—do you live?"

"A good ways." She pointed toward some wrecked houses that had been lined like soldiers on a side street.

Daniel looked at the girl more closely. "You never did tell me your name."

"I'm Gretchen."

"Nice name."

"Whatever your name is, I think you get used to it."

Daniel shrugged and smiled. "I'm Dan. Pleased to meet you." He rubbed the back of his hand over his mouth and glanced around. "When a dog runs away in a storm, it's usually the same way the wind was blowing. They do that to survive. You say Candy ran that way?" He pointed west.

Gretchen nodded.

"I'll tell you what. I'm going that direction. You wanna hop in the SUV and I'll drive you that way? Maybe up and down some of these streets where houses used to be, we can spot Candy."

The girl didn't hesitate. She smiled. "That'd be good."

"Might work," Daniel said.

He climbed in on the driver's side and unlocked the door for Gretchen, then helped her climb up into the SUV.

"You keep a sharp eye out," Daniel said, starting the engine. "So will I."

He drove west, meandering some to get a closer look at a ruined building, or simply a pile of wreckage.

After about ten minutes he saw a house that was leveled, near a barn that was damaged but still standing. Nobody was in sight in any direction.

"Think I might have caught a look at a brown and white dog," Daniel said, stopping the SUV. "Mighta gone behind that barn. Why don't we—"

But Gretchen was out of the vehicle and running toward the barn.

Daniel drove after her, making sure he didn't run over anything sharp. He parked the truck where it couldn't be seen from the highway.

He was smiling.

"I don't see her," Gretchen said. "She mighta gone inside the barn."

"Then let's go in and look," Daniel said.

He got down out of the SUV and followed Gretchen into the barn. It was dim inside, and there was nothing there but some old rusty tools and a tractor that looked as if it hadn't run in years. And a length of rope draped over a peg in a supporting beam.

"Take a look there behind the tractor," he told Gretchen.

While she was doing that, he went to the broad wooden door and tried to pull it shut. It wouldn't move much, and jammed a couple of feet short of closing. That was okay, if there was a little light beyond what was leaking in through the separated wooden slats.

"How come you're shutting the door?" Gretchen asked.

"If Candy's in here, we wouldn't want her running outside," Daniel said.

Something in his voice must have alerted Gretchen. She gave him a wide-eyed look and bolted for the barn door.

Daniel tripped her, then lifted her and held her upright

by her hair and marched her toward one of the stalls. She was surprisingly light and it was no effort.

He snatched the rope off the peg with his free hand along the way.

Gretchen was trembling with fear.

Daniel with anticipation.

9

The city was still in the sweaty grip of summer heat and humidity. Sal and Harold didn't find much relief inside Macy Collins's apartment building, but it was better than outside.

Macy had lived in 5E. Harold knocked on the door of 5D, and Sal took 5F. They would work their way in opposite directions around the hall. Usually old apartment buildings like this one smelled like urine, disinfectant, and over-fried bacon, in various mixture and degree. This building made a different and less offensive olfactory impression that Sal couldn't quite place.

Nobody answered the knock on 5F's door. Sal moved along to 5G and heard Harold meet someone and enter 5D. "Are you baking something?" Sal heard Harold ask, after identifying himself. "It smells wonderful."

"Carrot cake," said the voice of an older woman.

"I *love* carrot cake."

"Your nose seems to be running. Do you need a handkerchief, detective?"

"That's not—"

The door closed. That was fine with Sal.

The door he'd just knocked on opened, and a woman in her thirties smiled out at him. She was short and plump, and her dark hair, combed straight back as if she were standing in a stiff breeze, emphasized a sweet, fleshy face. She was perspiring heavily, and her apartment didn't smell as good as the one Harold had drawn. "You're with the police," she said.

"I'm usually the one who says that," Sal said.

"But I'm not," the woman said. "I mean, with the police. You see, if you said—"

"I understand," Sal said, wishing Harold had knocked on this door.

"I'm Charmain Graham," the woman said, stepping back so he could enter. "Do you want to know if I was home last night? Did I see or hear anything unusual? Did I know the dead woman well? Do I have something to say that might provide information about the murder?"

"Do you want me to sit under a bright light while you question me?" Sal asked.

She appeared puzzled. "Why would I—" A wide, wide grin. "Oh, I see. You wondered, was I going to hamburger you."

"Hamburger?"

"You know—grill you. That's police slang."

"I've never heard that one," Sal said.

"It was on one of those CSI programs."

Sal knew he was going to have difficulty with this woman. She seemed to see conversation as a kind of oblique jousting with rubber lances. She motioned for Sal to sit on a small sofa with a worn green slipcover. A ginger cat glared at him and then skulked away. "I won't do anything with a telephone directory," she said.

She had Sal there. Again. He sat and looked at her.

Charmain grinned. "Isn't that what the police do

sometimes with a stubborn suspect? Whack him in the head with a phone directory? So there are no marks?" She acted it out, swinging hard with her arms parallel to each other.

"That's right," Sal said, playing along. "The more serious crimes get the biggest boroughs."

"Now you are joking with me." Charmain Graham laughed. She had a nice, musical laugh. Sal found himself liking her, despite that fact that she might be certifiably insane.

"So did you?" Sal asked. "See or hear anything last night?"

"Anything suspicious, you mean?" She sat down in a small upholstered chair angled toward the sofa. The chair creaked a warning, but she ignored it. There was a low wooden coffee table between them, bare except for some back issues of *New York* magazine fanned out like a hand of cards. The apartment was cheaply furnished but impeccably clean and ordered. There was nothing superfluous. No gewgaws, no photographs. Sal had talked to plenty of potential witnesses like this; Charmain Graham was lonely and glad for the company, even if it meant there'd been a murder next door.

Sal shrugged and smiled at her. "Tell me anything that comes to mind. I'll figure out whether it's suspicious."

"The policeman who was here earlier said the murder took place in the park, but the killer came here afterward to clean up. How weird is *that*? They know that's what he did because of the blood all over—"

"Yes, we've already established that," Sal said, putting a little bite in his already gruff voice. He wanted some free association here, but he didn't want the conversation to go off a cliff.

Charmain got the message. She teetered for a moment as if about to lose her balance, and then righted herself, her fingertips touching the base of her throat, and assumed a new attitude. She was an actress in one of those *CSI* episodes now. "At approximately seven minutes after three this morning, I heard laughter from next door."

"You mean Macy Collins's apartment."

"It would be her bedroom, to be exact," Charmain said. "I couldn't sleep, like usual, and I woke up about quarter to three and just laid there. You know, tired but mostly awake and hoping I'd pass out altogether. But all I could do was keep changing positions. I had the air conditioner on high, but it wasn't doing much, so I went over to adjust it and found it had frozen up, like it does sometimes. It was shooting out little flecks of ice but not much of a breeze. Well, there's nothing to do then but switch it off and wait for it to thaw out, which it does pretty fast in this weather."

"So that's when the room got quiet," Sal said, trying to keep her on point.

"That's right."

"And you heard laughter."

"Not right away. I went back to bed, but I still couldn't sleep. Macy's bedroom is—was—right on the other side of my bedroom wall. They're thick walls, though, in this old building. Mostly soundproof. But there's a vent near my bed, and it sort of magnifies sound. I heard moving around in Macy's bedroom. Couldn't tell what it was. And now and then a voice."

"Voices?"

"No. Just a man's voice. At least, I think it was a man. I can't be positive. Nothing I could understand. Just a low murmur now and then. And then, after about ten minutes, he laughed."

"How do you mean? Like a big guffaw?"

"What's a guffaw?"

"I mean, do you think he might have thrown back his head and laughed real loud?"

"No, more like a chuckle."

"I'm not sure what a chuckle sounds like."

"More like he was amused than that he was slapping his thigh with laughter."

"Have you ever seen anyone actually do that?" Sal asked. "Laugh real hard and slap their thigh?"

"No."

"Did you hear Macy's voice at all?"

"No. Not a peep. She was already dead, wasn't she? In the park?"

" 'Fraid so." Sal folded his black leather-bound note-pad and stood up. "I'd like to see your room. Where you were when you overheard the laughing."

"Chuckling."

"Sure."

Charmain fought her way up out of her creaking chair and led the way into her bedroom.

"Did you know Macy well?" Sal asked.

"Hardly at all. She didn't live here all that long, and she was always busy, always on the go. Like she didn't have time to make friends. No, wait a minute. I did see her once with an older woman, eating at a diner over on Broadway. They seemed friendly enough, like they had lots to talk about."

"How old was this older woman?"

"In her forties, I'd guess. But she was one of those sort of larger women who might look older than they are. You know what I mean?"

"Sure. Did she often entertain men in her apartment?"

"Not that I noticed."

The bedroom was as neat as the living room. The bed and dresser were IKEA. There was a small TV on a table where it could be seen from the bed. The floor was bare hardwood but for a small black and red oval throw rug. In the one window, the air conditioner that sometimes froze up was softly humming away. The bed was tautly made with a pale blue spread. A tattered brown stuffed bear was lodged between the pillows. It looked uncomfortable.

"I've had Andy since I was a little girl," Charmain explained, noticing Sal staring at the bear.

"Do you sleep on the right side of the bed?" Sal asked. "Or does Andy?"

"I do."

"Near that vent?" Sal pointed toward narrow grillwork that had been painted over countless times and was now the same cream color as the walls.

"Near enough." Charmain seemed slightly embarrassed.

"When you heard noises from Macy's bedroom, did you get out of bed and put your ear to the vent so you could hear better?"

Her round face flushed. Then she seemed to gather herself and put on a don't-give-a-damn expression. "Of course I did. Wouldn't you?"

"To tell you the truth, yes," Sal lied. Or thought he lied. He smiled at her. "Stay right here." He moved briskly from the room.

Charmain stood where she was for a minute or so, and then sat down on the edge of the bed. Her back was rigid, as if she might leap up any second.

Sal returned shortly, glanced at his watch, then walked over and stooped low so he could place his ear against the vent.

Within a few seconds he heard Harold tell him that now was the time for all good men to come to the aid of something. Then Harold said, quite distinctly, "Ha, ha, ha."

Sal straightened up and stretched his back. Charmain

remained seated on the edge of her bed, smiling at him in a way he didn't like.

"If Macy talked in bed, you could hear her," he said.

"Yes."

"You've heard her before?"

Charmain smiled. "I said she didn't bring men home *often*, not never."

"You heard them through the vent? Having sex?"

"Why would you ask that?"

"It seems to deepen voices. Turned my partner into a baritone."

"When you say partner—"

"I mean fellow detective, just now, through the vent," Sal said, wanting no misinterpretation.

Charmain kind of half closed her eyes and regarded him. "I guess sex does change people's voices. A man like you, in your work, you must meet lots of women. . . ."

Sal knew where this was going and wished Harold was here. And just like that, as if wish were command, Harold walked into the bedroom.

"Did I come through loud and clear?" he asked.

"Loud enough, but not completely clear," Sal said. He introduced Harold to Charmain.

"Would you like a Kleenex for your nose?" Charmain asked.

Harold thanked her and accepted a tissue from a box by the bed.

"Was I any help?" Charmain asked.

"Sure were," Harold said.

"I mean, my testimony? Not the vent thing."

"I thought you meant the tissue."

"Yes and yes," Sal said. Charmain had heard the killer celebrating with himself over the recent murder. She had helped to establish the time of death, but Sal saw no point in telling her that. And if the killer had been bouncing around in Macy's bed, he might have left a good DNA sample. Or maybe he'd done that earlier in the evening, in the park. "You've been a big help," he said. He moved toward the door. Harold and Charmain followed.

At the door to the hall, Charmain winked at Sal in a way that Harold wouldn't notice. All this talk about murder seemed to have excited her. "If you need anything else, like more experiments with the vent, under more realistic circumstances, just let me know. I'm available."

Sal just bet. He thanked her politely and formally for her help, then ushered Harold toward the elevator.

"That was nice of her, with the Kleenex," Harold said on the way down to the lobby.

"It was because you smell like jet fuel," Sal said.

"It was because she likes me," Harold said, "and you're jealous."

Knowing Harold, Sal said nothing in reply.

10

There was something wrong with the air conditioner that caused it to run and not run in long cycles. Or maybe it was just overwhelmed by the heat wave. Right now it was in its not-run phase.

It was unnaturally quiet in the office, as if the warmth were smothering sound. There was a smell like wet paste, maybe from the plastic or wiring in Fedderman's computer heating up. If there still was any wiring in computers. Everything might be modular now. Sometimes Quinn felt like he was modular and didn't fit anywhere, a time traveler from the Bronze Age.

Quinn was working the phones. Only the intrepid, ill-clad Fedderman was there with him, at a desk fifteen feet away, facing Quinn's. Fedderman dressed somewhat better since his recent marriage, but his right shirt cuff still usually managed to come unbuttoned when he wrote with pen or pencil. And it would stay that way, flapping like a signal flag when he walked. He was busy transferring his written notes to a file on the computer. Both copies would be saved, to add to a growing physical as well as electronic file.

The jangle of the phone broke the silence and Quinn

picked up. The receiver of the landline phone was hard and slippery against his ear.

The caller was Pearl, checking in from the brownstone. She'd worked late last night, making connections with Macy's three roommates, who were out of town for the summer. Pearl, bearing the bad news.

Macy's roommates had been horrified when they learned of her death. Other than that, they didn't have much to add to the investigation. They were all college students, home for the summer. Two were in Chicago. The third was in Europe. None of them had really known Macy, though all of them cried during their conversations with Pearl. They'd had nothing negative to say about the dead, apparently thinking they might draw down an ancient curse upon themselves if they were anything but complimentary. Pearl had run into that attitude before, when the young were unexpectedly confronted with the death of someone who'd touched their lives.

It could happen to anyone.

Quinn thanked Pearl and asked if she was still in bed.

"Why?" she asked. "Are you interested in phone sex?"

"I didn't know phones had sex," Quinn said.

Pearl's cue to hang up, which she did.

Quinn had read Sal and Harold's respective reports. So far, the interview with Charmain Graham, Macy's neighbor in an adjacent apartment, had proved the most fruitful. She might actually have heard the killer in Macy's bedroom. No one else in the building other than the super seemed to have even met Macy other than to say hello or nod to in the hall. No one had noticed anything suspicious in or near the building during the weeks leading up to her death.

The killer had committed a clean and seamless crime, except for the soft laughter overheard through Charmain Graham's bedroom vent. That laughter so soon after the process of human slaughter infuriated Quinn. He kept imagining it, even though he'd never heard it. Had the killer laughed that way while butchering the gagged and still-alive Macy? Or while working the blue panties onto her corpse? *What the hell was that all about, with the panties?*

Quinn picked up a different sheet of paper and scanned it yet again.

What the CSU had removed from Macy's apartment yielded little of use other than the names and addresses of Macy's mother and father. Her mother lived in Davenport, Iowa. Her father in Oakland, California.

Quinn figured Pearl had done enough death notification.

He sighed and made the necessary calls. The reactions of both parents made rips in his heart. He thought of his own daughter, on the other side of the continent, in California. People didn't have children with the notion that they might be tortured and butchered by a monster. Across the office, Fedderman had heard sound but not substance. But he knew what the calls were about and his eyes had teared up. He quickly looked away from Quinn.

Another phone call, incoming, was also less than a pleasure. Nift from the medical examiner's office, with Macy's postmortem findings.

"Official cause of our girl's death was heart failure brought about by extreme shock," Nift said, getting right down to business.

"No surprise there."

"Slicing off her tits took a bit of know-how and skill."

"Medical skill?"

"No. More like practice-makes-almost-perfect skill. They were done antemortem. It's a wonder she didn't die of shock early in the process. The killer was expert at keeping her alive as long as possible. He was the one who chose almost the precise instant of death. I would imagine that was important to him."

"Try not to imagine," Quinn said. But he knew Nift was right. It simply irritated him that the smarmy little M.E. enjoyed playing detective.

Nift gave a low chuckle that reminded Quinn of Charmain Graham's description of the killer's laugh. "Macy's evening wasn't all bad," Nift said. "Stomach contents were steak, salad, red wine, consumed approximately five hours before her death. She was wined and dined and then—"

"Raped?"

"Maybe. Could have been consensual. But damage to the vaginal tract suggests otherwise. And there was residue of the kind of substance used on pre-lubricated condoms."

"You sure about that?"

"Positive. I see it over and over," Nift said, in an oddly cheerful voice.

"Our killer practicing safe sex," Quinn said.

"Whatever entered her might not have been a penis."

"A dildo?"

"Maybe. Or some make-do inanimate object that required lubrication."

"Or some object ceremonial to the killer."

"It could be we're making too much of it," Nift said. "We can't rule out simple, consensual sex. She might have been wined, dined, and reclined—and enjoyed that part of it, even though it had to have been rough. There's some frictional damage to the vaginal wall. But you know women."

"I wish."

"There isn't any sign of her resisting until after she was gagged and taped."

"The wine, maybe."

"Could be. If she wasn't used to it. And there are traces of an over-the-counter sedative in her stomach. Bruising on her arms is consistent with the killer straddling her and pinning her down. Maybe keeping her hands away from her face after slapping that tape over her mouth. He had to have taken some of the fight out of her before taping her arms to her sides."

"That would take a strong person."

"Average-strength man, stronger-than-average woman. He was probably seated on her boobs, then slid down toward her pubic area while applying the tape. My guess is he waited until she was stunned and exhausted from torture before he lopped off her jugs. There are small cut marks, or stab marks that barely penetrated the flesh, in sensitive areas all over her body."

"Made while she was still alive?"

"Definitely. He wanted her to see as well as feel what he was doing. Wanted them to experience it together."

"He wanted to take the trip with her," Quinn said, "but not all the way."

"Company loves misery."

"*Company* being Daniel Wentworth, aka Daniel Danielle, aka Danielle Daniel?"

"That would be my guess."

"Only a guess?" Quinn asked, holding in his anger at the killer, feeling slightly sick. The heat.

"At this time, yes. But I remember the original Daniel Danielle murders. Between us, this is the same guy."

"He's dead," Quinn said. "Nobody on foot where he was could have survived that hurricane."

"Zombie love. But if that's not a good enough explanation for you, we got some human flesh out from under one of Miss Macy's painted but broken nails. We'll have a DNA comparison shortly. You wanna bet some money on this?"

"No," Quinn said. "And what I heard was the Florida cops either didn't take or lost Daniel Wentworth's swab, and the DNA sample from under the nail of an original victim was too small and too old to be of much help. Most of it was used up during the trial."

"Same guy, though," Nift repeated. "It's very distinctive, his work with the knife. It had to take some thought, some practice." Nift paused. Quinn could hear him breathing. It was possible that Daniel had taken over a hundred victims, their bodies still lying in shallow graves or disposed of in ways unimaginable to the normal mind. "Something else I couldn't help thinking about when I was working on this one, Quinn. Something you really oughta keep in mind. Looking down at Macy, before I peeled back the face and did the brain pan—even after— she kept reminding me of Pearl."

Quinn hung up the phone hard, causing Fedderman to stare over at him.

"You okay?" Fedderman asked.

Quinn was sweating. Trembling slightly. He dragged the back of his hand across his clammy forehead and sat back. "Yeah. Just talking to Nift about the postmortem."

"That'll do it," Fedderman said. "Anything useful?"

Quinn related his conversation with Nift, now and then thinking about Pearl.

No doubt that was what Nift wanted, not knowing that Quinn would have been thinking about Pearl without being prompted.

Pearl herself entered the office an hour later. She was neatly dressed in gray slacks and blue blazer, shoes with slight high heels on them to raise her at least somewhat above her five-foot-one height. Her breasts didn't look so prominent beneath the loose cotton fabric of her white blouse. Her eyes were dark and alert, her pale complexion set off by her jet-black hair, which fell to below her shoulders. *Vivid* was the word most often used to describe Pearl. A sketch in black and white by an artist who loved women.

She nodded good morning to Quinn and Fedderman, and to Sal and Harold, who'd only just arrived themselves. Then she went over and poured herself some coffee in her initialed mug. She was glad to see that someone else, knowing she'd be coming in late, had taken the trouble to make coffee.

"We saved you a doughnut," Sal said, motioning toward a shallow white bakery box resting on the printer, "but Harold ate it."

"I didn't know it was Pearl's," Mishkin said quickly.

"That's okay," Pearl said. "At least there's coffee. The four of you must have pitched in and somehow gotten it made."

"Eat your doughnut," Sal growled. "We were only kidding about Harold."

"It's cream-filled," Harold said.

Pearl lifted the box's lid to reveal a small and broken cream-filled doughnut with chocolate icing. Lucky she'd taken the time to toast and eat a bagel in the brownstone. Letting the box lid drop back into place, she made sure they all saw her disdain for the doughnut.

"Since we're all here," Quinn said, "we need to have a meeting and coordinate what we know. Maybe get some kinda picture of what we're dealing with."

Line one rang on the phones. Pearl picked up the unit on her desk and turned away so her conversation wouldn't be a distraction. Also, it wouldn't be overheard.

When she'd finished talking and hung up, she turned back to the others. She was the one who looked distracted.

"That was Rena Collins," she said. "Macy's mother. She's flying into town today to talk to us, and to identify and claim her daughter's body."

"This is a homicide investigation," Quinn said. "We'll want to hold the body."

"I told her that," Pearl said. "I think she understands."

Quinn raised his eyebrows.

Pearl shrugged. "She wants to see her daughter. She'll wait for the body. She said she's bringing a dress."

No one spoke for a while.

Quinn said, "I'll call Nift and make sure he makes Macy presentable."

He immediately realized how callous that sounded, but he couldn't think of a better way to say that pieces of Mrs. Collins's daughter were either missing or needed to be fitted back together.

1 1

Quinn picked up Rena Collins at her hotel and drove her to the morgue. She was an attractive woman in her fifties, with a trim figure that looked like the result of fanatical dieting and exercise. Her hair was blond, unlike her daughter's, and she was tan, as if she'd been swimming or playing tennis within the past few days. Only the crow's-feet at the corners of her narrowed and sad blue eyes hinted at her age.

"You didn't have to go to this trouble," she said. "I could have met you there." Her voice sounded rough and worn, as if she was an incurable smoker. Quinn thought it was probably from crying.

"It's no trouble."

"I thought at first this was a hired limo," Rena Collins said. "It doesn't look like an unmarked police car."

"It isn't. It's my personal car, a 1999 Lincoln. It does look like a hired car. That makes it one of the least conspicuous rides in New York."

"It must be," Rena said. "Two of them just passed us."

"Newer models, but close enough."

Traffic was building up; almost lunchtime. The silence in the car became thicker and heavier. There wasn't much for the two strangers to talk about, other than the dead woman. Neither of them wanted to discuss her at the moment, even though her foreboding presence was with them as surely as if she were sitting in the backseat.

It wasn't easy, what Rena Collins was about to do. Identifying the corpse of a dead child was about the worst thing you could ask of someone. Quinn would be glad when it was behind her. Behind both of them.

He was relieved, mostly for Rena, when the dead face of Macy Collins appeared on the morgue monitor. The photo had been taken before the autopsy. Nift had done a good job of preparing Macy for viewing. The face on the screen didn't look much like her recent photographs that the hometown media had dug up, but maybe that was a good thing, that she didn't look like herself. Quinn recalled the horror that had been in her eyes, the constant silent scream that had been on her lips once the tape had been removed. At least Rena Collins was spared that.

"It's Macy," she said in a choked voice, and turned away from the monitor. Her breasts were heaving. "Christ! I need to get outside where I can breathe."

"So do I," Quinn said, glad she wasn't going to demand to see the body up close and not on a monitor, as some surviving family members did. There were family members who felt it their duty to approach the dead, to touch them, as if in a magical way some life remained that would be responsive. In this case, the photo had been enough, and the law was satisfied.

Quinn led Rena Collins back outside into the warm, exhaust-hazed air of Manhattan. It seemed infinitely better than the air inside the building.

She was perspiring. Her breathing had leveled out but was still slightly ragged. He could hear it in the brief intervals when traffic wasn't making itself known.

"Sure you're okay?" he asked, gently gripping her elbow to steady her.

She made herself smile and moved away from his grip. "I'm okay. Really."

He stayed alert, in case she showed signs of giving in to the heat and what she'd just endured.

In the car she said, "They won't let me take her home for burial right away, will they?"

"We'll need to hold her for a while," Quinn said.

"I wish I could—" She thought better of what she was about to say. "Never mind."

He turned the Lincoln's air conditioner on high, and after a few blocks she stopped sweating and her breathing was normal. Quinn wanted to talk with her about Macy. He drove slower.

"Need anything?" he asked.

"I want to call my ex-husband, but not yet."

"Macy's father?"

"Yeah. He's out in California. He wanted to come here, to New York, but it was impossible, he said. He thinks he can be at the funeral."

Thinks he can be . . . "I see," Quinn said. But he didn't. Macy had been the man's daughter.

Rena Collins stared out her side of the windshield for a while. At the windshield and nothing else, really. Her thoughts were directed inward. Then she looked over at Quinn. "Something to drink," she said. "Not alcoholic."

"There's a diner in the next block."

"I'd rather go to the hotel restaurant."

Quinn thought that was a good idea. The restaurant would likely be more conducive to conversation.

He found himself wondering if Rena Collins had something more than conversation in mind. He'd seen it work that way, the near proximity of death acting as an aphrodisiac, a lusting for its polar opposite. At the end, underlying everything, we all wanted to live. We wanted life for ourselves and for everyone we loved.

He told himself not to be an idiot. This woman didn't want a roll in the hay with an aging ex-cop. She wouldn't get one, in any event. She had just gazed on the remains of her dead daughter. He was at least partly responsible for having her do that, and he was responsible for whatever might happen after.

Quinn was still plagued by guilt for what he'd contemplated, when he turned the Lincoln over to a hotel parking valet. He let Rena go ahead of him and then stepped in behind her and provided most of the power for the revolving glass door. They entered the cool lobby.

The restaurant was serving lunch and was already crowded, so they went into the nearby bar and found a booth that afforded relative privacy. Three flat-screen TVs over the bar were showing last night's Yankees–Red Sox game, but the volume was off. Rena ordered a Diet Coke with a lemon, and Quinn asked for a cup of coffee.

When their drinks came, he added cream to his cup and stirred, and watched her squeeze her lemon wedge and drop it in the Coke. She stirred the ice deftly with her forefinger and then sipped from the glass, ignoring the straw that had been delivered with the drink. When she placed the glass back on its coaster, she pressed her cool hand to her forehead for a moment, then looked at him.

"Isn't it warm out to be drinking coffee?" she asked.

He smiled. "Cops would drink coffee in hell."

She sighed, knowing that even though this was her idea, they weren't there for small talk. Cops would be cops in hell. "You want to discuss Macy."

"There are things I need to know," he said. "You okay with that, or would you rather we do it later?"

"Now's all right." Another sip of Coke. Another cold palm pressed to the forehead.

"This might sound obvious," Quinn said, "but did Macy have any enemies?"

"Somebody who might do such a ghastly thing to a twenty-one-year-old girl? No, of course not. But then . . ."

"What?"

"Obviously she did have such an enemy."

"What about at school?" Quinn asked.

"We were in contact. I would have known about any sort of serious issue. Every indication was that things were going well at school. Macy liked being away from home, out on her own. She was proud of it. That's why she decided to stay in New York instead of coming home for the summer. And she was interested in her job, interning at a law firm. Enders and Coil. Do you know it?"

"Know of it," Quinn said. "Big firm."

"Odd that she'd be so interested in a job like that. She was always kind of a counter-culture rebel, more the public defender type."

"Did she know the girls she subleased from?"

"Not at all. She found the place on a school bulletin board."

"They aren't students at Waycliffe."

"True, but they know where to look for someone who can afford to sublease their apartment when they leave the city."

"Did they all leave town?"

"For the summer, yes. All but one of them."

"Jacqui Stoneman?"

"I think so."

"Stoneman left ten days ago," Quinn said. "The super and the other two girls said she's backpacking around Europe. She isn't due home for another month."

Rena nodded. She managed to sip her drink without using her palm to cool her forehead.

"So Macy knew no one in New York?" Quinn asked.

"Not well. Other than some of the people she worked with at the law firm. She did mention someone, an older woman named Sarah. And maybe she was a casual acquaintance of some of the girls from Waycliffe who live in the city and stay in New York year-round."

Quinn sipped his coffee and sat back in the upholstered booth. A smattering of cheering and applause came from the bar, where the recorded ball game was being shown. Someone hitting a home run and rounding the bases yesterday. "What about Waycliffe?" he asked. "Was Macy happy there?"

"She said she was. And just in the past year she seemed to be maturing, becoming more . . . practical. She was always a scholastic brain and made top grades. Waycliffe had her in their Vanguard program for gifted students. She seemed to have done a good job of adapting to college life."

"Did she mention any particular friends she'd made?"

"Some, but their names don't come to mind. Macy wasn't exactly a social butterfly, but people liked her." Rena's lower lip began to tremble.

Quinn guessed that the photo of her dead daughter was on the screen of her mind. Or maybe the murder itself, reconstructed from the horrible wounds. The recent past playing out again, like the ballgame. The Macy in the crime scene photos hadn't looked peaceful and composed, as in the morgue shot. Rena hadn't seen the crime scene photos, but she knew what had happened to her daughter, and she could imagine how it had been done.

She took a slow sip of her drink. "Last time I talked to her on the phone, Macy did seem to hint that something at her job was bothering her, that it didn't seem right."

"What does that mean, 'did seem to hint'?" Quinn asked.

Rena shook her head. "I don't know, exactly. I shouldn't

have brought it up. Maybe it was just something I inferred. Macy had a way about her. Maybe because she was so smart. When we talked, it was always like what she meant was floating somewhere between the lines. It was kind of unsettling. Like once when she phoned me from her dorm room."

"So what exactly did she say on the phone?"

"I can't quote her verbatim. One thing I remember: she said it was possible somebody'd slept in her bed while she was gone."

"Maybe her roommate."

"She didn't have one. The students in her dorm have small sleeping rooms without space for much more than a bed and a desk."

"Did she have a key?"

"Yes, but the door hadn't been locked. Hardly anyone in the dorm locks their room when they're only going to be gone for a short while. That's the sort of college it is."

"Everyone there is trustworthy?"

"Apparently. Or rich enough that they don't have to steal."

"Very exclusive?"

"You have to have brains, money, or connections in excess even to think about going there. In Macy's case it was brains. She scored perfect or near perfect on every aptitude test she took."

"Where had she been the evening of the bed incident?"

"She'd attended a group discussion at the home of one of her professors. You know, drinks, snacks, endless analysis or political posturing."

For a moment it struck Quinn that on a certain level Rena might have been jealous of her daughter's superior intellect.

"Maybe she just forgot to make her bed," Quinn said.

"And forgot she forgot? That wouldn't be like her."

Rena bowed her head and the lip trembling began again. She looked as if she was about to cry, but with great effort she gained control of her emotions. She methodically unwrapped her plastic straw and then plunged it like a lance into liquid and took a long series of pulls on her Diet Coke, almost emptying the glass.

Quinn didn't tell Rena that serial killers were sometimes driven to get into their intended victims' minds by learning intimate things about them, even sneaking into their homes and mimicking their experiences. Like sitting and watching their TVs, reading their e-mails, wearing their clothes, using their combs or makeup. Or lying in their beds.

"Where exactly is Waycliffe College?" he asked. "I mean, if I wanted to drive there."

Over another cool drink, she told him.

12

Fedderman and his wife, Penny, went out for dinner. Hot on a case as he was, he and Penny didn't get to eat together often.

This was a special treat, pasta and wine at D'Glorio's, a block down the street from their apartment. Penny's old apartment, actually. They'd moved in together after their marriage, choosing her place because it was larger and more of her furniture was worth saving. Most of Fedderman's flea-market ensemble was hauled away as junk.

In D'Glorio's you knew you were in an Italian restaurant, with its red and white checked tablecloths, wax-coated wine bottle candle holders, Verdi operas playing softly in the background, the scents of garlic and mystery spices wafting from the kitchen.

They were finishing their wine and waiting for their tiramisu desserts when Penny brought up the subject that had been nagging her for weeks, and almost unbearably for the past several days.

"It isn't getting any easier," she said.

Fedderman sipped his cabernet as if he knew good wine from bad, and raised his eyebrows. He'd known something was weighing on Penny lately. Now he was going to learn what it was.

"Whenever you leave," she said, "I can't help thinking it might be the last time I see you alive."

How many cops' wives have said that to their husbands?

He relaxed, but only slightly.

"Accountants' wives think that kind of thing, too," Fedderman said. He actually wasn't sure of that.

"Accountants' wives know the statistical probabilities and don't worry as much as I do."

"You've thought this out," Fedderman said.

"I'm just saying . . ."

"What?"

"I'm not sure I can keep living this way. Wondering daily if I'm going to lose you."

He smiled at her, unable to disguise his pleasure in knowing she loved him enough to worry about him so. Yet it was the intensity of her emotions that was a threat to their marriage. At least she seemed to be telling him that.

"It's not like being a cop on TV, Pen. The truth is, most of the time it's a boring job. Just like an accountant's."

"Accountants don't run around trying to confront serial killers," Penny said.

"Who are trying not to be confronted," Fedderman pointed out lamely.

"Don't try to tell me about serial killers," Penny said.

Fedderman nodded. Her sister had been the victim of a serial killer two years ago. That was how he and Penny had met, when he'd accompanied her to identify the body.

"What I'm trying to tell you about is my job," he said. "Tomorrow I'm gonna attempt to contact the parents of a murder victim's roommates, to see if any of their daughters mentioned anything we might find useful. That's the sort of thing I usually do, Pen. I'll be at a computer or on the phone most of the day. The only danger I'll face is carpal tunnel syndrome. It's more likely that a book at the library will fall from a shelf and injure you than that I'll be hurt on the job."

Penny finished her wine. She didn't look as if she believed him in the slightest. "Maybe you *should* worry about me, what with Henry James and Ayn Rand looming."

"Not really. Even Stephen King isn't much of a threat. And talking on the phone to the parents of the dead woman's roommates isn't likely to be dangerous for me. Damned unpleasant, but not dangerous."

Their tiramisu arrived, along with coffee. They ate and sipped silently for a while. The restaurant was warm, but it was a comforting warmth that had more to do with the scents of spices from the kitchen than with the summer heat outside.

"So tomorrow you shouldn't worry," Fedderman said.

"What about the day after?"

"Nobody knows about that one," Fedderman said. "Not accountants or airline pilots or salespeople or hedge fund managers or cops. There isn't much we can do about the day after tomorrow."

"Except try to live to it and through it," Penny said. "Both of us."

When they were finished with dinner, they went out into the night and strolled back toward the apartment. The evening had cooled down somewhat, and there was a nice breeze playing along the avenue.

In the apartment, they left the air conditioners off and opened a couple of windows. Night sounds entered from outside, along with a slight movement of air.

Fedderman encircled Penny with his arms, pulled her gently to him, and kissed her on the lips. She tasted like wine and garlic and sweet chocolate.

"I know how to free your mind from worry completely," he said.

"Feds . . ."

"I don't want to lose you," he whispered in her ear.

How many times have cops said that to their wives?

"Nobody wants to lose anyone," she said.

He kissed her again, and they went into the bedroom.

They made love as if it were their first time, or their last. Did this premonition of finality mean something? To Fedderman, everything meant something. And Penny was starting to think the same way.

Afterward she slept peacefully beside him, while Fedderman lay awake staring into darkness, braced for impending nightmares and aware that nothing had been settled.

He knew that Penny was the sort who, if there was a problem, did something about it.

13

The morning sun grew larger and more orange, dissipating the lingering haze. Quinn threaded the Lincoln through heavy traffic and drove from the city and into upper New York State. Pearl sat quietly beside him in the passenger's seat. The sun burning through the windshield was making her sleepy. The radio was playing softly and had lapsed into a rap tune:

> *You be the one*
> *I got the gun*
> *The favorite son*
> *Run, bitch, run*
> *You know I got the gun*

Pearl wondered if the lyrics had really been thought out, if they had any significance. She couldn't help doubting. She reached forward and switched the radio off, then glanced over at Quinn. "Do you mind?"

"Most of the time, if I'm told nice."

"What the hell do you think those lyrics mean?"

"Means he's got the gun."

She continued to stare at him but couldn't make out his eyes behind the dark lenses of his sunglasses.

Pearl settled back in the Lincoln's plush upholstery and crossed her arms. She tried to doze off, but couldn't.

Run, bitch, run.

The drive had taken them a little more than an hour. Waycliffe College was about a mile outside Putneyberg, a town easy to miss if you weren't paying attention and drove past the "Business Loop." The town proper was an assemblage of clapboard shops and shaded side streets. Quinn wouldn't have been surprised to see Andy and Barney patrolling.

Traffic was sparse. So was paint. The structures that weren't brick had taken on a gray, weathered look. Quinn decided what the hell, call it rustic.

As they drove along Main Street (what else?) the few people on the sidewalks didn't pay much attention to the Lincoln. They were probably used to luxury vehicles coming and going, many of them carrying present and future trust-fund babies. The loop off the highway was now mostly for the college.

Waycliffe wasn't large enough to transform Putney-berg into a college town. Only one of the two local bars looked like the kind of place Waycliffe students would frequent. A twenty-four-hours place called Price's. Of course, there was always the other bar, a dump called Eddies (without an apostrophe), if some dumb college kid wanted to pick a fight. Probably at either place they could score drugs.

The newest-looking object in Putneyberg was the big shiny sign informing Quinn and Pearl that Waycliffe College was one mile ahead, and that Putneyberg wished them good-bye. Quinn looked for a HELLO sign on the other side of the street where traffic ran the opposite direction, and there it was.

"No gown versus town here," Pearl said. "It looks like gown won a long time ago."

"I didn't see anyone of college age," Quinn said.

"Because it's summer."

"Still, only a mile away from a cold beer . . ."

The trees bordering the road suddenly looked a lusher green than the others, and they were well trimmed. There was a sign announcing the college turnoff was five hundred feet ahead.

Quinn braked and made the right turn, and they were on smooth blacktop winding through more uniformly trimmed trees. Quinn and Pearl, New Yorkers, offered a few guesses about what kind of trees they were, but they probably weren't even close.

And there ahead was the college, an assemblage of similar redbrick buildings, most of which were at least half devoured by ivy. The largest building, brick and with a column-flanked entrance, loomed before them. Where the ivy had been trimmed away, carved stone lettering identified it as the administration building. All the ivy and other foliage lent the grounds a lush look, but at the same time everything was neatly manicured. Waycliffe had about it the burnished quality of the old and invaluable.

There was a small gravel lot in front of the building. Half a dozen cars were parked in reserved spaces near the entrance. Quinn parked before one of the VISITORS signs on the opposite side of the lot, in the shade.

When Quinn and Pearl entered the building they were surprised by how cool it was. The only person in sight was a girl in her late teens or early twenties seated cross-legged on a lone wooden bench, diligently copying something from a netbook computer in her lap into a spiral notebook.

"We're looking for Chancellor Schueller," Pearl said.

The girl didn't glance up but pointed with a long, decorous fingernail to her left.

They walked down the hall about fifty feet, past a couple of blank wooden doors to a larger, six-paneled oak door with a brass plaque lettered OFFICE OF THE CHANCELLOR.

Quinn knocked and opened the door simultaneously.

They entered a small anteroom with book-lined walls and a narrow desk, behind which sat a gray-haired woman with a wasted look and a narrowed left eye that gave her a kind of shrewd expression. She'd apparently just closed a bottom desk drawer and sat up straight. She gave them a *May I help you?* smile.

"We have an appointment to see Chancellor Schueller," Quinn said. He and Pearl simultaneously flashed their identification.

"Oh, yes, the police," the woman said. "About poor Macy Collins, I would imagine." Without waiting for her assumption to be confirmed, she rose from her chair and strode to one of two oak doors like the ones connecting to the hall. She knocked gently on the door on her left, pushed it open a few feet, and announced them.

Then she opened the door wider, and Quinn and Pearl walked past her into Chancellor Linden R. Schueller's office.

Schueller was standing behind his desk, grinning widely, in meet-and-greet mode. He was a slender, handsome man, perhaps early forties, in a neat gray blazer with leather elbow patches. His dark hair was combed sideways with geometric precision from a perfect part. Gold cuff links flashed on white cuffs. His eyes, behind newly fashionable tortoise-shell glasses, were brilliant blue and aware. He looked too much like a rich playboy to be an academic

After introductions and hand shakes, he motioned with his arm toward two small but overstuffed chairs facing the desk, causing a gold watch to flash beneath a white cuff. "Detectives, please make yourselves comfortable."

Quinn and Pearl did, while Schueller settled in behind his wide, cluttered desk. There was a green desk with narrow leather edging of the sort people stuck business cards and odds and ends under. An array of envelopes, slips of paper, and business cards were wedged beneath the rich-looking leather. It struck Quinn as odd that Schueller would have such disorderly layers of paper on his desk; didn't college chancellors delegate most of the actual work?

"You mentioned that this was about poor Macy Collins," Schueller said. He shook his head and appeared genuinely sad. "Such a bright young woman. Such a terrible waste."

"Did you know her personally?" Quinn asked.

"Oh, we in administration know all our students, especially those with the potential Macy Collins possessed."

"Then you might know which students were her particular friends," Pearl said.

"She had many friends, but mostly on a casual basis. Students in the Vanguard program are kept quite busy. They're primarily here to learn, and they want to learn. They form fast friendships, but it takes a while. Macy hadn't been in Vanguard quite long enough to make those connections."

"She was a sophomore," Quinn pointed out.

"Yes, but a Vanguard program sophomore."

"She was that from the beginning?"

"Oh, yes. She was chosen for her exceptional abilities. Most of her qualifying and placement test scores were well above the ninety-nine percentiles group. Our Vanguard students quite often are recruited into responsible, high-paying jobs immediately after they obtain their degrees." He beamed, proud of his students. "Waycliffe alumni do quite well in the world. You might pause on your way out to examine our Wall of Fame."

"Macy Collins will never be there," Pearl remarked.

"Sadly, that's true." He looked at Pearl as if disappointed that she'd stated the obvious. Pearl would never make the Vanguard program.

"Macy lived in a dorm," Quinn said. "Is it unusual that she didn't have a roommate?"

"No. All our Vanguard students have private rooms."

Why am I not surprised? Pearl thought. Her college years before she'd dropped out were, to her recollection, a haze of arguments with her instructors, parties, and putting up with people who mostly infuriated her. And, oh, yeah, there'd been sex. The kind that didn't budge the earth an inch. Criminology courses had been her only refuge.

"We'd like to take a look at her room," Quinn said.

Schueller nodded. "Of course. It's relatively barren. She took most of her possessions with her to the apartment she subleased in the City. The apartment where she was living when she . . ."

"Died," Pearl finished for him.

Schueller stood up and absently buttoned his blazer. "Your professional scrutiny might find something pertinent."

They left the administration building and Schueller accompanied them along a curving concrete walk toward a three-story redbrick building with the requisite relentless ivy framing its entrance. The campus was almost deserted. A few people were strolling the walkways. A couple was seated side by side on a wooden bench beneath a shade tree, speaking to each other as if in rapture. A hundred feet from them a young man with a mane of curly blond hair sat cross-legged on the grass, working attentively on his upside-down bicycle. That was it for human habitation, other than Schueller and his two guests with guns. Pearl felt as if she didn't belong here.

"We have summer classes in session now," Schueller said, glancing at his watch, "so the place isn't as deserted as it seems." He drew a briar pipe from his pocket and clamped down on it in the corner of his mouth. "I don't actually light this thing," he said. "Bad example for the students. But I like the aroma of the unlit tobacco."

"You must have been a heavy smoker at one time," Pearl said.

The chancellor smiled around his pipe stem. "We won't talk about that."

And maybe a lot of other things, Pearl thought.

Macy Collins might have had a private dorm room, but it was small. There was room for a narrow bed, a desk, a closet with a tri-folding louvered door, a single window looking out on an area of green and meticulously tended lawn. In the distance were crowded trees and the dormered roofs of old but well-kept homes, some of them quite large and no doubt expensive. Some faced the street beyond, others the campus. Quinn supposed that was where some of the tenured faculty lived. There must be plenty of endowment money to augment the lofty tuition fees hinted at in the college brochures.

A flat-screen monitor with a blank screen was on a corner of the wooden desk, along with a full-sized keyboard. A small printer sat on the floor near a desk leg. Everything but the computer, just as there had been no computer in Macy Collins's apartment.

"It appears that she had a laptop she hooked up here."

"All of our students are furnished with laptops," Schueller said, holding the briar pipe in his hand now. It was for show, anyway. "There's no need to instruct them on their usage. Computer literacy is one of our prerequisites. Even our non-Vanguard students are superior in most respects. Mostly they come from the best families. I'm sure even a detective would recognize some of their names."

"Maybe especially a detective," Pearl said. This guy Schueller was about to make her puke.

"The full-sized keyboards and monitors are optional," Schueller said. "The monitors are for watching movies, or occasionally sports."

"Does Waycliffe have a football team?" Quinn asked.

Schueller smiled tolerantly. "We only play lacrosse."

"Ah," Pearl said.

Quinn was picking up her vibes and hoped she wouldn't mouth off.

They poked around for a while, but there was nothing of use in the tiny dorm room. Macy Collins hadn't possessed much, and most of it—including her laptop, which might have been taken by her killer—could have been transferred via backpack to her address in Manhattan. Macy had lived light, and probably mostly alone, at least somewhat isolated by her intimidating IQ and penchant for listening, watching, and learning.

"Are any of her friends on campus taking summer classes?" Quinn asked Schueller.

"No. Most of our Vanguard students take summer internships. Some travel for further enlightenment. Others visit their families. I understand that Macy Collins was working as an intern at a law firm in the city."

"It didn't strike me that she was from a wealthy family," Quinn said.

"She wasn't. But a student like Macy is eligible for a great deal of grant and student loan money. For the most part, our students work real summer jobs only because they wish to experience them. I'm sure that for them the extra money is negligible."

Maybe, Quinn thought. It was something to check with Macy's mother.

He and Pearl thanked Chancellor Schueller and drove into Putneyberg to try Feed'n'Speed, the restaurant they'd noticed on Main Street. It was a low tan brick building with a NASCAR décor. Front ends of race cars lined the front edge of the flat roof. Just inside the door was a large black-and-white photo of racing and bootlegger legend Junior Johnson.

The service was slower than the sign promised or Johnson would have approved. Lunch was tasteless, but apple pie for dessert was terrific.

"Why do places like this usually serve great pie?" Quinn asked, washing down his final bite of pie with tepid coffee.

"Maybe it only seems that way because of the rest of the food." Pearl glanced around at what passed for the lunch crowd. About a dozen people at tables, and five slumped on red vinyl stools at the counter. Most of them were over fifty. Nobody seemed to be from the college. She could understand why most Waycliffe students went elsewhere for the summer.

"Notice something about Chancellor Schueller?" Quinn asked.

"Other than he's the kinda guy who was probably born with a pointer in his hand?"

"He seems more upset about the loss of such a promising student than about a young woman's violent death."

Pearl thought about that. "True. What do you think it means?"

"Right now, it means I'm gonna have another piece of pie." Quinn waved to get the waitress's attention.

"Only lacrosse," Pearl said. "Jesus H. Christ!"

Chancellor Schueller had summoned two faculty members to his office. Summer classes were over for the day, and the administration building was otherwise unoccupied. They would not be overheard.

It was warm in the office. Schueller sat behind his desk. Elaine Pratt sat relaxed with her legs crossed in one of the two office chairs. She wore a fashionable lightweight beige pantsuit and darker brown Jimmy Choo high-heeled pumps. Around her neck was a dainty gold chain threaded through a delicate cameo. Professor Wayne Tangler, who taught literature, was there, standing. He had on a navy-blue Hickey Freeman blazer and a striped silk tie over a pale lavender shirt. He was lean, with a gray downturned mustache and calculating gray eyes. On his lanky wrist was a loose-fitting platinum watch on a linked band. The three academicians looked as if they belonged on a yacht rather than in a tradition-bound, ivy-smothered college.

"We have a problem," the chancellor began. "It has a name. Macy Collins."

"The other students are naturally upset," Elaine said.

"That's not exactly the kind of problem I mean." Schueller was obviously uncomfortable with what he had to say. The others waited patiently while he struggled with himself. Out came his briar pipe; then it returned back to his pocket.

"The police are as of now uninterested in anyone at Waycliffe as a potential suspect in the Macy Collins murder, and I see no reason that might change."

"But it might," Elaine Pratt said.

"Exactly. If it does, we need to be ready. We have secrets other than murder that we can't have revealed. Secrets that a murder investigation might lead to incidentally. If a Waycliffe faculty member—one of us—is even mildly suspected of this crime, it could lead to the ruination of this institution we all love. It could deprive our students, and it could end our tenure at this great place of learning."

"Not to mention," Elaine said.

"Not to mention."

Tangler stood hipshot like a duded-up western gunslinger. He became very still. Elaine Pratt cocked her head to one side, like an interested sparrow.

"It might not be that bad," Elaine said.

"Don't kid yourself," Tangler said.

Elaine uncrossed her legs and looked over at Schueller. "Any ideas?"

Schueller began absently toying with a sharp-pointed yellow pencil on his desk. "The solution to our problem is simple," he said. "This suspected faculty member was here with us, in this office, on the evening of Macy Collins's death."

"Maybe this person already has an alibi," Elaine said.

Schueller shook his head. "If he does, if he, say . . . was in another city with a married woman, the police wouldn't suspect him of being in New York murdering Macy Collins." *Or if his flight plan suggested he was in another city* . . . "The point is, we don't want that sort of information to get beyond us."

"And the married woman," Tangler said.

"Of course."

"You're suggesting that we lie to the police," Elaine said.

"Only if necessary. It would be a harmless lie that might as just as easily be true, and it might save this college from extinction."

"As well as our jobs and considerable financial interests," Tangler said. He squinted at the chancellor. "I understand the cops were here today. Did they ask you about this person?"

"Not yet. And maybe they never will. But I want to be ready, and I need to know we can continue to count on each other."

"You're not only proposing that we lie to the police, but that we do so in a murder investigation," Elaine said, as if to make clear to each of them what was happening.

"Exactly."

"That will make us accomplices."

"In for a penny . . ." Tangler said, smiling beneath his mustache.

"We're already accomplices," the chancellor said. "But as far as the police are concerned, not in murder."

Tangler rubbed his chin, tugged at his mustache. "All right, Chancellor. You can rely on me."

"And me, I suppose," Elaine Pratt said, after a slight hesitation.

"We can't simply suppose," Schueller said.

"Of course. Count on me." No hesitation that time.

Schueller smiled, nodded, and stood up.

"Are we going to cut ourselves and join hands to mingle our blood?" Elaine asked.

"Our needs are already mingled," Tangler said. "As is our duty to each other."

"Noble talk," the chancellor said.

"Noble purpose," Tangler said.

"Let's not kid ourselves," Elaine Pratt said. "Especially about the death of Macy Collins."

Nobody drew blood, but they did shake hands.

14

"I love your body," Lou Gainer said to Ann Spellman.

"You made that clear just a few minutes ago," Ann said. She was still breathing hard, and her twenty-four-year-old nude body glistened with perspiration. She watched her diet and worked out faithfully almost every day, but even though she knew Gainer was several years older than she was, it was all she could do to keep up with him physically. He appeared deceptively slender in clothes. The grace of his movements and cut of his suits made his lean, hard physique a surprise.

She was aware of Gainer watching her closely as she rose from where she'd been seated on the edge of the mattress. After veering to the window to turn down the thermostat on the air conditioner, she padded barefoot into the bathroom.

In the mirror she caught sight of her compact, busty body, dark eyes, and thick black hair. It had been amazing how Lou had used her body, how much pleasure he'd given her, and derived from her. She felt a brief uneasiness about how skilled a lover Gainer was, how experienced he must be. His knowledge and lovemaking skills weren't intuitive. They had to have been learned. Nothing about that concerned Ann, other than that someone had to have taught him.

Jealous. That's all I am.

She pushed her worries to the back of her mind, pinched the flesh of her waist to make sure she wasn't putting on any excess weight, and turned on the shower. Testing the water carefully with her hand to make sure it wasn't too hot, she thought about trying to preserve what was left of her hairdo. Then figured screw it. She'd dry her hair with a towel and then comb it damp.

The steady spray of water was lukewarm and soothing, making her sorry she couldn't spend more time under it. But it didn't really matter. Warm water in this building didn't last long before it began to run cold.

Ann had no serious misgivings about her affair with Lou. He was her boss at Clinton Industrial Designs, where she worked as one of half a dozen graphic artists. The other employees all knew by now that Ann and Lou were a couple. One of them, an attractive and immensely talented artist named Gigi, had even asked in a round-about way if Ann might be thinking about a wedding.

Ann hadn't been, until Gigi put the idea in her head. *Twenty-four already. I'm not so young anymore, and the clock is ticking.*

Standing beneath warm needles of water in the tiled shower, Ann had to smile. Sleeping with the boss was one thing, but marrying him was something else altogether. There was a sense of adventure in their affair, spiced by secrecy even if it was an open secret. She wouldn't want to undermine that with talk of marriage. She needed to be careful here.

She was still smiling as the shower curtain was suddenly swished and jangled aside.

Lou stepped into the shower with her. He kissed her wet forehead and fondled her soapy breasts. Began sliding his hands down her back and over her buttocks.

"You're trembling," he said.

"You startled me. Haven't you ever seen *Psycho*?"

"I had another kind of movie in mind. Ever think what a hit we'd be in a porno film?"

She laughed. "Is that a proposition?"

"Just an idle thought."

Deciding more soap was called for, he picked up the tiny oblong sliver from the soap dish and shook his head. "Times are hard," he said, showing the thin oval of soap to Ann.

"So's something else."

He reached around her and rotated the chromed knob to make the downpour from the showerhead warmer, simultaneously kissing the side of her neck. The thin wafer of soap slipped from his other hand and didn't make a sound as it was taken by the gauze of water rippling on the shower stall floor. Lou used his bare foot to slide it over where it was out of the glide of water toward the drain.

"Speaking of hard," he whispered in her ear, "there's something I need to tell you."

She felt the warm tip of his tongue in her ear and squirmed, grinning, to wrench her head away. "So go ahead and tell."

His hesitation, something in the sudden stillness of his body, warned her, but she didn't grasp the meaning of her sudden premonition.

"I'm going to have to fire you," he said.

She toweled dry in a fury and stood before him in her white terry cloth robe, her wet hair a dark tangle like her thoughts. Her brown eyes danced with anger. Lou finished putting on his pants, then his shoes.

"What else do you have to say?" she asked.

He looked up at her from where he sat on the bed. "That I hate like hell to have been the one to tell you. But I had to. It's part of my job."

"Is it something I did—or didn't—do?"

"For God's sake no, Annie! It's the economy. I wasn't kidding when I told you times were hard. You know we've lost some big accounts. The company simply can't justify paying so many employees."

"I'm not the only graphic design artist there."

"And I'm not the one who decided to let you go. It was a board decision."

"Aren't you on the board?"

"You know I am."

"Boards are just a way to dilute responsibility," Ann said.

"C'mon, Annie . . ."

"Did you fight for me?"

"Hell yes, I fought."

She didn't believe him. The lie was in his eyes like an ominous object floating just beneath the surface of dark waters. He wasn't leveling with her. He'd decided to end her employment, probably as a way to end their affair.

And there the bastard sits. On my bed.

"So you thought you'd drop by one more time and have one last piece of poor, dumb Ann before telling her she's being cut loose. Or did you expect to keep coming over here and dropping your drawers while I was drawing unemployment?"

"That's not in the cards, Annie. It can't be."

"Better damn well believe it."

"The board knows you're good, and you'll probably soon be working for the competition. How'd it look if you and I were still having this secret affair that everyone knows about?"

She had a hard time catching her breath. "Lou . . . I can hardly get my mind around this."

He hung his head. "Me, either. We just got caught up in circumstances." He raked his fingers through his damp hair and looked at her petite, tight body. But it was an oddly impersonal appraisal, as if he were assessing a piece of statuary rather than a real person. Ann realized he was fixing her in his memory. "You're still the most beautiful woman I've ever slept with."

She was still struggling with her comprehension.

"I'll have your stuff sent here to you," he said, "along with your final check. You know how they are. They don't want you in the office once you've been severed."

"*They?* You are *they*."

He stood up and looked at her sadly. "Did I ever say I wasn't?"

She rubbed her towel with vicious abandon over her mussed wet hair, squinting at him through flying droplets. "You are really a sack of shit, Lou."

He nodded in silent agreement, put on his shirt, and left.

15

Central Florida, 2002

Sophia wanted everyone to see what she had done. That was why the sky was a cloudless blue, and the only breeze was soft and cool. The air was so clean and clear it seemed possible to see details half a mile away, like looking through a pair of powerful binoculars.

It didn't require binoculars to see what Sergeant Ed Hall of the Florida State Police was looking at.

The sergeant stood staring down at a dead girl. She looked so frail beneath the wreckage of the barn. And there was something about her injuries, even beneath all that blood. There seemed to be dark rings around the flesh of her wrists, and the flesh was wrinkled. The same marks were around at least one of her ankles, too.

A length of rough-hewn beam lay across her mid-section, and it appeared that it had come down and smashed her rib cage. Not much doubt as to what had killed her.

But what had she been doing in the barn almost nude? It was possible that the fierce winds of the hurricane or a trailing tornado had stripped the clothes from her.

Except for another oddity, at least to Hall's way of thinking. She was wearing black thong underwear. A strange thing, for a kid her age. Unless she'd been older than she appeared now, dead.

The thing about the underwear that struck Hall as odd was that he'd just come from the eastern part of the state, following the wide swath of Hurricane Sophia, and he remembered the Ambersons being found dead in the wreckage of their house. One of the cops there had been saying it was hard to tell, what with the condition of the bodies, but it looked like Nathan Amberson might have been shot.

His wife, Flora, had been found nearby, her body also mutilated by fierce winds and debris. She'd been mostly buried in wreckage, and nude, like this poor as-yet-unidentified girl.

Hall had known the Ambersons slightly. Flora, though getting along in years, had been an attractive woman, and was rumored to have been sexually adventurous in her youth. Hall knew that some of the rumors were true. Husband Nathan, in fact, had once been talked out of shooting an unwanted suitor with a shotgun.

Hall stared down at the dead girl under the barn and rubbed his bristly jaw. A black thong on Flora Amberson, maybe.

On this girl, never.

But that wasn't the only thing about the girl that didn't set well with Hall. It was something about her eyes. Something that made it hard to look into them.

They reminded him of other dead eyes.

16

Professor Elaine Pratt stood tall and slim in designer jeans and a crisp white blouse, the practical kind of outfit she usually wore to teach summer courses. She had on her cameo necklace on its gold chain, and a gold bangle bracelet. Her dishwater-blond hair was shoulder length, her eyes brown and intense beneath a wisp of bangs.

There were only a dozen students in her business psychology class, seven female, five male, but they were among the brightest attending Waycliffe College. All of them were in the Vanguard program for advanced students. When they graduated, they would be more than ready for the world beyond the ivy.

The room was bright from a long bank of jalousie windows, and furnished with rows of small gray metal desks and a wooden table up front. There was a large flat-panel screen behind Professor Pratt, and an open laptop computer nearby so when necessary she could PowerPoint salient information. She believed imagery was crucial to learning.

A wasp droned persistently against the closed windows, bouncing off the glass, going nowhere.

"I can see that some of you are upset," the professor said to her class. "There are signs that you've been crying. It's a sad thing when someone as young and promising as Macy Collins dies. It's even more tragic because her life was taken from her violently."

There was no sound from the class other than a few sniffles. Three of the students showed no emotion at all, other than impatience. They obviously wanted to get the mourning over with so they could begin class.

"This is, despite its sad dimensions, positive," the professor said, "an opportunity to express and understand that whatever the circumstances, we must press on. There is a time for grieving and emoting. This is not it. That is not a coldhearted assessment of the situation, but a pragmatic one. In the wider world there will come times when you'll be faced with similar situations. What will be right won't *seem* right. Vestiges of childhood concepts of morality, of rights and wrongs, can haunt and cloud your logic. It must not. You can't let it. Your opposite number somewhere will be yielding to no such delusions. He or she will have long ago locked them away so that they're no longer a part of the decision-making process. The earlier you learn to compartmentalize, the better for all concerned."

"Except Macy Collins," Juditha Jason said. Juditha, known on campus as "Jody," didn't say it in a tone of disagreement. She seemed to be speaking thoughtfully, and mainly to herself.

"Macy will not lodge a complaint," Professor Pratt said. There were a few snickers. "In the military," she said, "there was an officer who, shortly before a major battle, stood before his fresh recruits, a dead enemy at his feet. He kicked the dead man in the head. Then he opened his canteen and poured water into the corpse's gaping mouth. He made his troops do the same. He was teaching them there was nothing to be feared from the dead. They had nothing more to do with the living. They would not feel nor benefit from your respect, your empathy, your regret, or any other emotion. They were simply . . . the dead." She met the gazes of each of her students. "He doubtless saved many of his troops' lives with that demonstration. They learned that there is a time for grieving, and then the dead are simply inanimate objects. Am I making myself understood?"

"If you aren't pragmatic, you're going to lose the battle," a tousle-haired boy in the last row said.

"Precisely," Professor Pratt said, pleased.

"I agree with what you say," Jody Jason said, "but we can't simply put what happened to Macy out of our minds."

"We can for the next hour," the professor said.

And for the most part, they did.

Professor Pratt considered that a breakthrough.

After class, Jody lingered and approached the professor, who was gathering her teaching materials and poking them into a brown leather bag that was a cross between a large purse and a briefcase.

"I noticed a man and woman talking with Schueller," Jody said.

"You mean Chancellor Schueller."

"Of course." Jody actually thought of the professor as "Elaine," and the chancellor simply as "Schueller." But she'd learned to be careful. Hierarchy and respect were important at Waycliffe. "I was wondering if they were talking about Macy Collins."

"I can't enlighten you on that," Professor Pratt said. "But I wouldn't be surprised."

"Were they police?"

"Yes. That's my understanding."

"Are they going to talk to any of the students?"

"I wouldn't know." Professor Pratt closed and latched her purse-briefcase. "Why are you so interested?"

"It's a puzzle," Jody said. "A murder case that cries out to be solved."

"How do you know it isn't solved? There might be an obvious perpetrator. Possibly a boyfriend none of us knows about."

"I wouldn't think so. And the way she was killed. Did you read about Macy's injuries, the awful things done to her?"

"Actually I haven't," Professor Pratt said. "All I've seen or heard about the case is from a capsule report on a cable news channel this morning. It was too hysterical to be very informative."

"The twenty-four-hour news cycle."

"Yes, it's changed the world," Professor Pratt said. "Not necessarily for the better."

"It's easier to find people."

Professor Pratt looked at Jody as if trying to decipher some code. "That's not always a good thing."

"I meant with the Internet. The social networks."

"More like antisocial networks."

"Sometimes, I guess. Do you happen to know the names of the two detectives who were here earlier today?"

"No. Sorry. Chancellor Schueller might be able to help you there, but I'm not sure you should bother him with business other than Waycliffe's."

"Macy was a Waycliffe student," Jody pointed out.

Professor Pratt laid a hand on her wrist and gave a little squeeze. "If I were you, I wouldn't talk to the chancellor, or to the police, about Macy Collins. Remember what I said about compartmentalizing. Well, this isn't the time for you to be distracted. Concentrate on your studies and let the detectives go ahead and detect. You shouldn't get enmeshed in a murder case, Jody. For a number of reasons, not the least of which is that nothing about this case involves you. As far as you're concerned, what happened to Macy Collins exists in another dimension, and one you shouldn't visit."

"I suppose you're right," Jody conceded, smiling as if the professor had persuaded her.

How wrong you are.

"So what kind of place is Waycliffe College?" Fedderman asked Quinn and Pearl, after they'd returned to the office.

Pearl had made a fresh pot of coffee and was pouring some into her initialed mug. "Kinda place where half the girls are nicknamed Muffy, and the boys Bunny."

"Like state prison," Fedderman said.

"I won't even ask what that means," Mishkin said. He and Sal Vitali had divided the notes from the interviews with Macy Collins's neighbors and were poring over them to find items of interest or contradictions.

"It looks like minor league Ivy League," Quinn said, leaning back in his desk chair. "Small and secluded."

"Very picturesque," Pearl said.

Sal growled something unintelligible.

"And it looks like money," Pearl said.

"That, too," Quinn said.

"But I think *secret* suits it better than *secluded*." Pearl sipped her coffee and made a face. "Maybe that's an odd word to describe it, but that's the impression it gives. Like there's some dark and musty secret hanging over the place."

Quinn swiveled slightly in his chair and said nothing. He'd had the same feeling as Pearl's, that something just beyond sight or sound was lurking in the ivy. Or maybe that was because it had been a long time since either of them had been on a college campus. The quiet, shaded grounds and buildings of Waycliffe were a detached world of their own. One conducive to pondering and discussing rather than conducting police interviews.

After all, the Collins murder had occurred in the real world, beyond the rows of oak and maple trees that marked the boundaries of the academic enclave. In the world of Waycliffe, everything had to make sense. In Quinn's world there was chaos.

"Are we going back there?" Harold asked.

"Right now we don't have a reason," Quinn said. "There doesn't seem to be anything connected to the college that figures into Collins's death. And there wasn't anything useful in her dorm room."

"No computer there, either," Pearl said. "And the crime scene unit didn't remove one from her apartment."

"No computer, few friends," Sal growled. "Makes things difficult."

"On the other hand," Harold said, "Macy hardly knew anyone in New York, so if a serial killer didn't do her, there aren't too many suspects." Harold, looking on the bright side.

"You don't have to know someone in New York to get murdered," Sal said.

Helen Iman, the NYPD profiler, came in, making the office suddenly smaller with her six-foot-plus height. She was wearing khakis and a white pullover shirt with a collar and looked like a women's basketball coach. Quinn wasn't sure if she'd ever actually played basketball.

She was sweating, as if she'd been running up and down the court.

"Hot out there," she said, pulling a plastic water bottle from a khaki pocket and taking a hearty swig. "I was by earlier and you weren't here," she said to Quinn, back-handing away water that was dribbling down her long chin.

"He and Pearl have been to college," Fedderman said.

Quinn described the visit at Waycliffe to Helen.

She seemed to become more interested as the account unfolded.

"You think the college president—"

"Calls himself the chancellor," Quinn interrupted.

"Okay. Whatever. You feel he was being evasive?"

"Yes," Pearl answered.

Quinn nodded, not as sure. He didn't want to go off in a wrong direction here. "It was only a feeling," he said. "We have no reason to believe he was lying about anything."

"The college itself looks too good to believe," Pearl said. "So picturesque, and isolated from the town. Snooty as hell, too. They play lacrosse and only lacrosse."

"I lettered in lacrosse," Helen said.

"I bet you played field hockey, too."

Quinn shot Pearl a warning look. If a spark was struck, the two women sometimes deliberately tried to get on each others' nerves. *Go easy, Pearl.*

"Good game, lacrosse, if you're up to it," Helen said, apparently primed for an argument this morning.

"We're not concerned about their athletic program," Quinn said, heading off trouble. "Anyway, it isn't the kind of place you'd think would have a bowl contender."

"Football," Pearl said. "Beats the hell out of lacrosse."

"Maybe we oughta go back up there," Fedderman said, coming to Quinn's rescue before Helen could reply.

"I don't think so," Quinn said. "Schueller might just have been nervous, like a lot of people when they come face-to-face with the law. Especially if it concerns a murder investigation. That sort of thing would be foreign to the Waycliffe campus."

"We would hope," Helen said. "What about Macy Collins's friends there?"

"She didn't seem to have any close friends. She was in something called the Vanguard program, for gifted students. Sounded to me like everybody in the program had to work too hard to have time for friends."

"Not like the jocks," Pearl said. *Jab, jab* . . .

"They must have a basketball team," Helen said, as if every institution with more than five people did.

"No," Quinn said. "Only lacrosse. I didn't see any obvious jocks. The women we saw looked like college types. Trendy, studious. The men were Ivy League types, or nerds. Everybody looked like they spent too much time on Facebook and Twitter."

"Of course," Pearl said, "we didn't see many students. Summer classes were in session. But Quinn's right; the few students we did see looked like nerds or future bond salesmen. The geeky kids who did all their homework in high school."

"Sounds like you need a perfect SAT score to get near the place," Fedderman said.

"Or perfect bank account," Pearl said.

"They should have a basketball team," Helen said.

"Only lacrosse," Quinn said, before Pearl could.

"Macy Collins have a roommate in her dorm?"

"No," Quinn said. "Vanguard students room alone."

"And die alone," Harold said. He'd been silent on the other side of the office, listening.

Quinn sat wondering if this conversation was getting them anywhere. It seemed to emphasize the paucity of hard facts in the investigation. A serial killer (if he was one) like Daniel Danielle who butchered his victims (if there was more than one) didn't seem to have much to do with an exclusive and secluded college, even though the dead woman had been a student there. Quinn was beginning to think they'd taken a wrong turn.

"I were you," Helen said, "I'd drive back up there."

"Why?" Quinn asked.

"No basketball team."

17

Something was wrong with Ann Spellman's laptop computer. Her wallpaper that formed the background of her desktop on her screen when she turned on the computer had somehow changed from blue sky to a news photo of victims lying under blankets on the side of a highway after a horrible head-on collision between a car and truck.

Her computer had been hacked. Great! Another disruption in her life.

Everything else seemed the same when she went online, so not exactly *wrong* . . . but different.

This was the third day of her unemployment. Her personal possessions had been delivered from her desk at work at Clinton Industrial Designs, and she was sure she'd be *persona non grata* if she ever so much as entered the building.

One good thing was that the worries of her job had melted away. Being among the unemployed was unsettling, even scary. Yet it was undeniably liberating.

She had to smile. *Being thrown out of a high window probably creates the same sensation, and where does that get you?*

One thing, though. Life was simpler now. All she had to do was find another job. And stop thinking about Lou Gainer.

She clicked on her computer's history and saw the familiar sites she'd recently visited. Various business networks. Matchmaking services. But were they in the same order as when she'd last left the computer?

They seemed the same. She didn't know a lot about computers, but thought you had to go online in order to change your wallpaper. Then it struck her that someone might not have hacked into her computer remotely, but could have gone online here, in her apartment, and simply noted her browser's history and visited the sites in the order in which she'd left them.

If they knew her passwords.

She reached over and tilted her heavy desk lamp sideways so that the weighted base lifted. There was her folded slip of paper with her handwritten passwords and screen names.

But was it folded in the same way? Hadn't the quarter-folded sheet of printer paper been pressed perpendicular to the desk edge, rather than at an angle?

She couldn't be sure.

She replaced the list beneath the lamp base, thinking how dumb it was to keep it hidden there. Probably half the people who used computers kept their passwords and screen names list hidden beneath the base of their desk lamp. It had to be the first place any self-respecting thief or hacker would look. Of course, as far as she knew, somebody who really understood computers could get to her sites without knowing the passwords. That was one of the reasons she'd decided on the desk lamp, with its heavy base. That, and the list was handy.

Who the hell would want to look at my computer?

Clinton Industrial Designs, maybe. Because they might

want to know who she was contacting in her attempts to find another job. Lou Gainer had told her they didn't want her taking trade secrets with her to use as leverage when interviewing for employment. The industrial design world was a shark tank.

She took several deep, calming breaths. This was silly, she told herself. Losing her lover and her job simultaneously was making her suspicious of everything. Wouldn't anyone get a bit paranoid after such an experience?

She leaned back and considered the items on the desk. Her laptop computer, a green, leather-bordered desk pad; a pen holder with compartments for paper clips, stamps, and whatever; a phone and answering machine; an Edward Hopper print mug that held pens and pencils; a cork coaster borrowed from Ellie's Lounge; and a small Rolodex. The symmetry of the objects' placement seemed the same as always.

A quick check of her desk drawers revealed nothing even slightly different.

Ann sat very still, aware of her heartbeat, and after a few minutes she felt satisfied that nothing had been moved in her absence.

A sudden thought sent a chill through her. She got up from her chair and hurried to the door to the hall. After opening the door, she stepped into the hall and glanced both ways, making sure she was alone. Had a shadow moved near the banister's turn in the stairwell leading to the foyer? Someone hurrying down the steps? In a far part of her mind she wondered if she'd been lured out of her apartment. Was it possible that someone very smart, and very malevolent, was manipulating her? Toying with her?

No, no, don't be an idiot!

For a few seconds she forgot why she'd come out into

the hall. Then she stretched up on her toes and felt along the top of the door frame. That was where she kept an extra key, in case she lost or misplaced hers and couldn't get inside. Lou Gainer had returned his key to her apartment. Did he know about the spare key? She wasn't sure.

Ann rubbed her fingertips over the lintel's rough wooden surface, ignored by generations of painters—and there was the key.

She took it down and stuck it in a pocket, then went back into her apartment. Closing the door firmly, she worked the dead bolt and fastened the brass chain lock.

The rest of the world was outside now, and she was inside, with a better handle on reality. She was safe, and had been since arriving home and walking through the door. Imagination could be such a bitch.

I'm so paranoid!

She felt slightly ashamed and embarrassed. She'd really gotten herself going, and over nothing but suspicion. Why should that be a surprise? After what had happened to her, could she trust anyone ever again?

Don't be a fool. You'll get over it.

She did feel better now, after this evidence of her security. She was imagining the worst and working herself into a fearful state over nothing.

Ann returned to her desk and sat back down at her laptop. She clicked on Facebook and there was her home page, her familiar profile photo.

And a posting that was from her.

From Ann.

Right beneath her photograph. The one with her cocking her head to the side and smiling:

I have this feeling something bad is about to happen.

Facebook said the message had been posted slightly more than a minute ago. Ann hadn't posted a Facebook message in over a week.

When I was out in the hall!

Suddenly the image on her computer screen faded and vanished. Her software programs began to appear, one after another, then roll and disappear, more and more rapidly, while she sat there stunned.

Some kind of virus!

. . . Something bad is about to happen.

"The best thing to do in a situation like this is unplug the computer," said a voice behind her.

A hand rested on her right shoulder and squeezed hard enough to hurt.

18

Jody Jason absently flipped her thick red hair and jogged up the wide concrete steps toward the impressive entrance to Jung Hall, known among students simply as the psych building.

It was warm in the building, but still a few degrees cooler than outside. Professor Elaine Pratt was waiting for her in her office. Jody doubted if the appointment had anything to do with her business psychology class, which the professor taught. Though Jody was majoring in law, the Vanguard program had assigned Professor Pratt to be Jody's counselor. Besides, the B-Psych class was a snap for Jody, like most of her other classes.

The office was small and cluttered, and lined with enough books to make it smell musty. Books were shelved wherever possible, including above the windows and doors. Most of the books pertained to law, psychology, and psychiatry. But there were also biographies, medical tomes, sets of general reference books, textbooks . . . even popular fiction. Jody had long ago made note of the fact that the professor was an eclectic reader. Elaine Pratt wasn't one of those indrawn academics constricted by narrow if long tunnels of knowledge.

She'd stood up behind her desk when Jody knocked and entered. Now she motioned for Jody to take a chair near the desk and sat back down. Jody cleared some books from the chair and moved it over so it was more directly facing the desk.

Professor Pratt was wearing a starched yellow blouse today with light gray slacks. Jody figured that the professor, if she wanted to dress for it, could achieve a stunning willowy attractiveness. Like a fashion model. Jody could imagine her strutting down a runway, drawing every eye like a magnet.

In the wall of bookshelves directly behind her desk was one of those huge two-volume boxed Oxford dictionaries, the kind that came with a tiny cardboard drawer that held a magnifying glass for reading the fine print. Staring at it, Jody decided you must really want to look up a word to wrestle with one of those mammoth, weighty volumes.

The professor smiled at Jody. "I can't reveal anything about it at this time," she said, "but I thought you should know that something good is coming your way."

Jody was surprised. "Good how?"

"I can't say, or I would. What I need to know is if you feel ready for a change in your life."

"Ready?"

"I need to know that you don't have plans for the rest of the summer that you've kept to yourself. That you're not pregnant. That sort of thing."

Jody laughed. "No other plans. And I guarantee you that I'm not pregnant."

"And I need to know if you're ready in other ways. If you've absorbed certain knowledge between the lines of text." Professor Pratt looked directly at Jody and didn't blink.

"I'm confident that I've absorbed those lessons," Jody said, knowing what the professor wanted to hear.

Telling people what they wanted to hear was a skill she'd mastered early and well.

"The chancellor and I have discussed you often," Professor Pratt said. "We think you have special abilities."

"I think I'm ready for whatever we're talking about here."

Professor Pratt stood up. "That's fine, Jody. I don't like keeping you hanging, but I needed to make sure you had that block of time free."

"I'm available," Jody said, smiling. "And thank you."

She maintained an erect posture as she went to the door and opened it.

She didn't glance back as she passed through into the anteroom and then into the hall. Nothing about her revealed her thoughts.

What the hell was that *all about?*

19

Choking to death!

That was Ann Spellman's first realization.

Then she began breathing deeply, noisily through her nose. Something—it felt to her tongue like tape—was clamped tightly over her mouth. She gagged, coughed, and worked the tip of her distorted tongue violently but couldn't budge the taut and tacky surface.

She forced calm on herself, made herself breathe evenly through her nose. Her mind refused to function fully as she tried to remember. The man, the drink . . . he must have put something in her drink. She remembered walking with him, supported by him. She hadn't been drunk—she knew that. She never drank enough to get drunk.

Had they walked to her apartment?

Had they just left her apartment?

Ann wasn't clear on any of it.

She attempted to move her arms and legs, and shuddered with painful, wracking cramps.

Where am I?

When she screamed almost silently into the unyielding

tape and opened her eyes wide, she realized everything was upside down. She was on a hard surface and staring at the night sky. She could see stars through the leaves of overhanging branches.

What an awkward, painful position she was in! How . . . ?

A man's voice spoke to her in memory: "The best thing you can do in a situation like this is unplug the computer."

Standing behind her, near her, when she was seated at her crashing computer.

He must have gotten in somehow and been hiding in the apartment when I locked the door. All the time I was thinking I was safe.

And now she was paying for her carelessness. She remembered now that she'd lost consciousness, and he'd forced her to drink, not wine. He'd said it was wine, but it was something else. It had made her dizzy, made her feel small, smaller, so that she did what he said, went with him somewhere. To a car?

She craned her neck and looked around. There were planters with brown, dead plants, a surrounding stockade fence with vines growing up it. There was a brick wall—dark, old brick. She seemed to be in something like a small courtyard. There was a moon. Light from somewhere else—maybe a streetlight.

A slight scuffing sound near her, where she couldn't see, made her muscles tighten with alarm. Her legs began cramping and she could do nothing to relieve the pain.

The fear, the dread knowledge she wanted so badly to deny, invaded her mind and body. Nausea expanded in her in waves and she had to swallow, terrified that if she vomited she'd choke to death. She began to tremble and felt her bladder release.

This is happening to me. To ME!

Make sense of it! For God's sake, concentrate and make sense of it so you can deal with it!

I'm not alone, but he hasn't done anything to me. Not yet. Maybe he won't. Maybe this is it. He's a sex nut who gets his jollies tying up women, then simply watching them, enjoying their helplessness.

It's possible. There are such men.

By the time she'd gathered her wild and errant thoughts, the cramps had subsided. She determined that she was on her knees with her wrists bound tightly behind her. A short, taut rope led from her bound wrists to where her ankles were crossed and tied together, causing her knees to splay out, her back to arch painfully.

Hog-tied.

She'd been hog-tied and then positioned so her upper body stretched backward, leaving her staring at the sky. There was a constant tension in her backward arched body that was in itself painful.

The natural urge to straighten her upper body to the perpendicular was in constant battle with the tautness of the rope that ran between wrists and ankles. She was drawn backward like a bow, as if to shoot an arrow into the night sky.

And it hurt. Her spine felt as if it might snap.

Now what?

A sole made a scuffing sound beside her. *Nearby.*

He loomed above her, and cold terror ran like a chill through the marrow of her bones. The violent cramps returned as her body strained again for its unattainable release. Her agony worked its way through the rectangle of duct tape over her mouth as a drawn-out keening plea, like the muted wail of a siren. Another soft wail, the tape playing in and out.

He showed her the knife, rotating the long silver blade so it caught the starlight, and smiled down at her.

"Let me know if you're uncomfortable," he said softly through the smile.

The knife's sharply honed blade found flesh, and then blood.

The muffled human siren wailed longer, louder, but not so loud that anyone nearby would hear.

Not that it mattered. The building was unoccupied. There was no one nearby.

They were in the small, brick courtyard of an East Village six-story walkup that was being rehabbed. Dawn had broken. CSU techs were busy doing their white-glove ballet, staying well away from Quinn, Pearl, Nift, and what was left of Ann Spellman.

"Shock, shock," said Nift, the pugnacious little M.E. "The victim has dark hair and eyes, and a great body with a terrific rack. Well, obviously *had* a terrific rack."

"I can see that," Quinn said, "even through the blood."

Nift, leaning over the awkwardly bound corpse, glanced sideways and let his gaze flick up and down Pearl. He didn't say what he was thinking, that the dead woman facedown on the hard paving stones, her back arched so drastically that she might have broken it in her death throes, was very much the same type as Pearl.

Pearl said nothing, but she stared unblinkingly at him in a way that would have embarrassed a man with the slightest sensitivity or consideration.

"After hog-tying her, he must have gripped her under the jaw and lifted so her breasts dangled. Then held her under the jaw and gone to work with the knife," Nift said. He was grinning. "Then he rocked her back on her knees and left her like she is, stargazing."

Quinn rested a huge and powerful hand on Pearl's shoulder, gently, but in a way that restrained her.

"She still has her panties on," Quinn said.

"Sure does," Nift said. "All pink and lacy, too. Dolled up to screw or die."

Quinn felt a sudden embarrassment for the dead woman, the way they were talking about her when she was right there with them. He was surprised. He'd thought he was past that. Somewhere in his mind it registered that this killer could get to him, make him feel that way.

"Rigor mortis has come and gone," Nift said, not seeming to notice that Pearl had almost sprung on him and sunk her teeth into his arteries—and still might do so. "I left her like this so you could see her before the paramedics removed the body. Her tits, incidentally, seem nowhere to be found. Like with the previous victim."

Quinn lifted his hand from Pearl's shoulder and patted her, then stepped forward and more closely examined the arched body on the redbrick pavers. The freeze-frame of terror in the woman's bulging eyes was something he'd dream about, even twenty years later, from time to time. If he made it that many more years in a world where people did things like this to each other.

"You should have seen the funny grin on her face before I removed this. It was jammed crossways in her mouth. I didn't know what it was till I got it out."

Quinn stared at a flat half circle of steel and then saw that it was marked. It was a protractor, used by draftsmen to calculate and draw angles.

"You should have left it where it was," he said.

"I know," Nift said. "Curiosity got the best of me. And I knew it was going to the morgue one way or the other. I found it interesting what the killer did. After everything that happened, he made her smile."

Both men looked down again at the dead woman.

The knots binding her were simple square knots of the sort anyone might tie. The rope itself looked like ordinary clothesline, impossible to trace even in this era when hardly anyone actually hung clothes out to dry. Here and there, the victim was cut for what seemed like pure meanness. The raw flesh and blood where her breasts had been made Quinn swallow bile and anger.

The rope and hog-tie were something new in Daniel's repertoire—and Quinn was becoming more firmly convinced that the killer *was* Daniel—but Quinn didn't find that surprising. Serial killers, even locked as they were in their obsessions, sometimes introduced variations in their methods. Often that was to mislead the police, but it could also be that Daniel had thought about ways to increase his pleasure and his victim's pain and fear, and come up with the hog-tie restraint. Classic serial killers were works in progress. That was what made them so terrifying.

Some of the simple knots were double tied, as if to make sure that rope crossed rope correctly. Simple but effective, like double tying your shoelaces. Quinn knew he was looking at precaution and not expertise.

"Our man's not a sailor," he said.

"Or Boy Scout," Pearl added.

"Depends on the kind of merit badge we're talking about," Nift said.

Fedderman came out the door into the courtyard, moving carefully so as not to interfere with the techs. He had on one of his cheap brown suits with the coat open and flapping. As he moved in his awkward gait, the coattails swung like pendulums, brushing and almost knocking over a pot of dead flowers on a rusty plant stand. He'd been talking to the super of the building next door, who'd discovered the body early this morning while searching for his runaway cat.

Quinn gave the okay to remove the body as long as the techs were finished with it, and then motioned for Fedderman to follow him back through the building and outside to the street. Pearl waited until Nift had finished packing up his instruments and was on his way out before joining them. As if she needed to stand guard over the dead woman to protect her from a necrophiliac. For years there had been whispered rumors about Nift.

Who'll protect her in the morgue?

As she was leaving, Pearl hesitated, then bent over the distorted corpse and looked at the label in the panties. They weren't an expensive brand, and were fairly new. She examined them more closely.

"So whadda we got?" Quinn asked Fedderman, when the three of them were standing out on the sidewalk.

Fedderman got out his leather-bound notepad, which he opened to the proper page and stared at as he spoke. "The super, a guy named Willy Fernandez, lives and has an office in the building next door. He's also been hired to keep an eye on this building while it's being rehabbed, and he has a key. His cat, Theo, took off and Fernandez had to go look for him. He saw Theo run into the next-door building with the door hanging open, so Fernandez let himself in and went looking for him. When he found Ann Spellman, he forgot all about Theo."

"I'll bet he did," Pearl said. "He the one called it in?"

"Yeah." Fedderman stuffed the notepad back in his pocket. "He's watched enough cop shows on TV to know not to touch anything, so he went back to his apartment next door and called the police."

"Not nine-one-one?" Quinn asked.

"No. He'd seen enough to know it wasn't an emergency."

"Where's Fernandez now?"

"In his apartment in the building next door. I told him we might wanna talk to him again."

"We do," Quinn said.

Fedderman stayed around to watch the body being removed, while Quinn and Pearl left to go to the building next door and talk to Fernandez the super.

An ambulance with its siren off but its red and yellow lights flashing was already coming down the block toward them. Ann Spellman's ride, picking its way through traffic. Fedderman could see the two paramedics behind reflections playing on the windshield.

He didn't envy them their job.

20

The foyer of the super's building was the same as that of the one next door, with a stairway falling away toward the basement, as well as ascending to a landing and a stairwell running up the rear wall. The walls had just been painted a pale green and there was no graffiti. An elevator had been installed in this building, but it had a hand-written OUT OF ORDER sign taped to its door. Quinn didn't mind, as he went ahead of Pearl down the steps and felt her lightly touching his shoulder as if for balance.

He pushed a button near a brass-lettered SUPER sign on the door, and it opened almost immediately. Fernandez had heard them descending the steps.

"I thought you'd be along soon," Fernandez said, as Quinn and Pearl flashed their IDs. He had a slight Spanish accent. He raised dark eyebrows. "You are NYPD?"

"Working with them," Quinn said.

"Closely?"

"Like lovers."

Fernandez grinned and stepped aside so they could enter. He was a short, handsome man in his forties, with sharp features and only a few gray strands in his jet-black hair combed straight back. He was wearing a green work outfit, but it was easy to imagine him in a tailored European suit playing a sleek gigolo in a play or movie.

Quinn had expected a modest basement apartment, but this one was spacious and well furnished, with a large flat-screen TV on one wall. A green recliner faced the TV directly. There was a small table next to the recliner with a beer bottle sitting on a magazine so it wouldn't leave a ring. Quinn could see a modern kitchen with white appliances beyond the living room.

"You live here alone?" he asked.

"I was with my wife until six months ago." Fernandez motioned with his arm toward a stiff-looking leather or vinyl sofa. "You want to sit down?"

Quinn and Pearl both declined.

"You and your wife separated?" Pearl asked. Fernandez hadn't struck a tragic note, so she assumed the wife hadn't died. Maybe the couple was divorced.

"She ran away with an electrician."

Pearl resisted asking him if it had come as a shock. She almost smiled.

Quinn, seeing something was going on with her, took over the conversation. "Did you know Ann Spellman?"

"The vic?"

Obviously Fernandez used his big TV to watch cop shows.

"The vic," Quinn confirmed.

"I never saw her before but to glance at her," Fernandez said.

A large gray cat entered the room, took brief notice of the presence of Quinn and Pearl, then ignored them. Quinn watched the cat effortlessly jump up onto a plush chair and curl into a ball, facing the other way.

"That Theo?" Quinn asked.

"The one and only," Fernandez said. "He slipped out when I was opening the door to go check and see if I had mail in my box. I forgot to look earlier, and I got a Netflix coming. *Lie to Me*. You ever see that one?"

"Constantly," Pearl said.

"So I go after Theo, up into the foyer, and damned if the street door wasn't open a few inches, the way it sticks sometimes, and I saw Theo squeeze through and outside."

"What time was this?" Quinn asked.

"About midnight."

"You wanted to watch *Lie to Me* at midnight?"

Fernandez shrugged. "What else I got to do, with the wife gone? I sure as hell couldn't get to sleep."

"Thinking about her and the electrician," Pearl said.

"You got it."

"Did you notice anyone coming or going at the building next door?"

"Just Theo. When I went outside to try to get him and bring him back, I saw him go into the other building. Its street door was hanging wide open."

"That was unusual?" Quinn asked.

"You bet. It might be an unoccupied building, but there's stuff to steal in there. Raw lumber, copper plumbing, even tools the workmen leave behind. That's why they hired me, to make sure nobody unauthorized came or went. The place is usually locked tight."

"But not tonight," Pearl said.

"No. The lock had been forced. Like somebody wedged a pry bar or something between the door and frame and leaned hard on it."

"A large knife, maybe?" Quinn asked.

"Yeah, that'd do it. The screws just popped out of the old wood door frame, and the lock wasn't worth diddly."

"So Theo was inside," Pearl said. She and Quinn could be a smooth team when it came to keeping someone talking.

"And I went in after him."

"You're a brave man," Quinn said. "Seeing the door had been forced, didn't you think there might be someone in there?"

Fernandez gave his little shrug. "I love my cat. And I did run back here and get a flashlight and a baseball bat. Then I went back next door and went inside. I knocked the barrel of the bat against the floor and kept calling Theo as I went, making plenty of noise so if there was somebody in there he'd have plenty of time to get away. I wasn't looking for trouble; I was looking for my cat."

"And?"

"I didn't find Theo, but I saw that one of the French doors out to the courtyard was open. I went to it, shined my light out there, and saw . . ." Fernandez stopped and swallowed.

"The vic," Pearl said.

Fernandez gulped again at the grisly memory. "Yes. Right away, I came back here and phoned the police."

"Not nine-one-one," Quinn said.

"*Madre de Dios*, I knew she was dead."

"Yeah."

"I waited till a police car came, then I told the officer what happened. He went in, then came back out and called for help. He asked me where I lived, then told me to come back here. First thing I saw when I stepped inside was Theo. He acted like he'd never been gone."

"Cats," Pearl said.

"Is there any way to get into the courtyard from the street?" Quinn asked.

Fernandez shook his head. "No, all these buildings, you got to go through them to get to the courtyards. They're built that way for security, I guess. That's why whoever took that lady—the vic—back there had to get through the door, then go through the apartment to the French doors."

"Are you sure you didn't notice anyone suspicious hanging around next door, or even in the neighborhood, the last few days or so?"

"Everybody in the neighborhood's suspicious," Fernandez said.

"Every neighborhood," Pearl said.

"Hey!" Fernandez said, as if jolted by his memory. "I did see someone last week. Mr. Kemmerman, in the apartment right across the street, he's been having trouble with his toilet leaking at the base. I been working and working on it. He seems to think it's the flapper, making the water overflow and run down the sides of the bowl when he's not around. Water pressure or something. I don't see how—"

"Never mind that," Quinn said.

"Anyway, I was leaving the Kemmerman apartment, looking out the window on the second-floor landing, and I saw a woman standing at the door to the vic's place. At first I thought it was a Jehovah's Witness—they been coming around—or maybe some kind of inspector. Then I saw her glance up and down the street and try the door. She gave it a good yank."

"It was a woman?"

"Oh, sure. I could see that much, even though there were some branches in the way."

"She see you?"

"No, I just stood still and watched, and she walked away."

"What'd she look like?"

"Blond, I think. But it was hard to tell in the light. And there were those branches and the leaves."

"What was she wearing?" Quinn asked.

"Jeans, I think. I don't remember up top. Light-colored

blouse or something. Thing is, I never saw her face. There wasn't much light, and she was mostly facing away from me. And the angle I was at, her hair got in the way."

"How was she built?"

"Looking down at her like I was, it's hard to say, but I'd make her to be tall average. On the slender side. Had on high heels. I do remember that."

"Would you describe them as extreme high heels?" Pearl asked.

"You mean like hooker shoes? No, nothing sexy like that. It's just that I recall high heels. I'm a leg man, I guess."

"I figured you for one," Quinn said, to keep him talking. He considered asking Fernandez why, if he was a leg man, he kept staring at Pearl's breasts.

Pointless question.

"I got the impression," Fernandez said, "just from her arms and the way she moved, she was older than the vic, like in her forties. The vic was like a kid, almost." He swallowed and looked grim. "She sure didn't look like a kid last time I saw her."

"You're positive you never got even a glimpse of this woman's face?" Quinn asked, keeping Fernandez on point.

"No, not the way she was standing."

"What time was it when you saw her?"

"Around two o'clock. I'd just come back from lunch, and I rested up a little and read the paper, then went across the street to check the toilet bowl in the Kemmerman apartment. There's no way that could have been the flapper. That's got nothing to do with—"

"Was Mr. Kemmerman home when you saw this woman?"

"No, he was at work. He's a teller at a bank. The people on this block, we know each other. They trust me. They know I don't pry, like some supers. I mind my own business."

"Too bad," Quinn said. "If somebody had seen the killer and his victim enter that building and not minded his own business, maybe a life would have been saved."

"I did hear one thing," Fernandez said. "My window on that side of the building was open and I heard somebody—maybe one of the cops—say the vic was some kind of designer. A very talented artist. Is that true?"

"I don't know," Quinn said. *That explains the protractor. It fits right in with the killer's ghoulish sense of humor, the protracted grin.* "We're still in the early finding-out stage. Know the name of the company where she worked?"

"No, I couldn't tell you. I didn't stand there and eavesdrop. I don't pry."

"Too bad," Quinn said.

Fernandez flashed his handsome grin.

Quinn and Pearl exchanged glances, letting each other know that at the moment they had nothing more to ask. They let Fernandez know, too, and thanked him for his time.

"Sorry I couldn't help," he told Quinn, as they were going out the door.

"Ah, you never know," Quinn said.

When they were back out on the hot sidewalk, Pearl said, "What do you make of it?"

"Fernandez might have seen the killer," Quinn said. "Or he might have made the whole thing up."

"You see Fernandez as the killer?" Pearl asked, surprised.

"Not likely. A lot of supers pry. He might have been lying about something to cover his ass, but I figure he's the guy who found the body, and he's nothing more. I'll have Sal and Harold check to see if he's got alibis for the times of the other murders, so we can cross him off our list."

"Fernandez doesn't *feel* like the killer." Pearl said. "He passes the gut test."

"Exactly."

They continued along the sidewalk to the entrance of the building where the murder had taken place. The uniform who'd stood screening visitors was gone, as were the radio cars and CSU van that had been parked in front. The ambulance was nowhere in sight. Ann Spellman was on her way to the morgue, where she'd be the subject of intense scrutiny and expertise by Nift, the nasty little M.E. Nift should have more to tell Quinn soon. Renz was seeing to it that these killings got top priority.

Quinn absently fingered the wrapped illicit Cuban cigar in his shirt pocket, then realized what he was doing and quickly lowered his hand. He'd thought there'd be a chance to be alone for a while and smoke the cigar today, not figuring on Ann Spellman interfering with his plan. He felt like smoking it in the car when they were finished here, but he knew better. Pearl might erupt.

"I'd like to know who that woman at the building's door was," Pearl said.

"Or *if* she was."

21

When the super let them into Ann Spellman's apartment, both Quinn and Pearl noticed a door near the end of the hall edge open a few inches and then close. Someone sneaking a peek at death.

Yet when the neighbors were questioned, they usually didn't want to get involved and had little to say.

Quinn dismissed the super and closed the door behind them. The super seemed to want a look around the dead woman's apartment, too. It made Quinn wonder if the man had entered and had his look-see earlier. It was odd how anything that had to do with a publicized murder victim held a certain attraction. Ann Spellman was dead and had died the hard way, so the super might have been unable to resist treading sacred carpet and hardwood, touching sacrosanct personal objects the recently deceased had touched.

The aftermath of violent death still resonated in the apartment, as if the tenant were sadly lingering and hesitant to leave. Quinn and Pearl each knew the other could feel it, and said nothing. The air was heavy and the only sounds were from traffic outside the building.

They set about carefully looking over the apartment,

not hurrying but not wasting motion. Pros who knew their job.

They found no computer, but there was a Lexmark printer on a small table by the desk. On the desk pad was what looked like an indentation where a laptop might have regularly sat when it wasn't traveling.

The contents of the desk did reveal that Ann Spellman had run up a sixteen-hundred-dollar Visa card balance, and that she worked for Clinton Industrial Designs, on East Fifty-fourth Street near Second Avenue.

With that information, and some personal notes and letters, they learned that she'd recently been fired, and gathered that she'd been having an affair with her boss, one Louis Gainer.

Damn him! Damn him! Damn him! was scribbled in pen on the top sheet of a Post-it pad. Quinn thought it was a good bet that the object of the scribbling was Louis Gainer, and the affair was over. The split had probably happened recently, since the note hadn't been disposed of when a better use arose for the pad.

The apartment's kitchen was neat and clean except for an empty carry-out pizza box stuffed into a wastebasket surrounded by a scattering of crumbs on the tile floor. The spotlessly clean oven and meager contents of the refrigerator suggested that Ann Spellman had eaten out often, or had food delivered. A hardworking career woman. Until last night.

Nothing unusual in the medicine cabinet. Tylenol, a bent tube of toothpaste, dental floss, a bottle of antibiotic tablets with an expired date, mint mouthwash. On a top shelf were some morning-after pills. Cautious Ann Spellman. Not cautious enough. The pills that prevented life couldn't prevent death.

The closet revealed a female mid-level executive's wardrobe: slacks and blazers, modest blouses, and at least half a dozen pairs of high-heeled shoes. Black was the predominate color. There was the expected basic black dress, with flimsy straps and a neckline low enough that the garment kept slipping from its wire hanger whenever Quinn touched it.

There were also faded jeans, worn-down joggers, and a pair of blue Crocs—for weekend casual wear, no doubt. But most of Ann Spellman's wardrobe wasn't casual; it was conservative business wear. Not high-end designer clothes, but nonetheless expensive. Possibly she was as talented as Fernandez the super had suggested, and had held—and been fired from—a fairly responsible job.

A search of the dresser drawers netted nothing of significance. Tucked beneath conservative slacks, and more folded jeans and T-shirts in the bottom drawer, were leopard-print thong panties and a vibrator shaped like a penis. *Big whoop-de-do.* No whips, chains, leather outfits, or anything of that sort.

There were a couple of Robert B. Parker books on the bottom shelf of a bedside table, along with a book of photographs of Frank Lloyd Wright homes. Wright was on the cover in an old black-and-white photo, looking grim. As if he knew what had happened to Ann Spellman.

Pearl, standing by the dresser with its drawers still open, said, "She wore lots of thong underwear."

"Do a lot of women wear that stuff?" Quinn asked. "It looks uncomfortable as hell."

"That's never stopped us," Pearl said. "But I can't answer your question. I've never seen a poll. I do know stores sell the hell out of thong underpants. Men go for women who like that kind of thing."

"You've seen a poll?"

"They conduct them hourly in hook-up bars all over the city."

"Hmm."

"The thing is," Pearl said, "Ann Spellman's panties were a size too large for her."

Quinn stood still and looked at Pearl, knowing where she was going.

"Right," Pearl said. "They were the right size for Macy Collins. The size of all her other panties."

Quinn should have realized it himself—Daniel Danielle usually left the corpses of his victims wearing the panties of his previous victim. For continuity, the Florida police profiler had said, which suggested the killer might be obsessive-compulsive.

Aren't they all?

"Judging by the panty count I just made," Pearl said, "the chances are better than fifty-fifty that the next victim will be wearing thong underwear the same size as what's in this drawer."

"I'd put it at sixty-forty," Quinn said. "She must have gotten some kind of kick out of it, wearing her conservative business clothes over a thong."

"Like half the working women in New York," Pearl said.

"You really think so?"

"That's what the polls say."

"Who do they ask?"

"Men."

"Ah."

Quinn cupped his chin in his hand and glanced around the room. Ann Spellman seemed to fall within the amorphous definition of normal. Quinn had found no drug paraphernalia, serious S and M equipment, or extreme pornography. Nothing in her life suggesting danger.

Except, maybe, her recent firing from her job, and her breakup with Louis Gainer.

Quinn wondered which had come first.

Damn him! Damn him! Damn him!

* * *

The killer always enjoyed sipping an espresso at a sidewalk table at one of the city's restaurants featuring outside dining. This Upper West Side restaurant, Spirit, had a wide, mustard-colored awning to ensure shade, and two large box fans providing something like a breeze. People were frequently walking past on the sidewalk beyond the black iron railing, a narrow passageway between the seating area and the traffic.

It was pleasant here, watching the hurrying pedestrians and the traffic on Amsterdam. The dinner crowd hadn't yet arrived. There weren't many other customers. A man and woman sat three tables away, leaning toward each other and engaged in intense conversation. The woman, with a small, shaggy dog resting at her feet, had her blond hair pinned up, and an oversized nose that made her unattractive. The man with her was also blond. He had a sparse ponytail, and was wearing jeans and a blue denim vest over a white T-shirt. They were both drinking beer from green bottles. Not far from them was a balding man who had a blue backpack resting beside his chair, and two men with heavy gray beards. The bearded ones were playing chess.

At a table near them sat a tall, thin man sipping what looked like iced tea and munching nuts from a small ceramic bowl.

The killer looked around his open netbook at the expanse of his glass-topped table and saw no nuts. Saw none on any of the other tables. He guessed you had to ask for them. He worked the computer's touch pad, clicking the netbook's cursor on the various pages of RomancerMate.com, one of the many websites that promised men the opportunity to meet whatever type of lonely woman they preferred. It was like browsing through a catalog. The killer found the website immensely entertaining. Tech was wonderful. Other people struggled with each new device or application that made its way to the market. Not the killer. He seemed to have been born to be a tech head.

"May I have some nuts?"

A waiter nodded and disappeared inside the restaurant.

The killer turned his attention to the two bearded men playing chess. They appeared to be in their sixties. Each was bent over the board, giving the game his rapt attention. One of them had several more pieces than the other. Traffic hummed and fumed past only a few feet from them, but they were oblivious to what was happening out in the street, beyond the shade of the awning. Right here, right now, the game was everything to them. Winning was paramount.

The killer had to smile. The chess players were completely unaware of him. They had no idea that going on very near them was a much more serious game of move and countermove. A game where lives were involved.

And deaths.

After another slow sip of espresso, the killer smiled even wider, at least on the inside.

He was contemplating how women, if you chose them carefully, became terrified and evasive when they knew they were being stalked, when they understood what was intended. They became truly desperate.

Then, at a certain point, they became played out and tired of watching and taking alternate routes, of double-checking locks, of constantly being cautious, of being afraid. They wanted it to happen, to be over. They welcomed it, whatever *it* was. They welcomed *him*.

Women. The perfect prey animal, surely made that way by God for the predators.

Of course, when they learned what it was really like, they changed their minds. Always. But too late.

They were like the prey animals on television nature channels that stood gasping and heaving after the chase, waiting for the inevitable because finally, on a primal level, they understood what and why they were. They would run no more. They accepted their predetermined end.

But when fang and claw were applied, when their last seconds arrived, they always struggled meagerly and futilely. A final and feeble burst of life force, not enough.

It interested him, that inevitable summoning of dying effort. Why did they cling so to every last tick of life? What did they know, or see, that frightened them so? A glimpse behind the curtain? Perhaps something looking back at them.

Or perhaps, nothing at all

He thought of Ann Spellman. Of how she'd fought so for her last few seconds of life. Of how her fingers had fluttered like a poignant good-bye at the end.

Of Frank Quinn and his dangerous band of misfit detectives.

Of Pearl.

God, he loved the game they were playing! A part of him worried that maybe he was beginning to love it too much and it cautioned him with inner voices. But for now he'd ignore those voices. He hated to use the word *fun*, because it seemed so inadequate to describe what he was capable of feeling. But the fact was—

The waiter reappeared, and the killer beckoned him with a languid wave of his hand.

"Some *nuts*, please."

22

The Times had the heat wave above the news about Ann Spellman being murdered. An odd order of importance, but Quinn guessed it made sense, depending on who you were.

While Pearl held down things at the office, and Fedderman, Sal, and Harold were in Ann Spellman's neighborhood talking to neighbors, merchants, and friends of the deceased, Quinn went to Clinton Industrial Designs to question Louis Gainer. He left the Lincoln parked outside the office, in a loading zone he knew was seldom used, and took a subway downtown to Third and Lex. Then he returned to the surface world and walked to East Fifty-fourth Street.

Clinton Industrial Designs occupied the top floor of a ten-story office building. A financial adviser and a dry-cleaner occupied the first floor. Quinn entered the building through a door located between them. He stepped into an ancient, creaky elevator, pushed the 10 button, and up he went with surprising smoothness.

A small, bustling woman scurrying about in a reception area informed Quinn that Louis Gainer didn't see people without an appointment. Quinn flashed her his ID and told her again he wanted to speak with Gainer.

The woman didn't seem impressed. But she thought things through for a moment, then hurried over to a desk and said something into a blue phone. She replaced the receiver, staring at Quinn and obviously wondering about the nature of his visit.

Then the blue phone jangled, and she picked up the receiver and talked and listened. Mostly listened.

When she hung up, she smiled and came over to Quinn at almost a dead run.

"Mr. Gainer will see you. I'll take you back."

Quinn had to walk fast to keep up with the woman. They went through a door in the back wall of the reception area, down a narrow hall, and then through another door that led to a large loft area with skylights illuminating desks and drafting boards. Three men and two women were at the boards, working away like kids taking a final exam. Another man, sitting at a desk, stood up when they approached.

He was average height, lean, and muscular, wearing a white shirt, and a tie with a loosened knot. His brown slacks were made voluminous by pleats. He had dark wavy hair, open Irish features, and an engaging white smile.

The kind of guy people would describe as a lady-killer.

Quinn wondered how close that description was to the truth.

He introduced himself and, when the woman who'd escorted him was gone, Quinn told Louis Gainer he wanted to talk to him about Ann Spellman.

At the mention of her name, Gainer seemed about to start sobbing.

But he didn't. Instead he simply nodded, his eyes moist, and led Quinn to a room containing a long table and ten identical wooden chairs down each side. There were matching black leather upholstered chairs at each end of the table. In one corner were a fax machine and phone. A computer with a large flat-screen monitor mounted above it was in another. The walls were adorned with framed color photographs of what looked like building lobbies. There were no people in any of the lobbies, only ferns.

Gainer sat down in a large leather chair at the head of the table, and motioned for Quinn to sit in the first wooden chair on his left. Some kind of power play?

Quinn lowered himself into the chair and was surprised by how comfortable it was.

"What exactly does your company do?" he asked.

Gainer seemed relieved that they weren't getting right to the topic of the late Ann Spellman. "We design and install both public and private common spaces, taking into account ambience as well as functionality."

"Ah," Quinn said. He leaned slightly toward Gainer. "And Ann Spellman was one of your designers?"

At the mention of the victim's name, Gainer winced. A normal enough response. They'd been close. "She was one of our best designers, and was in charge of one of our industrial units."

"Yet you fired her."

"No, no. The board fired her. We—they had no choice."

"Something about her work or attitude?"

"Something that became inevitable," Gainer said.

"Her reaction to being dropped by you?"

Gainer obviously didn't like where the conversation was going. "You mean on a personal level?"

"The most personal."

Gainer seemed to give that some thought, shifting position in his high-backed chair. "Well, yes. It was partly my fault for letting our relationship go as far as it had. She and I were good with each other, but in a temporary way. I knew that, and I thought she did. When I had to end it, I knew how she'd take it. Especially since I didn't give her the kind of explanation I owed her."

Quinn thought there were a lot of I's in that answer. "And what was that explanation?"

"I'm in love with another woman. We're going to be married." Gainer sighed and looked at a blank wall as if there were a window in it and he was gazing outside. There was a lot of light, but it was artificial. There were no windows in what had to be the conference room. "You can see the company's position. At least I could."

"Hell hath no fury . . . ?"

"Exactly."

"You might have told her the truth," Quinn said, "given her a chance to react. She might have surprised you and wished you well."

Gainer smiled sadly. "That would have been a surprise, all right."

"What did you tell her?"

"That the company was letting her go for economic reasons. That it was a board decision and had nothing to do with her competency."

"How did she react?"

"By calling me a sack of shit." He breathed in and out and looked ashamed. "Maybe she's right."

"And then you told her you and she were over?"

"No. She naturally assumed that. I mean, after I told her I was firing her. She thought I was cutting her loose from the company because I wanted to end our affair finally and forever. I don't recall which of us, or either of us, came right out and said it was over. But believe me, it was understood."

"And this conversation was when?"

"Three nights ago."

"And that was the last time you saw her alive?"

"Or dead," Gainer said.

"Where were you last night?"

"When Ann was killed? I was with the woman I'm going to marry. I have restaurant receipts. After we had dinner, we went with friends to the theater. I even happened to run into a man I went to school with. During intermission."

"You seem to be covered for every minute."

"Like it was planned?"

Quinn smiled. "Don't get ahead of me, Mr. Gainer."

"I mean, I *could* have paid somebody to kill Ann, and made sure I had an alibi. But I had no reason to harm her. She was gone from here, gone from my life." He wiped away what might have been a tear. "To tell you the truth, I miss her. We were lovers. We were also good friends."

"Friends or not, the company couldn't take the chance."

"No. We couldn't even let her come back for her things. Had them delivered to her." He looked beseechingly at Quinn. "You don't know how fiercely competitive this business is. You have to be a hard-ass just to survive."

"Like my business," Quinn said.

"Yeah. From what I've heard."

Quinn stood up. "Anything to add?"

"I don't know what it would be."

"Maybe a confession."

Gainer sat back as if struck by a blow. "Do I need a lawyer?"

"You're asking me?"

"I'm trying to be cooperative. I didn't do anything. I've got nothing to hide." Gainer wiped at his eyes again. "Go ahead and check my alibi."

"We will." Quinn saw the fear in Gainer's expression, along with the hope. This guy should never play poker. "I know what you think, Mr. Gainer, that maybe you should have lawyered up and gone mute. That you handled this meeting wrong. But you didn't. Not if you told the truth."

"Do you think I killed Ann? Or hired someone to kill her?"

"No," Quinn said. "Right now, I don't."

"Thank you," Gainer said.

Quinn went to the door. "But that's right now."

23

Since it was the last door, they were together.

In Ann Spellman's apartment building, Sal and Harold had knocked on all the doors but this one, 6-F. It didn't promise to open on any new or pertinent knowledge of Spellman's murder.

The slot in the mailbox down in the foyer had simply said A. Ackenheimer. The woman who opened the door said nothing. She simply stood and stared at them through rheumy, faded blue eyes. Her mousy brown hair was a mess, as was the baggy flannel nightgown or robe she wore even though it was four o'clock in the afternoon.

A close look at her suggested she was in her forties, but she was like a woman trying to appear older. An even closer look revealed a certain glint in her eye. Harold thought that if she really got it together, with makeup and a hairdo, she might be attractive. No, probably not.

Sal leaned toward her slightly, sniffing for alcohol. Found something like smoked salmon. It could have been fish for lunch, but she looked as if she could be high on some other substance. He smelled nothing potentially incriminating.

"Miz Ackenheimer?" Harold said, as if attempting to wake her.

"Right on the first try," she said in a throaty, fishy voice.

"A for Alice?" Harold said.

She smiled widely. "Amazing."

Harold grinned beneath his bushy mustache and shrugged. "I'm kind of psychic sometimes, Audrey."

She shook her head. "You, too? *Amazing*. Some people call me Amazing Ackenheimer. My given name is actually Audrey, but I've used the name Alice."

"Are you in show business?" Harold asked.

Sal had had about enough of this. "We'd like to ask you a few questions about Ann Spellman's murder," he told her in his rasp of a voice that was even deeper than hers.

"It sounds like you might juggle or something," Harold said, "with a name like that."

Sal glowered. Harold was being Harold here, with the last potential witness. It irked Sal.

"No," Audrey Ackenheimer said. "I'm not in show business, though I can juggle. And I know nothing about Ann Spellman's murder. She's not—wasn't—even on this floor. And wasn't she killed someplace else altogether?"

"Not necessarily altogether," Sal said. "Her apartment, her neighbors, might have something useful to tell us."

"I wouldn't think so," Audrey Ackenheimer said.

"Did you know her at all?"

"Only to nod to on the elevator about every two weeks." Suddenly she paused and looked off to the side.

"Something?" Sal asked.

"I was just remembering . . . last week I accidentally pushed the wrong button in the elevator and the door opened on her floor. Ann Spellman's. Well, there's a straight look down the hall to her apartment, and I saw a woman standing in front of Spellman's door. Then I looked again and she wasn't there. I suppose Ann Spellman let the woman in."

"This was when?

"Wednesday, I think."

"The day before Spellman's murder."

"Evening before," Audrey said. "About seven o'clock. I was on my way to meet someone for dinner."

"Could you describe the woman?"

"I was meeting a man."

Sal said nothing, looking at her hard.

Audrey Ackenheimer shrugged beneath her tent-like robe or night gown. "The woman was average height and weight, I suppose. Had on a light raincoat because it had been drizzling all evening. As she was entering she turned slightly, and I would have gotten a good look at her face, except . . ." She shrugged again in her noncommittal way.

"The elevator door closed," Harold said.

She looked at him and grinned. "Amazing!"

"That's you," Harold said. "I'm psychic."

"Hair?" Sal asked.

"Yes," she and Harold said simultaneously. They both laughed.

"Jesus!" Sal said.

"I think brown, light colored like mine, but I'm not sure. The lighting isn't great in the halls here. We keep telling the super about it, but nothing's ever done."

Sal rummaged through his notes. Harold had already talked to the super, a guy named Drucker who'd spent the murder evening with his wife in front of a blaring flat-panel TV that took up half his apartment wall. Sal had discussed him with Harold and read Harold's notes. Drucker knew nothing.

"Little guy with blond hair and a mole near the tip of his nose?" Harold asked.

"Yes. You've talked to him?"

"Never saw him or even heard of him before just now," Harold lied.

Audrey's eyes widened. "That's amazing!"

"No. You're ama—"

"Stop it!" Sal said. Harold could turn any interrogation into a shit storm.

"I wouldn't recognize the woman if I saw her again," Audrey Ackenheimer said, thinking it was time to get serious before Sal blew his cork. Harold, the nice one, looked at her and kind of rolled his eyes, letting her know he understood. "I have seen her around the building before. Once from a distance, coming out. Another time from the back as she got in the elevator."

"On her way to see Ann Spellman," Sal said. "If she was home."

"Might have paid her a visit, anyway," Harold said. "If she was *sure* she wasn't home."

"What about men?" Audrey said.

Sal looked at her. "What about them?"

"I did see a storybook-handsome guy, kind of stocky, with wavy dark hair, come and go a few times. Saw him and Spellman leave together once holding hands."

"I think we know who that is," Sal said.

"Any other male callers?" Harold asked.

Audrey gave them her shrug again. "Couldn't say yes or no."

It was the woman who interested Sal. He wanted to know if she actually existed outside Audrey Ackenheimer's and Fernandez the super's imaginations. No one else seemed to have seen this woman, except maybe Theo the cat. And cats were notoriously uncooperative witnesses.

"I don't spy on people's personal lives," Audrey said. "Poor Ann Spellman could have been chaste as a nun, or led a life of wild debauchery. It's something we'll never know."

Sal didn't agree with her, but didn't say so.

24

There wasn't much pain if she kept her little toe scrunched up.

Pearl was striding along West Seventy-ninth Street toward the office, wearing her New Balance jogging shoes. They were her most comfortable shoes for walking, but her left sock had bunched up and might be causing a blister. She figured she didn't have far to go, so the hell with it.

She had spent much of the day verifying Louis Gainer's alibi for the night of Ann Spellman's murder. Gainer's fiancée had been aware of his relationship with Spellman, and she described it as "long over." Pearl let that one pass. It looked like Gainer was innocent, so why screw up a marriage before it even started?

Restaurant receipts and witness statements indicated that Gainer and his fiancée were where he'd said they'd been, with the people he'd named. And the old college friend Gainer had run into in the theater lobby at the approximate time of the murder described their meeting the same way Gainer had. The play they'd attended was titled *Chance Encounter.* Gainer wouldn't have chosen that one to lie about. Unless he had a dangerous sense of humor, or no sense of humor at all.

If anything, Gainer was *too* alibied up for the night of Spellman's torture and murder. Something Pearl would keep in mind.

Does this job make you cynical, or what?

Pearl's cell phone, clipped to her belt beneath her light linen blazer, came to life and instinctively her hand moved toward it.

Then paused.

Pearl had a new phone that enabled the use of individual ring tones to identify callers. She stopped walking as she heard the musical strains of "You Talk Too Much," Joe Jones's old rhythm-and-blues hit from the sixties. When she looked at the phone's caller ID, sure enough, she saw Golden Sunset Assisted Living in New Jersey. Where her mother lived, and called from at the most inopportune times.

Not that this was one of those times. But still . . .

While she was debating whether to take the call, the phone fell silent.

Her mind had been made up for her. She told herself she'd been about to answer, even though she didn't feel like hearing her mother harangue her for everything from her job to not being married, or for being married to her job.

She decided she really didn't want to talk with her mother—or, rather, listen to her—even though she had a spare moment.

Pearl smiled. There was nothing like being honest with oneself.

No doubt her mother had left a message. She'd listen to it later.

As she clipped the phone back on her belt—turned off, just in case—the movement of her head caused her to glance behind her.

A tickle moved up her spine. Subtle, but she recognized it.

Something was wrong. She scanned the block she'd been walking along. Nothing seemed unusual. Yet in her initial glance, something hadn't been right. She knew it. Like many cops with a talent for tailing people, she had a talent for knowing when someone was tailing her.

There!

A woman, slim, average height, wearing yellow, one of those girly sundress outfits that were popular these days. Moving gracefully away from Pearl, slipping in among the throng of pedestrians coming toward her. Even in the bright yellow dress, she'd disappeared. Half a block away, and she made the last of the walk signal. It would be impossible for Pearl to catch up with her.

The woman was familiar, but in a way Pearl couldn't grasp. There was something unsettling about her.

Then it all clicked into place, how Pearl had caught glimpses of the woman on the subway platform, near the deli she frequented, crossing the street near the office. During the past few days, she and the woman had been in the same place at the same time too often for it to be coincidental.

The woman was a talented tracker, but not a pro. That was how Pearl had spotted her. A pro would have kept her wardrobe drab and wouldn't have worn the standout yellow dress.

Still, there was something about this woman that suggested she wasn't to be taken lightly. Something that triggered an emotion deep in Pearl's consciousness. *Fear?* She wasn't sure. Not of what it was or why she was feeling it.

Was the woman Daniel Danielle? It wasn't impossible. After all, the original Daniel Danielle was sometimes Danielle Daniel, a woman by all appearances. One who'd disappeared in a Florida hurricane decades ago, had never been seen again, and was listed officially as dead. One of the worst disasters in Florida history had done the job of the state and executed Daniel Danielle, clearing the docket.

Officially. There was a word that put Pearl on her guard. The presumed dead killer, or a copycat, appeared to be operating in New York.

Another possibility occurred to Pearl. The woman tailing her might be a confederate of the killer, working for him and with him. Helping him to learn about Pearl as he prepared to make his move on her. He might have done that with his earlier victims, stalked them, perhaps deliberately letting them know he was there so they would worry, become worn down by their anxiety to the point of surrender.

He'd be there to accept that surrender.

Pearl thought about that.

Be ready, you schmuck. I'm ready, too.

When she reached the office, Quinn was there alone, seated at his desk and reading something inside a yellow file folder. He glanced up when Pearl entered, and it registered on his face immediately that he knew she was distressed.

He laid what he'd been reading aside and sat back, waiting, swiveling his chair an inch this way, then that, causing a soft *eek, eek*.

"That isn't important?" she asked, pointing to the folder he'd put aside.

"Sal's report on his and Harold's interview of Audrey Ackenheimer, neighbor of the victim."

"Learn anything?"

"Yes. Sal's being driven insane by Harold."

Pearl had to smile. "It's been that way with them for over ten years, from when they were NYPD. But somehow they make a good team. Cops who partner for years sometimes get like old married couples."

"You're talking about Sal and Harold because there's something else on your mind," Quinn said.

He stopped swiveling and the chair stopped squeaking.

"More a feeling than something I know for sure."

"Share it so we both won't know it for sure," Quinn suggested.

She told him about the woman she thought was shadowing her. When she was about halfway through the account, Helen the profiler came into the office. Tall, red-headed, and sweaty, smelling like estrogen. She was wearing a running outfit with baggy shorts, a sleeveless red Fordham T-shirt, and New Balance shoes like Pearl's, only more expensive. She paused the way people do when they realize they've intruded in a private conversation.

Only there was no reason for this to be private. Pearl knew it was part of the investigation.

Quinn nodded to Pearl, reading her mind, and she started over.

When she was finished, Helen said, "You're certain it wasn't your imagination?"

"I'm certain. And the woman was too small to be Daniel. What I'm not certain about are my speculations as to why. It doesn't make much sense, a woman shadowing a potential victim for the killer."

"It makes a lot of sense," Helen said. "*Especially* if the woman being followed is already slated to be a future victim. We all know how charming and manipulative some serial killers are. We also know you're the killer's type. It's not unlikely that this woman's scouting you, learning all about you, and will turn the information over to him."

Pearl looked mad enough to spit. "I'm no teenage girl ready to be swept off my feet because some good-looking guy's done research and knows my sign."

Quinn was nudging his swivel chair this way and that again, making a rhythmic, almost inaudible squeaking. These two women were making him nervous. "None of it seems to fit."

"Interesting," Helen said, "that your gut feeling is different from Pearl's."

"I didn't say I had a gut feeling about who was following me or why," Pearl said, "only that I was being followed."

"By a woman," Helen added.

Quinn said, "Our killer's familiar enough with us to know that whoever he sent to shadow Pearl, Pearl would most likely spot her. Or him."

Helen crossed her arms and got more comfortable where she was leaning back against a desk—because of her height, almost sitting on it. "Oh, he wouldn't care if the tail was spotted. That might have been the idea."

"To let Pearl know she's being stalked?"

"To let *you* know."

"Playing a game."

"Very much a game."

"If he kills me," Pearl said, "the game's over."

"Maybe not for the killer," Helen said. "Taking you as a victim might be his way of focusing his opponent's concentration, making the game more interesting."

"Still doesn't feel right," Quinn said.

"Maybe at a certain point he lets all his victims know they're being stalked," Helen said. "He might derive pleasure from that. It isn't uncommon."

"This is an uncommon killer," Quinn said.

Helen nodded. She stood up straight, unwinding, surprising Quinn as she almost always did with her six-foot-plus height. "There is that."

"There's the other thing," Pearl said.

They both looked at her.

"I'm an uncommon victim."

25

Jody Jason had no idea why Professor Pratt wanted to meet her here, though it must pertain to their earlier conversation about some profound change in Jody's life. In a way, it didn't surprise Jody that Elaine Pratt had chosen this place. She probably knew it was one of Jody's favorite spots on campus, an oasis conducive to study and quiet. And private conversations. It was like Professor Pratt to know such things.

From where she sat on a concrete bench in the shade of a fifty-year-old post oak, Jody had a wide and impressive view of the Waycliffe campus. The green, manicured quadrangle, with its concrete paths and uniformly trimmed trees; its occasional lounging student; its encompassing ivy trellised brick buildings. It all looked like a painting by a master impressionist.

Though the afternoon was warm, there was a persistent soft breeze. It was pleasantly cool in the shade of the tree's clustered leaves, which rattled in the wind.

Jody often sat on this particular bench to read, and it always amazed her that there were never any bird droppings on it. Or, so it seemed, on any of the benches. Maybe maintenance had some special chemical that repelled birds. Or maybe the birds simply knew better, at a prestigious college like Waycliffe.

"You beat me here," a woman's voice said.

Jody looked over and saw that Professor Pratt had approached her unseen, at an angle.

"It was so pleasant," Jody said, "I thought I'd come early and sit here a while."

Elaine (as Jody informally and privately thought of the professor) glanced around and smiled. "It *is* beautiful. And useful. As beauty often is."

Jody scooted over to allow Elaine room to sit down, but the professor chose to remain standing.

"I hope I haven't screwed up," Jody said.

Elaine seemed amused. "Why would you think that?"

"This is . . . such a private and distant place, I thought . . . well, I don't know what I thought."

"That I chose a place where no one would observe us or overhear us shouting at each other?"

"Not that," Jody said with a smile. Might this be about something else altogether? A disciplinary measure? Did Elaine know about those times Jody had sneaked off campus to explore the town after dark? About that over-amorous associate professor she'd kneed in the groin at the annual Waycliffe anniversary party?

What the hell's going on here? I can think of a few possibilities, and I don't like them.

"Chancellor Schueller and I have ruminated upon you further," Elaine said. She seemed to be enjoying this, stringing it out and keeping Jody in the agony of curiosity.

Uh-oh. This didn't feel like a positive discussion.

Elaine waited. For maximum effect, Jody was sure. Was Jody going to be reprimanded? Cautioned about future behavior?

There should be suspenseful music here.

Jody felt momentarily pissed off. She knew the game now and put on an eager expression. Let Elaine think she was squirming inside. Actually, she was getting bored and at this point didn't much care where the game would end. Waycliffe wasn't the only college in the world.

"You've been approved for an internship at Enders and Coil," Elaine said.

Jody didn't have to fake her surprise. Two months ago she had, almost as a matter of routine, filled out brief applications for summer internships at some of the major law firms in the area. Not really holding out much hope. It wasn't easy to obtain internships. Usually, somebody had to know somebody for it to happen. Or . . .

"I'd be replacing Macy Collins," Jody said.

"Someone must," Elaine Pratt said.

The summer had started without any of the internships coming through. Jody had pushed the possibility from her mind. It had been a long shot anyway. But now, this late in the season, one of them had accepted her because of murder.

"Often in life, someone's misfortune is someone else's opportunity. Pick up the sword and use it, Jody."

"That sounds so . . . Roman."

"The Romans had a lot of things right." Elaine Pratt said. "And whatever you do will make no difference to Macy Collins."

Jody wanted to learn the particulars of what Macy had done at the law firm, and how well she'd done it. Obvious questions to ask, and difficult ones to answer. Jody knew that and remained silent.

Causing Elaine to smile. These two could understand each other.

"I pressed for you to be the choice," Elaine said. "The chancellor agreed and recommended you to the firm."

Jody could believe that. It seemed that the Elaine and

Schueller had a special relationship. Not romantic or sexual . . . but something drew them together. Maybe something kinky, after all. But Jody didn't want to even imagine that. Unless maybe the chancellor took Elaine up in his airplane and they . . .

Jody put on a big grin. Not all of it fake. "Thank you! Really! Thanks to both of you."

"You deserve it. Enders and Coil's offices are in Manhattan, but you won't have to commute. Though the internship doesn't pay, of course, it does include a small apartment near the firm."

"In Manhattan?"

"Of course."

"That's so great!" Jody said, and meant it. *An apartment in Manhattan. Holy shit! This could all work.* She had enough left of her student loan to be able to clothe and feed herself. She hoped.

Elaine drew a deep breath, then exhaled loudly and clasped her hands. "So, we're all set?"

Time to throw shit in the game.

"Professor Pratt, I hate to ask this, but would you mind if I thought about the offer?"

Elaine almost laughed out loud in surprise, but she held a neutral expression. Just like that, dominance had shifted and she was now the one on pins and needles. How would it look if she'd pressed so hard for Jody, and then Jody brushed off the internship? What would Chancellor Schueller think? How would Enders and Coil react? How would this affect Professor Pratt's career?

"Can you let me know tomorrow?" she asked, careful not to sound anxious.

Jody thought for a long few seconds—in control now and letting Elaine know it—and then nodded. "Sure. No problem there."

"Here, either," Elaine said.

When Jody got up, she gave her a big hug.

Jody sat back down and watched the professor's re-treating figure change shapes as it passed through length-ening shadows across the quadrangle.

She didn't know quite what to think other than *WTF?*, as they said on the social networks.

26

Deena Vess was tired of skating. She was sore mostly in the knees and ankles. Roller Steak, the restaurant where she waited tables, featured all its servers on skates. It did make for fast service, and sometimes spectacular collisions.

She liked her job, and the pay was good enough that she could rent a top-floor unit of a six-story walkup on Manhattan's Lower East Side. Her divorce from douche bag Danny in Chicago had been finalized last month. And on that very same day she got her job at Roller Steak.

New York wasn't so tough, if you started out with a little luck. She'd been cautioned about moving to the city, but Deena wanted to start over, and here. She stretched her finances a bit getting the apartment; then, just like that, she'd gained employment at the first place she applied.

Deena didn't kid herself. Maybe it wasn't all luck. Her looks helped. She was narrow-waisted and had muscular, shapely legs, qualities that were obviously very important to Ramon, the restaurant manager. And her ample breasts didn't hurt her chances. She might have to fight this guy off sometime in the near future, but if she was diplomatic enough it should pose no threat to her job. Ramon seemed to be a decent enough sort when he wasn't playing hard-ass to keep the personnel in line.

The third night she'd spent in the apartment, Empress arrived. The small tabby cat had squeezed in through a window Deena had left open a few inches for the breeze. The cat was friendly enough, and was darling and seemed to know it. Deena enjoyed watching it prance and preen.

The animal appeared to be cared for and well fed, but had no collar or tags. Deena had asked around, and nobody in the building recognized it or knew who owned it. So she'd renamed the cat Empress and took it to the vet for its shots, and to have it spayed. Then she'd bought a new red collar at a pet shop on Eighth Avenue and fastened to it the shot tags and a metal tag bearing Empress's name and new address. Empress, Deena thought, had gone from vagabond royalty to a feline citizen in good standing in a matter of days, and should be grateful.

But of course the cat displayed no sign of gratitude. She was affectionate, but only on her terms. Whenever Deena came home, Empress didn't appear at first, as if she couldn't be bothered. After a few minutes the cat would come yawning and stretching, as if she'd been napping, and present herself for holding and petting.

Empress became increasingly territorial and began sleeping with Deena, first making her rounds of the apartment and then curling into a fuzz ball near the foot of the bed.

Tonight, when Deena came home from work and shut and locked the apartment door behind her, there was no sign of Empress.

Deena called the cat's name (fat chance of that working) as she walked through the small apartment, checking windows. There seemed no way Empress could have gotten out.

"Empress!" Deena called again, knowing now it was useless. "Where the hell are you?"

She suddenly became aware again of how sore her legs were from skating over the hard plank floor at Roller Steak. She plopped down on the sofa and removed her shoes, stretched her legs, and wriggled her toes. Running her fingers through her thick dark hair, she glanced around again for a sign of Empress. She was beginning to get anxious.

Spend a fortune on a cat and this is what it does. Some investment.

But Deena knew it was more than the money. She'd become extremely fond of the haughty yet affectionate animal.

It was possible that someone had stolen the cat. Before Deena had moved in, the apartment had been vacant for a while as it was redecorated. People came and went during that process—painters, plumbers, carpenters, city inspectors. There must have been keys floating around. It would have been easy enough for one of the tradesmen, or even a prospective tenant, to come into possession of one. Deena decided she should have the locks changed. She would call about that tomorrow.

It was hard to imagine someone letting himself in and stealing a cat. And there seemed no way for Empress to have left of her own accord without someone opening a door or window.

Deena picked up the remote from the coffee table, and was about to switch on the TV, when she caught sight of tabby fur beneath the old wing chair across from her.

Empress!

Deena broke into a big grin and forgot her sore legs as she jumped up and crossed the room to scoop up the errant cat.

Empress withdrew from her so she couldn't be reached.

Deena got down on her hands and knees, then lay on the carpet and reached back in the darkness beneath the wing chair and grasped the red leather collar. Empress yowled and scratched her.

Shocked, Deena drew back her hand.

This was odd. Imperious though she was, Empress wasn't the sort of cat that would bite or scratch the hand that fed and petted her.

Deena moved more carefully, getting down lower now so she could see and wouldn't be working by feel. She clutched the cat by the loose flesh on the back of its neck and pulled it out.

Empress seemed docile enough now, and made no further attempt to scratch or bite her.

Deena petted the cat, then felt a quiet chill. She hefted Empress in one hand, and looked closely at the collar and tags. Same collar. Same tags. There was the cat's name: Empress. With Deena's address. Everything proper.

But Deena knew this wasn't Empress.

Not the *real* Empress, anyway.

Deena stared intently at the pattern of gray-striped fur flecked with brown. She saw now what she was sure were slight variations.

Quickly, she put the cat down and watched it hurry back to the wing chair and scoot beneath it.

Not like the sociable if superior Empress.

Deena swiveled her head, frightened now. Knowing she was alone, yet making sure anyway.

Someone must have been in here. He or she had for some reason switched cats, substituting this one, who looked almost exactly like Empress, for Empress.

But why?

There had to be a reason. This was insane.

It was that last thought that terrified her. Maybe it *was* insane. Either she was going insane, or some insane person had made this substitution.

A practical joke? Deena didn't think so. She barely knew anyone in New York, much less someone with this kind of sick sense of humor.

Someone had been in here while she was at work. Doing what? Seeing what? Feeling what?

She realized with a sense of dread that she was more afraid of what must have happened than she was sad about the loss of Empress.

She would probably never again see the real Empress. But at least Empress was the kind of cat that could take care of herself, a survivor in the jungle of the city.

Deena told herself to stay calm. There might be a reasonable explanation for all this. Even if there wasn't one, she had to act as if there might be. Whatever was happening, she'd cope with it. Hadn't she just made it through an ugly divorce in Chicago?

Another jungle, that city.

It was time to be practical. One thing Deena knew for sure was that, though it wasn't Empress, she had a cat. She went into the kitchen and got a can of liver-flavored cat food from a cabinet. As she used the electric can opener, she automatically looked toward the kitchen door for Empress to come strutting in.

No cat.

She scooped out the entire can of food into the heavy ceramic bowl on the floor. Surely the pungent scent would draw the shy animal from its shelter beneath the chair.

No cat.

She ran a glass of tap water and poured it into the bowl next to the food bowl. Then she moved to the other side of the kitchen and waited.

No cat.

The wall phone in the kitchen jangled and she went to it and snatched the receiver from its cradle on the second ring.

No one was there.

After a few seconds she heard a click, and then the dial tone.

Deena hurried to her small desk in the living room and checked caller ID on her other phone. She pecked out the unfamiliar number and waited.

Her call was answered on the fifth ring with a man's tentative, "Hello . . ."

"Who the hell are you?" Deena asked.

"I don't think you need to know, lady. Who am I talking to?"

"You know damn well."

"This is a public phone, dumb-ass. It was ringing so I picked it up. Thought maybe somebody might be in trouble. You in trouble?"

Deena didn't know what to say.

"Listen, are you in trouble?"

Deena hung up.

Someone was deliberately doing this to her.

Definitely, someone is messing with my mind.

For laughs?

Or something else?

Who do you call about a missing cat that isn't missing?

No one, she decided. There was no one to call for help. No one who'd believe her, anyway.

. . . Am I in trouble?

Am I?

27

The Q&A office, 9:15 PM.

Sultry despite the rattling air conditioner mounted in the window with the iron bars, illuminated in yellow light from the glowing desk lamps.

They were talking about murder.

Quinn was behind his desk, leaning back in his swivel chair, his fingers laced behind his head, as he listened to Sal and Harold describe the neighboring super's sighting of a woman emerging from the boarded-up apartment building where Ann Spellman was later murdered. Then the conversation with Spellman's neighbor in her building, Audrey Ackenheimer.

Quinn said, "Why do they keep doing it?"

"You mean killing people?" Harold asked.

"No. Why do the neighbors only remember later seeing something that might be useful to us, and then never remember seeing the faces of the possible perpetrators?"

"If they saw the faces, they might remember."

Quinn stared at Harold. The guy looked like a malnourished accountant, with his slightly stooped figure and oversized graying mustache. Quinn could understand why he got on Sal's nerves. But he knew Harold was smart, and a tough enough cop. It intrigued Quinn, the way sometimes the most unlikely people were the ones who could reach deep inside and find what they needed in a crisis. Quinn knew that one of those people was Harold Mishkin, however he was wrapped.

"The woman was described as older than Spellman," Sal said. "But then, Spellman was only twenty-four. Most of the three hundred million people in the country are older than her."

"Narrows it up," Harold said.

Quinn couldn't tell if he was joking.

"Any info on whoever might be shadowing Pearl?" Sal asked.

"No. But Pearl's hardly ever wrong about something like that. If she says she's got a shadow, there is one."

"You think she should have two?" Harold asked.

It took Quinn a few seconds to understand what he meant. "I suggested we should take shifts in watching her back. Pearl said definitely not. Doesn't wanna spread us thin while we're on the trail of a serial killer."

"Maybe we should ignore what she wants," Sal said.

Harold looked at him and swallowed.

"We should," Quinn said, "except that if we do put a second tail on her, she'll know. And she's right: if this is the killer, we wouldn't want to spook him before she gets some kind of line on him."

"Still and all . . ." Harold said.

"That's what I'm thinking," Quinn said.

"Jody Jason," Professor Elaine Pratt said, when Chancellor Schueller asked why she'd come to his office.

Schueller remained seated behind his desk, absently using both hands to play with a yellow number-two pencil. Elaine noticed that it had an extremely sharp point.

"You *did* say she accepted the Enders and Coil internship," Schueller said.

"She accepted, then took a train into the city for an interview. When she returned we talked, and she was unsure again."

Schueller was quiet for a moment, thinking. "Do you suppose the murder of Macy Collins is giving her pause? I mean, we couldn't blame her for that." The chancellor shivered as if the office had turned cold. "It must have been like being attacked by an animal."

"I think she feels like most of the students about that," Elaine Pratt said. "They regard it in the way they would if Macy had been struck by lightning."

"An apt comparison. It's a tragedy they'll have to put behind them."

"They're young enough to do that," Elaine said.

Schueller touched the tip of the pencil as if testing for sharpness. "So our sticking point is simply that Jody is a fickle one."

"Not usually," Elaine said. "Coil wasn't there, and Jack Enders interviewed her. He didn't make a good impression."

"I thought Jody was supposed to worry about impressing them."

"She seems not to see it that way."

Schueller smiled. "What did he say or do that turned her off?"

"She knows the firm is representing a client who owns three blocks of property in lower Manhattan. Old warehouses and deserted office buildings. Also a couple of rundown apartment buildings. The client wants to finish clearing the property so work can be started on a new complex of office buildings. Jody knows there's a holdout tenant who refuses to move, preventing them from razing one of the buildings."

The chancellor frowned, troubled. "She knows about Meeding Properties already?"

"Yes, but not much. That sort of thing is a matter of record and can't be kept secret within the confines of the firm. Not telling her would arouse her suspicions later on. And the firm has taken extra steps to hide Waycliffe's involvement."

"Those eminent domain cases," Schueller said, "don't they always end the same way?"

"Not always. This woman claims her lease has a clause that precludes them from making her move in the event of eminent domain."

"Doesn't eminent domain by its nature transcend that kind of lease?"

"Her argument is that it doesn't. It's a specious legal position, but not so much that she can't tie up the project for months if not years."

"So if she's got a case, they make her an offer."

"She's refused all offers. She and her late husband lived in the apartment for twenty years, so it's an emotional thing with her."

"Money can also be very emotional," Schueller said. He began tapping the sharpened pencil on the desk, making a constant slight ticking sound. When he realized what he was doing, he drew his briar pipe from his pocket, tamped down the tobacco in its bowl with a forefinger but, as usual, didn't light it. "So our young idealist has sided with the old lady."

"I don't think the tenant is an old lady," Elaine said. "That's the problem. She seems to be an attorney in her forties. Sophisticated and eager for the fray."

"Still, she's the underdog."

"Yes, and that's what's bothering Jody. Meeding Properties." The big development company was an Enders and

Coil client. "But she knows only so much. What we expected."

"Davida against Goliath," Schueller said. "Starring Jody as Davida."

"Something like that." Professor Pratt moved closer to Schueller. "I know Jody. She and Enders and Coil are on the same page we're on. It's just that sometimes she doesn't realize it. I understand our students, young girls especially."

"If you feel that way, Elaine, I wouldn't worry too much."

"Enders and Coil need to feel that way. And so do you."

"There's no need to have any doubts about how I feel. I'm aware that Jody is wicked smart. The same youthful idealism that's causing her to hesitate will also cause her to review the fact that everyone deserves legal counsel. That's the beauty of our system. She'll realize that Enders and Coil clients are true and deserving citizens being targeted simply because they have money."

"I hope you're right," Elaine said.

"They'll realize what an asset she can be."

"Jody's a stubborn one. And there's something else. She didn't like the way Jack Enders looked at her."

Schueller clamped the unlit pipe between his teeth. "He was coming on to her?"

"She thinks he was. Or that he almost surely will."

"Well, she'll have to learn how to handle that." He sucked on the pipe stem. "You know, Elaine, you were the one who recommended Jody to me to parade for Enders and Coil."

"I don't regret it," Elaine said. "Jody's an idealist, but she's also smart, practical, and in some ways cynical."

"Yet you come to my office because now there are doubts."

"I thought you should be kept up to date," Elaine said.

Schueller removed the pipe from his mouth and smiled. "And up to date I am," he said.

When Elaine Pratt was gone, he sat for a while and thought about Jody Jason, and whether she could be a fit at Enders and Coil. She was hamstrung so much by idealism. But then, that was the condition of so many bright young people. Sooner or later, they learned. And the sooner the better.

Idealism, he mused, was the bane of his existence.

He swiveled in his chair and looked out the window. Whatever clouds there'd been had fled, and the sky was a soft, unbroken blue.

A perfect day for flying, he thought. When he was in the air, things on the ground seemed so much more patterned and controllable.

More and more, he enjoyed flying.

28

Quinn was going to stay late at Q&A. Pearl left the office by herself.

The evening was pleasantly cool and she was walking to the brownstone. There was leftover pizza in the fridge there, along with diet soda and the makings of a salad. Also, she was sure there was an unopened bottle of blush wine. That could be enough for them tonight, unless Quinn wanted a late supper out.

Pearl had crossed Amsterdam when she noticed the woman again. She didn't have on the yellow dress this evening. Instead she was in jeans and a blue blouse. Pearl caught a glimpse of springy red hair poking out from beneath a blue baseball cap. Changing her appearance so Pearl wouldn't recognize her. Pathetic. The way the woman stopped and turned away with feigned casualness to look into a show window where real estate flyers were taped to the glass was so obvious. There was no doubt in Pearl's mind that the woman was on her tail.

Pearl picked up her pace, which was easy to do because her blood was up. She crossed the street, walked in the opposite direction, went in one door of a store, and out another. The woman stayed with her. She was either an amateur with a gift for being sticky, or she wanted Pearl to know she was back there like a persistent shadow. That last possibility bothered Pearl. It was the kind of game the killer might play, openly stalking his prey, instilling a fear that could eventually grow potent enough to paralyze.

Was Pearl amusing herself by leading her shadow on a merry chase, or was her shadow the one controlling the game?

Either way, Pearl had had about enough of this being-followed business.

Dusk had enveloped the city, but there was still enough light for the woman to see her. Pearl didn't glance back as she turned down a side street. There was very little traffic there, and only a few people on the street. Half a block down, Pearl slipped into a narrow walkway between two gray stone apartment buildings.

The woman behind her would figure her to pick up speed once around the corner, and if the narrow passageway went through, to dash to the next block and finally shake herself free. The smart thing for the woman to do was to run to the corner and cut to the next block, rather than pursue Pearl into a possible ambush. Or try to get close enough so she could follow her through the passageway.

Pearl stopped a few feet into the passageway and stood still, pressed against a brick wall. Beyond her she could see a chain-link fence and some stacked plastic trash bags. She couldn't get through to the next block if she had to. Was she the one who'd been outsmarted?

She fished into her small leather strap purse and pulled out her nine-millimeter Glock.

She waited, gun at the ready. You never knew what might come around a corner.

The rapid tapping of what sounded like flapping

leather sandals sounded faintly on the pavement, drawing nearer.

Pearl waited.

The footfalls ceased, nearby. She could hear rapid breathing.

Waited silently . . .

The woman rounded the corner, said, "Huh!" as Pearl lowered a shoulder and went into her hard, knocking her back against the brick wall. She braced her left forearm against the woman's throat and pointed the Glock at her head so she could see it. The woman was all high-pitched breaths that were almost shrieks. Impossibly round blue eyes. Her blue baseball cap fell off, a Mets cap. Pearl kicked it away in disdain.

"Turn your ass around," Pearl said, as she withdrew slightly and spun the woman so she was facing the wall. She made her place her hands high and wide against the wall and then with a series of short, abrupt kicks moved the woman's feet back and apart so she was braced at an angle against the wall and couldn't make a sudden move.

"Why are you following me?" Pearl asked.

"I wasn't."

"Bullshit!" Pearl grabbed a handful of springy red hair and held it. "You've been behind me for blocks, crossing every street I crossed, turning every corner I turned."

"You say."

"Damned right I say. You were wearing a yellow dress yesterday."

"Wasn't." Angry now, like a petulant teenager.

"Was."

"I don't own a yellow dress." The woman started to push herself away from the wall to get more comfortable. Pearl tightened her grip on her hair and shoved her back into position, hard. "Knock off that stuff!" the woman said. "I'll report you."

"*You'll* report *me*? I'm going to place you under arrest for harassing a police officer."

"I want to talk to my mother."

"You get one phone call."

"What's your number?"

29

"**B**ullshit!" Pearl said.

"You keep saying that," the woman told her.

Pearl no longer had the young woman with the springy red hair up against the wall and was pacing, fast, three steps each way, breathing hard and glaring at the woman. She wished her heart would stop hammering.

The woman bent down and retrieved her Mets cap that Pearl had knocked off her head and then kicked. She dusted it off on her thigh, then put it on perfectly straight and tucked strands of unruly hair beneath it.

"Cody's girl," the woman said calmly, staring straight at Pearl from beneath the cap's curved brim.

The past came rushing at Pearl and hit her like a wall. She'd been twenty, pregnant, and in love with Cody Clarke, who studied music at NYU and supported himself playing saxophone in night spots around the city.

Cody Clarke. The first one. Jesus!

Pearl's mother had warned her not to try living on her own in New York. Warned her about this very thing. How could Pearl have gone home to New Jersey and told her what happened? That she'd made the biggest, most blundering mistake possible?

Pearl could see Cody now in the clarity of time, sitting in his underwear on the mattress laid out on the floor, the covers bunched around him, his wild red hair a jumble of curls. The roach-infested apartment's ancient radiator was hissing and spitting. *Why am I remembering that?*

"We can't get married, babe," he'd told her.

"That wasn't in my mind," she'd lied. She went to him, sat down next to him on the mattress, and they hugged each other.

"You're sure?" he asked.

"Don't ask me that. Of course I'm sure."

"You been—"

"To a doctor? Yeah. He confirmed it."

"I know another doctor," Cody said.

"Don't even think about that."

"Okay, I won't." Breezy Cody. "I gotta leave next week for California. The tour with the guys." The guys were Happy, Joey, and Tex. Happy played the drums, Tex the bass guitar. Joey played about everything. They were all mediocre musicians except for Cody, who could play saxophone like a wild man. Cody was the glue and the draw. He had to go to California.

"So go," Pearl said. "Don't let me interfere with your plans. You're not gonna interfere with mine."

He looked at her almost as if he loved her. "What are your plans, babe?"

"Adoption."

He squeezed her. "That could be hard on you. I know a girl who . . ."

"What?"

"Never mind. Are you gonna tell your mom about this?"

"I won't have to. She'll know. But we'll never talk about it. She doesn't want to disown me."

"God, Pearl!"

"I'm gonna have the baby, Cody. Don't try talking me out of it."

"I wouldn't do that. It's your choice."

"You don't have to worry."

"About what?"

"Child support, whatever. I'm gonna put it up for adoption. Not even gonna look at it."

"You might change your mind about that," Cody had said.

But she didn't. The next week she saw him and the guys off to California in the beat-to-hell Volkswagen bus they'd found somewhere. Somebody had painted yellow stars all over the thing. She could see it now. And hear it. And feel the tug of the parting. Cody . . .

"Pearl?" The woman's voice. Her daughter's. The bitter-sweet past was gone.

"Yeah?"

"You do believe me, don't you?"

I believe you. I dreamed about you. I searched for you during the first few years of your life. When I look at you, every part of me believes you.

"Yeah. I think so. How'd you find me?"

"I've been looking for you off and on. Finally came across you on the Internet. 'Least I thought it was you. It seemed like you. Then I saw you on campus with that other cop."

"Quinn."

"Whatever. I figured you were investigating the Macy Collins murder. So I asked around. Learned it *was* you. I decided to find and follow you."

"Why?"

"Curiosity, I guess."

"You been curious about your father?"

"Not for a while. He died fifteen years ago in a nightclub fire in Holland, along with a dozen other people. He was there playing music. I never met him."

Pearl wasn't prepared for the way her heart dropped. She began to sweat and felt dizzy.

"You okay?" the woman asked.

Pearl straightened up. *I'm not okay. You dropped a nuclear bomb on me. I feel sick.* "Yeah. Listen, what's your name?"

"Juditha Jason. People call me Jody."

"Juditha . . . ?"

"I think somebody wrote my name down with a flourish."

"And you're a student at Waycliffe?"

"Studying law." She grinned. "You find 'em, I put 'em away."

"Lame," Pearl said, dabbing perspiration off her forehead with the back of her hand.

"Yeah."

"Er, Jody? Your time growing up? I mean . . ."

Jody smiled. Pearl saw Cody and almost keeled over. "It was good. I loved the Jasons. They loved me." The smile widened. "You did right by me. The right thing."

"Are they . . . ?"

"Both gone now. Mom of breast cancer two years ago. Dad had a stroke six months later."

Mom . . . Dad . . . Would Pearl ever get her mind around this? "I'm sorry, Jody."

Jody gave a sad smile. "Thanks. And thanks for giving me my time with them."

Pearl took a deep breath and felt better, as if she'd been carrying around a weight most of her life and it had been lifted, though in truth she'd outlived the guilt she'd felt for putting Jody up for adoption. Yet here, along with surprise and joy was—not guilt, but something like guilt.

She hadn't even seen her daughter before the Jason family had obtained her. Of course Pearl hadn't known their names. Or her baby's. Nobody knew anybody then. The agency wanted to keep it that way. It had made sense to Pearl then. Still did.

For a few seconds she felt a deep anger directed at Jody. Then it passed. What had the girl done other than grow up well and search for her mother and father? She'd found her father. At least his memory.

And now . . . what? Could all this . . . disruption . . . be true?

Pearl looked hard at Jody, who grinned and shrugged her shoulders to great effect but without much movement. The way Pearl shrugged her shoulders.

"We need to talk," Jody said.

"One of us was bound to say that."

"It figured I'd be the one."

"I know a quiet place near here," Pearl said.

She touched Jody's elbow lightly to lead her out of the passageway, and found that she couldn't release the elbow. She *couldn't*. Her legs were numb and weak. Jody could feel her trembling and moved closer to support her. The two women hugged, and both began to sob.

God, Pearl hated this!

30

Deena was skating fast with a tray full of food. Hamburgers, mostly. The famous (so the restaurant claimed) Roller Burger. There were two beers on the tray, a small egg cream, and two orders of fried onion rings. She didn't see Rolf, one of the busboys, with his tray full of plates and stacked cups, speeding toward the kitchen.

"Hey!" a man at one of the tables yelled, seeing the imminent collision.

Both Deena and Rolf turned their heads to look at him, which is why they collided with such force.

Deena was sure she'd blacked out for a moment. Her back hurt, just below her shoulder blades. And her head was throbbing. When she opened her eyes she was looking up at one of the slowly revolving ceiling fans. There was also a circle of faces above her, staring at her. Most of the faces wore concerned expressions. She caught two of the men and one of the women obviously enjoying her pain and embarrassment.

That was when she felt the real pain. Her right ankle sent spasms of agony up her leg.

"Could be sprained," she heard a man's voice say.

"It's not sprained," Deena said. If she could get upright, the pain might go away. She might not lose her job. "I'm telling you, it doesn't hurt."

"It's gotta hurt, Deena," her boss said, though she couldn't see him.

"Gimme a chance!"

Hands reached for her, levitated her, and set her on her skates.

And the pain did go away. Her ankle felt numb, though. One by one the hands removed themselves from her arms and shoulders.

She stood still for a moment, and then attempted to take a step.

Pain ran like electricity up her leg and she heard herself scream. She landed hard on her ass and sat leaning back on her elbows. The woman who'd been enjoying her pain was grinning at her now.

I'll remember you, bitch.

"Call nine-one-one," Deena heard her boss tell someone.

"Hey! What about me? I'm hurt, too." It was Rolf, the busboy. Deena looked over at him. He was lying among a mass of broken plates and cups, but she knew he wasn't really hurt. He was making a joke of it.

"If we saw bone sticking out of your leg like Deena's," a woman said, "we'd take you more seriously."

Deena's stomach lurched. She looked down at her ankle. Looked away.

And passed out.

31

Pearl was still in shock.

She finished cleaning up after dinner, which took about five minutes. She fed what was left of the reheated pizza to the garbage disposal, resealed the plastic bag of pre-washed salad ingredients and placed it in the refrigerator, then dropped the paper plates and beer and soda cans into the trash. A quick wipe-off of the table with a damp dishcloth, and she was finished. This was the way to eat and clean up afterward, second only to dining out and letting someone else clean up the mess.

Quinn, seated on the sofa, could see into the kitchen and watched her curiously. She was moving like an automaton, with no wasted motion. On automatic.

Pearl had been quiet during dinner, thoughtful. He wondered what was occupying her mind. He knew something was. He also knew this was the time to hold his silence. If Pearl wanted to talk something out, she'd get around to it.

She came into the living room and sat down in a gray wing chair, curling her legs under her. Light from the streetlight in front of the brownstone filtered through the sheer curtains and softened her pale features, darkened her black hair and eyes. She was observing him now, weighing what she was going to say. He wondered if he was going to like hearing it.

"I met my daughter tonight," she said.

"Huh?"

"You heard me."

Well, he thought. *Well . . .*

"Quinn?"

"But did I hear you right?"

She smiled with a new wisdom. "Yeah, you did. Want me to tell you about her?"

"Maybe later."

A widening of her eyes. Then the familiar smile. "You bastard!"

He listened intently, not moving a muscle, as she told him about Juditha Jason who was called Jody, about Cody Clarke and the pregnancy and adoption. About the Jason family, who had loved Jody and had been loved by her.

Luck, Quinn thought. *It sounds like the kid was lucky.*

"I was seventeen, Quinn. I didn't know myself or the world. All I've known all these years is that my baby was a girl."

Quinn didn't know what to think. What to say. Other than, "It's all right, Pearl."

"Gee, thank you."

"I mean . . . well, it's great, I guess. This Juditha—"

"Jody." Pearl swallowed. "Jesus, Quinn. She's really something."

Forces Quinn didn't quite understand were at work here. He knew he'd have to come to grips with this and was working on it. Pearl a mother. The father, her long-ago lover, dead. Her daughter, a twenty-two-year-old girl—woman—was here in New York.

Pearl, a mother . . .

Pearl must have seen the consternation on his face. "You two'll get along fine," she said. "I know it!"

"When am I going to meet her?"

Pearl shot a look at her watch.

The intercom rasped. Someone downstairs in the foyer.

"That would be Jody," Pearl said, and got up to go buzz her daughter in.

Quinn thought, *Holy Christ!*

"I don't understand it," Fedderman said to his wife, Penny. But he did understand. He'd just hoped it wouldn't happen to them.

"I see you go out in the morning, and all day I keep wondering if I'm ever going to see you again."

Fedderman nodded. *Like so many other cops' wives.* "You knew I was a policeman, Pen. Hell, I'm not even actually that now. I'm a private investigator."

"And look what you're doing, Feds. You're tracking the most dangerous killer in the city. You're *trying* to be in the same place at the same time he is."

"It's my job."

"I'm not asking you to quit. And I'm not about to quit on our marriage."

"But you might change your mind about that."

"I go crazy thinking you might be hurt or dead somewhere, Feds."

"So you went out and got a job to fill your time."

"To fill my mind. Is that so crazy?"

"I guess not."

"I talked to Ms. Culver at the library and she told me there was an opening."

"Getting your old job back."

"Not exactly, but close. The library has a big DVD section now."

"I guess they would," Fedderman said. In truth he was kind of surprised. The Albert A. Aal Memorial Library didn't seem large enough for such an addition. Maybe they had fewer books.

"I start day after tomorrow," Penny said. She came to him and snaked her arms around him. "Can you put up with me, Feds?"

He hugged her back, kissed her lips, and gazed down at her. "Question is, can we put up with each other?"

"I know the answer to that," Penny said, and kissed him back.

Fedderman hoped she was right, but he wondered.

"Are you any closer?" she asked.

"To what?"

"Finding the killer."

He didn't know the answer to that, either.

32

Rory was fourteen years old and didn't have a driver's license. That didn't mean he was a bad driver. Or so he told himself. Hadn't he had almost a dozen lessons from Jack Smith, an older brother of one of his friends? Even Rory's mother had let him drive, with her along, in the Leighton Mall parking lot. When the mall was closed.

His mother was at the citizens' meeting about the proposed new dam tonight, like half the adult population of Leighton, and she'd gone with a neighbor and left the family car in the garage. So it seemed a perfect time for Rory to test his wings—or wheels. After all, he'd never gotten much chance to drive at night. He wasn't surprised to find it just as easy as daylight driving. Probably he was a natural driver.

He was a bright kid, and while not big for his age was well built, so he could pass for older than fourteen if anybody saw him driving the big green Chevy Impala. The car was three years old, and his mother had bought it used two months ago, trading in the old Volvo that had almost two hundred thousand miles on it. She liked the Chevy. Its styling was bold, and a pleasant change from the staid and solid Volvo.

Rory imagined how he'd look from outside the car. Pretty damned dashing. He pushed a button and the driver's side window glided down out of sight into the door. He rested his arm on the open window, causing the bicep to spread. He had to steer with one hand, but that was okay; the big Chevy almost steered itself. And he was familiar with the road. It was Oaks Road, which ran parallel to the train tracks for a while and then veered off into lightly wooded farm country.

He made the turn, away from the tracks. Less traffic now. No one was likely to see him. He ran the speedometer up to forty, fifty. The speed limit was fifty miles per hour, which meant sixty was okay. Seventy if you weren't caught.

Most of the Leighton police department was at the meeting about the dam the state wanted to build. And the state police hardly ever patrolled here, well off the main highway.

Okay, seventy.

Rory edged his foot down on the accelerator and the Chevy responded as if it would like to run up to a hundred miles per hour.

No thank you, Rory thought. He was a risk taker, not a fool. A man has to know his limitations.

A car passed him going the other way.

Another.

Even though there was a full moon, all he saw of the other two vehicles were their headlights. There was nothing ahead of him now traveling either direction. Nothing in the rearview mirror. He relaxed and sat back in the comfortable seat.

The road straightened out like a black ribbon. It had

been recently asphalted, and the tires hit the seams with soft slapping sounds. *Neat.* Rory liked that sound. Warm air came in the open window and swirled around the inside of the car. Trees lined the road here and there, and the car flashed past steel crash guards on each side where there was a culvert. Rory had chosen the right road. This was a cinch.

It was because he was so relaxed that he didn't see the medium-sized shaggy black dog that trotted from the high weeds out onto the road. Rory noticed the dog only when it was in the car's path. It stopped and stared at him, its eyes glowing in the reflected headlight illumination.

God, no! Rory thought, sitting bolt upright behind the steering wheel. *Move, won't you? Move!*

But the dog didn't move. There was a solid thump and what sounded like a yelp.

Shit!

Rory braked the car and parked on the grassy shoulder. He found that he was shaking.

Gotta stop that!

He drew some deep breaths and did manage to regain control of his jangled nerves. The smart Rory kicked in.

A quick examination revealed no apparent damage to the car, thank God. His mother would kill him if she found out about this.

He walked back toward the point of impact.

The moonlight was bright enough to show that there was nothing on the road. Maybe he'd actually missed the dog, and that's why the car wasn't damaged. Maybe the whole thing hadn't happened. Had he seen something that only *looked* like a dog? A possum or coon, maybe.

But there was a streak of what looked like blood on the pavement. Rory knew then that he'd hit something, and probably not a possum or coon.

He followed the trail of blood into the weeds, and found in the shadows beneath some trees a black dog lying on its side, panting and whimpering.

Trembling again, his heart in his mouth, Rory knelt beside the dog and examined the wound. He could see white bone, maybe a rib, and the dog's front right leg was terribly twisted. It had a red leather collar but no tags.

Damn! Time for smart Rory again. Calm Rory. Analyze and act.

Rory straightened up and stood in the moonlight with his fists propped on his hips. *What now?* He felt sorry for the dog, but it obviously didn't have long to live. And it was suffering. He could put it in the car and drive it into town to a vet. But he was sure a vet would simply put the dog down. Stop its suffering, at least.

But there would be blood in the car. Rory's mother would know he'd driven it despite her strict instructions to leave it parked in the garage.

The dog whimpered and gazed over at Rory. Its tail wagged.

Rory set his emotions aside, and his quick and logical mind came up with what he should do. It would be best for everyone, including the obviously suffering and dying dog.

Act!

He didn't hesitate. He walked a few feet away to where he'd seen a large rock and pried it up from the ground. It weighed at least five pounds—large and heavy enough. It also had an edge.

Rory kneeled down beside the dog, raised the rock, and brought it down three times on the dog's head. The dog let out only a faint whimper. Its legs trembled and thrashed as if it were running in death, and then it lay still.

The plan was in action and there was a directness and

purpose to all of Rory's decisions and actions. Buzzards would find the dog and their circling might draw someone's attention. He left the dog where it was, and went back to the car and got the tire iron. Using the hard end of the tool, he scraped and dug a shallow grave near the dog. He dragged the dog over to the grave, removed the red collar, and shoved the animal into the hole. It took him only a few minutes to hurriedly scoop dirt over the dog, then brush some of last year's dead leaves over it. It was unlikely that anyone would find it even if the buzzards did somehow get to it and circle. And if the remains ever were found, the conclusion would be that the animal had been struck and killed by a car, which was in fact the truth.

Rory wiped the bloody rock on the grass and then threw it as far as he could. It bounced once and made no sound. Then he rolled up the red leather collar and threw it in the opposite direction.

He looked around, satisfied, and then trotted back to the Chevy. He was high on adrenaline now. And something else. He was fooling them. All of them. He'd be the only one who knew about this. It was an unexpected, exhilarating rush.

The Chevy's cooling engine was ticking in the warm night. He clambered back in and drove.

He was careful to stay well within the speed limit, and was glad traffic was light and his mother's car, with him behind the steering wheel, wasn't likely to be noticed.

Every second of the drive home, his mind was working.

When the car was safely in the garage, Rory sat and waited for the overhead door to lower, then got out and switched on the fluorescent light mounted on a crossbeam. He cleaned the tire iron with a rag and replaced it in its bracket with the jack. Then he reexamined the right front of the car where the results of any impact might be found. There was what might have been a dent, but it was barely noticeable. It might even have been a reflection. Also there was some kind of dark stain near the dent, maybe blood. Rory wiped it off with the same rag he'd used to clean the tire iron and then threw the rag away.

He looked again at the dent and where the stain had been. Good as new, he thought. Good as three years old, anyway, which was all that mattered. Even if his mother or someone else noticed the slight dent, they'd think it had been there and they simply hadn't seen it before. They'd attribute the damage to the car's previous owner.

Rory undressed in the garage and went into the house through the connecting door. He saw no sign of blood on his clothes, but he put his T-shirt and jeans in the wash, just to be sure. Sometimes he helped out his mother by washing his own clothes. This was the perfect night for it.

By the time the clothes were in the washer, thumping reassuringly as they were agitated, Rory, wearing only his socks and Jockey shorts, was seated at his bedroom desk doing his homework. John Cougar Mellencamp was singing "Lonely Ol' Night' on FM radio, but advanced mathematics occupied Rory's mind and he barely heard the music. It was a level of math taught only to "top track" students.

The incident with the dog was already pushed to a distant part of his consciousness. It might as well never have happened, so it *hadn't* happened. Not as far as Rory was concerned. He'd run through his possible choices and done what was best for everyone and everything involved. There was no doubt as to the righteousness of his actions.

Don't look back. Additional speculation or sentimentality was pointless. He'd done the smart thing, which was the right thing, and that was that. Tonight's episode in his life was closed, would be known to no one else, and would soon be forgotten even by him.

Very soon, when he drove that stretch of Oak Road it would hold no special significance for him.

33

New York, the present

Quinn's immediate thought when Pearl went to the door and let in Jody Jason was that she looked nothing like Pearl.

Then he realized that was her attitude. Whoever this girl—woman—was, she stood like a wayward waif, her springy red hair sticking out over her ears as if there might be a mild current of electricity running through her. She was wearing jeans and a pale green blouse. Once you looked more closely at her, at the angle of her nose, the shape of her head, her ears, the look in her eyes—yes, Pearl was there. She was busty like Pearl, though the rest of her was much thinner than her mother. When she moved toward him, she moved like Pearl.

Quinn stood his ground. *What the hell am I supposed to do?*

Jody continued toward him, visibly gaining courage as she came. When she reached him she didn't hesitate, but gave him a brief, hard hug that almost made him whoosh out a breath of air. He couldn't help but think it: *Her breasts feel like Pearl's.*

"There hasn't been time to have heard much about you," Jody said through Pearl's smile, "but everything I've heard has been good."

Quinn grinned stupidly. Felt like it, anyway. "All true," he said. *When in doubt, be witty. Sure.*

"Of course," Jody said, stepping back. "Mom wouldn't lie."

Oh-ho! "No," he said, "she wouldn't."

Pearl was giving him a look he was glad Jody couldn't see.

"Come all the way in," he said, "and sit down. Something to drink?"

"A beer, if you have it," Jody said.

"Easy," Quinn said, and went into the kitchen.

He could hear the two of them talking while he got three Heineken cans from the refrigerator and opened them.

"Glass?" he called in.

"For sissies," Jody called back. Or maybe it was Pearl. Quinn smiled. Suddenly, unaccountably, he liked this unexpected development. Like that. *Flip*. That was how it worked. Jody was a fact, and he'd have to learn to deal with her. Maybe it would be more than tolerable. Maybe it would be fun.

He returned to the living room with the three beer cans held in one huge hand. Jody and Pearl quickly relieved him of two of the frosty cans. Quinn raised his beer, grinning, and they clicked the cans together in a metallic toast. He felt some of his beer run down between his fingers, but he didn't care.

"Welcome to the almost family," he said.

Pearl was grinning her widest grin, nodding at Quinn as if he'd passed some kind of test. *Good boy!* said her eyes.

The landline phone rang, and he went to the table by the sofa, lifted the receiver, and identified himself.

"Captain Quinn?" said the voice. "I've been calling and calling Pearl's cell phone, but there's always a click and a message saying half of something, and then there's a terrible buzzing noise. Technology will kill us all."

Quinn held the receiver out toward Pearl but was looking at Jody when he spoke: "It's your grandmother."

Jody's eyes widened and then took on a look of comprehension. Quinn couldn't help but notice that she'd grasped this sudden overload of information fast.

Pearl thought, *Jumpin' Jesus!*

Pearl went to Quinn slowly. She took the receiver from his hand as if it were a live thing that might bite her any second.

Quinn heard Pearl's mother's rasping voice even four feet from the phone.

"It's your mother, dear, checking to see if you're alive or dead, and if you are alive—and God willing you are— what is going on in your life?"

"Well," Pearl said, feeling her nerves vibrate like cello strings, "there is some news."

Penny and her supervisor, the austere Ms. Culver, were alone in the library except for a few people browsing the stacks, and a man operating one of the microfiche machines in the research department. The Albert A. Aal library had never computerized its newspaper and periodical files.

Penny was pushing a cart stacked with returned books to be replaced in their correct order on the shelves. The library was familiar to her. Working here was almost like having returned home.

When she was finished replacing the books, she wheeled the cart back to its place behind the front desk, where it could gradually be reloaded as books were returned.

Ms. Culver was wearing a severe gray dress with black low heels, had her mud-colored hair in a bun, and was as impeccable as ever. If librarians were manufactured somewhere, Ms. Culver must be the prototype.

Yet there was something in her severity that didn't ring true. Penny thought she saw a slight tremor in Ms. Culver's right hand when she dropped a copy of *Pride and Prejudice* onto the cart Penny had just wheeled up. Or maybe it struck her odd that Ms. Culver didn't place the book down in the cart more gently, and square it neatly in a wooden corner. Ms. Culver worshipped symmetry.

"Is anything wrong?" Penny asked.

"Wrong as in what?"

"As in not right," Penny said.

Ms. Culver placed both her hands flat on the return desk. She seemed to be debating internally whether to confide in Penny.

"DVDs," she said.

Penny stared at her.

"Last week, for the first time, we had more DVDs out on loan than books."

"Kids love them," Penny said. "Video games with car chases and shootouts and violence. The comic books of today."

"It wasn't only kids that borrowed them. Same with audiobooks. More and more people are *listening* to books while they sit in traffic, or do something else that demands half their attention, or fall asleep in their recliners."

"You might be right."

"I am right. I know by the declining percentage of actual books we loan. And by the decreasing number of library patrons who come and go here because they go someplace else. And that someplace else is the Internet.

They use Wi-Fi, whatever that is. Where they can download e-books for their electronic readers or computers. There's no *paper* involved in any of this, Penny. It's as if we've reverted to oral history and fiction, storytelling passed down through generations while sitting around campfires. We read something on a screen, and then it goes from substance to memory, just the way those ancient stories did. They're nothing but electronic impulses. When they're deleted from the machines, they no longer exist. There are fewer and fewer actual, tangible *books*."

"Yes, what you say is true. So we're worried about unemployment."

But both women knew Penny wasn't worried about it. She had a husband, another wage earner, and there were other kinds of jobs she could get. Ms. Culver was a librarian, had always been a librarian, and always would be. The way an obsolete buggy whip would always be a buggy whip.

Ms. Culver was watching Penny through rimless glasses as if reading her thoughts. "I'm worried about the future," she said. "I have nieces, nephews."

Penny hadn't known that.

"We're just dipping our toes in a new era," Penny said. "Like the era following the invention of the printing press, only everything's moving faster. Your nieces and nephews will adapt."

"That's the problem. They have adapted. They don't type; they keyboard. They've made *keyboard* a verb, Penny. They've made *text* a verb. They don't read text in books, and hardly ever do on a computer screen. Not for pleasure, anyway. It's distressing."

Returning to her job at the library might have been a mistake, Penny thought. She'd sought solace and security here, a shelter from the world of worry about all the things that could happen to Feds and to her, to their mar-

riage. Maybe Feds was right and there was no real security. If you lived, you risked. Even if you weren't a cop.
Feds's enemies were the bad guys. Ms. Culver's enemies
were e-books.

"You know how the French say the more things change
the more they stay the same," Penny said, trying to
brighten Ms. Culver's mood. "Books are books, even if
they're electronic books."

"All the books in this library could be stored on one
chip," Ms. Culver said. "And I'm not French. Now I suggest you go straighten up the magazines."

Penny did, but she was thinking about this evening,
when Feds would be working late. She'd told him she didn't
mind, that she wasn't worried about him. But she was.
Only now she was doing something about her worries.
Something for others but, ultimately, something for Feds
and herself and their marriage. He wouldn't approve.

But then, he didn't know.

34

She liked imagining herself in the old movie she'd watched last night, *Rear Window,* but she'd rather have been Grace Kelly. Instead she was James Stewart, sitting at a window with his leg propped up, helplessly watching the world go by.

Deena Vess's ankle had stopped aching, but it itched like crazy under the plaster cast. Day after tomorrow she was supposed to go back to the doctor and get the cast removed, to be replaced by a plastic one that could be taken off occasionally and was sure to be more comfortable.

From where she sat, she could look out her apartment window at the street below if she strained herself. A fly buzzed frantically and futilely against the lower pane, trying to get on the other side of the invisible glass barrier. She knew how it felt.

It was a hot day, and there were fewer people than normal down there on the baking sidewalks. Traffic wasn't very heavy, either.

But there was the foreshortened figure of Jeff the postman, crossing the street to his mail truck. He stepped up into the truck and drove away.

Okay, something to do! Get the mail. A chore that required her attention.

It would hurt slightly, but it was worth the pain. And worth it to escape daytime television. Or roaming Facebook or Twitter. She'd tired of sending out messages about her aching ankle. The social network didn't want to hear you bitch any more than people standing right next to you.

She used one of the metal crutches she'd bought at Duane Reade to brace herself as she stood up from her chair. Then she hobbled toward the door. From the corner of her eye she saw the cat that wasn't Empress stretch and edge toward the kitchen door as if stalking something. She still couldn't work up any fondness for the cat, and how it had taken Empress's place was still a mystery that sometimes kept her up at night, wondering. The longer she and the cat shared the apartment, the less the animal looked like the real Empress.

But what you couldn't understand you at last got tired of thinking about. She'd posted a status on Facebook asking if anyone could explain the bizarre cat substitution. The answers from her "friends" strongly implied that she might be insane and should seek help. Sure, Deena should hobble into a psychoanalyst's office with a cat under her arm and say it was impersonating another cat.

She reached the door to the hall, opened it, and clattered out into the tiled hall on her crutches. After closing the door, she used the crutches to make her way to the elevator. There was some pain, but it was bearable. And going down to the foyer and getting her mail was one of the few things she looked forward to these days. She needed to get off these damn crutches and back on her skates, if she was still employed at Roller Steak. The boss had assured her the job would be there for her, but what was that worth?

Deena hobbled out of the elevator and over to the bank of brass mailboxes. She glimpsed white through the slot in her box. *Mail!*

A disappointed Deena discovered that her mail consisted of an ad for Viagra.

She returned to the elevator, pressed the up button, and momentarily got one of her crutches caught in the crack between elevator and floor. Finally safe inside the elevator and leaning on the wall near the control panel, she pressed the button for her floor.

By the time she was back in her chair, facing the muted TV playing *Sex and the City* reruns, her ankle was throbbing. Probably these mail-fetching missions every day weren't the best thing for the ankle, but she had to do *something* to get out.

She'd been sitting there for almost an hour when it occurred to her that she hadn't seen the Empress imposter since returning from her mail pickup. She knew she'd closed the door behind her and—

Someone knocked on her apartment door hard enough to startle her, then continued to knock, softer but insistently.

Deena cursed, snatched up her clattering crutches, and hobbled over to look out the peephole.

An eye was staring right back at her. She hated it when people did that.

A male voice in the hall said, "I have a cat somebody told me was yours."

Deena peered through the peephole again. This time a guy was standing back, farther from the door. He was holding up a cat that, even distorted by the peephole glass, looked more like Empress than the imposter.

Deena worked the dead bolt, then opened the door, leaving it on the chain.

The man looked in at her and held the cat up again for her inspection. Definitely the real Empress.

But then—

"I ran some *found cat* ads in the paper," the man said. He was a good-looking guy, storybook handsome but not effeminate. "I'm a cat person, and I knew this one was loved and had an owner in the neighborhood who must be worried stiff about her."

Empress waved a paw at Deena and mewed.

Deena detached the chain lock and opened the door all the way. "It's odd," she said. "There was this other cat—"

The man threw a yowling Empress into Deena's face and at the same time kicked her injured ankle and pushed her backward. She fell with a sharp intake of breath and a clatter of aluminum.

He was on her while she was too shocked to utter another sound. She saw and then felt the sticky gray rectangle of duct tape slapped over her half-open mouth. He gripped her wrists and kept her hands away from her face while she struggled and tried to scream. He was laughing. That was what for some reason terrified her more than anything, his soft, amused laughter.

He stood up, crouched over her, still squeezing her wrists hard enough that her hands were twisted into claws. She couldn't stop working her legs, fighting to stand up despite the agonizing pain in her ankle.

Smiling, he waited patiently until he had the opportunity and then kicked her broken ankle again, this time as hard as he could, grunting with the effort.

The pain carried her to a place where she could no longer hear her muffled screams.

To where she melted to nothing and consciousness stole away.

35

It was done mostly by computer now. The law library in the offices of Enders and Coil was primarily for show, a casualty of LexisNexis. But Jody knew that not everything in the vast body of recorded law was online. There simply hadn't been enough time and work hours to have scanned it in. Useful precedence could exist in obscure legal tomes, and the library at Enders and Coil was comprehensive and marvelous in its way. There were decisions long forgotten but useful, if someone had the time, patience, and instinct to know where to look.

"It's six o'clock. You should have gone home an hour ago," Jack Enders said.

Jody looked up from where she was sitting at a mahogany table stacked with fat law volumes she'd borrowed from the shelves above and around her. The room was square, with a series of catwalks angling upward toward a high, arched ceiling. Almost every inch of wall space was packed with books. Enders was standing just inside the open wood-paneled door. There were no windows in the room. Light was provided by fixtures dangling at the end of chains of varying lengths strung from the ceiling, and from large reading lamps at each of the three tables.

"I've been researching Dash-Meeding," Jody said.

"Why that one?"

Jody shrugged. "I was browsing, saw it was an eminent domain matter, and thought it might be interesting. Property rights cases have always intrigued me."

Enders smiled. "That one's almost automatic."

"Finding for the defendant? Not actually. There's a 1912 finding that eminent domain can be nullified contractually if the prospective enacting entity is specified."

Enders grinned. A handsome man over six feet tall, impeccably tailored and with flowing black hair just beginning to gray, he was an intriguing combination of dignity and virility. "1912," he said. "That's the year the *Titanic* went down. I don't think a decision in the Edwardian era will in any way influence a multimillion-dollar New York commercial real estate transaction."

"I don't know," Jody said. "The specificity clause. Isn't there one in the Dash-Meeding case?"

"Not one the former owners of the property authorized. That's why the first judge brushed the claim away without a second thought."

"Is it under appeal?" *As if I don't know.*

"Yes. But only as a matter of formality."

"But I don't see how authorization—"

"Look, Jody, I don't want to discuss Dash-Meeding. I came here to see if you wanted to go to dinner. You don't have to starve yourself to work here, especially if it's work done on your own concerning an action that's been all but decided."

"I appreciate the offer," Jody said, "but I've got another dinner date in a few hours."

Enders gave her his handsome white smile. "A beautiful young woman like you, I should have known."

Jody smiled. "It was nice of you to ask, sir."

Still smiling: "Oh, a distancing *sir*. Are you afraid to socialize with the boss?"

"I'm just remembering he's the boss," Jody said. "And I meant it when I said I appreciate the offer."

Enders reached behind him and gripped the brass doorknob, but he didn't turn to leave. "You really do have potential, Jody."

"Thank you." *What kind of potential are we talking about?*

He started to open the door, and then hesitated. "A bit of advice?"

"Always."

"Your time would be better spent dining with the boss than working on an all but decided case."

Jody smiled at him. "That makes sense."

He nodded. "I'm not surprised you came to that sensible conclusion."

He left and closed the door behind him.

Jody knew there was another sensible conclusion to be reached here. There might be a good reason Enders didn't want her learning more about Dash-Meeding.

Enders had tried to give her advice, but instead given her motivation.

When Jody left Enders and Coil she took a subway uptown and walked to Quinn and Pearl's brownstone on West Seventy-fifth Street. She liked Quinn a lot; he was like some kind of Bible-illustration Old Testament guy who'd gotten a shave and haircut and looked pretty sexy. Seemed to think like one, too. But at other times he was surprisingly modern in his attitude. *Contrast*, Jody thought. *The world's full of it.*

Like with her mom, who had turned out to be not at all what she'd expected. Pearl had a hard surface, but know her for a little while and you realized that beneath that surface she was even harder. The thing was, she hadn't any real meanness in her; she was simply realistic. Nothing she knew or did was tinged with false hope. That was what Jody liked about Pearl—she was a person who met the truth head-on. It was the way Jody thought of herself, though she knew she wasn't completely like that. Emotion got in her way. She'd inherited it from Pearl, probably—getting pissed off when somebody you might not even know got the dirty end of the stick. Maybe that was why Pearl was a cop. She'd figured out how to use that emotion for energy and determination. *Maybe I should go into criminal law*, Jody thought.

Odd the things you think about when you let your mind wander while you walk.

She took the steps up to the brownstone's stoop and pressed the buzzer button that let her into the foyer. Quinn and Pearl were expecting her, so she didn't have to use the intercom to be buzzed up.

Pearl was wearing her gray slacks from work, black leather moccasins, and a white blouse. Quinn had on pinstripe brown pants that looked like half of a suit, and a blue pullover golf shirt with a collar. Socks but no shoes. He seemed unconcerned that he was breaking several fashion laws.

Pearl smiled at Jody and kissed her on the cheek. Quinn did the same. Jody thought she might faint.

Where am I going? What am I doing? And is it real?

The dining room table was set for three beneath the gigantic antique crystal gas chandelier that had sometime in the past hundred-plus years been converted to electricity.

Jody realized she was staring at it.

"It won't fall," Quinn assured her.

Pearl and Quinn together brought the food in from the kitchen. Some kind of noodle and meat casserole, tossed salad, warm rolls. Quinn brought in a bottle of Australian red wine and filled three glasses with it, then placed it on the table, where all three of them could reach it.

When they were seated, he raised his wine and they clinked glasses and toasted the future.

After they were finished eating, but still drinking wine, Pearl looked across the table at Jody and said, "We have a proposition."

Quinn cut in before Jody could say anything. "You aren't crazy about the apartment that the school and law firm provide for your internship."

True, Jody had bitched about it. The roaches, mainly. Also, Jack Enders had taken to dropping by. He had one thing in mind, and Jody was getting bored with the challenge of fending him off without losing her internship.

"The place has pests," Jody said.

"It seems . . . *right* that you should take one of the upstairs bedrooms here," Pearl said.

"She means live here," Quinn said. "With us."

Jody looked at him. There was no way to read this man's thoughts.

"What do you think about the idea?" she asked him.

"I think you're family."

That struck Jody as a wild and wonderful thing to say, considering he wasn't officially married to her mom.

"It's only a short subway ride from here to Enders and Coil," Quinn said.

"I'll take that ride," Jody said. "And thank you. Both of you." She knew her eyes were moist, but she didn't touch them.

They sat silently like that. Jody's eyes almost watering, Quinn stone-faced.

Pearl said, "Goddamn it!" and wiped away a tear.

"I do have another favor to ask you," Jody said, when she'd been shown her room and a date had been designated moving day. "I mean, besides the free room and board." She had to smile at her own chutzpah.

"You are definitely Pearl's daughter," Quinn said.

The three of them were seated in the living room, with its tall, draped windows facing the street, its inlaid hardwood floor, and red carpet. Substitute horses clopping outside for traffic sounds, and it might as well have been 1885. Jody didn't know when she'd been more comfortable.

"Fire away, Jody," Pearl said.

"Following you around the way I did, Pearl"—she still vacillated between *Pearl* and *Mom*—"I got kind of interested in what you were doing. And since I've gotten to know you, and Quinn, I've become even more interested. I'd like to shadow you."

"Didn't you do that for several days?" Pearl said.

"Yeah, and not very well. But that's not what I meant. I want to shadow you when you work, observe you on the job. I want to go to a crime scene with you."

"I don't know if that's a good idea," Pearl said.

Jody gave Quinn a smile. "She's protective of me."

And you're working me, Quinn thought. *How did I get mixed up with these two females?* "She's right," he said to Pearl, choosing sides. "Maybe we should let the kid tag along."

"The *kid* might see things she'll dream about the rest of her life."

"I'm willing to take the chance," Jody said.

"Of course you are."

"And I'm not actually a kid," Jody said to Quinn.

"That was what I was trying to say," Quinn lied to the kid.

"Do you really want to let her do this?" Pearl asked Quinn. "Do you want her to see what we see? Meet the people we meet?"

"No. But Jody wants to do it, and I think she can handle it. And if she can't . . . well, she'll find out."

"It might turn all her dreams to nightmares."

"You're being overdramatic, Mom." *Huh? It just slipped out.*

Pearl studied her for a long time, and then said, "Okay, if that's what you want."

"Thanks to both of you again," Jody said with a wide grin.

"You might change your mind," Pearl said.

"I've done that before," Jody said.

"So has your mother," Quinn said.

Pearl gave him a look that Jody decided to imitate and practice in the mirror.

"Don't expect a lot of excitement," Pearl said.

The phone rang.

36

The troops had arrived before Pearl and Quinn—and Jody. There were three radio cars parked at forty-five-degree angles to the curb. Just beyond them was an ambulance, lights out, with two paramedics sitting in it, waiting for the work to be done upstairs.

Quinn felt his throat tighten as he observed the two white-clad men. *Taking out the dead. Some occupation, always to arrive at a crime scene when the battle's lost.*

Beyond the ambulance a black Chevy was parked properly at the curb. Quinn recognized it as Nift the M.E.'s car. Pearl had noticed the car, too. "He's put himself on all these cases," she said.

Quinn nodded. "He always does."

"Who is he?" Jody asked, walking alongside Pearl.

"Dr. Nift," Quinn said.

"Think of a cross between Napoleon and Frankenstein," Pearl said.

Jody didn't quite understand that, but she didn't push it, reminding herself she was here as an observer.

A big uniformed cop was standing sentry at the building entrance. Quinn knew him. His name was Harmon and he lifted weights and could pass for thirty even though he had to be about Quinn's age. Quinn wondered why he, Quinn, didn't work out, as he always wondered when he saw Harmon.

"Apartment's on the fifth floor, right where you get off the elevator," Harmon said to Quinn and Pearl, pointing and making a huge bicep stretch the material of his shirt. He looked at Jody and smiled. It was scary. "Journalist?"

"Observer," Quinn explained.

Harmon didn't press. If the young woman with the springy red hair was with Quinn and Pearl, that was good enough. But she had that look about her, like a journalist. Curious as a cat that had used up about eight lives.

They entered the building and took the creaky old elevator to the fifth floor.

When the door slid open, there was the crime scene.

The opened apartment door had 5-A on it in those luminous stick-on parallelogram labels. A tech guy with white gloves looked out at them as he passed the door carrying a plastic evidence bag. There were two more techs in the room, one of them a woman. The corpse was in the middle of the room, centered on the carpet as if on display.

Beside Quinn, Jody said, "Holy shit!"

Everyone in the room except the dead woman looked at her.

"Observer," Quinn said, by way of explanation.

After a few seconds, the rest of the room's occupants turned back to their work.

Fedderman came in from a hall that led to the back of the apartment. He came over to stand by Quinn and Pearl. "Her name was Deena Vess. Twenty-four, single, occupation food server." He glanced over at Jody, back to Quinn.

"This is Jody Jason," Quinn said. He turned toward Jody. "This is Larry Fedderman. Don't let his casual sloppy persona fool you. He's even worse than he seems."

Jody nodded hello to Fedderman with a sickly smile.

"She's an observer," Quinn said.

"Really?" Fedderman might never have heard the word before.

"Pearl's daughter," Quinn said.

"Huh?" Fedderman stared at Jody. Everyone alive in the room stared at her. Deena Vess stared straight ahead. The expression on her face made you wonder what she might have been looking at when she died.

"Explanations later," Pearl said. *Mind your own damn business!*

Everyone dutifully looked away. Even Nift, though he looked away last. He smiled. "I can see the resemblances."

"It'll be the last thing you see if I shove those tweezers up your ass," Pearl told him. Jody stared at her.

Nift shrugged and continued to pick with the tweezers where Vess's left breast had been.

Jody swallowed loud enough for everyone to hear. No one spoke. Quinn looked at Jody and she looked back, knowing what he was wondering. She subtly shook her head no and he smiled.

The victim, who was wearing only panties, had been hog-tied in the same manner as the previous victim, tilted back on her knees so her breasts would have jutted out, if she'd still had breasts. A rectangle of duct tape was fixed firmly to her mouth. Quinn didn't want to ask Nift if she'd been alive when her breasts were sliced off. He already knew the answer; she'd been alive, like the other victims.

"It looks like what he did to her was the same as with Ann Spellman," Nift said. "Hog-tied her, then stood straddling her, grabbing her by the hair or under the chin, and bent her up toward him so her breasts dangled and he could reach down and remove them easily and completely."

"You pretty sure about that?" Pearl said.

"It's how I'd do it. Unless . . ."

"What?"

"The victim's breasts were very firm. Then I'd have her on her knees, bent back and facing up. Looking at the ceiling." Nift's mind seemed to have drifted. He came back abruptly. "Our killer's certainly a breast man," he said. "Likes his women with long dark hair, too." He pointedly did not look at Pearl.

"How long's she been gone?" Quinn asked.

"I'd say only a few hours."

"Same guy?"

"Same guy, and probably the same knife. He made small torture cuts on her. Some of them are beneath her panties."

"Which are the size worn by Ann Spellman," Quinn said.

Nift looked at him in faux admiration. "Damn, you're smart."

"Sometimes," Quinn said.

"He puts the previous victim's panties on them," Pearl said softly, explaining to Jody.

"Why?"

Pearl shrugged. "Why does he kill them in the first place?"

"Something different here, though." Nift had held something back, as he often did for dramatic effect.

Quinn arched an eyebrow. "Oh?"

"She had a broken ankle."

"*He* broke it?" Pearl asked.

"I don't think so. Be a good detective and look over there."

"The cat?" Pearl asked, seeing a tabby-striped gray cat slide around the corner of the sofa and disappear. Sometimes she wondered if she was the only person in New York who didn't own a cat. *City of cats.*

"Not the cat. Though she might be the only witness to the crime. Over there."

Pearl looked where Nift was pointing and saw a metal cane and a plastic cast. The cane was leaning in a corner. The cast was near it on the floor as if it had been carelessly tossed there. "Looks like the killer removed the cast and used the ankle to torture her. A broken bone must have been like a gift to him."

"You would understand that," Pearl said.

"Another thing," Nift said, ignoring her. He pointed to a small metal object near where the victim's long hair spilled onto the carpet from her thrown-back head. "That was balanced on her forehead when she was discovered."

"What is it?" Quinn asked, looking closer.

"It's a roller-skate key," Pearl said. "The sort that tightens the kind of skates that fit over your shoes."

"What the hell could that mean?" Fedderman asked. He looked at Jody as if she might supply the answer. She felt flattered that he was including her in the conversation. "The key to the case . . ." she offered.

There was a ripple of laughter.

"She might be right," Quinn said, in such a way that all laughter stopped. *What the hell am I doing now, getting protective?*

"One thing it might explain," Pearl said. "She might have hurt herself skating, and the broken ankle is why he wasn't able to lure her someplace and decided to kill her in her apartment. She's the first victim found indoors."

"How many of Daniel Danielle's victims were found indoors?" Fedderman asked.

"Two out of twelve," Pearl said. "Of course, he might have murdered over a hundred women, so we don't know for sure how many were indoors when they were killed."

"More than a *hundred?*" Jody asked.

Quinn stared at her somberly. "It's a dangerous world."

She looked dubious and shook her head. Even let slip a slight smile.

Oh, God! He was beginning to feel like a parent again, not being taken seriously.

Pearl was looking at him in a kind of surprised way. Had she experienced the same sensation?

She had, he was sure.

It was disconcerting.

"I've got a question," Jody said. "What's going to happen to the victim's cat?"

"No!" Quinn and Pearl said simultaneously.

37

Jody, unaware of a similar cat that had run away, re-named this dark gray tabby cat Snitch, after a cat she'd had when she was ten years old. She would feed it and it would sleep in her room. Everyone agreed to that but the cat. The food plan was okay with Snitch, but she slept where she damn well pleased. Sometimes that was at the foot of Quinn and Pearl's bed.

Living in the brownstone was light-years better than living in the cramped apartment Jody'd had. And she was allowed to keep the rent money allocated to her. The only downside was that she had to travel farther to get to work, across town to the East Side.

Jody stood now in the Enders and Coil conference room with the firm's avuncular and wise senior partner, Joseph Coil. Well-padded black leather chairs rimmed the long mahogany table. There was on the table a large crys-tal vase of incredibly realistic silk roses as a centerpiece that was removed when the room was being used for seri-ous business. That Coil hadn't sat down, or invited Jody to sit, indicated this was to be a short, informal conversa-tion.

The light was at Coil's back. Behind him stretched a

panoramic view of the East River. He politely shifted position so the light wasn't in Jody's eyes, as if to assure her he wasn't going to subject her to that obvious strategy of domination. He wasn't playing games.

Coil smiled at her in a way so genuine she had to smile back. His blue eyes shone with bonhomie, and his lips curved upward in a way that suggested he smiled even in his sleep. His hair was expensively trimmed and gray, his cheeks so rosy they appeared almost rouged.

Jody assumed this was going to be a conversation about her unwarranted interest in the Dash-Meeding eminent domain case.

But it wasn't. Yet.

"I realized," Coil said, "that the two of us had never had a serious friendly conversation. I wanted to talk to you about the law in general. To get your views on it."

Jody was surprised. Why would a man like this be interested in the views of a lowly intern? "I agree with the position that our legal system is fallible, but it's the best there is." *Yada, yada*. But she did believe it.

"And possibly the most pliable and useful," Coil said. The smile never left his face.

"I suppose," Jody said. "Truthfully, I hadn't thought about it in those terms."

"Well, it takes time to understand the utilitarian side of the law." He bowed his head and shook it slowly side to side, as if amused. "You *have* grasped by now that it is quite malleable?"

"Oh, yes."

"The law is in fact so malleable that at a certain high level it is more about how to manipulate the system within the penumbra of the law, than about the law itself."

Jody struggled for a moment with that one. "I can see how it might be used that way," she said.

"The longer you practice the law, and the more importance your duties take on, the more you come to understand the law's true and most important purpose. It's like higher math: the loftier and more complex it is, the further it moves into the realm of what might be thought of as a more sublime logic."

"It becomes more and more malleable," Jody said.

Coil fairly beamed. "Smart woman. At a certain plateau, that malleability is what it's all about. It's vitally important that you comprehend that. Justice, truth, guilt, innocence, those all lose their meaning under the sword of the law; and the clay of malleability is worked in ways never imagined at the beginning of a legal process. Malleability is the king of the court."

"I think I—"

"No, no. Give it some thought before you decide you really do understand."

Jody smiled. "All right, I will."

"I won't insult you by reminding you it doesn't matter whether our clients are guilty or innocent."

"Everyone deserves the best counsel they can afford," Jody said. "For that matter, the most malleable."

"Ah!" Joseph Coil said, obviously pleased that he might have an apt pupil here. Well, that was what Jody was supposed to be, coming out of Waycliffe. And with Elaine Pratt and Chancellor Schueller's recommendations.

He didn't say anything else for a few seconds, and Jody thought their conversation might have ended.

But it hadn't.

"It's come to our notice that you've shown an interest in Dash-Meeding," Coil said.

Uh-oh.

"I do find it interesting," Jody said. "I've always been drawn to eminent domain law."

"Oh? Something in your background?"

"No, nothing like that."

"It seems like the rich stealing from the poor?"

"I'm not that naïve," Jody said with a grin.

"Yes, no reason to single out eminent domain. But the Mildred Dash case seems to command your attention."

"I suppose that's because it's sort of a classic situation: a large developer and a holdout old lady standing her ground. All she's asking is to continue living in her apartment, where her life unfolded. The place holds special significance for her."

"It holds a special significance for Meeding Properties, too."

"I understand that," Jody said. "I guess it's the familiar story, and the familiar emotion—sympathy for the old lady guarding the gate against progress."

"I suppose you could call it progress. Meeding is going to build a lot of retail space and condominiums and overcharge its tenants. Meeding will make a lot of money."

"There's nothing wrong with that," Jody said.

Coil raised his shoulders and crossed his arms as if hugging himself. "Not for Meeding. Not for us."

"Especially not for us," Jody said. "It's just that there's the valiant old lady fighting insurmountable odds."

"Things aren't always what they seem, Jody."

"But this seems to be exactly what it seems. "Meeding Properties is gigantic; Mildred Dash has lived in her apartment for twenty years, and there she stays while demolition goes on all around her building. She seems to have enough legal claim to hold the developer at bay." Jody couldn't help herself. "She must have a lawyer who knows about malleability."

Coil's mild blue gaze fixed on her and his smile held. Such a charming man. "Mildred Dash isn't an old lady unless you count forty-eight as old. She's a cutthroat corporate attorney with inoperable pancreatic cancer. And she doesn't want to live in her apartment, she wants to die in it."

Inoperable cancer. Jody could think of nothing to say other than, "Oh."

"These things are unknowable. If she does get her wish and dies at home, it might cost Meeding Properties millions of dollars. Millions," he repeated. "The clock is already ticking on that money."

"Oh," Jody said again.

Joseph Coil nodded a smiling good morning and moved toward the door. He paused going out. "Keep thinking malleability, Jody."

"Yes, sir."

I'm malleable, she added, to herself, not without a certain degree of disgust.

Sal Vitali called in just before noon. The call was on his cell phone, but Quinn was sitting at his desk in the Q&A office. Pearl and Fedderman were across the room at their desks. Fedderman was working the phone. Pearl was on her computer. Knowing she owed her mother a phone call, Pearl had waited until she knew it was time for *This Is Your Life* reruns at Golden Sunset and her mother wouldn't be able to answer her phone.

Pearl left a cryptic message and hung up, feeling better. Feeling free. Obligation fulfilled. Her mother and Jody could explore their relationship without her.

But Pearl's mother wasn't watching *This Is Your Life.* That was because her granddaughter had taken a long lunch and then a long cab ride, and here she was in the spacious carpeted lobby of Golden Sunset Assisted Living in New Jersey. Handshakes, smiles, and stiff hugs had been exchanged.

Jody found her maternal grandmother to be a heavy-set, formidable-looking woman with a rigid hairdo and searching dark eyes. She had on a perfume that didn't mingle well with the food scents wafting in from the nearby dining room.

The two women were seated facing each other, Jody in an uncomfortable wooden chair with upholstered arms, her grandmother in the corner of a soft leather sofa.

Jody noticed all the liver spots on her grandmother's arms and then glanced around. "This looks like a nice place."

"Let me tell you, sweetheart," said her grandmother, "if I may call you that, you being the one precious issue of my barren offspring, that perhaps it looks nice but so, when you first arrive, might hell."

"You mean the people—"

"Are disguised as people, if you mean the staff, and some of the inmates, if I may call them that. People? I would say right out of Dante's imagination."

"Really? Everyone I've talked to seems nice. And Pearl—Mom—said you have your own apartment."

"Own cell, I would say with knowledgeable accuracy. Like they have on Devil's Island."

"That's terrible," Jody said, "that you should feel that way."

"You're such a smart girl. If only your mother would listen and learn."

"Mom can be stubborn." Jody stared at her grandmother, looking for herself in her, perhaps seeing it, trying to figure out what she thought, how she felt.

"Are you all right, sweetheart?"

"Yes." Jody forced a smile. "Maybe we should go into the dining room and have some lunch."

"That isn't food they serve in there. Come to my apartment and I have at least, learning of my granddaughter's arrival, prepared some good and healthy soup. Not without crackers. Even croutons."

"That sounds wonderful."

Jody's grandmother produced an aluminum cane that had been propped out of sight against the back of the sofa. She planted the cane's rubber tip in the carpet and began struggling to her feet. Jody rushed to help her.

After a little dance they were both standing. Jody's grandmother was breathing hard, even softly wheezing. "That's fine, dear. Thank you. There are some people I want you to meet, so I can show you off, then we can have our soup and talk about your mother. Did I say croutons?"

"I think you did," Jody answered, and found she had to move fast to keep up with her grandmother, who walked surprisingly fast for a woman with a cane.

The office's air-conditioning unit was humming and rattling away, making phone conversations private. Fedderman wouldn't be disturbed by Quinn speaking in a normal conversational voice.

"Whaddya got, Sal?"

"Victim's full name is Deena Maureen Vess," said Sal's gravelly voice. "Neighbors say she worked at Roller Steak. That's a restaurant where the servers zip around on skates while they juggle the food. Deena had a collision and broke her ankle. They liked her at Roller Steak and were holding her job for her."

"She have any special friends at the restaurant?"

"Naw. She'd only been there a few weeks."

"Love can be capricious," Quinn said.

"From what we heard, there was no capriciousness there with Deena. At least we know now what the roller-skate key on the body meant. The killer's sick joke."

"Nift mentioned at the crime scene that he probably used the ankle to torture her. That'd be broken bone end against broken bone end. He might have thought that was funny, too."

"Holy crap! We do need to catch this guy. What do you want for me and Harold to do now?"

"Have some lunch, then chat again with Deena's neighbors. Widen your canvass. See if there's anywhere in the area where the killer might have bought a roller-skate key. You don't see many, if any, people using the kind of skates that require a key these days. There can't be that many places where they're sold."

"Nift call with any more info from the lab?"

"I'm still waiting," Quinn said.

He didn't have long to wait. A few minutes after his conversation with Sal, the desk phone rang. Caller ID said it was the morgue. Nift.

"Like we thought," Nift said, "the murder weapon was almost surely the same knife used on the last victim. She was tortured with small, painful stab wounds, and apparently by rubbing the ends of her broken ankle bones together. Looks like the ankle was broken several days ago, then reinjured. As if he struck her with something there, maybe kicked her."

"What about the rope and duct tape?"

"Both common brands, not traceable. The tape is probably off the same roll as last time. It appears to have been firmly sealed over her mouth all through her ordeal."

Her silent ordeal.

Quinn thought that must have been the most terrible kind of loneliness.

"Her breasts never did turn up at the crime scene," Nift said. "They were sliced off antemortem, as with the earlier victims. He likes his victims alive when he separates their breasts from their bodies."

"Was it done fast or slow?"

"I can't tell for sure, Quinn, but I can guess. So can you."

"He'd want to take his time."

"That's what I'd do."

Quinn could hardly believe what he'd just heard. But that was often the way with Nift. "Why does he want them?" Quinn asked, trying to assume the same sick mind-set as the killer's. "What does he do with them?"

"I don't know, but they were obviously a great set. You can easily judge by the cut patterns, and what little is left."

"*You* can tell," Quinn said, feeling a little queasy.

"Well, I'm a professional." Nift was silent for a moment. There was a sound as if he might be shuffling through some papers. "No indications that the victim struggled. No flesh caught beneath her nails. And there were no lacerations other than those made deliberately by the killer. Looks like she didn't so much as scratch him."

"That's too bad," Quinn said.

"No indication of recent sexual intercourse."

"Except maybe with himself."

"No indication of that, either. This killer is a perfectionist." Nift said. "He leaves nothing behind he doesn't want to leave."

"Everybody eventually overlooks something," Quinn said. "We just have to find it."

"So they say on the TV cop shows."

"And they always end well," Quinn said.

"Sooner or later they get canceled. Tell Pearl I said hello."

"I think not," Quinn said, but Nift had hung up.

Over dinner in the brownstone that evening, Jody didn't mention her conversation with her grandmother. She didn't understand why it should be kept secret, but her grandmother had extracted a sworn oath that their conversations would remain private and special. Jody, who had never had a best friend, agreed.

She did tell Quinn and Pearl about her conversation with Joseph Coil.

They both listened attentively. Pearl speared a bite of salad and considered while she chewed and swallowed.

"What Coil told you about the total malleability of the law," she said, after washing the salad down with a sip of wine, "is bullshit."

"Unfortunately," Quinn said, looking across the table at Jody, "I think Coil is right."

Jody leaned back in her chair and sipped her wine, regarding them. The gray head of Snitch the cat became visible above tabletop level. Snitch squinted at Quinn and seemed prepared to stare him down. Quinn realized Snitch might have been in Jody's lap all through dinner.

"You guys are a lot of help," Jody said.

"We try," both Quinn and Pearl said almost simultaneously.

Jody grinned. "And I appreciate it." She sat forward again. Snitch's head disappeared. "Do you have any more information about the vic?"

"That depends," Quinn said, "on whether you want dessert."

38

Leighton, Wisconsin, 1986

Rory was slouched behind the steering wheel of his mom's Impala, about to turn onto the county road near Cheever's Hardware, when he saw one of the posters. It was tacked to a telephone pole and headed MISSING in large black letters, and beneath that was a photo of a shaggy dog as black as the letters.

At first Rory felt no connection with the poster, so deep into a corner of his mind had he pushed the night he'd struck the dog and buried it. After putting the poor animal out of its misery, he reminded himself. *The humane thing to do.*

He couldn't help it. The sequence of events that night flashed through his brain. How and why they had occurred. What they meant.

No, there was nothing he'd do differently after the car had struck the dog. His actions had been harsh but right.

A horn blasted as he almost ran a stop sign.

He felt a stab of panic. He wasn't supposed to be in the car. If his mother for some reason left her book club and found out he'd borrowed it and was driving without a license again, she'd be plenty mad.

The man in the pickup truck that crossed the intersection ahead of him glared at Rory and gunned his engine. Rory felt no surge of anger, only worry about his mom turning up and ruining his day. But he'd already figured the odds of that happening and accepted them before getting into the car. So he stopped worrying about his mom. It wasn't logical. He again concentrated on the dog incident.

He pulled the car to the road shoulder and put the transmission in park. He'd assumed he'd never have to think about the dog again, but obviously he did. The owner was going to be proactive.

So where does that leave me? How should I feel?

No, the question isn't about how I feel. What should I do?

The answer came immediately: nothing.

The dog, with its head crushed by a rock, hadn't been found (which was how he'd planned it). There would be nothing that might publicly connect the dog with him, even if it was found (which was how he'd planned it). The owner missed the dog (no surprise) and was tacking up MISSING DOG posters all over town (should be no surprise).

Logical course of action? Forget about the dog incident again—except when you have to look at one of the damned posters.

He smiled. This new development, the possibility of which he should have foreseen, posed no danger whatsoever. His initial reasoning, and his actions, had been correct. Nothing fundamental had changed.

Rory put the Chevy in drive, glanced in the rearview mirror and then over his shoulder, and pulled the vehicle back onto the road.

He glanced at the dashboard clock. His mother's book club would be ending in half an hour, which meant he could safely drive another twenty minutes.

He drove down High Street, in the general direction of his house. A few people were walking along the sidewalks, going in and out of the shops, despite the temperature pushing ninety.

Rory settled back into the soft upholstery and steered with one wrist draped over the wheel. The air conditioner worked well; the motor was smooth, and there were no rattles. He pressed the radio buttons until he found some rap, then turned up the volume.

And saw the girl tacking up a MISSING DOG poster.

He recognized her immediately and slowed the car, staring at the way the breeze pressed the material of her blouse and slacks against one side of her body, the way her back arched as she held the poster high with one hand and hammered with the other, how her dark ponytail swayed slightly as the breeze blew and she worked her arm to drive the nail into the wooden telephone pole. It was a pole pecked with dozens of nail holes from notices of garage sales or other missing-pet appeals. There was a canvas bag at her feet that probably held more posters. Rory was in love with her, and she . . . well, she liked him. No, she more than just liked him, he was sure. He hoped. Sherri Klinger was her name. The more he repeated it to himself, the more he found it oddly melodious.

She was in advanced studies, smart like him. He could talk to her and she understood. And he understood and agreed with almost everything she said.

He hadn't known she owned a dog.

When the car slowed to a complete stop just behind her, she turned and recognized Rory. She dropped the hammer into the canvas bag, picked up the bag by its strap, and walked smiling toward the car.

He switched off the radio, then held down the button to drop the window.

"Rory," she said, leaning down to look at him. She seemed glad to see him. "Don't you know you're too young to drive?"

Rory gave her what he thought of as his dynamite grin. "Too young for a lotta things I do."

"I'll just bet." Her face, which he thought about so often before he slept, became serious. "You haven't seen Duffy, have you?"

"Don't know him."

"My dog, dumb-ass."

"That him on the poster?"

"Good guess."

"Haven't seen him." *How easy it is to lie, when you know it's saving someone you love from pain.* "He run away?"

"Yeah. It's not the first time. But it's the first time he didn't come back."

How much more terrible she'd feel if I told her the truth. "And now you're going around town tacking up posters."

"That was the last one." She motioned with her head toward the poster on the phone pole.

"Wanna drive around for a while and look for Duffy?"

"I dunno."

"I've got a little bit of time before I have to get the car back."

"Your mom even know you've got it?"

"Ask me no questions and I'll tell you no lies."

She grinned.

"Hop in," Rory said. "For Duffy."

"For Duffy," she repeated. She hitched the canvas bag's

strap over her shoulder and walked around the front of the car to get in.

He watched her walk, the way her hair flounced, the subtle rhythmic sway of her breasts, feeling a mixture of desire and satisfaction.

This dog-poster thing, he'd turned it his way.

39

New York, the present

Neeve Cooper sat alone on a bench in Central Park and read more manuscript pages of *Overbite,* the vampire novel Paranormal Books, a small publisher, had assigned her.

She wielded a sharp red pencil in her right hand and from time to time made a mark or jotted a message on the pages. Whatever she penciled had to be legible. This would be published as an e-book, but also in audio and print forms. Her editing would find its way into all formats.

For almost five years Neeve had been an associate editor at Noir and More, a publishing house with offices on Hudson Street. Then Noir and More had been bought (absorbed, the execs liked to say) by Schmelder and Kott, a large German publisher and distributor of skiing equipment. The problem was that half the Noir and More employees, including Neeve, hadn't been absorbed with the rest of the company.

So she had become a freelance editor, copyediting

manuscripts for publishers that, like Noir and More, were short of employees during this hard time for publishers. Neeve considered herself lucky to have hooked up for freelance work with Paranormal. She could make enough to eat and pay the rent, but she sure got tired of reading about vampires and zombies. Her book before this one had been about a vampire cat. The worst part was, halfway through, she found herself enjoying the damned thing.

She glanced at her watch, then took off her reading glasses and brushed back the lock of long dark hair hanging down one cheek. She was a pretty, brown-eyed woman in her mid-thirties who looked younger and had at one time considered pursuing a career in ballet. She had the powerful, lithe body for ballet, and the balance. Then she'd been horrified to find that she was growing boobs, and large ones that the other girls envied. But those girls didn't want to be ballet dancers. Neeve had considered surgical reduction, but her mother said that was insane, and besides, she'd known women who'd had breast reduction and their breasts had grown large again.

At eighteen, Neeve was finished as a ballet dancer. She enrolled in college and pursued an English degree.

Some of the grace from her ballet days showed as she bent effortlessly and stuffed the rubber-banded vampire manuscript into the computer case on the ground. Neeve used the case for print manuscripts (it was the perfect size unless they ran over six hundred pages). She draped the case over her shoulder by its padded strap, then picked up her knockoff Gucci purse and stood up from the bench. Several people observed her walk away. A few of the men seemed hypnotized. It was like watching a dance.

Neeve knew she'd have to hurry to get to the Pig in a Poke restaurant on time. She was meeting three friends there at twelve-thirty, which was only fifteen minutes away. She lengthened her stride and her legs seemed long even in her flat-soled jogging shoes. The long stride emphasized the artful turn of her ankles and the musculature of her calves. Some shape on this woman.

At the first intersection outside the park she had to stop with a knot of other people to wait for the walk light. She noticed she was breathing hard. Out of condition.

It also occurred to her that she didn't have to hurry. If she was half an hour late, her friends would still be there. This wasn't a business lunch of the sort she'd gotten so used to at Noir and More. There was no *need* to be on time. She was self-employed, and that carried with it some definite advantages.

She walked slower and smiled. *Self-employed.* In business for herself, by herself.

The future was uncertain, but she'd been getting enough work lately. Reading vampire novels wasn't all that bad. And one of the large publishers had agreed to e-mail their manuscripts to Neeve, which meant she could use the editing software on her computer. This lugging around of pounds and pounds of paper would cease, and she could still get out of the apartment from time to time. She could take her laptop with her. It wasn't half as heavy as a text-on-paper manuscript.

Neeve tried to think around her trepidation and the moodiness she'd fallen into. She decided she could use a little uncertainty and adventure in her life. Publishing was changing, and no one could predict exactly how. Once she learned to get used to the uneasiness that accompanied that situation, she might learn to enjoy the world of the freelancer. Maybe this was one of those times when opportunity visited in disguise.

Suddenly *Overbite* didn't seem so heavy.

* * *

The Alfred A. Aal Memorial Library smelled exactly as a library should—of perspiration-infused wood and old books. It was also suitably hushed.

"We don't have to be as careful about Ms. Culver as we used to," Penny said to Feds, after he'd timed pecking her on the cheek when the chief librarian was looking the other way. "She's depressed these days."

"Too bad," Fedderman said. "Library business down?"

"You could describe it that way. She's worried about e-books."

"Aren't we all?"

"It isn't funny, Feds. It would be like you being edged out of work by robotic cops."

"That's already happening." He glanced toward the front of the library and the distraught Ms. Culver. "She should have learned by now to deal with progress. And libraries aren't going to simply disappear overnight because all of a sudden some people are reading books on little screens. She needs to lighten up, for her own good."

"Ms. Culver tends to catastrophize," Penny said.

"Is that a word?"

"It is now. It might not make much sense for her to build what is a very real problem into some kind of dilemma, but everybody has a pet issue."

"It can be that way in my work. With Quinn. He doesn't catastrophize, but he sure gets obsessed with the job. He kind of locks in, not so unlike Ms. Culver."

"Speaking of your job, I saw in the news that a patrolman was shot to death by a car thief in the Village last night."

"Young guy named Messerschmitt," Fedderman said. "Been on the job less than a year."

"Was he married?"

Fedderman figured Penny already knew the answer to that one. He was getting used to her methodology. "Married and with an infant son," he said.

"See what I mean about being a cop's wife?" Penny said. "I don't even know this woman and I broke out crying when I saw that on TV news. I found myself identifying with her."

"You don't have a baby, Pen."

"Being a smart-ass doesn't make this a less weighty subject, Feds. You tell me I shouldn't worry about you, and this poor guy wasn't even on the job a year and he's dead."

"He pulled his gun when he didn't have to," Fedderman said.

"How could you know that?"

"Word gets around fast. The car thief was cornered and panicked, and had a gun of his own. He was sixteen years old."

"Are you saying it was this Messerschmitt's fault?"

"I'm saying he made a mistake I wouldn't have made. And *he* wouldn't have made it after spending more time on the job. And you're wrong, Pen, in thinking the longer you go as a cop and don't get hurt or killed, the more the odds turn against you. It's the other way around; the longer you go, the less likely you are to do something that bites you."

"Anything can happen," Penny said.

"Even to people who try to live their lives in a bubble of safety. Like a library."

"You're impossible, Feds."

"I want to show you there's no reason to be afraid for me."

Penny looked exasperated. "You carry a gun. The people you deal with carry guns. Enough said."

"Maybe your sister should have had a gun." The moment he said it, Fedderman knew he was in trouble.

And he was wrong: Penny's sister, Nora, probably would have been murdered by the brutal serial killer who'd taken her life, even if she'd owned a gun. The aggressor, the one who moved first, almost always won the struggle. They knew this, the predators of the world. The Sullivan Act made it difficult to own or carry a gun in New York. The predators knew that, too.

"Don't stand there and give me a lot of Second Amendment bullshit!" Penny said.

"All right. I'm sorry."

Penny turned around and busied herself shelving books. He knew she was plenty angry, and she'd be thinking again and talking again about how he should consider changing occupations.

"Pen . . . ?"

She wasn't going to answer. She slammed a book into place so hard the shelves swayed. A man browsing in Biographies gave her a stern look.

Fedderman knew there was nothing to be done until she calmed down. All because Messerschmitt hadn't kept his gun in its holster.

It was impossible to talk with Penny when she was feeling, and acting, this way. He turned around and trudged toward the library exit, up near the checkout and return counter, silently cursing.

He didn't like the way this point of contention was going with Penny. Each time they talked about it she seemed to become more and more worried. Madder and madder.

One thing he'd learned about Penny: she usually did something about her anger.

How the hell was this going to end?

He knew how cops' marriages too often ended.

He reached the tinted glass door, leaned heavily into the metal push bar, and felt the heat from outside.

When he looked back he saw Ms. Culver glaring at him as if he were an e-book.

40

Sal said, "I think we need to talk to Pansy Lieberman again."

"Not a name you often hear," Mishkin said, "Lieberman."

Sal looked at him. It was hard to know about Harold.

The two of them were on the street in front of Deena Vess's apartment building. They'd been canvassing the surrounding buildings, and in the one next door Sal had encountered Pansy Lieberman. Unlike most of Deena's neighbors, she'd talked. Maybe it had been worthwhile. "She claims she saw a woman who might have been leaving Deena Vess's apartment unit at around the time of the murder."

"If she's from the building next door, how did that happen?" Harold asked.

"I'll let her tell you, Harold. That way we can see if her stories are the same."

"If they're exactly the same—"

"I know, Harold. That suggests she's memorized the story and she's lying."

"I was gonna say we wouldn't need a second set of notes," Harold said.

Sal doubted that. "Let's go talk to Pansy," he growled.

Pansy's apartment was on the same floor as Deena's, with a view of a window in Deena's building that might be on a landing. Sal wondered if that had anything to do with anything. If Pansy Lieberman was one of those people who wanted to be part of a homicide investigation just for a brush with their idea of celebrity, she would have probably taken advantage of that window to the building next door to embellish her tale. But she hadn't. The window didn't figure into it.

"Come on in," she said with a wide grin. She was one of those beautiful women who seem not to know it. Or maybe they take it for granted. Pansy was in her early thirties, wearing dark slacks and a gray and white striped blouse that made her look like an extremely attractive convict. She had dark hair almost short enough to be called a buzz cut. Beauty that she was, her ears stuck out almost at right angles from her head. The ears, with her wide grin, gave her an elfish, mischievous expression. She was wearing floppy slip-on sandals. Sal noticed that the toenails of only her left foot were painted, with brilliant red enamel. Had they interrupted her?

She noticed him staring at her feet and read his mind. "I don't paint the nails on that foot when I'm practicing," she said. "It makes them slippery."

"I see," Sal said, but he didn't.

Harold had been looking past him at the glossy, open *New Yorker* spread out on the floor by the sofa. "You've been turning pages with your foot," he said.

Pansy smiled brightly. "How astute of you."

Sal wondered how Harold knew that. Then he noticed the way the magazine's pages were crumpled, and that there was a scant but definite print of a bare foot on one of them.

"You slipped on your sandals to answer our knock on

your door," he said, realizing with a tinge of dismay that he was trying to keep up with Harold and impress this woman.

"I only had the right sandal off," she said. She smiled again. "I didn't want to greet you walking crookedly. You might have insisted on a breathalyzer test."

Sal found himself wondering what kind of witness she'd be in court if the case went in that direction. "Could you repeat to Detective Mishkin what you told me?" he said, wanting to get back on point.

"I assumed that was why you were here," she said. She drew a deep breath, as if she might be planning to tell her entire story without inhaling. "Mrs. Metzger, who lives in the building next door, is visiting her daughter in Minneapolis," she said, "and I went to her apartment to feed Lewis, because that's our agreement.

"Lewis a cat or dog?" Harold asked.

"Fish."

"Uh."

"I look after Lewis," Pansy continued, "and when I'm gone for any length of time Mrs. Metzger waters my plants."

Harold looked around and saw some scraggly-looking geraniums, along with flowers he didn't recognize, in plastic pots and trays.

"Anyway," Pansy continued, "I was on my way back here and I took the stairs, like I do sometimes for the exercise. When I was on the landing near Deena's apartment, I glanced down the hall and saw a woman walking away from her door, toward the elevator."

"Had she just left Deena's apartment?" Harold asked.

Sal gave him a look that meant *No prompting*.

"I couldn't say for sure," Pansy said. "But she might have."

"Could you describe her?" Sal was pretending to take

notes. It wasn't necessary. So far, the stories matched up okay.

"Actually, I couldn't. She was facing away from me both times."

"*Both* times?"

"Yes. I'd seen her once before, on the street, when she hurried to get into a cab at the corner. I recognized her light blue raincoat and umbrella."

Here was something new. In the corner of his vision, Sal saw Harold jot it down on his notepad. "Had she come out of Deena Vess's building that time?"

"I can't be positive."

"But you're sure it was the same woman?"

"Yes. She passed right by me on the sidewalk, but it was fast, and I'd been looking the other way. Besides the coat and umbrella, there was something distinctive about her. Something that didn't seem *right*. Maybe it was because for some reason she seemed too old to be one of Deena's friends. I imagined her as almost middle-aged. And she moved with a kind of confidence."

"If we showed you photographs . . ." Harold said.

"I honestly don't think I could identify her. She might be in her forties. Indeterminate hair color. There was nothing distinctive about her walk. And I never did actually get a good look at her face."

"But you were close to her for a while."

"Only for a moment, when she stepped on my toes. And on this foot, as luck would have it." Pansy held up her bare right foot. "I was in too much pain, and looking at my poor, poor toe instead of noticing what was going on around me. The woman apologized but didn't slow down and was walking away when I looked up to tell her that was okay, that I walked on that foot all the time."

"Anything memorable about her voice?" Sal asked.

"Not really. A little deep and throaty. It could be she's a smoker."

"What about scents?" Harold asked.

"Pardon?"

"Did she smell any particular way? You know, like perfume, tobacco?"

"Not that I can recall."

"Was this other encounter also the day of the murder?" Sal asked.

"No, I'd say about a week earlier. That's why I didn't remember it right away." She sat down in a beige chair with wooden arms and tucked her trim legs beneath her. Sal wished his legs were still that limber. Well, actually they never had been.

He looked at Harold, who gave an almost imperceptible nod. They had no more questions. That is, about the case.

"Why?" Sal asked.

She appeared puzzled.

"Why were you turning *New Yorker* magazine pages with your bare toes?"

"To make my toes more dexterous."

"And to get to the next cartoon," Harold said.

"That, too."

"That doesn't exactly answer my question," Sal said.

"True." Pansy smiled. "I've gone back to school to major in anthropology. I was wondering what it might be like to learn to use our feet the way our primal ancestors might very well have done. When you get in the habit of using them like hands, you'd be surprised how natural it comes to feel."

"Our primal ancestors wouldn't have understood those cartoons," Sal said. He didn't understand some of them himself.

"Oh, you might be surprised. Many of the cartoons don't require language in order to be understood. "

"That they might have understood the cartoons isn't her point," Harold said quickly. Kind of testily, Sal thought. How men must love rescuing or defending poor little Pansy. How she must manipulate them.

"And the point is?"

"Empathy," Pansy said. "I want to experience at least some inkling of how our ancestors must have thought while performing delicate tasks with their feet. What they must have felt." She smiled and shook her head. "I guess you think that's crazy."

"No," Sal said, wondering how many of their primal ancestors had subscribed to the *New Yorker*.

"We do that ourselves in our work," Harold said. "We try to empathize and figure out why some of them killed. Why some are still killing."

"That could be dangerous," Pansy said. "We have roots that might be deeper than we know, and set in soil that would terrify us."

"That's why empathizing is as far as we go," Harold said. "That's the key difference between us and the people we're trying to find and stop."

Pansy aimed her warm glow at him, obviously pleased. "You are a very perceptive man."

"It's my job," Harold said. "It makes me that way."

Sal thought he might retch.

"Can you stay for some tea or coffee?" Pansy asked. "Both of you." But she was looking at Harold.

"Thanks," Sal said, "but we've got more calls to make."

"Another time?"

"If you think of something pertaining to the case," Sal said. "Call me. Leave a message if you have to, and I'll get back to you. You have my card."

Pansy followed them to the door and watched them for a while before moving back out of sight and locking herself into her apartment.

On their way down in the elevator, Harold said, "I wonder what else she can do with her toes."

"That woman might be twenty years younger than you, Harold. Harold?"

"Sorry. I was empathizing."

Jerry Lido, Q&A's resident computer genius, came over to Quinn's desk, shaking his head. If it could be traced anywhere on the Internet, Lido could find it. He seemed to possess some kind of innate GPS.

"Whaddya got?" Quinn said, looking up and noticing the expression on Lido's face. He knew Lido had stayed up most of last night, drinking and communing with his computer. Now he appeared exhausted but triumphant.

"I found a few places where the skate keys could be bought on the net, hacked into their records, and came up empty. It was near six o'clock this morning by then. I took a short nap, then cleaned up some and had breakfast at a place down on Houston." Lido was grinning.

Quinn was getting impatient. "And?"

Lido dropped a skate key on the desk. It looked identical to the one pressed into the flesh on the forehead of Deena Vess's corpse.

"I got it at this little bike shop in the Village, also sells skateboards and such. Also roller skates, though not the kind that need keys. But they do have a bunch of those keys in a little bin near the front of the store." Lido's smile slipped away. "That's the problem. Anybody coulda come in and stole one."

"Did you ask if they'd sold any lately?" Quinn already knew the answer.

"They haven't sold any in almost a year," Lido said. "The guy let me have that one for free."

"A dead end," Quinn said glumly.

"Yeah. Not the key to the case."

Quinn returned to his paperwork with the doggedness of a man getting accustomed to frustration, not liking it any more for the familiarity. "Go have some more breakfast, Jerry."

What *was* the key to the case?

41

It was like watching dinosaurs at play, if you overlooked the huge, knobby tires.

The roar had awakened her at eight o'clock sharp and continued steadily for the last three hours, so she never got back to sleep. Mildred Dash stood at her apartment window and watched the earth-moving equipment across the street.

The brick and stone walls of the buildings had come down days ago. Now the dinosaurs were scooting the wreckage around, even moving some of it with cranes (so like a brontosaurus, a crane), so it could be scooped up, loaded into squat and powerful dump trucks, and hauled away.

Mildred was tall and a bit *too* statuesque to be attractive. Though refined, even regal, in bearing, she was too rough hewn to be feminine. Her gray-tinged black hair was coarse, her features chiseled but not finely. Her nose was slightly too prominent, her chin too pointed. When she was very young, the boys had considered her a knockout. Now those same boys would have found her a little scary, like a dreaded substitute teacher.

Meeding Properties, and Enders and Coil, had learned not to take her lightly.

She was still wearing her robe, and wasn't planning on going out today. There was no way she could escape the feeling that if she left her apartment, left the building, the neighborhood, even for a short while, the dinosaurs would attack. She would return not to her home but to ruins.

As a former practicing attorney, she knew the value of a *fait accompli*. The destruction of her building wouldn't harm anyone, if the building was completely unoccupied. Even if she'd had enough legal claim to delay demolition almost indefinitely, her arguments would become moot in the dust of debris. Mildred Dash knew how the law worked—and how it didn't work.

As matters stood, Jack Enders would continue his attempts to intimidate her, and kindly rattlesnake Joseph Coil would continue his folksy charm assault. They continued in their attempts to assess her, to read her motives and her intentions. It didn't make sense to them. Of course it wouldn't—to them. Even if she were to explain it to them, they'd nod their supposed understanding and then offer her money. Or at least try to talk her out of her intransigence. Become her saviors instead of her pursuers.

Mildred understood the puzzle piece that was missing, and whose absence caused all their other assumptions to be off the mark. Meeding Properties, and Enders and Coil, knew about the limited time she had left. They didn't see why she wanted to spend it here, in the midst of demolition and debris. This had been her life, with her husband, her children, her tragedies and joy. Her meaningful life had been here, was still here.

Still here.

It was so simple, so foreign to them, that they overlooked it, couldn't see it.

She refused to end her life before she died.

* * *

Jody found herself alone in the offices of Enders and Coil. Dollie, the receptionist, was up front in the anteroom minding the phones, but that didn't count. Dollie didn't venture back into the main offices unless she had a good reason, and with Jack Enders and the associates in court, and Joseph Coil on his way to Philadelphia to take a deposition, there wouldn't be a good reason.

Jody took one of the two flash drives she'd bought on credit from an office supply and computer shop on East Fifty-fourth Street, and slipped into Enders's office.

It was more than merely quiet in there; it was hushed. Jody had been told the offices of Enders and Coil had been specially insulated so they were virtually sound-proof. That wasn't quite true. If she listened closely, Jody could hear the rushing sound of Manhattan traffic.

Enders's desktop computer sat blankly on its oak table nestled to the side of the desk. With a glance out through the slatted blinds covering the window to the hall, Jody booted up the computer. She'd lightly searched the office a few times and had no trouble coming up with the list of passwords Enders used. *Genius9578* gave her access. She slipped the flash drive into a USB port on the side of the computer and copied the files and e-mail contents of Enders's hard drive.

It took less than five minutes.

She removed the flash drive and returned it to her purse, then repeated the process with the second flash drive in Joseph Coil's office.

So much more convenient than rummaging through paper files in steel cabinets, Jody mused. She regarded technology as her friend.

Jody and her friend were going to see what they could learn in addition to what she already suspected about Enders and Coil. And Meeding Properties.

Safely back in her own shoebox-sized office, she had to smile. She also had to admit to herself that she enjoyed what she was doing. It wasn't only trying to right a wrong. It was also the secretiveness, the spying, the taunting of fate. She liked figuring the odds, then proving she'd figured right by experiencing the danger and accomplishing her goal. The danger. God help her, she loved the danger.

If either Enders or Coil had caught her copying the contents of their computers, all hell would not only have broken lose, it would have run riot.

Jody understood that what she'd done was illegal, and there would be no point in pretending she hadn't known. Not only would she have lost her internship, she would have lost all possible chances for a position at a respectable firm. If she'd been caught copying files, she probably would have been arrested and charged. After all, this was a law office.

On the other hand, the law was malleable.

42

The Happy Noodle was within easy walking distance from where Neeve had been working on the *Overbite* manuscript in the park. Still, she was slightly late when she walked into the restaurant for lunch with her friends and former colleagues.

Melanie, who arranged these occasional lunches, had made the reservation and was sitting at the head of the white-clothed table. Rhonda and Lavella were on either side of her. Each woman had before her a drink along with folded paper napkins, twisted red plastic swizzle sticks, and a few squeezed lime wedges.

"Train delay," Neeve said, by way of explaining why she was fifteen minutes late. The truth was that her purse, and the heavy computer case containing the *Overbite* manuscript, had slowed her down, and she'd felt faint. She'd found a doorway to stand in, where the swarms of people on their lunch hour wouldn't buffet her and she could catch her breath. She figured she might be experiencing a sugar crash, after only a doughnut for breakfast.

She'd felt around in her purse, found what was left of a wrapped Tootsie Roll, and popped the chocolate morsel into her mouth.

It did seem to help, as she proceeded more slowly to the restaurant, feeling her energy level gradually rise.

She sat down next to Lavella and placed her purse and computer case on the floor, propped against her chair leg.

Lavella was a beautiful black woman who worked as an associate editor at one of the big publishing houses. She glanced at the computer case.

"If the food server steps on that stuff, you're gonna need a new computer," she said.

"No computer in the case," Neeve said. "Manuscript."

"New thriller?"

"Vampire novel."

"Surprise, surprise. Any good?"

"It sucks."

The server, who looked a lot like a young Susan Sarandon, arrived. She didn't step on the computer case, and jotted down Neeve's order for white wine, and a fresh round of drinks for the others at the table.

The four women fell into easy conversation. They talked about the fact that Rhonda and Neeve had been forced into the ranks of the self-employed by the shrinking and consolidation of major publishers. About the encroachment of e-books. About a new book Lavella's publisher was bringing out that claimed there was a secret government plan to cause the bond market to crash. About a launch party at a mystery bookstore. About Melanie's new boyfriend, who used to play in the NBA and whom the other three had never heard of but pretended they had. All four women decided they liked a new bestselling thriller about a serial killer in New York. They were smart, strong women who enjoyed a good vicarious scare.

Though Neeve was a drink behind the others, she still felt slightly tipsy as they finished their lunches of soup and salads and left the restaurant. Beneath a large sign that indeed depicted a happy noodle, they wished each other luck, hugged each other, and went their separate ways.

Neeve was in a much better mood and was pleased to notice she was easily walking a straight line, so must not have drunk too much. What? Three glasses of wine? Four? Well, she'd had pasta with her drinks. Rather, drinks with her pasta—an important distinction, in Neeve's mind.

The afterglow of drink and food was making her sleepy. By the time she'd reached her building and stood before her apartment door, she knew her plans to work some more on *Overbite* were going to be put on hold. A short nap was in order.

Self-employment. It has its advantages.

43

Quinn sat at his cherrywood desk in his den, reading Sal and Harold's respective reports, wishing he could smoke a cigar. His Cubans remained unlit in a small humidor in the desk's bottom drawer. If he actually lit one anywhere in the brownstone, even *near* the brownstone, Pearl would smell the tobacco smoke and bitch at him. And now a second nose was in the picture. Jody wouldn't actually say anything to him about the scent of tobacco smoke, but she would regard him with a sad and disdainful expression that was very much like Pearl's.

Quinn absently touched his shirt pocket where a cigar wasn't and reflected that it would be nice if eyewitness accounts were actually as accurate and useful as they were in TV police shows and the movies.

If ifs were skiffs we all would sailors be.

Something his daughter, Lauri, used to say. She lived in California, where she was doing okay, according to her occasional letters or cards. A few times she'd sent some e-mails, with photographs of her and some guy she was dating. Gary, Quinn thought his name was. There were palm trees in the backgrounds of all the photos, as if she was trying to make a point. She'd never return to New York.

Quinn wondered if Lauri and Jody would get along.

Separated by a continent, it was possible that they would never meet.

Made melancholy by such thoughts, Quinn considered phoning Renz and seeing if the NYPD had any new information that might help in the investigation. It could be a good idea to remind Renz that information flowed both ways.

On the other hand, it was always annoying to talk with Renz. If Renz wanted to pass on information to Quinn, he'd call, so why should Quinn subject himself to having to listen to the conniving and ambitious commissioner?

Why would anyone willingly subject themselves to Renz? Such encounters left an odor of corruption and had a lasting effect, like radioactive garbage.

Quinn decided it would be better to feel melancholy.

Renz lay on his back in the hotel room bed, still panting. He knew if he didn't start losing weight, sex with Olivia would kill him. He grinned. On the other hand, if he kept having sex with Olivia he was bound to lose weight. Hell, Olivia might kill a healthy man.

He could hear Olivia tinkering around in the bathroom, then the faint hiss of the shower. Renz wondered if she had another appointment booked. He knew Olivia was one of the highest-paid call girls in the city, though he never found out exactly how much she charged. That was because she was free for Renz, as long as he kept the vice squad away from the supposedly honest escort service where she was employed. It was odd, Renz sometimes thought, how the fact that no money changed hands made things different. A real relationship had developed. For Renz, anyway. He wasn't sure about Olivia Dupree, which wasn't her real name.

He knew her real name, and more than that about her.

Olive Krantz had been raised by strict Baptist parents in St. Louis, where she started getting into trouble with the police when she was fourteen. By the time she was eighteen, marijuana possession and peace disturbance had become breaking and entering and prostitution. Even at fourteen she'd looked more like a beautiful woman than a teenager. By eighteen she'd been devastating. And she'd devastated the lives of two mall security guards who were caught on video exchanging merchandise for sex. The woman in the grainy security camera video hadn't been identifiable, and Olive Krantz had walked away without being charged.

She apparently liked prostitution, and before she was twenty she was in New York, working for one of the big escort agencies. She was twenty-nine now, and probably rich in her own right, because she'd never been a fool.

Renz knew she was simply doing her job, keeping the police commissioner—a very important client indeed— off her employer's back.

She and Renz had become something like friends one night, not while they were screwing, but while they lay in bed together afterward, talking.

Renz knew it was all bullshit, pumping him for information. This woman was smart and knew information was power and protection, so she wanted some about him. He didn't care. He knew what not to tell her while telling her plenty. He realized he would never really possess a woman like Olivia. Not all of her, anyway. No one could.

They talked more and more often, sharing each other's secrets. Or so it seemed. Most of what Renz told her were lies, and he wondered if she ever checked to see if any of it was true. She seemed so trusting, but he knew she wasn't.

She emerged from the bathroom nude, still rubbing her short blond hair dry with one of the hotel's huge white towels. The brisk action with the towel made her breasts jiggle.

"Wanna come back to bed?" Renz asked, wondering if he'd be able to get it up again so soon after the last time.

"You're insatiable."

"For that I need inspiration," Renz said, "and that would be you."

Olivia smiled.

Still holding the towel, she walked over to the bed and kissed his forehead. He felt her bare nipple brush his arm.

"Really," he said, "why don't you hang around for a while? We can talk."

"I would if I could, baby, but I promised a girlfriend I'd babysit her two kids for her." She glanced over at the clock on the dresser. "And I'm running late already."

Renz nodded and smiled. *Oh, you beautiful liar.*

He watched her finish getting dressed, and they kissed good-bye before she left.

Renz had over an hour before checkout time, so he lay back on the linens that still smelled of sex and rested peacefully, forgetting about the pressure on him from the pols and higher-ups, the sicko Daniel Danielle (Quinn's problem), the blizzard of paperwork that was his constant annoyance, his plush but lonely penthouse apartment in the Financial District.

He thought only about Olivia and their relationship. About how they gave each other exactly what they both needed and didn't ask too many questions, knowing the answers would be lies anyway.

What could be better than that?

Renz's cell phone played a trumpet cavalry charge in his pants pocket. The trouble was, his pants were folded over the back of a chair across the room. He hesitated, then decided the call might be important and reached the phone in three large steps away from the bed, reaching it just before the charge was over. His pants dropped to the floor as he dragged the phone from their left-side pocket. They'd be wrinkled now, which irritated Renz.

He glanced down and saw that the call was from Q&A. Quinn.

When the connection was made, Renz said, "We need to make this fast, Quinn. I'm at a meeting."

"Sure. Sal and Harold widened their canvass in Vess's neighborhood and came up with a witness that saw a woman who came around the victim's apartment."

"You mean when the victim wasn't home?"

"Could be," Quinn said. "And her actions were furtive. What I want from you are some uniforms to really cover that neighborhood and see if anyone else has something to add. I'd like to put this woman with Vess, and maybe get a better description."

"Whaddya need, six officers?"

"That would do it," Quinn said, surprised by Renz's generosity.

"Anything else?"

"No, I'll let you get back to your meeting."

"It's over now," Renz said, glancing down at his flaccid self. "But there'll be another one pretty soon."

Hanging up the phone, Quinn thought that was an odd thing for Renz to say. He supposed that as police commissioner, Renz's life had become one meeting after another.

Renz had stepped out of the shower and was toweling himself dry when he heard his cell phone again. He'd brought the phone into the bathroom with him and rested it on the edge of the washbasin. The trumpet charge was deafening bouncing off all that tile.

He reached the phone with a wet hand and squinted at

it to see who was calling. Quinn, maybe. Wanting something more.

But he saw that the caller wasn't Quinn. It was an aide to the mayor, no doubt calling for a progress report on the Daniel Danielle investigation. Pressure, pressure.

Renz's puffy cheeks rounded with his slight smile. He knew how to deflect pressure. And where to deflect it.

And who would feel it next.

44

The knocking on Neeve's apartment door turned out to be a middle-aged man with the looks and bearing of someone thoroughly beaten down by life. He asked for Herb Moranis.

Neeve informed him that Moranis had lived on the first floor but moved away last month. He looked crestfallen, thanked her for the information, and walked meekly toward the stairs.

Neeve stood with her hand still on the knob of the closed door. *See, what you were so afraid of? Nervous Neeve.*

Someone had chided her with that long ago in her childhood. She couldn't remember who.

Nervous Neeve.

"I've read about your organization in the papers," Penny said.

Genna Sinclair, a stern-looking woman of forty-five who looked as if she should be carrying a yardstick and terrorizing students, smiled in a way that caused her chin to jut out and convey a definite menace. "Shadow Guardians is having an effect," she said. "We make it safer for

the individual police officer by phoning in crime as we
see it develop. Our central office has direct lines to every
precinct house in the city."

Keeping her voice low, since they were in the library,
Penny said, "But I don't know exactly what you mean by
crime developing."

"Say someone is getting bullied on the subway and it
looks as if it's going to develop into a fight or beating. Or
a car alarm goes off and you see someone walking away,
and the owner of the car hurrying to catch up. Or someone has shoplifted something in a jewelry store and you
know the store's security is going to confront him on the
sidewalk, and the security is an old man unarmed. Those
kinds of things. You realize they happen more often than
you think, once you learn to look for them. And if the police know soon enough about crimes developing—or just
committed—they'll be able to close on the spot sooner
and in greater numbers, and be safer." Genna tapped a
button on the dark lapel of her business suit, lettered
SOONER IS SAFER.

"It makes sense," Penny said.

"Too many cops get hurt or killed because they arrive
on the scene without proper backup following in time.
And when they get there one at a time, it emboldens the
bad guys. A cop might be the only one who knows what's
going down, find himself alone and outnumbered, and
bang."

"That's my recurring nightmare," Penny said.

"You contacted us, so you must think our kind of organization is needed."

"I saw you interviewed on TV and decided to look at
your website."

"And?"

"It seems to make sense."

Genna flashed her indomitable chin-out smile. "You

should come to one of our meetings, then make up your mind. If you think our police should be safer—"

"I do," Penny interrupted. "My husband is a sort of cop."

"Sort of?"

"He's an ex-homicide detective. Now he's private, with Quinn and Associates Investigations."

Genna nodded. "Q and A." She seeming impressed.

"In a way," Penny said, "it's more dangerous than regular police work."

"Then you should definitely attend one of our meetings. We tend to snuff out violence before it has a chance to begin. *Preventing* violence is the key."

"Where do you meet?"

"Different places. Sometimes libraries." She glanced around. Hit Penny with the smile again.

"We don't have much space," Penny said, "but maybe after closing time."

"That would work. I'll let you know when the next meeting's scheduled."

"Fine. Anything I'll need? I mean, to join?"

"I know it's hard to get a license," Genna said, "but it might be a good idea if you owned a gun."

45

"**M**eeding is getting impatient," Jody heard Jack Enders tell someone in his office as she walked past the door.

The words made Jody slow down, then stop a few feet beyond the closed door.

She went back and stood near the door and pretended to be shuffling through the papers she'd been taking to the printer, listening and watching. It wouldn't do for a lowly intern to be caught eavesdropping on one of the partners.

She could neither see nor hear clearly. The standing figure she assumed was Enders's visitor was a dark shape on the frosted-glass window in the door. The two voices were muddled and barely understandable.

Jody stayed very still, trying to tune in. Hearing but not comprehending. Sometimes catching phrases she wanted to hear.

The voice that definitely wasn't Enders's did say clearly, "She has a cat, right?"

Enders said something about the cat keeping her spirit up. The "her" might well be Mildred Dash.

"It's keeping her building up, too," the other voice said.

"What if—"

"Lose something?" Dollie the receptionist asked Jody. She'd approached Jody unheard.

"I might have." Jody shuffled through the papers faster, the transcript of a boring deposition in an illegal corporate takeover case. "I need to make a copy of this." She held out the sheaf of papers. "You do that while I go back to my desk and see if I forgot or dropped one."

Dollie wasn't quite sure if an intern outranked a receptionist, but she couldn't take a chance. Her expression made obvious what she thought about Jody giving her instructions. That was fine with Jody. Dollie's irritation was what Dollie would remember most about their encounter in the hall near Enders's office door.

Dollie visibly fumed for a few seconds, then snatched the papers from Jody's hand and strode away in the direction of the copy machine.

Jody returned to her desk, in what was more a cubicle than an office. From where she sat she had a glimpse of the hall, but when Enders's visitor left she caught only a brief look at him from the back. He was average height if a little on the short side. Slender but fit. His body contained strength. In the few seconds that she saw him, Jody thought his walk was vaguely familiar. She thought, but couldn't imagine who the man might be. Someone with Meeding Properties? More likely, someone who couldn't be traced to Meeding Properties. Or to Enders and Coil.

Jody noticed Dollie approaching with the copies and originals of the deposition transcript she'd handed her. Dollie kept her expression neutral as she laid the neatly stacked papers on Jody's desk. "I wasn't mad at you a few minutes ago," she said. "It's just that seeing you like that . . ."

"Like what?"

"Somebody else kind of sneaked around here like you for some reason."

"I wasn't sneaking."

"She'd have said that, too."

"Who we talking about here?"

"You know . . . Macy Collins."

Jody felt a tremor run through her body. "You saying Macy—"

"I'm not saying anything about anyone," Dollie interrupted, and then turned and left the cubicle.

Which didn't prevent Jody from finishing her sentence.

"—found something that got her killed?"

At lunch that day, Jody sat in bright sunlight at an outdoor table at a corner restaurant. She picked at her Cobb salad, mulling over the brief snatch of conversation she'd heard wafting from Enders's office. Something beyond Mildred Dash's cat had been mentioned—possibly. Jody had heard the muted exchange just before Dollie had approached in the hall.

She couldn't be sure, but she thought she'd made out the words *Waycliffe College.*

She'd overheard those words in an earlier conversation at the firm, but in a hushed manner, and not in any context she understood. There seemed to be some kind of need for secrecy that excluded even a future alumna like her.

Maybe, she thought, she was making a fool of herself, sneaking about eavesdropping and leafing through files. She could do the simple and obvious thing and ask Jack Enders or Joseph Coil what work the firm was doing for Waycliffe.

But she had a strong suspicion that would be a mistake. Instead she would keep studying the files that she'd copied from the firm's computers. Most of it was stultifying legal boilerplate, but now and then a crack of light shone through.

She did know what she had to do about what she'd overheard today. Jody had something like a photographic mind and remembered Mildred Dash's phone number from the Meeding Properties file.

She got her anonymous throwaway cell phone from her purse and pecked out the number. It was no surprise when she got no answer.

Jody knew the number had to be to a cell phone. There hadn't been landline phone service to Dash's apartment for weeks. That was part of the strategy of isolating her.

Jody called the number again and texted a simple message: **if u have a cat don't let it out.**

When she'd replaced the phone in her purse, she finished her salad and ordered a wedge of chocolate cake.

Diet and dessert in one meal.

Fighting fat to a draw.

But she knew better.

"Ms. Culver," Fedderman said to the head librarian, "I'm Larry Fedderman, Penny's husband." They'd met before, but being in the vicinity of Ms. Culver seemed to call for a measure of formality.

"Of course you are. I congratulated you after your wedding," Ms. Culver said, from behind a formidable stack of books she was sorting. Her round rimless glasses reminded Fedderman of some kind of military equipment allowing her to see into the enemy's mind.

"Er, yes," Fedderman said. "I remember."

Ms. Culver managed a smile, but it seemed forced. "Penny seems to have made a good choice."

Fedderman was surprised. "In husbands, you mean?"

"Of course. What did you think I meant? Suits?"

"No, no," Fedderman said, wondering if he'd just been insulted as well as complimented with one swipe. "What I wanted to talk to you about was Penny's mood lately."

"Must we stay in the past tense, Larry?"

"Everyone calls me Feds."

"You wish to talk to me about Penny's moodiness."

"Her fear," Fedderman said.

"She's afraid of *you*?" Ms. Culver seemed to find that less than credible.

"*For* me," Fedderman said. "She fears I'm going to get shot. Or hurt some other way. You know, my job . . ."

"Ah, the policeman's wife's dilemma. I believe we might have that one in stock."

"I haven't read it, but I've seen it plenty of times in other marriages."

"What usually happens?"

"Divorce."

"And the alternative is?"

"Pen needs to learn to live with her fear," Fedderman said. "To put it aside. Like all of us do about something." He wondered what fears Ms. Culver might be putting aside, hiding behind her books.

Ms. Culver smiled. "You've apparently given this some thought, Larry."

"Plenty of thought."

"And you think everyone must learn to set aside some fear or other?"

"Sure. That's life. There's risk in everything, which means possible fear. We simply have to learn to live with it."

"Or divorce it."

"Or accept it. Like you're going to have to do with e-books."

A stiff smile from Ms. Culver. "I'm aware that Penny thinks I'm obsessive about e-books. But they *are* something to fear."

"Something to accept."

"Ha! Shelley and Shakespeare for ninety-nine cents!"

"But you lend them out free here."

"We lend *books*. Not bits and bytes of electronic impulses, or whatever they are."

"It's text," Fedderman said. "Stuff people read rather than watch like pictures."

Ms. Culver stared at him.

"We have to embrace the future," Fedderman said. "We've got no choice."

"I accepted that you married my friend Penny."

Fedderman thought that was an odd thing to say.

Ms. Culver adroitly adjusted her glasses, as if bringing him into sharper focus. It made Fedderman uneasy. "I think what you're suggesting," she said, "is that I set an example for Penny. I'll no longer walk around in fear of e-books, and she'll take my example and no longer walk around fearing that some night you won't come home from work."

"Something like that," Fedderman said.

"Do you think these fears are comparable?"

Fedderman shrugged. "Fear is fear."

"Is love all the same?"

"More or less."

Where was Ms. Culver going with this conversation? It seemed to be getting more and more obscure.

"And you're sure you love Penny?" she asked.

"I've never been more sure of anything."

That creepy stare again. It was unnerving.

"What?" Fedderman asked.

"Nothing," Ms. Culver said. "Just an unfinished thought. You're right. I'll try to set an example. We do have to learn to put our fears aside. We have to learn to do that with lots of emotions."

"I guess that's true."

"I've never been more sure of anything," Ms. Culver said.

PART TWO

That a lie which is half a truth
Is ever the blackest of lies

—ALFRED, LORD TENNYSON,
"The Grandmother"

46

"I don't quite know what you mean by that," Quinn said to Jody, over supper in the brownstone that evening. They were having ravioli along with a salad Pearl and Jody had spent over an hour preparing in the kitchen. Quinn mused that Jody had awakened in Pearl a domestic side that was new to him. Not that she wasn't in other matters still the old Pearl.

Jody swallowed a bite of ravioli. "I think what they're doing to Mildred Dash could be interpreted as illegal."

"Interpreted?" Pearl said, taking a sip of the merlot Quinn had bought on the way home from the office.

"Mildred has a clause in her lease requiring *all* the tenants' permission before the building can be razed in the event of eminent domain, and for at least six months' notice before having to leave the property."

"That doesn't make sense," Pearl said. "Especially that first part."

"Sounds illegal," Quinn added.

"That, or we're talking about the penumbra of the law," Jody said with a wicked grin.

"Seems it wouldn't hold up in court," Pearl said.

"Of course not, but it would take a while to wend its

way through the legal process. And for Meeding Properties, time is money."

"And that's what Mildred Dash is counting on," Quinn said. "We understand that, but what's her endgame?"

Jody swallowed too big a bite. She was excited. Her face was flushed and her red hair seemed to be standing on end. Quinn was enjoying this. And he couldn't help but notice that, except for the wild and colorful hairdo, Jody sure looked like Pearl when she was argumentative.

A sip of wine, another huge gulp, and Jody was calm enough to talk. "Mildred is no fool. She's an attorney herself. My guess is that she's trying to stall them long enough that they'll be losing so much money by *not* building, they'll be forced to change their plans so the development doesn't require that particular patch of ground."

"If I'm not mistaken," Pearl said, "Meeding Properties owns that patch of ground, compliments of the city of New York."

"But the terms of the sale specified that the leases went with the property. Mildred became a Meeding tenant on closing; Meeding is held party to the lease, and they want to evict her illegally."

"Maybe."

"Meeding must think so, or they would have forcibly removed her," Jody said.

"She has a point," Quinn said. "Mildred Dash might not have a chance in hell legally. But every day Meeding doesn't evict her, her position grows stronger."

"Playing for time is an accepted and even heartily endorsed legal process," Jody said.

Quinn doubted that but said nothing.

"How are you getting all this information about the case?" Pearl asked.

Looking at Jody, Quinn tried not to smile.

"You're snooping around where you shouldn't be, aren't you?" Pearl said.

"I'm monitoring the files to see if I might perceive something illegal."

"*That* is illegal, no matter how you pretty it up with obscure language. At the least it will get you fired for snooping."

"You might call it snooping. I regard it as investigating. Something you and Quinn do."

"You got some idea of what we do when you went with us to that homicide scene," Pearl said. "That's the sort of thing that justifies our snooping."

"And illegally evicting a poor woman doesn't?"

Quinn backed his chair away from the table and stood up.

Was he about to run out on his responsibility to help Pearl deal with Jody?

Pearl glared at him. "Where do you—"

"To smoke a—"

"Oh, no, you're—"

"I'm only kidding, Pearl."

Jody stood up abruptly, as if to say, *I've had enough of this!* She wiped her mouth with her napkin as if trying to remove her lips, and then stomped out of the dining room and upstairs.

Pearl started to go after her, but Quinn laid a big hand on her shoulder. "She's only trying get out of helping with the dishes," he said.

"She's gonna screw up her internship, with this Mildred Dash crap," Pearl said.

"That's how she'll learn to control her temper."

Pearl gave him a look and then sat down again and took a sip of her wine. Quinn sat back down across from her.

"You haven't figured her out very far," Pearl said.

"No, I haven't."

"She wasn't as angry as she seemed."

"I know. She'd rather be up in her room in a snit than down here helping with the dishes."

"That's not what I mean. She was working us. She cares about the Mildred Dash business, but not *that* much. She's using that case for an excuse to snoop at the Enders and Coil offices."

Quinn didn't quite follow Pearl. Not a new sensation.

"She's wants us to know she's onto something," Pearl said, "but my guess is it's bigger than some stubborn woman who might get evicted in the name of progress. What Jody was fishing for was our tacit permission to go ahead and sneak around where she's working, and you gave it to her."

"I did?"

"Yes. It obviously amused you that she was taking risks for some youthful empathetic reason she didn't begin to understand. And remember you bought into that penumbra-of-the-law bullshit."

"I wouldn't say I bought into it."

"Jody would. She's on to something bigger," Pearl said. "Believe it."

Quinn considered what Pearl had said. For it to be true, Jody would have to be a damned good actress. And how could they know how good she was? She didn't have a track record with them. "Maybe we should talk to her about it."

"She wouldn't talk. Remember, she comes already lawyered up."

Quinn nudged half-eaten ravioli with his fork. "You should know," he said. "You're her mother."

Upstairs in her room, Jody read again some of the Enders and Coil files she'd pirated from the firm's computers. She'd broken the encryption code easily, and was now trying to make sense of what she suspected.

If it turned out to be true, what did it mean?

"You're gonna ruin your figure with this pizza," Jorge, the kid from Mexitaliano, warned Mildred Dash.

Jorge was nineteen and skinny enough that he'd never had to worry about eating too much pizza. The regular deliveryman when Mildred ordered food from the restaurant, Jorge had developed an obvious crush on the hermit-like Mildred, trapped as she was in her apartment.

Mildred, acutely aware that she was almost old enough to be his—my God—grandmother, kept him at a polite distance. Not that he'd have nerve enough to make his feelings known.

She paid him for the pizza, and the soda in its tall white foam cup with its plastic lid, along with a generous tip. He was, after all, one of her only lifelines to the outside world. Though she did sometimes leave the apartment, she always took great care not to be seen or followed. She didn't put it past Meeding Properties to have her under almost constant observation.

Jorge gave her a large smile and a lingering look at her ankles extending from beneath her long robe. "Thanks, Missus D."

"You're welcome, Jorge. By the way, have you seen Cookie?"

Cookie was Mildred's large golden tabby, a cat she'd shared her life with for the past several years.

"Ain't seen him," Jorge said. "But I'll watch for him when I leave, bring him back to you if I see him." The big smile again, meaningful. "Maybe there'll be some kind of reward."

Jorge, Jorge . . .

"He isn't really lost, Jorge, just not home." Mildred hoped that would throw cold water on Jorge's naïve sexual ambitions.

"I'll keep an eye out for him anyway. Anything for you, Missus D."

Mildred thanked him and watched him pocket the money and go out the door. She locked the door behind him, then went to the window overlooking the street in front.

Jorge came into sight below, mounted his delivery bike, and pedaled away, weaving through construction and destruction debris. It was dusk, and she hoped he'd be clear of the vast and unlit deserted area before it became dark enough to be dangerous.

She stood at the window for a while after Jorge was out of sight, looking for some sign of Cookie, telling herself not to worry, he was probably happily hunting mice or rats.

It wasn't like Cookie, though, not to appear this time of evening for his regular tuna-flavored meal.

Mildred went to the kitchen and ran the electric can opener, just in case Cookie was hiding somewhere in the apartment. The sound of the opener was usually an irresistible invitation to dine.

No cookie.

She remembered that when she'd called for the pizza there had been a text message on her phone. She went to the phone and read the text.: "if u have a cat don't put him out."

The anonymous message was from yesterday. Written in time but read too late.

She waited. Hoping. A lump of worry in her throat.

No Cookie.

*   *   *

Just before midnight Mildred was awakened by foot-falls and what sounded like muffled laughter out in the hall. Then something soft but not completely soft slammed into her door and *thump*ed to the hall floor.

She knew what it was. She worked the doorknob, opened the door a few inches, and looked out into the hall with the chain on to be sure. She returned to her bed and wept.

47

Leighton, Wisconsin, 1986

The lost dog posters had brought no response. They faded in the sun and wrinkled in the rain and mists of mornings. Rory no longer felt a twinge of guilt when he walked or drove past them.

In fact, the posters lifted his spirits now in an unexpected way. He knew logically that he'd done the right thing with Duffy the dog, so there were no longer twinges of regret. Now the posters reminded him of Sherri Klinger. Sometimes when he drove past them, he smiled.

Rory suspected his mother knew he was sneaking off with the car when she was away, and sometimes even when she was in the house asleep. She was becoming worn down, and simply didn't want to confront him again.

He was driving better all the time, obeying traffic laws so he wouldn't have a run-in with the law, parallel parking with greater skill so he no longer bumped up on the curb or dented cars in front of or behind him.

She must know he was driving more frequently and becoming better at it. Or maybe his mother was looking the other way when he "borrowed" the car because she approved of him seeing Sherri Klinger.

Yes, that was possible.

Sherri was, in everybody's estimation, a Nice Girl. Meaning she was possibly still a virgin. She would be good for Rory.

Well, he went along with that.

On the pretense of searching for Duffy, Rory would pick up Sherri at a prearranged spot—sometimes Creamery Curb Service, near the back, where people drinking soda or milkshakes in their cars were facing the other way and she wouldn't be noticed getting in the car—and they would simply drive around, Sherri keeping an eye out for the lost Duffy, Rory pretending.

They talked as they rode, getting to know each other better. After a while, Duffy was seldom mentioned, though they carried on the charade of searching for him.

"Gas is expensive," Rory told Sherri one day, as they were tooling along the county road in his mother's Impala.

Sherri laughed. "What is that, a news announcement?"

Rory smiled and took a curve a little too fast. It was a nice sensation. "What I mean is, maybe we oughta park a while and search for Duffy on foot."

"That doesn't sound very efficient."

"It's getting harder and harder to keep the gas gauge off empty," Rory said.

"So you're saying we don't have much choice."

"My wallet's saying it."

"You don't have a credit card?"

"I used one my mom gave me, but she confiscated it when it got up near a thousand dollars."

"Jesus, Rory! She's got some nerve. I mean, it's *your* card."

"It does have her name on it."

"So?"

"Anyway, it's a nice day for a walk."

Rory found a place where they could pull off the road and the trees were spaced out so they could drive the Impala into the woods just far enough so that it was invisible from the road. The underbrush might have scratched the paint on the side of the car, but not so much that Rory's mom would notice. And if she did notice, she'd probably think she'd done it herself.

Rory leaned over to work the door handle for Sherri just as she was leaning forward to grip it herself. Unexpectedly, they were close. This had to be more than coincidence. This was *fate.* They kissed. Then kissed harder, using their tongues.

The kisses became more than kisses. And then became something wonderful.

Afterward Rory folded his shirt so Sherri could sit on it and not get blood on the Impala's seat.

"What are we going to do now?" Sherri asked.

"That," Rory said. "Again."

They both laughed.

"God, Rory!"

"Nobody has to know," he said.

"In a way," she said, "I want everybody to know."

He stared at her, horrified.

"Don't worry," she said, and patted his knee.

"We're acting like an old married couple," Rory said.

She punched him hard in the side of the neck and then hugged him. They hugged each other, not wanting to let go. This was fine. This could be perfect. If no one would ever disturb them. Ever.

Finally they pulled apart.

"Ready to go back to the real world?" Rory asked.

"As I'll ever be."

"I'll put the window down so it won't look funny, me driving without a shirt."

"You are so devious."

"I guess we both have to be devious now," he said.

"Maybe everyone learns that sooner or later. It's called growing up."

As he maneuvered the Chevy back out onto the road, Sherri was thinking how her mom and dad would wring her neck if they ever found out about this. She had already been taking birth control pills she'd gotten from Hattie, the school nurse, without anyone knowing.

Rory noticed they weren't far from where he'd killed and buried Duffy. Now here they were, him driving shirtless, and the untouchable Sherri Klinger sitting beside him with her wadded panties and his shirt under her bare rump so she wouldn't get blood on his mom's car.

Some wide and wonderful world.

Some future!

"Want to stop at Creamery Curb Service and get some milkshakes?" he asked.

"Rory!"

48

New York, the present

They were driving in Quinn's black Lincoln, on their way to pick up Sal and Harold. The sun was low and the shadows stark and angled. The day's ferocious heat was hanging around with the remaining light, but the big car's air conditioner kept the interior comfortably cool. Now and then a smattering of rain spotted the windshield, taunting with the notion that the brutal heat would be broken.

Ordinarily Pearl would complain about the lingering cigar smoke smell in the car that meant Quinn had been puffing on one of his precious Cubans, but this evening she had things on her mind that made the cigar problem seem minor.

"Sometimes I wonder if it's worth it," Pearl said. "Then I wonder if it's not just me, but that's the way it is—you can't stand the obnoxious twerps, but you know if they were gone you'd miss them so much it would hurt."

"You talking about Sal and Harold?" Quinn asked.

"You know damned well I'm talking about Juditha Jane Jason," Pearl said.

He switched on the wipers. Switched them off. He was aware of her watching him as he drove. He hadn't known Jody's middle name was Jane, but he should have. But then, no one had told him. He kind of resented that.

"You raised a daughter," she said. "Being a parent? Is it like that?"

Quinn thought about Lauri and smiled without realizing it. "Sometimes it's tough. Other times it's grand."

"You're proud of Lauri. You love her and you're proud of her. I can tell."

"I am," Quinn said. "And sometimes she could drive me nuts, just like you know who."

They drove for a while without talking. Quinn cut off a cab at a gridlocked intersection and the driver yelled and cursed at him and made obscene gestures. Quinn ignored him. Sometimes, Pearl thought, he was like something made out of marble. But she knew his warm and beating heart, and part of his soul.

"How do you feel about Jody?" she asked.

He didn't divert his gaze from the madness of Manhattan traffic. "I'm beginning to feel possessive."

Pearl scooted across the Lincoln's big bench seat and snuggled up to him.

He glared down at her. "Pearl, you're a cop."

"Private," she said. "Very private."

Jody stood in the lobby of Enders and Coil and looked through the tinted glass at a patch of sky. Even through the tinting, low-hanging dark clouds could be seen. Rain clouds. Or a tease? Probably it wouldn't rain, but it might.

She placed her purse on a nearby leather chair and put on the light raincoat she'd had the foresight to bring to work. She had stayed late, letting her penchant for romping through Enders and Coil's up-to-date files and recent correspondence pass for hard work and ambition.

There was a full-length mirror at the other end of the lobby, and she went and stood before it, making sure the coat, which had never fit her well, hung low enough to cover her skirt and didn't look ridiculous.

A little short, but still okay. She'd have to be moving for the skirt to show.

She'd walked only a block from the law firm's building when a drop of rain landed on her eyelash. The clouds hadn't been bluffing. She felt similar cool pinpoints on her bare forearms. Great! Though she'd brought her raincoat, she had no umbrella and wasn't wearing the kind of shoes suitable for jogging to her subway stop.

She squinted and glanced skyward, though she had no idea what she expected to see. *Yeah, more clouds.* Based on the increasing number of drops, this didn't seem like the kind of summer shower she could escape by ducking into a doorway and waiting it out.

It began to rain harder.

Jody knew how it was in Manhattan when it rained. Occupied cabs were the only yellow vehicles you saw.

She didn't like spending the money, but the temptation of getting into a dry cab and being transported to the brownstone was irresistible even if it was a strain on her limited budget.

And there was a cab. Occupied. Followed by two more. Both occupied. Jody felt like she was being messed with. It was as if every damned cab in the city had cardboard pop-up figures in their rear seats that sprang bolt upright with the first drop of rain.

Something cool touched Jody's ankle. A spray of water from a puddle. Close to her on the left, a cab had pulled to the curb. One of its rear doors swung open like an invitation, as a voice said, "Miss?"

Jody leaned down and peered into the back of the cab, and there was a middle-aged, attractive woman smiling out at her.

Immediately Jody wondered if the woman was a cop or security guard and had been following her. Maybe because she still felt somewhat like a criminal for having examined Enders and Coil's files.

"I noticed you plowing through the puddles," the woman said. "That's not necessary. Come in out of the rain."

Jody hesitated.

"Besides, you might want this." The woman was holding something up for Jody to see.

Jody's purse!

My, God! She must have left it sitting in the chair in the law firm building's lobby. She recalled walking past the chair on her way out, but had no recollection of pausing and picking up her purse. As if it hadn't been there to see.

The woman's smile grew more benevolent. "Come on. We're obviously going the same direction. Lucky for you I looked out the window and recognized you as the person who forgot this, and who I'd tried to catch up with on foot. I wasn't sure at first."

Jody pushed aside whatever reservations she had and climbed into the cab's backseat next to the woman. She accepted the purse. "It's mine, all right. Thanks so much!" She reached into the purse. "Can I give you—"

"Nothing, really," the woman said.

"We'll split the fare," Jody said.

"Not on your life. We're going to the same place, anyway."

Jody looked at her curiously.

"A restaurant," the woman said, "where I'm going to

buy you dinner. I've been a young girl alone in the rain in New York myself."

"No . . . really," Jody said, thinking she *was* suddenly hungry. Maybe the woman's suggestion had worked on her in some Pavlovian way.

"I'm Sarah Benham," the woman said. "With an 'h' and an 'h.' This is where you tell me your name and say you're glad to meet me."

"Jody Jason. And I am glad."

Sarah showed her benevolent smile. "It looks like fate meant for us to be friends."

But Jody wondered if it might not have been coincidence, this charitable cab ride and then dinner. On the other hand, what was the harm? This woman, who seemed perfectly nice, who'd returned her purse, wasn't about to attack her. And even if she did, Jody could handle herself. It was a miserable evening, Jody was starving, and the truth was, she loved an adventure.

"No argument, please," Sarah said. "I want to impress upon you that New York isn't such a callous city. And it looks to me as if you worked hard and late this evening. Such industriousness should be rewarded. You need a good meal, and I'd like to introduce you to apple martinis."

"But I wasn't working for you," Jody pointed out, thinking that apple martinis sounded interesting.

"You were if you were working for truth, justice, and the American way," Sarah said, grinning.

"I suppose I was doing exactly that," Jody said, playing along, getting hungrier. It was odd how Sarah Benham could take on an almost motherly manner, even though she wasn't *that* much older than Jody. Then it struck Jody that yes, Sarah might actually be old enough to be her mother. It was difficult to tell for sure these days, what with all the cosmetic surgery and beauty aids. Possibly Sarah was even older than Pearl.

Wow! That was one Jody had to think about to grasp. Here she was sitting next to her new friend—acquaintance, anyway—who was more or less her mother's age. Manhattan was a special place, all right.

"Besides," Sarah said, "it won't hurt me to make points with Enders and Coil."

"Are you an attorney, too?"

Sarah laughed. "Heavens no. I'm in insurance. An adjuster."

"An Enders and Coil client?"

"Not at present, but I might need a good lawyer someday. And I believe in thinking ahead. Italian okay?"

"Sounds wonderful!"

"We'll enjoy a nice comfort-food meal and a chat, and then share a cab again, if it's still raining."

A motherly touch again. Or maybe that was all in Jody's mind. Maybe her new friend Sarah wasn't at all as she imagined.

49

"I received a phone call this morning," Professor Elaine Pratt said to Chancellor Schueller.

The sun was shining brightly outside the chancellor's office window, making the Waycliffe campus look pristine and green as a souvenir postcard. A student couple strolled past out on the quadrangle, hand in hand, assuring Elaine that the scene was real and not painted or Photoshopped.

"Subject?" the chancellor asked. He didn't ask who'd called.

"Juditha Jason," Elaine said. "Jody."

"I assume her internship at Enders and Coil is still not going well."

"She often works late," Elaine said, giving him a look as if she were peering over her glasses, though she was not wearing glasses.

"I see."

"She still seems to have a special interest in Meeding Properties' efforts to evict a pesky client."

"Youth," the chancellor said, peering out the window now that Professor Pratt was staring at him. "All those windmills to tilt at."

"Don Quixote wasn't young," she said. "On the other hand, Joan of Arc was."

"Meaning?"

"Jody's curiosity and efforts might be broadening beyond the eminent domain case, and in a way that might become serious."

"Oh. I thought it was going to be something about windmills. You think she . . . *suspects*?"

"Not at this point, or we'd know about it."

"You're sure?"

"Definitely. Nevertheless, Enders and Coil are getting uneasy about Jody's presence at the firm."

"And Meeding Properties?"

"They're unaware of any discord within the triumvirate."

Schueller shrugged and turned back toward the professor. "Well? Enders and Coil know what they can do if they're uneasy."

"They'd be even more uneasy if they ended Jody's internship. It would seem to confirm her suspicions."

"Think she's smart enough to know that?"

"Oh, yeah."

"Then cutting her loose would make her even more active," the chancellor said. "And in a more effective way." He picked up a sharpened pencil, as he often did when ruminating, and drummed out a tiny staccato riff on the wooden desktop. Elaine was sometimes tempted to tell him what he should do with that pencil. "At this juncture," he said at last, "I think we should let the matter ride."

"I agree," Elaine Pratt said. "As long as we remind ourselves from time to time."

"Remind ourselves?"

"That Jody Jason might be even smarter than we thought."

* * *

"So what is this?" Quinn asked, when he and Pearl were at their desks in the office and Fedderman came in with the mail that had been in the box since yesterday.

"What it looks like, I guess," Fedderman said. He appeared not to have had much sleep. His brown suit was more wrinkled than usual, and what hair he had left needed a trim. "A package addressed to you personally. Brown paper wrapping, neatly sealed with brown packaging tape." Fedderman hoisted the small rectangular package with one hand. "Doesn't weigh much." He held it to his ear. "Not ticking."

"Give it here," Quinn said, holding out his hand.

Fedderman tossed the package to him. He was right. It wasn't very heavy.

Quinn examined the label. Unadorned black felt tip printing on a plain white label.

"There's no postage marking," Fedderman said.

"Meaning it was placed rather than delivered," Pearl said, standing up from behind her desk. She looked worried. "Where exactly was it, Feds?"

"On the floor just beneath our brass mail slot, where the postman usually leaves packages."

"What's the return address?"

"No return address," Quinn said.

"Don't open it," Pearl said.

Quinn looked at Fedderman, who shrugged.

"We can't call the bomb squad to open all our mail," Quinn said.

"Don't be stubborn," Pearl said. She picked up her desk phone and began pecking out a number.

"Who are you calling?"

"Harley Renz."

"For God's sake, Pearl. Don't stir him up."

But it was too late. She had called Renz's direct line.

It took her only a few minutes to tell Renz about the package. Then she listened for about ten seconds and hung up.

"What'd he say?" Fedderman asked.

"He's sending somebody over from bomb disposal."

"What?" Quinn said. "One of those robots to open our mail?"

"That robot," Pearl said, "would be the second smartest person in the room."

The street door swished open, then the door to the office.

"Fast work," Fedderman said.

But it wasn't the bomb disposal guy; it was Lido, come either to report or to work on the high-tech NYPD computer Renz had loaned Q&A. He was wearing dark slacks almost as wrinkled as Fedderman's. His white shirt was untucked and buttoned crookedly.

"You already been at the sauce?" Quinn asked him.

"It's how I do my best work," Lido said.

Quinn looked him up and down. They weren't talking about hot sauce. "Jesus, Jerry! It's ten in the morning."

Lido made a dismissive motion with his right hand, as if shaking liquid from his fingers. And maybe there really was liquid on his fingers. "I just pretend I'm someplace where it's some other time," he said.

"Does that work?" Pearl asked.

"In some other place it does." Lido's bleary eyes fixed on the package Quinn held. "What's that?"

"We think it might be a bomb," Pearl said.

Lido stared at all three of them, and then turned around and left.

When they heard the street door again five minutes later they thought Lido was returning. Instead it was the bomb disposal guy, who turned out to be a woman. She was about forty, sweetly pretty, and slightly overweight.

Or maybe it was the uniform and all the gear dangling from her belt that made her just look overweight. At her side, held lightly by a short leather leash, was a large German shepherd.

"You the explosives expert?" Quinn asked.

"He is," she said, nodding down at the dog. The dog looked at Quinn as if daring him to question his expertise.

"What's his name?" Pearl asked.

"Boomer."

"Of course," Fedderman said.

"Can I pet him?" Pearl asked.

"If he'll let you."

That was a vague enough answer to keep Pearl where she was in her desk chair.

"I'm Darlene," the bomb disposal cop said. She fixed her blue gaze on the package on Quinn's desk corner. "That the suspicious package?"

"If you want to be suspicious," Quinn said.

"I do," Darlene said. "It's how Boomer and I stay alive."

No one spoke for a few seconds.

"That was sobering," Fedderman said.

Darlene and Boomer had crossed the room and were standing in front of Quinn's desk. Darlene brought her forefinger close to but not touching the brown package, and the dog looked up at her and then began sniffing the package.

Quietly, calmly, it sniffed for several seconds, and then backed away.

"It doesn't contain explosives," Darlene said. "But just in case, why don't the three of you leave while I open it." She didn't pose it as a question.

"I thought you said it didn't contain explosives," Fedderman said.

"There's only one way to be absolutely sure," Darlene

said. She had opened a case made of black plastic-like material with gray lining. There were various tools fitted inside. There appeared to be more tools than were needed to do the job. "Boomer and I won't be long," Darlene said. "Don't let anyone inside." She stood motionless, waiting for them to leave.

They went outside and stood on the sidewalk, about twenty feet away from the door. Darlene was right: there was only one way to be sure.

"Whaddya think?" Fedderman said.

"Candy from an admirer," Pearl said. "In which case, I want to see the card."

"Cigars from an admirer," Quinn said, just to get under Pearl's skin.

"Maybe something to do with the case," Fedderman said. "Like a clue."

The door opened and Darlene motioned that they could come back inside.

Fedderman's guess was closest to the truth. The brown paper and tape lay folded neatly on the desk corner. Near it, on a plain white sheet of paper, lay something Quinn didn't immediately recognize.

"That was inside," Darlene said. She pointed to a smaller slip of paper that was creased from being tightly folded. Beneath it was something beneath white tissue that Quinn would get to after dealing with the folded paper. One thing at a time. Darlene would approve.

Barely touching the paper with the tip of his retracted ball point pen, Quinn examined both sides.

There was nothing on the paper other than a small black printed question mark. Admirer or not, the sender was secret.

Quinn used the pen to move the tissue out of the way so they could see what was beneath it.

Again, no one spoke for a few seconds.

"It looks like a pouch," Fedderman said, "made of soft leather with a leather drawstring on top."

"I think it's a tobacco pouch," Darlene said. "But it would do for jewelry." She reached out with an exploring fingertip. "That leather's like butter. It's pretty high-quality goods. Boomer sure wouldn't mind chewing on it." She pointed with her pink-enameled nail to the bottom of the pouch. "What's that gnarly looking thing on the bottom?"

"That's a nipple," Quinn said.

Darlene and Boomer stood staring at the pouch. Darlene's expression began to change.

Pearl pointed toward the half-bath over by the coffee machine.

Darlene and Boomer crossed the room so fast that Boomer stepped with a heavy paw on Pearl's toe.

Quinn picked up the folded paper by its edges to look again at the question mark.

50

Quinn was back behind his desk. Darlene and Boomer had gone and taken the pouch with them. The lab would doubtless be able to match the DNA with one of the victims.

Unless the pouch had been fashioned from the breast of one of Daniel's earlier victims. Was that what the monster was doing with his victims' body parts? Using them for some kind of grotesque hobby?

It seemed too horrible to be possible, but Quinn knew that human beings were capable of any nightmare they could conjure.

Helen the profiler had come in to the office. Quinn wanted her to be in on this. Her short, carrot-colored hair was ruffled and looked soft, as if she'd just washed it and sat under a dryer. Probably, Quinn figured, she'd rubbed it dry with a towel and forgotten about it. Her denim shorts made her long legs look even longer. She had on blue jogging shoes and a sleeveless Fordham sweatshirt. Quinn didn't think she'd attended Fordham, more likely some college in the Midwest where they played basketball. He'd asked her once if she'd played basketball and she told him no, but she was a fan. Just because a woman was over six feet tall didn't mean she'd played basketball.

Quinn had wondered why not.

"He's trying to taunt us," he said.

"More to it than that," Helen said. She was wearing either no makeup or scant makeup skillfully applied.

Pearl returned from the coffee machine carrying two steaming mugs. "It's goddamned gruesome," she said, handing one of the mugs to Helen.

Helen accepted the mug and moved away a few feet to sit on a different desk. She'd been perched on Pearl's. Now Pearl sat down at her desk and placed her coffee mug on a cork coaster.

"If the killer's trying to send someone a message, it's probably Quinn," Fedderman said.

"And it's probably more than a simple taunt," Helen said.

"I don't know if it's complicated," Quinn said. "He wants to get me mad so I screw up. He's playing chess."

"The chess analogy goes only so far," Helen said.

"Maybe the idea is to make you feel vulnerable," Fedderman said, thinking back on his recent conversations with Penny.

"That's closer," Helen said. "But it's also possible that he wants to demonstrate how vulnerable Pearl is."

Fedderman appeared puzzled. "Why Pearl in particular?"

"Because he knows we're living together," Quinn said. "He sees Pearl as my possession and wants to show me he can take it away whenever he chooses."

"Women as toys for the sadist," Pearl said.

Fedderman sipped his coffee, which had become cool. "I dunno, Pearl. It could simply be that you're his type and he wants you the way he wanted those other women.

That's what the pouch might signify—he's objectifying you. You're no more to him than another souvenir pouch."

"Thanks," Pearl said.

"Or some other kind of souvenir," Helen said.

"No, he's a breast man," Fedderman said.

Pearl shot him a glance that would have stung a more sensitive person.

"The package was addressed to me," Quinn reminded them.

"He wouldn't send something valuable like that direct to a mere possession of yours," Helen said.

"That might well be," Quinn admitted. Once you figured out where Helen was coming from, she tended to make a lot of sense.

"Men!" Pearl said. "It's always about you."

"Helen's the one that worked it out," Fedderman said, "and she's a woman."

Pearl had no adequate response to that, but she wished now that she hadn't fetched Helen's coffee.

"Whatever is in this sicko's mind," Quinn said, "Pearl is in danger."

"And she's being followed," Fedderman said.

"That one's been worked out," Pearl reminded him.

"That's right," Helen said. "Your daughter." She smiled. "I'd like to meet her."

"I'm sure you will someday," Pearl said.

She wondered as she spoke, had Jody been active in any kind of sport?

51

This was odd, Renz thought.

Jim Tennyson, an undercover officer on the vice squad, had requested a private interview with him. Ordinarily Renz would have told him to go though the proper channels; scroungy undercover cops didn't just call their way up the telephone ladder to Harriet Gibbs, Renz's secretary, and have the unmitigated—or maybe it was mitigated—gall to leave a message asking for an appointment with the police commissioner. It was one word in Tennyson's rambling message that caused all of Renz's orifices to draw up: *Olivia*.

He'd granted Tennyson the interview.

Olivia's name also prompted Renz to request Tennyson's file and learn what he could about the undercover cop. These undercover guys could get too close to the goods sometimes and cause problems. Could, in fact, *become* the problem.

Tennyson had been in uniform for five years before becoming a plainclothes detective, then had almost immediately transferred to Vice and undercover work. He'd requested the transfer.

He'd used his gun once, winging a dealer who was

waving his shotgun at the occupants of a crowded subway car. Renz thought about that. A close call, deciding to fire a shot in a crowded subway car. Turning loose one bullet to keep a scattering of deadly buckshot from being fired. Took some balls.

The shotgun had turned out to be empty. As far as Renz knew, Tennyson had had no way of knowing that. The review board had seen it the same way. Tennyson had not only been cleared by the board but had received a commendation.

Renz had to admit, the man's record indicated he was a good cop. Still, those undercover guys . . . especially the ones who'd infiltrated the drug world.

Here he was standing slouched in front of Renz's desk, wearing a dirty sleeveless T-shirt lettered CRASH CAB, equally dirty jeans, and worn-out brown shoes tied with white laces. Renz noticed that the bows were double knots. The shoes wouldn't let Tennyson down if he found himself on either end of a footrace. Renz saw that the UC wasn't wearing socks, and his ankles were dirty. All in all, he looked like Robert De Niro playing a role.

"Nice disguise," Renz said.

Tennyson smiled. A front tooth was missing. Probably only during working hours. "It gets me by." He didn't seem at all nervous, even though he was seriously out-ranked. That worried Renz.

Renz said, "What the hell do you want?"

Tennyson looked genuinely confused. "I don't want anything."

"You mentioned someone named Olive Krantz."

"Olivia. I came across a conversation about her."

What was this? Blackmail? Renz thought he'd get out ahead of it.

"Came across?"

"In an indirect but reliable way."

"If you're here to tell me Olivia's a call girl, I already know that. And I know she's damned good at her job."

"She works for Prime Escorts," Tennyson said.

"Right again. Now get to the point."

"Word is she's playing you."

"We play together."

"Different games, maybe."

"You mentioned a word? Whose word?"

"I don't know the source, and that's the God's truth."

"Leave God out of this." Renz leaned back in his desk chair and expanded his already bloated physique. He looked almost as dangerous as he was.

Tennyson's bearing changed. He was a pro who could see a storm coming. Doubt had found its way in. Maybe he'd mishandled this.

"I'm not interested in any word from any drug fiend or psycho who doesn't know shit about what he's yammering," Renz said. "Why should I be?"

"Olivia might be a fine person, sir. I don't care squat what she does for a living. But she's in the trade, so I came across her, and what she was doing. What was the source? Like I told you, I don't know. But it might've been Olivia herself, when she was under the influence."

"Influence? What trade we talking about?"

"Coke, heroin."

Heroin! Jesus! Why did Tennyson have to come walking through that door?

"Olivia's not a user." Renz heard the hollow defensiveness of his own words.

Tennyson said nothing. His self-assurance had returned.

Renz deflated and sat forward again, his elbows on his desk. His stomach felt like rats were running in it. He didn't look so threatening now. More threatened.

"I'm not wearing a wire," Tennyson said.

"I know you're not. I got a little thingamajig that detects those and electrocutes anyone coming in here wearing a wire."

"Really?" It was impossible to know if Tennyson was asking a serious question. Toying with Renz now, the asshole.

"Of course."

"Like I said," Tennyson told him, "I only wanted to let you know. Avoid any possible trouble. It goes no further than me, whatever you decide to know or not know."

"You gonna name a sum?"

"I don't want a sum," Tennyson said, almost angrily.

"But you wouldn't mind an angel looking over you from the dizzying height of the police commissioner's office."

"Sure, I wouldn't. Let's be honest. I wouldn't mind at all if promotions came to me a little easier. Or more fairly. I don't want anything I haven't earned."

"And you think you're earning something coming here to me with this bullshit?"

A thin smile ran across Tennyson's lips. "I took a helluva chance."

"You did," Renz said.

"My good deed for the year."

"Humph! Loyalty. That's what you're selling."

"I don't think you can put a price on loyalty."

"And it should work both ways," Renz said.

Tennyson nodded. "It'll run both ways. If you want, I can see that nobody repeats the word, that nobody bothers this Olivia."

"That's Harry Primo's job."

"He's an asshole."

"So many of us are." Renz stared hard at Tennyson, who seemed unperturbed. "You all done here?"

"That's it."

"Now leave."

Tennyson took his time sauntering to the door, going out.

Renz thought, *There's a young copper with a bright future.*

What exactly does he know? How much does he know? How brief is that future?

52

C *razy Legs. Weird.*

Neeve hadn't been crazy about this new manuscript, a biography of Elroy "Crazy Legs" Hirsch, when she'd picked it up from the editor at Hamilton Publishing. *Who the hell is he?* Neeve had wondered. It had sounded like the book's subject was a gangster, like Legs Diamond.

But Crazy Legs hadn't been a gangster. He'd been a football player, and a great one, known as Crazy Legs because he ran so wildly and unpredictably he was difficult to tackle. Neeve was a football fan, so how was it she'd never heard mention of Crazy Legs Hirsch? Well, people often ignored four-leaf clovers they were standing over.

Truth was, Neeve felt lucky. She'd really gotten into *Overbite,* and wound up enjoying it immensely. And now here she was back on her bench in the park and all wrapped up in *Crazy Legs: Elusive Legend.* Two good books in a row to copyedit. Life was at least okay.

She did wish *Crazy Legs* was on disk rather than paper, or had been sent to her electronically. Instead of using her computer, here Neeve was again lugging around a thick stack of twenty-weight copy paper.

Suddenly she realized she was chilled. Leaves rattled above her, and she looked up to see that the sky had darkened and a breeze was wafting through the park, swaying the foliage. Dark leaves silhouetted against the gathering gloom did their restricted dance in the wind. Off in the distance, a man and woman hurried side by side along the trail, in the direction of the exit onto Central Park West. The man had his arm around the woman's waist. Neeve felt a pang of . . . what? Envy? Loneliness?

She pressed down on the manuscript in her lap, making sure none of the pages would be caught by the breeze, and looked up at the sky. Stars were becoming visible, and a pale moon was almost full. There were only a few wispy clouds, so the breeze was a bluff; it didn't figure to rain.

Unhurried, she gathered up her things, sliding the thick manuscript into her computer case, along with pencil, eraser, sharpener, and a paperback *Merriam-Webster's Collegiate Dictionary* that she needed a magnifying glass to read.

She was about to stand up when a figure suddenly sat down beside her, and something was clamped over her mouth and nose.

Startled, she gasped and inhaled something that made her dizzy, and then relaxed, and then very, very sleepy.

Neeve opened her eyes.

Terrific! I'm in Central Park after dark.

None of that wondering where she was, or what had happened to her. Neeve almost instantly remembered exactly what had happened. Only it was much darker now, with shadows moving slightly on the grass of her near and low horizon. She had no idea how much time had passed.

Jesus! I'm twisted like a pretzel.

She was lying on her stomach, her wrists bound behind her, and apparently tied to her ankles that were drawn up close to her wrists and also tightly bound. Hogtied. The awkward position put a terrible strain on her back, and her movements were restricted to none.

Neeve was breathing through her nose because something—it felt and tasted like tape—was fixed firmly over her mouth. Her lips were mashed open by the suddenness of what had happened. And there was the faint smell she'd experienced moments before passing out. Chloroform was her guess, though she'd never before smelled chloroform.

The way her body parts that touched each other felt, the subtle movement of air over her body, made her sure she was nude. No, she felt *something*. Her assailant hadn't removed her panties.

A voice said, "Ups-a-daisy," and warm hands were placed beneath her shoulders. She had no illusions that this was a rescuer. She was tilted back onto her knees, her spine still bowed, so that she was staring straight up at a full yellow moon visible between overhead branches.

The warm hands cupped her breasts, hefted them, and then released them. There was a darker dark above her that blotted out the stars. Movement. And then a hand held a knife before her eyes so she couldn't help but stare at it. The hand rotated the blade deftly so it glinted silver in the moonlight.

"You know who I am?" a voice asked.

Neeve made a soft whimpering sound. She read the papers, watched the news. She understood who had her.

Her feet, her painfully bent legs, her brain, her *soul*, wanted to leap up and run. She heard herself grunting with effort that resulted in no movement other than a shuddering that ran through her body.

The hand without the knife patted her cheek fondly.
The pain began.

Quinn lay next to Pearl in the dim bedroom, aware of
the subtle movement of her body as she breathed evenly
in deep sleep. She was facing away from him, still nude
after their lovemaking, covered lightly with the sheet as if
in modesty. It was cool in the room, and the air conditioner had cycled off. The varied sounds of the sleeping
city haunted the night, as well as nearer noises of the old
brownstone.

Quinn often thought that if houses could indeed be
haunted, New York's brownstones of the 1800s would be
among them. During the day he sometimes felt lonely in
the looming old building, but at night he seemed somehow not to be alone even when Pearl wasn't with him.
Jody, upstairs, almost didn't seem to count, so insulated
was she by the thick walls and floors of the old brownstone.

Well, if there were ghosts about, there should be no
reason to fear them. He might even thank them for the
company.

Oddly comforted by that thought, he fell asleep.

A huge wasp was chasing him down a long dirt road,
sometimes buzzing past him and circling again behind.
The damned thing was as big as a bird, and its buzz
sounded like a model airplane engine. Quinn lengthened
his stride and ran faster than he thought possible. His
heart was pounding.

Then he tripped and fell on the gravelly dirt road, skin-
ning bare arms and elbows. And the harsh buzz of the
wasp grew louder.

He scrambled to get up, knowing the wasp meant business now. Its droning didn't vary; it was no longer circling. It was coming right at him. He forced himself to turn and look at it.

There it was on the bedside table, beyond it morning light piercing the edges of the blinds. He realized he was awake, but the damned wasp . . .

His cell phone, set to vibrate, was buzzing and droning as it danced over the hard wood surface of the table, not falling to the floor only because it kept coming into contact with the lamp base.

The fright of Quinn's dream dissipated. The clock radio's glowing red numbers said it was a little past 6:00 AM.

Christ . . . !

He was alone in the bed. Pearl must be up already, maybe in the kitchen. Quinn tried to wake up all the way, shook the numbness of sleep from his right arm, and reached for the buzzing, vibrating phone.

He grasped it, flipped the lid up, and silenced the damned thing.

His sleep-fogged eyes were too unfocused to make out who was calling, but he immediately recognized Renz's voice.

"Time to get up, sleepyhead. Time for a walk in the park."

53

The sun was barely up, shining through a low, glowing haze that lurked between tall buildings. Half a dozen steps outside the brownstone, and already Quinn's shirt was sticking to him. When he got into the car, the leather upholstery felt comfortably cool on his back. For about five seconds.

Pearl got into the passenger seat and fanned herself with an old playbill from *Catch Me If You Can*. The humidity was going to be a bitch. Maybe Pearl was, too. The heat.

"It smells suspiciously like cigar smoke in here," she said.

"Don't start."

"You talking to me, or the car?"

"Depends on which one of you gives me a lot of shit."

They were both quiet the rest of the way. Neither of them liked where they were going.

Quinn and Pearl left Quinn's big Lincoln parked on Central Park West and entered the park on foot. Renz's directions were easy to follow. Yellow crime tape was visible ahead and to the left, along with one of several uniformed cops posted to keep people away from the scene. It was something they'd realize in an instant that they'd rather not have seen.

Nift was already there, along with a police photographer and the crime scene unit. Renz stood back about twenty feet from all the activity, wearing an expensive blue suit that made his corpulent body look almost svelte. He was standing away because he was calmly smoking a cigar and didn't want to contaminate the crime scene. The scent of the cigar immediately made Quinn want to smoke one. That sure as hell wasn't going to happen. Not with Pearl within half a mile. He absently touched his shirt pocket, seeking a cigar, and found only a ballpoint pen.

"Sorry to rouse you two so early," Renz said, winking at Pearl.

"We were already up and back from our morning jog," Pearl lied.

Renz didn't know if she was kidding. He looked confused for a moment and puffed on his cigar. Blew some smoke.

"Is it still legal to smoke in the park?" Quinn asked.

Renz shrugged. "Who the hell cares?" He motioned with his head toward whatever was on the ground and the center of attention just beyond the small rise of dew-damp grass.

Quinn squinted in that direction. "Who found her?"

"Pair of young lovers," Renz said. "Or so they say. They might have been young muggers. One of them was carrying a sock full of marbles."

"The girl have a weapon?"

"They were both girls. The one without the marbles let out a scream that attracted attention, so they slipped into the mode of good citizens." Renz flicked his cigar, holding it well away so ashes wouldn't drift onto his suit. "They're at the precinct house making a statement. You can talk to them if you want, but they're just who they say. I called there and neither one has a sheet. One's an artist and one isn't, and they both get money from mom or dad."

"What kind of artist?" Pearl asked.

"The kind you won't find in a gallery." Renz ground out his cigar on the sole of his shoe and flipped away the still-glowing butt. "You two had breakfast?"

"Earlier," Pearl said. Whatever happened, she didn't want to wind up having breakfast with Renz.

"Good luck," Renz said, and led the way to the body.

The victim was hog-tied, like the others, staring up at what would have been a night sky when she was killed. Though obviously beautiful when she was alive, her pale body, nude but for a pair of twisted pink panties, had the waxy sheen of death where it wasn't smeared with blood. Her well-structured face with its once strong features now wore an expression of fear and distraction, her dark eyes focused on something far above where she lay contorted on planet earth. Her breasts had been neatly removed, leaving only a few jagged rags of flesh.

"God, almighty!" Pearl said, as they stood staring down at the corpse. "You'd think we'd get used to looking at this."

"They're individual people," Nift said. "That's what makes each one interesting."

Pearl didn't know quite how to take that. Had Nift said something compassionate?

"She had a great rack, like the others," the nasty little M.E. added.

There was the familiar disgusting Nift.

Pearl refused to give him the satisfaction of a reaction.

"The panties look like they fit her," Renz said. "Maybe they're actually hers."

Quinn didn't see how Renz could hazard a guess at that, considering the way the nylon panties were twisted.

"I don't think they were put on postmortem," Nift said. "Looks like he either put them on her himself, or made her put them on before she was tied up."

"Looks like the same kind of rope he used on the others," Quinn said.

"It is," Nift confirmed. "The ends cut with a sharp knife, like with the other rope. And she was tied up using simple but effective square knots, same as with the other victims."

"Same asshole," Pearl said.

"Without a doubt," Nift said. "Almost surely the same knife." He grinned at Pearl. "And of course there's that other thing."

Pearl glared at him. "What would that be?"

"She's a dead ringer for you, Pearl."

Quinn rested a hand on her shoulder. "He's pretty much right about that, Pearl."

"I can't say I see her that way," Pearl said. "But then maybe I wouldn't, being me."

"Daniel Danielle liked them with dark hair and eyes and big boobs," Nift said, leering at Pearl.

Quinn gave him a warning look that made him concentrate again on the victim.

Renz had been over talking to the CSU people and a uniformed patrolman. He came back now carrying a black computer case and a purse.

"She has a name," he said. "Neeve Cooper. And a West Side address within easy walking distance or a short subway ride from here. Purse had some of her business cards in it. They say she was a freelance editor."

"Worked at home?"

"Or in the park," Renz said. "There's a bunch of paper in this case looks like it could be turned into a book. Red and blue pencil writing on some of the pages. Here and there, what might be somebody's name." He handed the purse and computer case to Quinn. "See if she knows anybody name of Stet."

"Could be Steve," Quinn said.

"Naw. It's in there half a dozen times."

Quinn assumed the crime scene unit was finished with the purse, so he put his right hand into it, felt around among wadded tissue, a comb, a Metrocard with an angled corner, and a wallet, and found some keys on a ring. One of them felt like a door key.

When he looked up he saw that Nancy Weaver had joined them and was standing alongside Renz. She and Quinn exchanged nods. Weaver, known among the NYPD as the woman who put the "cop" in "copulate," had slept her way up the bureaucratic ladder. There were even rumors about her and Quinn, but Pearl had never believed them.

Weaver had been out of town, recovering from serious injuries she'd received during her last case with Q&A. She'd been back for several weeks.

Now Weaver acted as the sometimes liaison between Renz and Q&A. Another way of saying rat.

"I've been filled in," Weaver said.

Numerous times in numerous ways, Pearl thought.

"We'll go have a look at Neeve's apartment, talk to her neighbors," Quinn said to Renz.

"I already sent a crime scene unit over there," Renz said.

"We'll stay out of their way."

"I'll go with you," Weaver said.

"Good idea," Renz said.

Nobody said anything for a while.

"Couldn't hurt," Pearl said.

Her gracious contribution to diplomacy.

"I need to know her panty size," Quinn said.

"I wrote it down," Weaver said. "Figured it couldn't hurt."

Pearl gnashed her teeth.

54

"**D**aryl Smith told me they found Duffy," Sherri's voice said on the phone.

It was Saturday morning and Rory had slept late. He sat up in bed and wiped his eyes. His mother had answered the phone downstairs on the eighth or ninth ring and yelled up the stairs that it was for him and it was past time he got up and what was he going to do, sleep all day? Rory woke up all the way, trying to comprehend what Sherri had just said.

Found Duffy?

"How could they have?" he asked. "And how would Daryl know?"

"He's working for that construction company that's widening the county road, and the bulldozer scoop turned over some earth, and there was Duffy. That's what he said, anyway."

"So how'd you—"

"Daryl just called me on his car phone. I've got no way to get out there, Rory. I need for you to drive us."

*Us. I gotta wake up all the way, learn more about this.
Duffy . . . still making trouble.*

"I think my mom's gonna use the car to go shopping,"
he said. "She wants to go to Antoine's."

"Can't you talk her out of it?"

"Talk my mom out of shopping? Are you kidding?"

"For God's sake, Rory, this is Duffy!"

"Okay. I can try to talk her into staying home," Rory
said.

"You will talk her into it, sweetheart. You can talk anyone into anything. I oughta know."

"It's not like I have an actual driver's license, Sher."

"There's no car here, Rory. If you can't get your
mom's, I'm gonna start walking."

"That's miles, Sherri."

"It's for Duffy, Rory."

Goddamnit!

At that moment Rory wished that he could run over
Duffy again.

"I'll go downstairs and talk to her," he said.

"Thanks, sweetheart."

Rory wasn't used to being called sweetheart—by anyone. He thought it might be nice to get used to it.

"You sound kinda foggy," Sherri said. "Are you still in
bed?"

"I was about to get up."

"My God, Rory, it's almost ten-thirty."

"I'm on my way." He stood up as he talked and took a
few stumbling steps.

"Hurry, please!" he heard Sherri say, just before he
hung up.

*   *   *

"So how'd you deal with your mom?" Sherri asked Rory, as she slid into the Impala front seat beside him.

"Told her this was super important, and it involved you. She likes you. Then I said I was just going two blocks to pick up Teddy Boylston first. He's a eighteen and has a license, so I'd be okay with him with my learner's permit."

"Will Teddy lie for you?"

"I know where he keeps his stash, so he'll cooperate."

"You oughtn't use that shit," Sherri said.

"It's not heroin."

Rory and Sherri had argued about this before, and both knew where it would end. She wasn't going to use drugs, and Rory was into moderate use of marijuana and coke. She couldn't talk him out of it. He couldn't talk her into it. They lapsed into silence as Rory drove toward the county road.

They'd turned and driven about three miles when they saw the red cones on the road, and a WORK ZONE sign. A small Bobcat earthmover was jolting and jerking back and forth while two darkly tanned guys without shirts stood leaning on shovels watching. One of them was Daryl Smith.

When Rory steered the Chevy to the shoulder and parked, Daryl nodded to Sherri and pointed precisely toward the spot where Rory had buried the dog.

Sherri clambered out of the car and ran to it. Rory followed. He looked over at Daryl, who shrugged and walked toward the Bobcat to shovel and smooth a mound of dirt it had left.

Rory stood beside Sherri, and there at her feet was what was left of Duffy. The remains were rotted and unidentifiable as a dog except for the once fluffy black coat, now lackluster and coated with dirt.

"You sure it's him?" Rory asked.

Sherri sobbed, did a half turn, and dug her forehead into his chest. She began to sob, then quickly gathered herself, straightened up, and swiped her arm across her nose. She nodded. "It's Duffy. But he had a collar."

"This dog doesn't have one. Maybe it's not—"

"It's Duffy," Sherri said firmly. She began to look around. "They've moved so much with that little bull-dozer."

But Rory knew they hadn't moved enough. The Bobcat had gone nowhere near where he'd thrown Duffy's collar into the brush. If the collar was still there, Sherri was sure to find it. She was moving slowly, head down, playing her lead foot back and forth through the weeds with each step as she advanced toward where the collar must be. Rory knew that if the collar was still there, it would look better if he found it.

He mimicked Sherri's slow, dragging walk and pretended to search with her, but moving at a different angle. The terrain was unchanged enough that he was pretty sure he knew where the collar had landed when he tossed it the night of Duffy's death.

Damn! There it was, a touch of faded red in the green-brown undergrowth. He considered leaving it there, but knew it would be found. If not by Sherri, then by someone else. Maybe Daryl. He might be able to bend down and slip the collar into one of his pockets. He also might be seen. And if he did manage to transfer the collar to a pocket, what then? Sherri might be all over him, even if the outline of the collar didn't show in his tight Levi's.

He made his decision and thought no more about it. The wisest alternative would be to find the collar.

He went to it, kneeled down with his back toward Sherri, and rubbed the dust-covered metal tags on his pants. Half turning out of his stoop, he held the unbuck-led and weathered red collar high. "This it?"

She hurried toward him.

He rubbed the tags with his fingers as if cleaning them so he could read them. Now his would be the only prints on them, only smeared.

"Says Duffy," he told her sadly.

She took the collar, held it to her with both hands, and started crying again.

"I'm being stupid," she said after a while.

Rory held her and patted her back. "No, not stupid. You loved your dog, is all."

Daryl Smith walked over and leaned on his shovel near them. "It yours?"

Rory thought that should be obvious, but he said nothing as Sherri nodded.

"Thanks for calling and letting me know," she said.

Daryl shrugged, still leaning with both hands on the long wooden shovel handle.

"She'll be okay," Rory said.

Sherri stood straighter and moved away from him. "There's a place in the backyard where I wanted to bury him."

Daryl glanced at the Chevy. "Maybe I can get you something so the trunk don't get messed up."

"I brought a plastic bag in my purse," Sherri said. "If you can get Duffy into it. I . . . don't want to watch."

"That's fine," Daryl said.

Rory waited with him while Sherri went to the car and got the black plastic bag from her purse. She handed it to Daryl and walked back to the car, standing by it and staring down the empty road.

The Bobcat ceased its clanking and roaring, and the other two construction guys watched as Rory held the bag open and Daryl used his shovel to move the dead dog into the bag. Rory fastened the bag tightly with its yellow plastic pull ties.

Daryl stooped and picked up the red collar. "She musta dropped this. You want it?"

Sherri was standing by the open trunk of the Chevy, watching them.

"I better take it," Rory said, and accepted the collar. "She might wanna save it."

"Women," Daryl said.

"Dogs get like kids to them," Rory said.

Daryl nodded toward the plastic bag. "I'm glad that's just a dog and it ain't my kid."

"Yeah, well . . . we'll get him buried, maybe even say a few words."

"Put up a little marker. Here lies Duffy. Fetch in peace."

"Don't let her see you smile," Rory said, starting with the bag toward Sherri and the car's open trunk.

Rory dug Duffy's second grave at the far end of Sherri's backyard. Her ten-year-old brother, Clyde, watched somberly from a distance.

When the grave was finished, Rory placed the plastic bag containing Duffy in it, as well as the collar and tags. Sherri mumbled a few words that Rory could barely hear, then picked up a handful of dirt and tossed it on the bag. Then she backed away, and Rory went to work again with the shovel.

When he was finished, Clyde came closer. "You gonna put a cross on the grave?"

"No," Rory said. "That'd just make people curious and they might disturb it. This way Duffy will rest in peace."

"Do dogs do that?" Clyde asked. "Wouldn't they rather be running around?"

"Ask your sister."

"She went on in the house. She was crying."

"Well, she's upset."

"I miss Duffy, too. I don't cry about it."

"Girls are different."

"No shit, Sherlock."

Rory put the shovel back in the garage, then went to an outside faucet and began washing off his hands.

Sherri was back outside now, and stood close to him. "Take one of these, why don't you?"

He saw that she was holding three small white pills in her pink palm.

"I thought you were so against drugs."

"These are prescription. They're different."

"So what are they?"

"Loraza-something or other. My mom takes them to help her sleep. If you take them, they'll make you feel better. Not so sad."

"Have you taken any?"

"Yeah. Two. I brought you three because you're bigger."

Rory didn't want to admit he wasn't terribly broken up about Duffy's passing, so he accepted the pills and put them in his mouth, then ran faucet water into his hand and scooped water into his mouth and swallowed.

"You got water all over your shirt," Sherri said. Her dark eyes were red and swollen.

"You gonna be okay?" he asked, turning off the spigot.

"I think so."

"Your mom home?"

"No, but Clyde is. We can't mess around."

"Guess not."

"I'll thank you later for doing this for me," she said. "Thank you properly."

She kissed him on the lips and he felt an immediate erection.

Sherri must have felt it, too. "I better not do that," she

said, smiling up at him. "And you better get the car back to your mother."

Rory waved good-bye to Clyde, who'd been standing watching them, then got into the Chevy and backed it down the driveway and into the street. So far he didn't feel any different from taking the pills. He ran a stop sign near his house, but managed to get the Chevy parked back in the garage.

When he went in through the kitchen he saw a note from his mother beneath the salt shaker on the table. She'd gone shopping with a neighbor in the woman's car and would be back soon.

Rory got a soda from the refrigerator, went into the living room, and slumped down on the sofa. He used his cell phone to call Sherri and they talked for a while. Sherri was the one who started giggling and talking crazy, then they both started making less and less sense so they each kissed their phones and then broke the connection.

Leaning back in the sofa, Rory sighed happily. It had been a hell of a day, but looking back on it, not such a bad one. He and Sherri were closer now, that was for sure. All in all, his world seemed pretty good, its pieces all in place.

He rested the back of his head against the sofa cushion and wondered . . .

It seemed like five seconds later when Rory woke up. It was dark outside. He struggled to an upright position and took a sip of soda. It was warm and fizzy and some spilled down onto his shirt.

He looked around for a clock, then remembered that there was none in the living room. That was where he was, in the living room of his house.

Reassuring, familiar territory.

After unremembered dreams?

He took a few deep breaths and decided he felt pretty good. Maybe a little confused, and sort of . . . heavy.

Light played over the living room walls. Headlights. Tires scrunching gravel. A car in the driveway.

Voices. A car door slamming. High heels clacking on the concrete porch. Paper sacks crackling. A soft jingling and then the ratcheting sound of a key being inserted in a lock.

The light came on, causing his eyes to ache.

"Why on earth are you sitting there in the dark?" Rory's mother asked. She was standing near the door, clutching several large Antoine's bags.

"I was watching TV. Musta fell asleep."

"I hope you didn't spill any of that soda on the couch."

"Nope. I was careful."

He suddenly realized he had to piss, and urgently, so he stood up, swaying gently. He couldn't get his legs to work for a moment; then he trudged heavily toward the hall and the bathroom.

"You're still half asleep," his mother said.

"I guess I am. TV does that sometimes." He plodded on toward the bathroom. How did it get so far away?

He still felt heavy. More like three-fourths asleep. Drugged.

Sherri and her little white pills.

But they *had* worked. He remembered feeling much better not long after taking them. The tension, his fear that he might say something wrong, or that in some other way Sherri would find out what really happened to Duffy, had seemed suddenly unimportant and then left him.

If the pills worked this time, they'd work again. People expected so much from him. It wasn't as if he lived a life without pressure.

He bumped into the small table in the hall, causing it to scrape against the wooden baseboard.

"For God's sake, turn on a light," his mother said behind him. "I hope you don't drive that way at night. You're liable to kill somebody."

55

Dr. Grace Moore's office was on West Forty-fourth Street, in a building attached to The Lumineux, a swank hotel with European décor. The idea was that some of the tasteful mood and environment might rub off.

Her office was furnished much in the manner of the hotel, with minimalist style and obviously expensive furniture. Matching taupe carpet and drapes set off—but barely—mauve furniture and throw rugs over a hardwood floor. Deep blue was, here and there, an accent color. The tan leather sofa where her patients sat was incredibly comfortable. She thought that in sum the office gave her patients confidence in her, and engendered a heightened tendency to share secrets.

Linda Brooks, a twenty-nine-year-old woman Dr. Moore had been treating for two years, had seemed exceptionally upset when she'd arrived for her appointment today, but now, sitting back on the sofa with her head resting against the cushions, her eyes half closed, she'd obviously calmed down.

Linda was an attractive dark-haired girl with well-defined features and a cleft chin that helped to lend her a habitual sincere and determined expression. Her teeth seemed always clenched, her jaw muscles almost constantly flexing. Linda had been diagnosed five years ago as mildly schizophrenic with episodes of paranoia. Lately, the paranoia had been increasing in frequency and seriousness.

"Have you been taking your meds as required?" Grace asked, seated in a soft swivel chair with her legs crossed. As usual, she was composed and calm.

"Of course I have," Linda said. "That's what they're for, aren't they?

"Do I sense hostility?"

"Toward you, no," Linda said.

"Toward yourself?"

"God, let's not get into that."

"Isn't that why you're here?"

"I *knew* you were going to ask that."

"Of course you did; it's the obvious question."

"So is my reply. No offense, Dr. Moore, but you don't know the right questions."

"So what are they?"

"The questions I'd ask."

"Such as?"

"Will I ever again look forward to getting out of bed when I wake up? Am I ever going to be able to develop a loving relationship with a man? Will I ever have to live on the streets because my parents' money and my insurance have run out? Will any of these shitty medicinal cocktails you dream up actually cure me? Is it possible I'm imagining being stalked by the same man?"

"What was that last one again?"

Linda smiled, pleased to have piqued Dr. Moore's interest.

"He's average height, built like a young Frank Sinatra,

wears a baseball cap sometimes, like he thinks it's some kinda disguise. But I see him. I know him. I recognize him. You think he's a hallucination, but he's not."

"Frank Sinatra . . . I would have thought you'd say Mick Jagger, or somebody more to the musical tastes of people your age."

"Okay, Mick Jagger. Even though he's older than both of us."

"This man who's following—"

"Stalking."

"What's the difference?"

"Where he appears, how he moves, how he looks at me. Have you ever gone to the zoo and tried to outstare one of the big cats?"

"Believe it or not, yes," Dr. Moore said. "A long time ago. A panther. I found it impossible."

"Because if the bars hadn't been there, the panther would have consumed you. Both of you knew that. And now one is stalking me. There are no bars."

Dr. Moore felt a chill of fear, and pity, for what Linda must be going through. "Where do you see this man, Linda?"

"The street, subway, park, my apartment . . ."

"*Inside* your apartment?"

"Once, for just an instant, when he was leaving out through the kitchen window. There's a fire escape out there." Linda opened her eyes all the way to match stares with Grace. *Like the panther*, Grace thought. "He *wasn't* a hallucination."

"Was the kitchen window closed and locked?"

"Of course."

"Okay. How could he get in?"

"Key. I leave my spare key under my doormat out in the hall."

"That's the first place anyone would look, Linda."

"Right. And when I get home I always look to make sure the key's still there. If it is, that means nobody's used it to get inside. Then I'm not afraid to go in."

Grace wasn't going to cross swords over that one. "Was the key under the mat the day you saw the man in your apartment?"

"Of course not. So I used my key and went in. I was going to see him, talk to him, make sure he was real. But he was already halfway out the window."

Something with countless legs crawled up Grace Moore's spine. "Did he say anything before he left?"

"No. He was more interested in getting out of there. He left the key, though. I found it on the corner of the kitchen table. I put it back under the mat." Linda laced her fingers behind her head and regarded the doctor. "Now you're wondering, was there really a man? Might he even have followed Linda here? Or is this simply more of Linda's usual paranoiac bullshit?"

Grace smiled. "Of course you're right."

"I get so tired of not being believed."

"I didn't say I disbelieved you."

"Word games. I bet you're good at Scrabble."

"I'm unbeatable," Grace said.

"Well, you've never played anyone crazy."

"But I have. Maybe someday you and I can—"

"No. You probably know too many seven-letter words."

"You know you do sometimes hallucinate. And you don't always take your meds as prescribed. It's easy to forget. And you do hear voices. So what makes you think—"

"If he hadn't been real, don't you think I would have given him a voice?"

Grace was a bit startled by that observation, because it was a reasonable question. "Let's make him this real," she said. "I think you should find a better place for your spare key."

"Then I wouldn't know if it was dangerous to go inside the apartment. I'd no longer have my key-nary in the mine shaft, if you know what I mean."

"I do. And it's good you still have your sense of humor."

"If I didn't have that I'd go cra—hey, wait a minute!"

Grace had to laugh. Linda was, in her own way, often the brightest person in the room.

"The son of a bitch is real," Linda said. "Believe it."

Dr. Moore knew better.

56

It was cool and dim in the lounge off the Lumineux Hotel's lobby. The lounge featured lots of black leather, tinted glass, and brushed aluminum. A few business types sat here and there, talking deals, making excuses, their drinks before them like ceremonial potions on square white coasters. Futures could be made or lost here in ways profound but barely noticeable.

The killer sat at the bar and periodically checked his watch. Linda Brooks hadn't suspected he was following her. At first he'd thought she might enter the hotel, which could have provided some interesting aspects. Each quarry was, after all, an adventure.

Instead, she'd walked past the hotel and entered the Cartling Towers, a glass and steel monstrosity adjacent to the Lumineux. He'd managed to squeeze into the crowded elevator she'd ridden to a high floor, and exited after she did, turning the other way in the hall and then stopping and watching which door she entered. He could perform that maneuver adroitly and without attracting attention. He'd had practice.

A psychiatrist's office. Wonderful!

He glanced at his watch. It was a few minutes before the hour, so it was likely she had an appointment.

Linda had entered the office of a Dr. Grace Moore, according to the brass lettering on the door. So probably she was under analysis, learning to cope with her problems. She hadn't realized her primary problem was close behind her, watching the play of her nylon-clad calf muscles as she strode in her high heels, the pendulum sway of her hips, the graceful elbows-in swing of her lissome arms.

He made a study of her, as he did with all of them.

The killer considered entering the doctor's office, perhaps taking a seat in the waiting room, if there was one. Pretending, if necessary, that he'd accidentally entered the wrong office. Linda wouldn't recognize him. Not for sure. She'd only seen him from a distance, and then only briefly. He'd never moved in close without being positive he wasn't spotted. And she'd never imagine he could pop up here, of all places.

He would artfully make his exit while her mind was still working and wondering, leaving her frightened and unknowing. Oh, he was tempted. It would be daring and fun and productive. And it would certainly confuse, and maybe rattle, her analyst. But he had second thoughts about that idea. It might be a mistake for her to see him in such close quarters.

This wasn't the time to take risks. There was no reason to prod the increasingly muddled mind he was making uneasy, or to stir the will he would soon break. This hobby—oh well, obsession—of his fascinated in part because it always became a joint venture. Eventually his quarry would long for the suspense to end, and would join in the process.

Standing in the hall outside Dr. Grace Moore's office door, he'd decided to have a drink at the bar in the hotel next door, and then go to Linda's apartment while she was still on the couch—if her analyst actually used a couch—and rearrange some things in her refrigerator and medicine chest. Not drastically, but unmistakably, so she'd strongly suspect—but not *know*—that someone had been in her apartment during her absence.

He could picture her, still rattled by what she'd seen in the fridge, standing in front of the rearranged medicine cabinet where she'd gone to take one of her tranquilizers, and seeing the bottle of pills for some reason resting on the wrong shelf—and upside down. How soon she'd be off the track, almost immediately after a session with the good doctor. It would be enough to shake her faith in science.

He paid for his drink and dismounted his bar stool, then left the hotel and had the doorman hail a cab.

As he gave the driver a cross-street destination, he thought he might spend a little time in Linda's apartment, go through some of her papers and perhaps find out why she was seeing a shrink. She'd be on the couch (if Dr. Grace Moore used a couch) at least another half hour or so, and it would take her a while to arrive even if she came straight home.

"Keep in touch with Quinn and Q&A," Harley Renz told Nancy Weaver, "but I've got something else important, and confidential, I want you to do."

Nancy Weaver, seated in one of the chairs angled toward Renz's desk in the commissioner's office, was keenly interested. And alert. She didn't actually trust Renz. Not all the way. He'd sacrifice her in an NYPD minute if it suited his purpose. He was a valuable but tricky ally.

Knowing when to keep her mouth shut, Weaver waited silently for Renz to continue.

"There's an undercover cop named Tennyson, working Vice in Midtown right now."

Weaver came up with the vague image of a tall, lanky cop. "Jim Tennyson?"

"Yeah. You know him?"

"Seen him around, is all."

"Would he recognize you?"

"I doubt it."

"Take precautions anyway."

Weaver waited again, seemingly unconcerned. Renz would make known what sorts of precautions were necessary.

"I want you to put a loose tail on Tennyson, find out where he goes, who he sees. You're going to have to be careful. He crosses paths with some pretty mean assholes."

"When you say *put a loose tail . . .*"

"I mean you by yourself, Weaver. And whatever you learn, you'll share with me and no one else. It'll be worth your while."

Weaver was sure of that. She also knew it would be a bad idea to refuse the commissioner's request. Renz would slit his grandmother's throat if it might help him in his relentless bureaucratic climb. No, it was a political climb now. Even better, if Weaver stayed on Renz's good side. Especially if she learned something about him that made him vulnerable.

If she had something on him that made him *have* to trust her, she knew it could go one of two ways: her future would be secured, or he would destroy her so she'd no longer be a potential danger to him.

It was a rough game she was playing.

"I understand the necessity for confidentiality, sir. You can trust me."

"I know I can, Weaver, or you wouldn't be sitting here."

Their gazes locked and something passed between them, an unspoken understanding between takers but not givers. The only two types of humans on this earth. Or at least in the city of New York.

Renz made a tent of his pudgy fingers and said nothing more, so Weaver stood up to leave.

"Do what you have to do," he said behind her.

She nodded.

Story of my life.

Concrete walls bearing indecipherable graffiti, steep grades overgrown with weeds, cars moving along on trackside roadways, all flashed past the window wherein the killer could see his somber reflection.

He was on the train back into New York City from Stamford, Connecticut. It was only a forty-five-minute commute, and it had taken less than an hour to visit a hardware store in Stamford where duplicate keys were made.

He'd had to do this. There was no certitude. Linda Brooks might at any time remove her spare door key from beneath the welcome mat outside her apartment door and change her locks. If she was seeing an analyst, she might well receive that very sound advice.

He'd explained to the girl behind the hardware counter that he had to leave the original key with his wife so she could come and go in his absence, but he'd made a wax impression of their house key. Could she duplicate it?

Of course she could, but it would cost more than a simple reproduction.

He gladly paid the extra charge.

While the key was being made, he browsed around the

store and bought a kit for hanging pictures. Let the girl working the key machine, who also had checked him out, draw her own conclusions about him and his fictitious wife moving or redecorating.

He was soon out of the hardware store and on his way back to the train station, a copy of Linda Brooks's door key in a small envelope deep in his pocket.

He knew that having the key, feeling its warm, light weight and presence against his thigh, hastened the date when it would be used for the last time.

The train slowed and took on passengers at one of its stops along the way. Then it picked up speed again and rocketed along the rails toward the city and Linda Brooks and her destiny.

57

Usually Linda Brooks wandered, walking the streets as if she might stumble across some answer there.

The killer sometimes thought her meanderings matched the random madness of her mind. It made her more interesting to follow. His projections of where she was headed were usually wrong, not from any fault of his own, but because her mind was a fickle navigator.

But today was different. Linda was walking faster and in straight lines, her chin thrust forward. Today she conveyed an obvious sense of purpose that was almost caricature.

The killer easily followed her without being seen. She didn't glance behind her once, as she usually did. Her focus was forward.

She crossed Amsterdam and strode north on Columbus, headed for the Upper West Side. The killer almost had to struggle to keep up.

When they reached West Seventy-ninth Street he realized where she was going. He hung back and watched her pause, and then enter the redbrick and stone building that housed Quinn and Associates Investigations.

* * *

Quinn heard the street door, then the office door, and watched from behind his desk as the woman entered. She had long dark hair, and was medium height and slender. Standing framed in the doorway as she was, in her tight jeans and yellow T-shirt, he couldn't help but notice she was buxom. The T-shirt was lettered MIND YOUR OWN BUSINESS across the chest.

Once Quinn got beyond her general description and focused on details, he was struck by the haunted quality of her dark eyes. The pale flesh of her face was taut over good bones. She was youthful yet haggard, as if she'd just gotten over a serious illness. Quinn could almost smell fear emanating from her.

"This *is* the investigative agency?" she said.

He smiled. "You're in the right place."

"Whew! Haven't been there for a while." She gave him a narrow look. "You should be Captain Frank Quinn."

"I am. Not a captain any longer, though."

"Wow. Right place, right person." She advanced closer to his desk and he motioned toward a chair. Something told him he shouldn't stand up and loom over her. She might take flight like an exotic bird.

She rolled the chair closer to the desk and sat down, assuming a prim posture. Nearer to him now, the fear in her was even more evident. As was a sadness.

"First of all," she said, "let's get it on the table that I'm crazy, but not all the time."

"Noted," Quinn said.

She waved her slender arms. "Schizophrenic is the diagnosis. Voices, hallucinations, the whole bag of agony."

"We can work around that," Quinn said.

She grinned. "You sound like my analyst."

He was glad to hear she was in treatment.

"My name is Linda Brooks," she said, "and I'm being followed." She leaned slightly forward as if to give the words more impact. "Not just today, right now, but for about a week. It's like I have a shadow, only it's not a shadow. A shadow doesn't keep its distance. Or disappear suddenly even though no light has been switched on. No shadow I've seen, anyway."

"Okay, Linda. Have you gotten a good look at him?"

"How did you know it was a him?"

"I surmised. I do that a lot."

"Yeah, you would. He's about five ten or so, thin and fit looking. He wears a blue and gray sweat suit some of the time. Other times jeans and joggers. Some of the time a suit and tie. If I saw him in a photograph, I'd probably recognize him."

Quinn raised a forefinger, motioning for her to wait a moment, then rummaged through one of his desk drawers. He drew out a copy of an old photo of Daniel Danielle from a *Miami Herald* news item and laid it on the desk.

Linda edged closer and peered at it. "That's him."

Quinn got another photo, this one a shot of Jerry Lido taken for Q&A files.

"I told you, that's him," Linda said, glancing at the photo.

"Okay," Quinn said. The two men weren't completely dissimilar. They were about the same size and each had dark hair. Daniel was wearing what looked like a prison shirt, the booze-emaciated Lido a blue shirt with a loosened tie.

"They're not the same man," Quinn pointed out.

"I know that. But they could be at different times."

It took Quinn a few seconds to understand what she meant. "You mean following you at different times?"

"Of course. I'm not stupid. I don't think they change identities, just that the same man can look different in different photographs. I mean, I'm not crazy all the time."

"You said that." He suspected it was her mantra.

"Now you sound like my analyst."

Time to get off this track. "I won't be analyzing you, just helping if I can. By the way, who is your analyst?"

Without hesitating, she gave him the name and address of a psychoanalyst he'd never heard of but who had a respectable address.

"I have good medical insurance," she said, while Quinn was still jotting down the information. "My mother saw to that before she died. My father died the year before she did."

"Natural deaths, I assume."

"Sure. None of that forty-whacks stuff."

"Other relatives?"

"None who'll have anything to do with me. I stole from all of them."

"How long have you been seeing Dr. Moore?" Quinn asked.

"Years and years. I'm not crazy twenty-four-seven. When I take my meds I'm perfectly normal for a while."

"Is this the first time you've been followed?"

"By someone who wasn't from the OSS, yes. You know who they are?"

"A long time ago, they became the CIA," Quinn said.

"That's if you accept the lie that they were ever completely disbanded."

"I've often wondered," Quinn said.

"I know you're not the cops. You'll want money. I can't pay you."

"We'll do it pro bono." *Because the city is paying me, and because you resemble Pearl.*

"It would be best if you could catch him in my bed."

"He sleeps in your bed?"

"Naps, maybe. I can see that *somebody's* been lying in it. When I'm not there, of course. He stays in my apartment sometimes when I'm not home."

"How does he get in?"

"Windows sometimes, if they're unlocked. And he probably has a key that opens all doors."

"Have you and he ever been there at the same time?"

"Once, when I saw him leaving through a window. But time and place always intersect someplace, don't they?"

"They do," Quinn said.

"So here's my place." She dug in her purse for a paper and pencil and wrote down a West Side address a few blocks off Broadway, uptown from where they sat. Beneath the address was a phone number. "I know how you work," she said, pushing the paper toward him over the desktop. "I've read the literature. I won't know you're around, but you'll be there. If he comes around again, whoever's watching over me will tackle him. Bend his arm behind his back and he'll talk. You can make him tell you who he is. We both know who he is. The wind told me who he is."

"Is that where you hear voices, in the wind?"

"Not always. But pretty often, actually. If the wind is blowing on stone."

Quinn thought that would be almost all the time, in New York. "What have the voices been telling you?"

"To be careful. For God's sake, be careful." She stared at Quinn with those eyes that had seen way too much that wasn't there, but in her view had to be *somewhere*. Whatever happened in her world became twisted and sharp before she could get a proper grasp of it. Her mortal enemy roamed the interior of her skull. Probably the pressure never ceased.

Quinn understood that he couldn't imagine her pain.

58

The killer watched Linda leave Q&A. Linda looked up and down the block but didn't notice him. Perhaps she'd seen him but didn't want to admit he was there, and so let her gaze slide past.

It was wonderful that she'd come here. She understood, and without knowing who or what was stalking her. And on some level Quinn would know what Linda knew, that he was meeting the woman whose violent death he'd soon be investigating. Of course, probably neither of them had talked about it. Not directly, anyway.

The elephant in the room was no less invisible and unmentioned because it was preparing to charge.

The Shadow Guardians meeting at the library had gone well. Penny felt better about it when she learned that Ms. Culver wasn't going to attend. She had a seminar on e-books at another library that evening.

Penny had come away assured that the Shadow Guardians weren't a group of far-right or far-left nutcases. They were wives and children of cops who wanted to make sure their loved ones had every advantage in a war against crime that was becoming more and more one-sided. The bad guys—the drug dealers, muggers, gang-bangers, and plain old thieves—were winning. And had the police outnumbered and outgunned. The Shadow Guardians were there to help and to prevent, that was all. But there was no doubt that even that could be dangerous.

The guest speaker at the meeting, a woman with sprayed, helmet-like hair, from California, talked about how this concept was working in some of her state's large cities. The organization wasn't an extension of the police force, but a simple aid in the critical time before confrontations and arrests. It helped to put time and numbers on the side of the law. It had saved some lives.

Though she'd been advised to sleep on her decision, Penny joined the Shadow Guardians that evening.

It was Penny's day off at the library. She kept her destination a secret from Feds, and from everyone else. Feds didn't really understand the pressure she was under because of his job. He certainly wouldn't understand how what she was doing would relieve that pressure—at least for a while.

Penny had roamed the Internet until late last night, contacting several Shadow Guardians via their websites, searching for answers. She'd been referred to a woman named Noreen, an ex-cop's wife who ran a blog about and for cops' wives. Sensing a kindred spirit, Penny had messaged Noreen.

She'd been surprised when she got a reply early the next morning. Surprised again by something Noreen recommended.

Penny took the subway to Grand Central, then a short train ride to a spot in New Jersey outside Newark. She was wearing jeans, a darker blue blouse, her worn jogging shoes, and dark sunglasses. All very unobtrusive. It wouldn't be the end of the world if she was recognized, but she'd have a lot of explaining to do. Mostly to Feds.

It would be better all around if he never found out about this. And, she hoped, she wouldn't always need it.

She hailed a taxi and gave the driver an address.

Half an hour later she was on the line at Shooter's Alley, a public firing range. Penny used a house gun. She didn't own or want a gun, and using a rental precluded Sullivan Act violations and crossing state lines and sundry other problems a gun could cause.

What surprised her about the firing range, and the nine-millimeter Walther semiautomatic that she used, was that she loved to shoot. The bullets went into a paper target on which was the outline of a man. Life-sized, from the waist up. He had broad shoulders and an oval face without features.

She could imagine the man to be whomever she chose. Usually it was the man who'd killed her sister. Sometimes it was the killer Feds sought. Sometimes it was simply a stranger.

Penny wore earplugs, but she liked the heavy bark of the gun, the feel of it kicking in her hand.

When the electric winch brought the target back to her on its track, she enjoyed seeing that most of her shots had gone where she'd aimed. Usually it was the target's head. Sometimes the heart.

The experience was, as Noreen on the Internet had promised, stress relieving and liberating.

Not that she ever wanted to use the gun on someone, or even carry the bulky, oily thing in her purse.

But somehow it helped her to know that she could.

If she wanted to, she could.

59

Jody stood up so Sarah Benham would notice her on the other side of The Happy Noodle.

Sarah, smoothing back her hair and patting this and that into place after coming in out of the cooling summer breeze, saw her immediately and smiled and waved back. She began weaving among the tables of the crowded restaurant, holding a general direction toward Jody like a ship in a storm.

Jody sat back down with her apple martini and watched her. The two women met for lunch every now and then. Despite—or possibly because of—their age difference, they had become very comfortable in each other's company; each knew the other wasn't a competitor in either work or love.

Sarah was still attractive, for a woman past the edge of middle age. She took good care of herself, spent money on it. Jody had decided weeks ago that Sarah might well have employed the services of a cosmetic surgeon. There was a subtle stiffness to her features, and deepening lines running from the corners of her mouth to her chin.

"I ordered you a drink," Jody said, as Sarah sat down

on the chair across from her. "An apple martini. I hope you don't mind."

"It's what I would have ordered," Sarah said. "That's why I introduced them to you." She settled deeper in her chair, leaning briefly to rest her purse on the floor, then did a lot of fidgeting and rearranging, like a bird settling into its nest.

The server came with her drink. Sarah accepted it, then raised her glass. Jody followed suit.

"To good friends," Sarah said.

Jody smiled and repeated the toast. She took a sip of martini. There were a lot of people she'd choose *not* to lunch with before Sarah.

Sarah smiled and licked her lips. The way she always did after the first sip of any kind of drink. She seemed very much to enjoy the moment. Something Jody would have to work on.

"So how are things in your life?" Sarah asked, placing her glass on the table but leaving a fingertip touching it, as if she'd be aware if it started to wander.

"If you mean love life," Jody said, "I'm too busy for anything like that."

"It's been my experience," Sarah said, "that love lives pretty much take care of themselves, and in their own time. There isn't much to be gained by planning."

"Good. Because I don't."

The waiter returned and Jody ordered penne pasta and a salad, Sarah only a salad.

"Not hungry today," she said. "The heat."

Jody took a sip of her martini, which prompted Sarah to do the same.

"I never asked you about your family," Jody said. "Do you have—"

"Children?" Sarah grinned. "Not me, and not ever, at

my age. I suppose you're wondering if I ever married, whether I'm widowed or divorced."

"I don't want to pry," Jody assured her.

"Of course you do." Sarah touched the back of Jody's hand. "We all do, but we don't want to step on someone's feelings."

"Would I be doing that?"

"Not in the slightest, dear. Both my parents have been dead for years. My mother had a fatal heart attack while swimming. My father died a month after that. He was in an auto accident. A one-car crash. I've always wondered if he'd made it happen, if he was simply ready to go to a place without grief."

"You were left an orphan," Jody said sadly.

"For a few years. I was sixteen when I found myself without parents. Or siblings. I lived in an institution—it was never called an orphanage—for about two years, then I found a job that would allow me time to also go to college. I was good at math, and was drawn into the insurance business. Started out with mortgage insurance, then life and property for several years. Then I got a job offer and moved to Manhattan. I'm an adjuster, mainly. Mostly art."

"Art insurance. That's fascinating."

"Not really. Not once you get used to staring at damaged Van Goghs and Kandinskys and calculating their market worth. Which is sometimes much different from the worth placed on them by their owners."

"Still, you must know a lot about art."

"I know more about insurance, and how to adjust it. That's really what I'm doing, just like with insurance on cars or, in some questionable cases, life insurance. It's all about odds, and settling on a number."

"Lots of things seem to be about that. Life isn't much different from gambling."

"We can do something about the odds, though. See me if you ever come into possession of a damaged valuable painting or sculpture, and I'll show you what I mean."

"Someday when I'm rich."

The food arrived, and both women concentrated for a few minutes on arranging plates and passing this or that across the table to each other.

"You have the capacity to become rich, Jody. I really believe that."

"I've been told so, often enough," Jody said.

Sarah was obviously very interested in Jody's future.

And Jody was interested in Sarah's past. Had Sarah been trying to sell Jack Coil art insurance that time she'd visited the offices of Enders and Coil?

Jody wondered, did Sarah also sell insurance on property development projects?

60

S herri Klinger said, "I've been thinking."

They were sitting in Rory's mom's Chevy with all the windows rolled down, letting the summer breeze wend its way through the car's interior. The Chevy was parked well off the road and shielded from view by large pine trees. The woods they faced were beginning to fill with twilight's shadows. Rory picked up the scent of tobacco smoke. His mom had been smoking again, even though she swore she quit months ago.

"We didn't come here to think," he said.

"Yeah." Sherri smiled. "We took care of that other thing, though."

"You're not gonna tell me you forgot your pill, are you?"

"Of course not."

"So what's your famous brain been working on?"

"Now that you're finished with my famous body."

"Not finished. It's just time out."

"God, Rory!"

He settled back where he was sitting behind the steering wheel, aware that he was already getting an erection just talking about sex with Sherri. And it had been . . . what, twenty minutes since the last time?

"I've been thinking about Duffy," she said, leaning her head against the point of his shoulder.

Rory's erection was immediately lost. "Not much to think about now," he said. He hoped. Sherri was a brilliant girl, but she seemed fixated on the dog. What was she going to suggest, a Duffy memorial?

Sherri snuggled closer. The breeze working through the car was cooling. "I mean, like the way his collar was discovered about a hundred feet from where somebody buried him. It was unbuckled, so he couldn't have slipped it before he died. Somebody must have taken it there. Or thrown it. How could that have happened? And why?"

"Maybe he laid there a while before somebody found him, then they took the collar off before scooping dirt and leaves over him."

"But why?"

"I don't know. Or it could be a fox or something dug Duffy up and moved the collar."

"A fox couldn't unbuckle the collar, and there were no tooth or claw marks on it. Somebody must have removed it either before or after Duffy was put in the ground the first time."

"Why would anyone do that?"

"I've been racking my brain trying to figure that one out. It was like they didn't want Duffy to be identified if he was found."

"But he was identified."

"A little longer underground and we wouldn't have known him. I think whoever killed him got scared, hid the body, and threw the collar far as he could into the woods thinking nobody would ever find it even if they *did* find Duffy."

Rory found himself squirming. He coughed to disguise his reaction to Sherri's words. She had it figured exactly right.

"Either way," he said, "the result is the same."

"But I remember the way Duffy's head was flattened on one side."

"God, Sherri—he was hit by a car."

"But maybe only injured, and whoever hit him finished him off."

"Why?"

"They didn't want to go to all the trouble of dealing with a hurt dog. It might bite them. And they wouldn't want it bleeding all over their car if they tried to pick it up and take it to a vet. It would be simpler just to get rid of the dog and drive away."

"You're saying they had a kind heart, or they would have just driven on and left Duffy injured and dying on the road. Instead, they put the poor animal out of its misery."

"I'm saying whoever ran over Duffy and hurt him might have then gone ahead and murdered him."

Rory faked a strangled kind of laugh. "You really think anyone would go to that kinda trouble over a dog?" He knew immediately the words were a mistake. He understood how Sherri's mind worked. She'd ask herself why indeed someone would take that kind of trouble. The possible answers would include that they might know Sherri and fear she'd blame them for killing her dog. The next step in her logical process might lead her straight to Rory. "Whatever happened," he said, "Duffy's dead and you have to put the whole thing behind you."

"I can't. It isn't Duffy's death I keep thinking about; it's like death in general. About how in this amount or that amount of years one or both of us, and most of the people we know, will be gone forever." She looked up at him. "Do you ever really think about forever, Rory?"

"All the time."

"Don't laugh at me."

"I'm not, Sherri, believe me!"

She moved away from him, rooted through her purse, and fished out a small brown vial with a pop-off white plastic cap. Rory saw a prescription form stuck to the bottle.

"These help me. You know they can help you."

"Yeah. We've gone through this before, with the pills. I almost wrecked the car. This time it's no thanks."

Sherri held the vial up and read the label: " 'Lorazepam.' The only way I can get to sleep now is by taking one of these, or by sneaking some of my dad's scotch. But the whiskey doesn't work as well. When I drink it I can fall asleep, but I can't stay that way."

"I know how that works," Rory said.

Sherri smiled. "My mom'd never dream I took these and have been using them."

"Didn't she ask you about them?"

"Just if I knew where they were. I said no, and reminded her how she misplaces things. She had a lousy night's sleep and then had the doctor call in a new prescription."

"They're easy to fool, aren't they," Rory said. "Doctors and mothers."

"Too."

She opened the vial and shook a small white pill into her hand and held it out to Rory. "Take one. You'll like the way this works. It like makes you stop worrying instead of making you sleepy. Then if you want, you can go to sleep on your own."

"I don't want to go to sleep."

"I just told you they don't make you tired, just re-laxed."

"I'm relaxed enough."

"You don't seem like it." She popped the pill into her mouth and swallowed it, as if she was used to taking pills without water.

"I know how I can get more relaxed," Rory said.

"Forget that."

He sighed. He knew she was thinking about what had really happened to the dog. She'd never let it alone. That was the way her mind worked. He knew that because his mind worked the same way.

They'd professed their love to each other. Why couldn't she look ahead instead of backward? Was this how life worked? Dragging around the past like chains that made you raw and tired and eventually brought you down.

Rory was a realist. He understood that when Sherri figured out what had really happened to her dog, that Rory had lied to her, and that he'd even used the dog's death to help him to seduce her, what they had together would be gone.

It was enough to make a person squirm. Lying to friends was one thing, but lying to someone you loved was different. Those were the lies that became chains.

Do you really think about forever? Sherri had asked him.

All the time.

61

"**I**'m used to him now, because I know he's not real."

"Used to him in what way?" Grace Moore asked her patient.

"It's almost like he came with the apartment," Linda said. "When I enter I catch a glimpse of him crossing in the hall from the bathroom to the bedroom. If I'm in the kitchen and can't see him, I know he's still back there. I suspect he hides under the bed."

"Have you ever looked?"

Linda stared at her. "Are you kidding?"

"You told me you know he's not real."

"But he could become real, and then where would I be?"

"If he wasn't real when he went under the bed," Grace said, "he wouldn't be real when he stared back at you if you bent down and looked to see if he was there."

Linda looked incredulous. "He could reach out and get me. Have me by the throat in half a second so I couldn't make a sound, then he'd do whatever he wanted to me. If you were me, would you take that kind of chance?"

Grace thought about it. "No," she admitted. She crossed her legs and sat back in her chair. "Does he ever talk to you?"

"No. Not him. Just the voices in the stone."

"If he could talk, what do you suppose he'd say?"

"You mean if he *would* talk."

"I suppose I do mean that," Grace said.

"He'd say, 'I'm here to torture and kill you.' "

"Why would you think he'd say that?"

"You know why. I'm a paranoid schizophrenic. And besides that, I'm his type."

"Oh?"

"I keep up with the news, all the stuff about the serial killer, Daniel. I look like the women he's killed. Same size and build. You know, with big boobs. Same brown eyes and brown hair." She decided not to tell Dr. Moore yet about meeting with someone who might believe her, might help her.

Grace smiled. "Linda, if I didn't dye my hair blond, I'd look like that. Well, maybe not so much in the boobs department, but I have brown hair and brown eyes. Like millions of women in New York. Why do you think that killer would settle on you?"

"He's in *my* apartment."

Grace tilted her head and nodded. The logic of the irrational was difficult to refute. "Have you tried talking to him?"

"Yes. He doesn't answer, only smiles or shrugs and goes someplace where I can't see him."

"You mean disappears?"

"Of course not. He simply walks into another room."

Grace regarded Linda for a long moment. "Do you think he'll be there when you leave here and go home?"

"He almost always is, after a session."

Grace smiled. "You have him trained."

"Or he has me trained. Same difference. He's my—"

"Your what?"

"My fate."

Grace shook her head. "Oh, Linda, that isn't so. You have control of your own life."

"Then what am I doing here?"

"Getting the help you need. Our sessions, your medications. Have you been taking your meds as prescribed?"

"Of course. He stands somewhere behind me and watches in the mirror as I take each pill."

"Hmm. I have an idea, Linda. You say he's almost always in your apartment when you come home from these sessions. How about if I go home with you and meet this man?"

"You mean after one of our sessions?"

Linda was going to be elusive now and protect her hallucination. Not uncommon. "I mean after this session."

"I doubt if he'll talk to you."

"Does he know about me?" Grace wanted a chance to examine Linda's medicine cabinet and see which pills and how many were in her prescription vials. Linda was displaying symptoms that her medications should be alleviating.

"Oh, he knows," Linda said. "He's followed me here. I watched him once hanging back behind me in the elevator and watching to see which door I entered."

"You mean my door, to my office?"

"Right. He stood down the hall a way and watched."

"Then he and I really should talk."

"You'll be doing most of the talking," Linda said. "But if that's the way you feel about it, okay."

Grace was slightly surprised by Linda's acquiescence. And pleased. It might mean she was ready to face up to what, on a basic level, she knew wasn't actually real. This might lead to what the TV psychoanalysts called a break-through. She looked at her watch. Ten minutes to eleven.

"I don't have another appointment until two o'clock," she said, standing up from her chair. She smiled reassuringly at Linda. "Let's go."

Linda braced herself with both hands on her chair arms, levered herself to her feet, and smiled back.

"Just sit for a minute in the anteroom while I shut things down here in the office, and I'll be right with you."

Linda went out and settled into a comfortable chair, and the doctor didn't take long at all.

Linda led the way out of the office and down the hall to the elevator. Already she was acting as the hostess, and would in subtle ways be in charge of this visit.

Dr. Moore considered that a good thing.

"If you don't mind," Dr. Moore said, "I'd like to drop by my apartment first and get out of these high heels; I've got a blister and they're killing me."

"I hear you on that one," Linda said.

"There are two messages for you," Pearl said, when Quinn returned to the office from lunch. "Both from women who think someone's following them."

"We've had more than a few calls like that," Quinn said.

"Since the media have made you the big hero and serial killer hunter."

Quinn made a sound somewhere between a snort and a laugh.

He ambled over and lowered his large self into his desk chair hard enough to make the cushion hiss. Pearl wondered if he'd been "lunching" with Jerry Lido. "Either of these calls sound like the real thing?" he asked, already sure of the answer.

Pearl shrugged. "One didn't make much sense, or maybe I couldn't understand the caller because of her accent. The other seemed okay at first, then she asked that no one contact her doctor to let her know she'd called."

"She say what kind of doctor?"

"She didn't have to."

Quinn punched a button on his desk phone and listened to both messages. The first was in a high-pitched voice speaking in what sounded like some kind of middle European accent he couldn't begin to understand.

The second caller was understandable, a woman speaking with what sounded like deliberate and fragile calm, explaining how the same man had been following her, how sometimes he let himself into her apartment. She then said that she didn't want her doctor to know yet that she was going outside the rules, calling someone who might believe and help her. Her doctor, the woman said, didn't think the man was real. Then she explained that it was true that he wasn't real all the time, but only sometimes.

Neither woman left a name, but the voice of one was familiar.

Quinn sat for a moment mulling over the calls. He'd received dozens like them over the past several weeks. There was something about the second woman, something in her voice that signaled real if sublime fear. Perhaps she had mental problems, but that didn't mean she couldn't be a potential victim.

And the woman with the accent? How could he judge if he couldn't understand her?

He looked at caller ID. The first number was that of a large insurance firm with a Midtown office. He called there and talked to three people who had no idea of the identity of a woman with a heavy European accent who might be trying to contact him.

The second number displayed no name but had a Manhattan prefix. He called it and got no answer and no invitation to leave a message.

After hanging up, Quinn stared at the phone, then dug through the note papers beneath a paperweight on his desk. The second caller's number was that of Linda Brooks, with a West Side address.

Linda Brooks, the woman who'd approached him in the office because she thought someone might be following her. The one who was under analysis.

She'd also left her doctor's name and address.

Quinn jotted down the information on a piece of scratch paper and tucked it into his wallet with similar folded slips of paper.

He wasn't quite sure why, considering how many women like Linda Brooks there were in the city. Seldom were their monsters real.

Real enough to them, however. He felt a pang of pity for Linda Brooks. Started to reach again for the phone.

But she hadn't wanted him to call her analyst. About that she'd been specific.

Yet she wouldn't answer her phone. And who was to say she needed more help than the woman with the European accent who'd called? Or any of the other troubled and frightened women, most of whom weren't in any actual danger?

Quinn wished he could help them all, the fearful and delusional, but he couldn't except in general ways. Like trying to stop a very real killer.

He turned his mind to his job.

62

It had taken only fifteen minutes for Dr. Grace Moore and Linda to cab from Grace's apartment to Linda's. Grace had changed into more comfortable shoes, and left the thumb drive video of her session with Linda with her other home files.

The phone was ringing inside Linda's apartment, but it stopped just as the two women got to the door.

"Do you have an answering machine?" Grace asked.

"Not anymore. It talked to me sometimes when it shouldn't have."

Linda unlocked and opened the door but stood back, allowing Dr. Moore to enter first. Grace did just that, smoothly and confidently. She took in the apartment with a glance: neat, neutral furniture that was carefully arranged, a small flat-screen TV resting on what looked like an antique table, hardwood floors that were scratched and dented but glossy with a recent coat of wax, a bookcase stuffed with books and stacks of magazines (so Linda was a reader), and a window with half-lowered white blinds. A lineup of small, potted geraniums spanned the marble sill.

"I bought those yesterday," Linda explained, noticing

the geraniums had caught Grace's attention. "Now no-body can climb in through the windows without disturb-ing my flowerpots."

Grace simply nodded, thinking the flowerpots didn't provide much security.

Linda was only halfway into the apartment, as if she was still considering staying out in the hall. Grace gripped her gently but firmly by the arm and guided her the rest of the way in. She could feel tremors running through Linda's body.

"Why are you so nervous? You're home. I'm here."

"And *he's* here," Linda said.

"The reason I'm here," Grace said, "is to demonstrate to you that he isn't."

"Hah!"

"So how does he get in?"

"Obviously, he has a key."

Grace almost smiled. "Tell me, Linda, is this person part of the secret government organization you men-tioned during our last session?"

"Oh, no. He's on his own. I'd know it if he was with the government."

"How?"

"He'd be dressed differently, for one."

"Like the government agents you see on TV or at the movies?"

"I don't go to the movies very often. That stuff isn't real." A click and a low, soft humming made Linda's body jerk.

"That's only the refrigerator," Grace told her.

"So maybe he's getting something from it. A glass of milk."

"Has he done that before?"

"Of course. He's left the glass out where I could see it, with just a little milk left in it. I know why he does stuff like that, so it creeps me out. He wants me to hope he goes ahead and does whatever he's planning, wants me to give up and put my fate in his hands. Work with him."

Grace raised her eyebrows. "Work *with* him?"

"You know what I mean."

Grace did. Linda was referring to the theory that victim and killer sometimes fell into a mutual rhythm and cooperation. The killer wanted his prey. The victim wanted the terror and anxiety finally to end. In a sick sense, their goals became the same.

"Is it possible that it was a glass of milk you drank and then forgot about?" Grace asked.

"Possible? Sure."

The apartment was silent except for the refrigerator's soft hum. The air was warm and still. Grace walked to the doorway leading to the small galley kitchen and stood staring while Linda watched.

"Nobody in there," Grace said. "No empty glass."

More geraniums in green plastic pots, though, lining the windowsill. Some of them still had price tags on them.

"I didn't say for sure he was there," Linda pointed out.

Grace turned so she was facing her patient directly and made eye contact. "What do you think he wants, Linda?"

"To do the most awful things to me."

"Have you been reading the papers about those women who were killed?"

"Now and then. And I see things on television." She didn't tell Dr. Moore about her conversation with the detective, Quinn, who was hunting the killer. He seemed, if not to believe her, not to totally *dis*believe her.

"Television can stimulate your imagination," Dr. Moore said. "Especially if you haven't taken your meds."

"It's difficult to remember to take them," Linda said. "And he comes when I'm not here and moves things around. Sometimes I have to hunt and search for my meds."

"Do you want me to look through the apartment while I'm here to convince you we're here by ourselves?"

"I wouldn't ask you to do that."

"But if I did it, would you be convinced?"

"I suppose so, but—"

"There aren't that many places he could hide. It will only take a few minutes. Do you want to come with me?"

"No. And I'd rather you didn't go looking for him."

"When you think he's here like this, do you ever simply leave?"

"Of course I do. He just follows me. Sometimes he's already waiting for me when I arrive wherever it is I go."

This interested Grace. Hallucinations weren't uncommon in schizophrenia. Linda had reported them before.

"How is that possible, Linda?"

Linda shrugged and gave Grace a look that suggested the answer was obvious. "He understands me so well he knows most of the places where I go." A glitter of fear played in her eyes. "How would you like to live with something like that?"

"Sometimes," Grace said, "it helps to face your problem squarely and it won't seem so intimidating." She began moving toward the hall leading to the rear of the apartment.

"I wouldn't go there," Linda said, starting to follow her. Three steps and a pause.

"There's no need to come with me," Grace said. "I'll look every place anyone could possibly hide, then I'll call for you." She walked a few feet down the hall and glanced into the bathroom. The plastic shower curtain was closed. She went to it without hesitation and yanked it open.

"The drip isn't in here," she said, and heard Linda, who'd been peeking around the door frame, laugh.

Grace didn't like the tone of that laugh. She moved farther down the hall toward the bedroom. Linda, who was torn between keeping a safe distance and not being left alone, was hanging back and looked frightened.

"He isn't in there," Grace said, when she was at the bedroom's open door.

"He is. I can feel it."

"The room feels *un*occupied to me," Grace said. She entered the bedroom without hesitation. She smiled as she saw the familiar geranium sentries on the windowsill. Beyond them the window was open a few inches, letting in a subtle breeze.

Linda had made it to the doorway and was staring into the bedroom, her eyes wide, her fists clutched tightly at her sides.

"Did you open the window?" Grace asked.

"Of course I did."

Grace looked on the far side of the old walnut wardrobe; she even opened the twin doors and looked inside. The wardrobe's interior contained nothing but clothes on hangers. It emanated a clean, cedar scent.

"Nobody's here," she said reassuringly, glancing over at Linda.

She went to the closed closet door.

"Don't—" she heard Linda say.

Sure. They're always hiding in the closet.

Grace yanked the door open.

There was a sagging wooden rod supporting more hangered clothes. Above them on the closet shelf were cardboard shoeboxes and a stack of self-help books. Seeing that she had Linda's full attention, Grace stuck her arm into the darkness between the clothes so she could feel around behind them in the depths of the closet, where she couldn't see.

Her fingertips found only roughly plastered wall.

She closed the closet door and, smiling, moved toward Linda. "No lurking monsters anywhere," she said. "Now let's have a look in your medicine cabinet and make an inventory of what it is you've been taking."

"It's what you prescribed."

"I'm sure. But I'm wondering about over-the-counter drugs. You take them sometimes, too, don't you?"

"Sometimes," Linda admitted. "To help me sleep."

Grace took a step toward the door.

Linda hadn't moved. "You didn't look under the bed."

"True enough," Grace said.

She went to the bed, got down on her knees, and bent forward, making a show of it for Linda. She lifted the bedspread and peered into the dimness beneath the bed.

A pair of eyes stared back at her

63

It was three o'clock in the morning, already hot in a way that made the Lincoln's windshield fog up on the inside. Renz was still at this crime scene. He'd phoned from there and given Quinn the cross streets, and remained there, waiting.

The scene was easy enough to find. Three radio cars and a CSU van were nosed in toward the curb. An unmarked blue Chevy that Quinn was sure was NYPD was parked with one tire up on the sidewalk.

A uniformed cop was stationed like a stern doorman at the building's entrance. He directed Quinn and Pearl to an apartment on the fifth floor. The cop said it belonged to L. Brooks, which caused Quinn to stop so abruptly that the soles of his clunky black shoes made a slight squeaking sound.

A simple first initial was common among women who lived alone and didn't want to display their gender on their mailbox.

"Linda Brooks?" he asked the uniform.

"Couldn't tell you, sir."

Quinn continued into the small lobby, Pearl at his heels. "Isn't that the woman who phoned earlier?"

He nodded.

"Don't blame yourself for this one," Pearl said, thinking ahead. She knew how Quinn would feel about this. The Brooks woman had called him yesterday and asked for help, protection, and Quinn the great protector had put her down as another nutcase or publicity junkie.

"I blame the bastard who did it," he said in a low, flat voice.

The apartment door was propped open with what looked like an umbrella stand. There was a certain smell wafting out into the hall, one Quinn and Pearl recognized. Death had visited here, and not long before they'd come calling.

Renz and the CSU techs were inside. Quinn and Pearl entered, careful not to get in anyone's way.

The living room was a busy place. The techs were in there, moving in their usual choreographed fashion. They barely missed bumping into each other. A flicker of brilliance like miniature lightning illuminated the walls along a narrow hallway. Quinn knew it was a camera flash.

"The police photographer and Nift are back there with them," Renz explained.

"Them?"

Renz ignored the question. "The killer called the *Times*, and had the paper call me. The guy at the *Times* said the killer told him he might make me a leather product like he made for you."

"He knew about the victims' breasts being removed?"

"That so-called secret information meant he was the real thing. That's how he got through to me instead of being brushed off as a head case."

"You get a voice print or phone trace?" Quinn asked.

"A voice print, yeah. But he musta made the call with one of those cheap-ass throwaway phones. I listened to a recording. The voice was normal, and so was his phrasing, like he had some education. Even apologized for waking me up. He knew about the tits being cut off. I asked him how he knew, and he told me. I asked him, 'Did you cut off the tits this time?' He said yeah, he did it to one of them.

"*One of them.* When I got here as he advised me—as if I wouldn't have come anyway—I saw what he meant."

Another flash from down the hall.

"Whaddya mean, 'what he meant'?"

"C'mon," Renz said. "I'll show you."

He started leading the way to the back of the apartment, then stopped and looked at Pearl. Then at Quinn.

"Jesus!" Pearl said. "I'm a cop. I've been to dozens of murder scenes. I'm not gonna faint or puke at the sight of a dead body."

"Nice of you to think of her, though," Quinn said to Renz. *Not acting like yourself at all.*

Renz gave his nasty fat man's smile. "I just don't want her upchucking all over the crime scene. Making a mess."

When they entered the bedroom, Pearl did feel a queasiness she hadn't expected. On the bed kneeled an almost nude dead woman in the usual hog-tied, bodybowed pose. Her wrists and ankles were wrapped and then tethered so that she was trapped in her awkward position, body arched, staring with unseeing eyes at the ceiling. She was gagged with a rectangle of gray duct tape. Her breasts had been removed. She looked afraid but not surprised.

Next to her lay another bound woman, this one flat on her back, her arms knotted by a rope to a belt cinched tightly around her waist. It was gray cloth and looked like a woman's belt. There was identically colored material showing in a jumble of clothes that looked as if they'd been tossed into a corner. Her ankles were tied. She'd been stabbed in the heart, and her throat had been slashed. There was surprisingly little blood, suggesting that the stab wound had been first and fatal. Near the stab wound, just above her sternum, her breasts lay spread and flaccid against her torso, still attached and apparently uninjured. As with the first woman, a rectangle of tape was plastered over her mouth.

The kneeling victim was wearing blue panties, and also appeared to have been stabbed in the heart.

Nift, who'd been poking at the hog-tied victim with something resembling a large dental pick, said, "Looks like he went for the best of the pair. This one"—he pointed at the prone woman—"has got considerably more years and mileage on her."

"They're not used cars," Pearl said through clenched teeth.

"They're pretty damn well used, though," Nift said, absently prodding the dead hog-tied woman with the steel instrument. She didn't object, as Pearl halfway expected she might.

The supine woman seemed to be staring at the ceiling with half closed eyes that had the stillness of marbles. Blue eyes. She had blond hair, but it was obviously dyed. She hadn't been bad looking but was nothing special.

The hog-tied woman next to her, festooned with the familiar knife nicks of violence, had dark eyes and genuinely dark hair, and appeared to have had large breasts.

"Have you guessed which one was Linda Brooks?" Renz asked.

"The one who looks like Pearl," Nift said, from where he knelt on the floor in a position suggesting he was about to do some gynecological examination.

Pearl started toward him, but Quinn held on to her elbow.

"Damn it, Quinn, that hurts. All I want to do is twist his head off."

Nift smiled. "By head I presume you mean—"

"Never mind that," Renz said.

"What about her panties?" Quinn asked.

"Same size as the last victim's," Nift said. He smiled. "That was the first thing I checked."

"I'll bet not," Renz said. He looked at Quinn. "How do you figure the second dead woman?"

"Offhand," Quinn said, "I'd say she happened to be at the wrong place at the wrong time."

"She probably knew the dead woman."

"Most likely," Quinn said. "A visiting friend."

"Maybe he didn't have to undress them," Nift said. "Maybe they were getting it on together and he interrupted them."

Pearl gave him a hard look. "Listen, you scumbag—"

Loud noises, raised voices out in the hall, made everyone in the apartment stop what he or she was doing.

Nift gave Pearl a superior little smile and stood poised and motionless with a stainless-steel implement in his right hand, like a figure in a wax museum. Part of the Famous Assholes exhibit.

There was more noise from outside, down in the street. A man's voice yelled something Quinn couldn't understand.

"What the hell's going on? Quinn asked.

"That would be a media wolfpack," Renz said, looking at his wristwatch. "The killer said he'd wait an hour so the *Times* could have its scoop, then he'd call the rest of the papers and television news."

"Did he say anything else?" Pearl asked.

"Only to give his best to you," Renz said.

It didn't take long to identify Linda Brooks's visitor. Her purse with identification and seventy-three dollars in it was found beneath the pile of clothes in the bedroom corner.

"A doctor," Quinn said.

"Not just any doctor," one of the CSU techs said. He handed a white business card to Quinn. "This was in one of the victim's desk drawers."

The card identified the dead woman as Dr. Grace Moore, psychiatrist and psychoanalyst.

A further examination of the desk, Linda Brooks's checkbook, and a nearby file cabinet, indicated that Dr. Grace Moore was treating Brooks, and had been for some time. There was a home file of rough and incomplete notes, but its contents, including documents signed by Grace Moore, described Brooks as a paranoid schizophrenic.

"That explains the pharmacy in the bathroom medicine cabinet," Renz said. "The lady lived on pills."

"I'll send Feds to Moore's office, see what else there is to see," Quinn said. "No need for a warrant. Doctor-patient confidentiality doesn't apply when both have been killed by the same madman."

Questionable legality. Quinn was glad Jody wasn't along on this one.

"Sounds right to me," Renz said. "But I didn't know you were gonna send somebody over there."

"Send somebody?" Quinn said. "Over where?"

Renz placed his hands over both ears and turned away.

PART THREE

And to die is different from what anyone
   supposed,
And luckier.

> —WALT WHITMAN,
>   "Song of Myself"

64

Time passed, and no one ever found out what really had happened to Duffy. Maybe there weren't enough clues. Or maybe it was because no one cared. No one other than Sherri, anyway.

The road repair was finished and looked much the same, only the trees began slightly farther from the gravel shoulder. Rory wasn't sure what drew him there, but sometimes, at night, he went alone to the spot near where he'd buried Duffy. Gotten away with murder, Sherri would say. If she knew.

He didn't like to admit it to himself, but maybe that was something he enjoyed, having gotten away with murder. Here on this desolate stretch of road, with its nearby concealing woods and very private clearing, was the perfect spot for it.

It was also the perfect spot for secret sex. Rory had often made use of it with Sherri, once he'd gotten her past her hesitation because Duffy had died nearby. *Mostly* past her hesitation, anyway. She still sometimes tried to talk him into parking elsewhere for their hurried trysts, and often he'd comply. But there was something special about this remote place beneath and among the trees, with only an occasional flicker of headlights from passing traffic as a reminder of the outside world. Things happened as usual out there. Not in here, to Sherri. Not to Rory.

Sex was definitely better here.

And so was quiet contemplation.

Rory wasn't the only one who appreciated this secluded area. Alone there one moonlit night, he'd parked the car out of sight among the trees, and was standing and smoking a cigarette, when he heard the sound of a car stopping on the gravel shoulder. He moved farther back into the woods and waited.

Tires crunched louder on gravel, and he saw the dark shape of a car with its lights out moving slowly to where it wouldn't be seen from the road.

Rory smiled. Somebody parking here to make out, probably. And Rory's car was parked where it couldn't be seen. Should he stay and watch? Was he a Peeping Tom as well as a dog slayer?

He saw the dark form of a slender man—or maybe a teenage boy—in jeans and a dark T-shirt—get out of the car, walk around to the back of the vehicle, and open the trunk.

He removed a nude, bound woman and laid her gently on the ground, then stood with his hands on his hips and glanced around. His gaze traveled smoothly past Rory, who was standing in shock, well concealed in the deep shadows.

Rory became aware that he was breathing heavily. He swallowed so loudly he was actually afraid the man might hear. Motionless, he watched transfixed, as if he were seeing a movie scene unfold.

The driver of the dark car had set to work. He bent over the dead or unconscious woman, untied her, then re-arranged her body, making sure that her legs were bound tightly with rope. Then he propped her in a kneeling posi-tion, looped rope around her elbows behind her back, and pressed her upper body backward so her spine was drawn like a bow and she was staring up at the stars where she might point an arrow. Her eyes were open wide, focused upward as if seeking some message of hope. So she wasn't dead. Even from this distance Rory saw her blink and move her head slightly. The man pressed something, some kind of tape, over her mouth and unreeled it and fastened it behind her head. Rory could barely hear her making desperate humming noises, trying to shake her head from side to side. But so tight was the tape and the tension of her bound body that she was barely able to move her head, and completely unable to move anything else other than her fingers, which writhed and flexed in search of any sort of tactile contact. She was seeking any-thing that she could touch, grip, hold on to. But nothing was within reach.

Rory's heart was pounding and his mouth was dry, and he couldn't stop watching. He knew he should yell, or go get the cops, or do anything that might help this young woman. It wasn't going to happen.

He could see that she was attractive, with bountiful breasts and long black hair. Dark eyes fixed in an expres-sion of sheer horror. Her frantic attempts to move caused her breasts to jiggle slightly, which seemed to amuse the man, because he briefly cupped one in his hand and pinched the nipple. The frightened humming grew slightly louder. Rory was aware that he had an erection. He had to do *something*. But he couldn't budge. He was as immobilized as the woman in the clearing. Even if he wanted to take some sort of action, he knew his limbs wouldn't respond.

He couldn't stop watching.

Not even when a knife glinted in the moonlight and there was little doubt about what was going to happen.

The man squatted beside the woman. He was wearing a cap with a bill, and Rory couldn't make out his features, but he was smiling as he held the blade so it glinted in the moonlight before the woman's face. No part of her moved other than her horrified eyes, which rolled wildly.

He began using the knife with delicate skill, making tiny, twisting cuts. The humming changed little in volume but was more desperate and slightly higher pitched, almost a monotone that yet expressed what must be going on in the helpless and doomed woman's mind.

Rory's own body was almost vibrating.

He couldn't stop watching.

The man with the knife began to work on the woman with intensity. Rory's hand moved to his crotch. *He couldn't stop watching.* This was wrong, he knew, and he'd never be able to tell anyone about it. He'd be some kind of accomplice if he did. He knew that all he had to do was remain silent and unmoving, and he'd see everything. Probably even the man burying the woman not far from where Rory had buried Duffy.

The all-encompassing power of the killer was stunning. Watching him was like watching God at work. Who wouldn't kill to exercise such power? Who wouldn't idolize such a creature?

Even the woman in the clearing—especially the woman in the clearing—must in her terror submit to and pray to the ultimate power of life and death, at the point when death would become a gift.

The humming grew more desperate and the woman's body shimmied with pain in the moonlight. Almost like an engine racing and vibrating toward an explosion. The man shifted position slightly, then crooked his elbow and turned the knife blade sideways. He began to remove the woman's breasts. Rory didn't blink, couldn't swallow, couldn't move.

He couldn't stop watching.

65

Jerry Lido said, "We've got a problem."

Quinn and Pearl were in the office with him. They stopped what they were doing at their desks and looked at him.

"Someone's been here," he said.

Quinn glanced around as if to find what Lido was talking about.

"Not *here*," Lido said. "But *here virtually*. Our virtual here."

"On our computers?" Pearl asked.

"Of course." For Lido the virtual world of computers *was* the real world. Then there was Lido's world where other people lived. And his world when he was drinking.

"My computer's been acting a little funky," Pearl said, wondering how Lido kept it all straight.

He grinned at her. "Exactly! We've been hacked. In fact, we're in the process of being hacked right now."

Helen the profiler entered the office, looking tall and lean as a fashion model, only a little too muscular. As usual, there was a fine sheen of perspiration on whatever bare flesh showed, as if she'd been working out. She'd caught the tail end of the conversation. "Somebody wants to know what's on our computers," she said.

"Somebody knows," Lido corrected her. He explained to her about having been hacked.

"Can you find out who he was?"

"Is," Lido said. "And that's what I've been trying to do the last two hours. He's put up Chinese walls, firewalls, indestructible walls. Our computerized information is going only one way—out."

"He's toying with you," Helen said.

Pearl immediately started to close down her computer.

"Better unplug it, too," Lido said.

She did. Quinn and Helen went around unplugging the other desk computers.

"You think he could turn them back on if they were plugged in?" Helen asked.

Lido grinned. "He might have installed the software to do that without us knowing about it. He might be online here at two in the morning, for all we know."

"If he can do that kind of thing to us," Quinn said, "can we do it to him?" Like Quinn to go on the offensive.

"If we knew about him what he knows about us, yes," Lido said. He stood up from his darkened computer screen.

"Where you going?" Pearl asked.

"Home, where I don't have to work using this limited equipment."

"I thought you installed new memory in our computers," Quinn said.

Lido gave him a pitying look.

"Doesn't Q and A have virus protection and firewalls and Chinese walls and all that stuff?" Helen asked.

Lido's expression turned to one of contempt. Not for Helen, but for whoever had trespassed in his world and made his skills seem minor. "The hacker got in somehow, then deleted all possible links, so a trace, even by an expert like me, is impossible. Supposedly." He snatched up a few items from his desk and then stalked out.

"His alcohol-tainted blood is up," Helen said.

"I wouldn't bet against him learning everything about this hacker," Quinn said.

Helen went to the desk Lido had just vacated and perched on the edge. Quinn couldn't help noticing her legs could use a shave. "Think about this," she said. "The hacker might have been secretly browsing your computers for information for a long time."

"He probably has been," Quinn said. "But Lido inevitably caught up with him."

Helen gave him her thinnest of smiles. "That's one way of looking at it. Another is to figure that if the hacker had the skills to hack into your system without being noticed, then circumvent your high-tech security and learn what you were doing, wouldn't he also have the skills to withdraw unnoticed?"

"Probably," Quinn said. "But that would mean—"

Helen's smile widened. "That the intruder wants you to know your computers have been hacked."

At two minutes to midnight Lido called Quinn's cell phone and woke him up. His words were slurred, and it took him a while to arrange his sentences with enough order for Quinn to understand that whatever precautions the mystery hacker had employed, they had worked. Lido gave Quinn a lot of tech talk he wouldn't have understood even if Lido was sober and speaking clearly. The message was, there was no way to backtrack the hacker's online footprints to the source.

Quinn lay awake in the dark for a long time after the phone call, wondering who would have the ability to out-fox Lido on a computer.

Every possibility he came up with was a worry.

66

After an uneasy night of patchwork dreams, Quinn was eating a late breakfast with Pearl in the brownstone's kitchen. Waffles and sausage patties, all pre-prepared, and the finished issue of toaster and microwave. Pearl's idea of cooking. It didn't smell bad, though. The faint haze suspended in the warm kitchen was pungent and conducive to the appetite. But it didn't fool Quinn or Jody. They'd been tricked before.

Jody had already left, explaining that she wasn't hungry and would stop on the way to her job at Enders and Coil for a bagel. Smart young woman, Quinn thought, not unlike her mother.

He wondered if, when he left the brownstone, he'd smell like waffles and sausage. And if so, for how long?

Quinn's cell phone played a cavalry charge trumpet tune and he dug it out of his pocket to see who was calling. Nift at the morgue. Quinn swallowed what he suspected would be his last bite of sausage and pressed the talk button.

"Mornin', Nift. Whaddya got?"

The annoying little M.E. didn't bother saying hello. "You talking with your mouth full, Quinn?"

"None of your business."

"I was you, I know what it would be full of," Nift said. Quinn could somehow hear the nasty grin on the little bastard's face.

"This a business call?" Quinn asked, with a hint of warning.

A hint was enough to scare Nift into a strictly business mode. "Linda Brooks died from a heart attack, no doubt caused by shock. Like the other victims when the killer played his games with them. By the time he got around to administering the *coup de grâce*, she was already dead."

"I hope that was a disappointment to him."

"No doubt it was. But he worked clean as usual. No usable prints, no DNA traces. Not even indefinite ones like with Macy Collins."

Quinn had never had much hope for the meager Collins sample that might have been mostly her own blood.

"There was a slight residue of condom lubricant in the vagina," Nift said. "The murder weapon was probably the same knife. Also used to remove Linda's substantial knockers. No sign of those, by the way."

"What about Grace Moore?"

"Probably not enough of a rack to interest our killer. He's definitely a breast man with high standards."

"At least she wasn't mutilated," Quinn said. He looked across the table and saw Pearl watching him intensely, interested in his end of the conversation.

"My guess is her death was comparatively easy," Nift said. "A quick choke to silence her, then a single, accurate stab wound to the heart. I think she was simply in the way. Unlucky in the extreme."

"Torture wounds have any commonality with the other victims?"

"You saw them. They almost had to have been the result of the same knife, the same killer. And they resemble morgue photos of Daniel Danielle's work so many years ago. He loves to carve."

"Yet he left Grace Moore untouched in that regard."

"She wasn't in his plans," Nift said. "I can understand that."

My God, so can I, Quinn thought. *What's it doing to me, getting into the heads of these sickos? Hunter thinking like prey, a part of him living inside their skulls. The killer is doing that with his potential victims. It's part of his game. But I'm not playing a game. Am I?*

"Speaking of commonalities," Nift said, "the panties on Linda Brooks were the same size and brand as the previous victim's. We even found a pubic hair for analysis that confirms the fact they were hers. Also, elastic marks, the lay of the material, looks like he temporarily untied the victim's legs and did the panty exchange postmortem, but before rigor mortis set in."

Quinn couldn't help imagining the killer maneuvering dead limbs into various positions to work off and on the panties. A complicated task, but it might be a chore he for some reason immensely enjoyed. One he was compelled to do as an exercise in total control. Quinn's stomach did a loop.

Pearl was giving him her narrowed eye look. "You okay?"

"Yeah."

"What?" Nift asked on the phone.

"Anything else we might deem important?" Quinn asked.

"No. Let me know if you happen to find the boobs. And say hello to Pearl."

Quinn flipped the phone shut without replying.

"Nift?" Pearl asked.

"Yeah."

"Want some more sausage?"

"No."

Jody stopped for a bagel at a Starbucks near Enders and Coil. She'd often had lunch with Sarah Benham, but this was their first breakfast. The two women had become even closer friends, though Sarah was still something of an enigma to Jody.

They were at a table near the back. Sarah had a cinnamon scone, Jody a toasted everything bagel with cream cheese and strawberry jam. Both had tall lattes. Jody couldn't help thinking how much better this was than her mother's toasted frozen waffles and microwaved sausages.

"So how's your mom doing on the Daniel Danielle investigation?" Sarah asked, and took a cautious sip of her steaming latte.

The question caught Jody off guard. "I'm surprised you're interested?"

"Why?"

"You never seemed interested before."

"The killer's apparently branching out," Sarah said. "He killed two women this time, according to the news. I was just wondering what that might mean."

"We didn't have time to talk about it this morning."

"I thought you were intrigued by your mom's work."

"I am." Jody took a bite of bagel and chewed.

Sarah smiled. "But you'd still rather be an attorney than a cop."

"As of now, yes."

"That doesn't sound like a very strong commitment."

"It's not."

Both women sipped their lattes, thinking about the answer that had popped out.

Jody, not committed?

"Something about Enders and Coil?" Sarah asked.

"About one of their cases. A woman refusing to move out of her apartment so the client, a big development company, can tear down her building."

"Sounds like the plot of a movie."

"Or a novel."

"Why do they want to tear down the apartment building?"

"They want the entire block for some big project. Office buildings, condos . . . they have no moral—or possibly legal—right to just plow this poor woman under."

"What about eminent domain?"

"It's not that simple," Jody said. "Believe me."

"Lots of times, when you've finally finished thinking things through, they *are* simple. That's when you make up your mind."

Jody laughed. "I'm not there yet."

Sarah looked at her more seriously. "How important to you is this woman's plight?"

"Very."

"But why? Do you know her?"

"I feel that I do."

Sarah frowned. "Does anyone at Enders and Coil know how you feel?"

"To a degree."

"I think you should give this a lot of thought before siding with a woman who's going to have to move out one way or the other. You might be risking your career, your future."

"How do you know she'll have to move?"

Sarah shook her head, her expression sad. "They always do, in these kinds of cases. It's in almost everyone's best interest."

"Everyone's but hers."

"There's no denying that. But maybe they'll offer her a large settlement to agree to move."

"They've done that and she's refused.

"Did she say why?"

"No. But it isn't about money."

"What money can't do, maybe more money can. Or some other kind of persuasion."

"What makes you think so?"

Sarah leaned closer across the fake marble table. Steam from the lattes rose as if the two women were engaged in some sort of alchemy. "I know someone who has a connection at the developer, Jody. I can't recommend strongly enough that you disassociate yourself from this case, and this woman's hopeless cause."

Jody was surprised, but she realized she shouldn't be. She actually didn't know much about Sarah Benham. "You know something Enders and Coil doesn't?"

"Probably." Sarah studied Jody and then shook her head. "You know I *can't* tell you, Jody. It would be betraying the confidence of a friend. I wouldn't betray *our* confidences that way."

Jody sampled her latte and still found it too hot to sip. "See?" she said.

"See what?"

"It really isn't that simple."

Fifteen minutes later Sarah left the coffee shop first.

Through the window displaying pastry, Jody watched her join a sunlit crowd of people massed on the sidewalk, waiting for the traffic light to flash a walk signal so they could cross the intersection. The signal appeared like a silent command. After an aggressive cab bullied its way through a right turn, Sarah disappeared in the flow of pedestrians.

Jody still had time to spare, so she opened her laptop. But she didn't tap into the coffee shop's Wi-Fi. Instead she inserted a thumb drive containing copies of Enders and Coil files and began rummaging through them. If someone from the firm, which was only a few blocks away, happened to enter the coffee shop and saw what she was doing, it would probably mean immediate dismissal. And less immediately, but just as likely, prosecution.

Well, life wasn't without risk.

Jody thought about Mildred Dash trapped and terrorized in her apartment, waging the good fight against an evil manifestation of capitalism, and pressed on.

She enjoyed the challenge and couldn't help becoming engrossed in what she was doing. She came across no actual evidence of criminality, but she was surprised to find e-mail exchanges with Waycliffe College. All the e-mails were encrypted, and she was unable to break the code. But she did notice that some of the messages bore Elaine Pratt's email address. That surprised her, and kept her at her task longer than she'd intended.

Futilely trying to decode the e-mails made her almost twenty minutes late when she arrived at Enders and Coil.

That didn't seem to matter, though, in light of more important events. Word had arrived that Mildred Dash had been terrorized by an intruder last night and had been found by a watchman early this morning in a coma. She was hospitalized and in intensive care.

Associate attorneys were dashing about or yammering on the phone. Jack Enders and Joseph Coil both appeared somber and determined, and totally in control. Jody had never before seen or been part of an event of such urgency at the firm.

She was assigned to continue calling the hospital and family to learn the seriousness of Mildred's condition. Meanwhile, litigators at Enders and Coil would be busy discussing the legal ramifications of razing her apartment building while her unit was unoccupied.

Here was opportunity, if they seized it.

Hours counted. Maybe minutes.

No one actually came right out and said it would be best if Mildred Dash died, but it was on the tips of a lot of tongues.

Jody was disgusted, but like everyone else at the firm, hanging in suspense. The mood was contagious and oddly, undeniably, pleasurable. She could see it on the faces of her coworkers. They loved being part of the drama.

Suddenly Jody wondered, was this what Sarah Benham had known about when she'd cautioned her at breakfast?

67

"**Y**ou're sure your mother thinks you went to visit your aunt in Milwaukee?" Rory asked Sherri.

"She saw me get on the Greyhound bus. What she didn't see was when it stopped to pick up more passengers, and let some off, down the road in Grantville. I got off along with some other people. Nobody noticed."

"So how'd you get back here?"

"Hitchhiked." She flashed him a wicked grin. "And you know why."

Rory did. His mother was out of town, in Milwaukee with a new boyfriend, and he and Sherri could make good use of her house. Rory simply had to be home now and then in the evening, so he could answer the phone if his mother called to check on him. And he would be home. With Sherri.

That was the plan.

They were standing now outside Rory's mother's Chevy, parked near where Duffy had died and been buried. Where that other girl—the one only Rory and the killer knew about—had been tortured, murdered, and then buried. It gave Rory a kind of chill when he walked holding hands with Sherri and stood kissing her over the dead girl's grave. It was a feeling he found he liked.

Sherri thought she was having that effect, and kissed him back hard, using her tongue.

Rory almost immediately had an erection. Beneath him was a closely kept secret only he and one other person knew. And the other person—the killer—thought only *he* knew what had happened here.

Rory remembered how the girl had been bound and gagged, staring straight up at nothing. The expression on her face when the killer began to do things—such small, delicate things at first—to her with the knife. The faint movements she made. Her quivering, unfeeling fingers. The pleading sounds emanating from her taped lips. The way her nude body vibrated near the end. Most of all, her eyes . . . her eyes . . .

What really got him was that she looked something like Sherri. Same type, anyway. Different hair, but definitely the same type.

". . . Take one," Sherri was saying. "They'll definitely make you feel good."

He looked down and saw that she was holding those same pills from her mother's medicine cabinet.

"I feel good already," Rory said. *If you only knew . . .*

"Don't be such a pussy," Sherri said, and pushed the vial of tablets toward him.

His manhood having been questioned, Rory shoved them away, causing several to spill out onto the ground.

Sherri punched his shoulder, a glancing blow, but it hurt. "Now look! You dickhead! You spilled them!"

She was angry with him. *How angry will she be when she figures out I killed her precious dog?* Rory knew she was smart. She *would* eventually find out about Duffy.

He bent down and began picking up the small white tablets, digging some of them out from beneath dead leaves.

"Get them all!" Sherri demanded.

When he had all or most of the dropped tablets in his cupped hand, Rory straightened up and threw them out toward the deeper woods.

"What the fuck, Rory?" She came at him in anger, batting at him, and the nail of her little finger scraped the corner of his left eye. The sharp pain enraged him.

He slapped her face hard, thinking about the girl beneath them in the earth, how she'd died. When she'd died. *How she'd died.*

When Sherri, stunned, bent over to spit out blood, Rory brought up his knee and drove it into her midsection. He caught her to break her fall.

He hadn't actually *planned* any of this. It was simply a sort of alternate sequence of things he could do. A work of imagination, really.

But damned if that imagined sequence hadn't begun. And he knew he would let it play out. It was like it was meant to be.

If it *wasn't* meant to be, why had he prepared for it without even thinking about it?

Maybe it had something to do with what he'd seen in the clearing, the god, and the girl in the ground.

Maybe he now had the secret knowledge and was acting on it. Nothing in this world really mattered compared to *this*.

The girl in the ground, she didn't matter anymore. All she was now was memory. Secret memory.

He went to the Chevy and opened the trunk, got the rope he'd brought, and the roll of thick electrician's tape.

It had only taken seconds, and Sherri was still curled on the ground, still struggling to catch her breath.

Rory stood over her, listening to her labored, gasping breathing, thinking about the dead girl. He bent down, lashed her ankles together, and cut the long end of the knotted rope with his pocket knife. Odd that he didn't recall taking the knife from his pocket and opening it. He maneuvered Sherri's body around on the leaves and tied her wrists tightly behind her back. *Hurts? Too bad.* He yanked her up and adjusted her body so she was kneeling, then ran a rope between the knotted ropes on her ankles and wrists. Thinking about the dead girl. He pulled that rope tight, bending back Sherri's body like the dead girl's had been. She'd almost recovered enough to scream, so he picked up the tape he'd gotten from the trunk, reeled off a long strip, and wrapped it firmly over her mouth, around to the back of her neck, thinking about the dead girl.

Rory used his knife to cut away Sherri's clothes. He watched her dark and desperate eyes, thinking about the dead girl. Then he straightened up and looked around. The moon was almost full, and there was plenty of light in the clearing. But no one around to see what he was doing. Not out here in this desolate part of town, on this remote road.

He moved around in front of Sherri and looked intently into her face, seeing the terror and incomprehension there. She stared back, pleading. He smiled, thinking about the dead girl.

He stood where she could see him wipe the knife's blade on the thigh of his jeans and then test its sharpness with his finger. He rolled her forward, onto her stomach, and began using the knife on her back as he'd seen the killer do to the dead girl. Sherri made the same horrified, muted noises the dead girl had made.

After a while, he put her back on her knees, her body

bowed in an almost impossible arch. Perhaps someone with a powerful telescope, on some distant star, could see the horrified expression in her staring eyes.

There must be someone out there in the cosmos who can help you.

Well, maybe not.

He began working again with the knife, keeping his thumb and forefinger low on the blade, the way the killer had done with the dead girl. The screams she made now were like the dead girl's had been, full throated but able to travel only as far as her taped mouth before changing to a frenetic low humming that barely escaped into the night.

He worked on her for quite a while there in the otherwise silent, isolated clearing, thinking about the dead girl. Her body began a frenetic bouncing and vibration, her bare breasts jiggling and heaving. This wasn't a surprise. Rory got comfortable and watched her eyes, watched them very carefully until all light and comprehension went out of them. Like the dead girl's eyes.

Then he used the knife to remove her breasts. It was easier than he'd imagined, no bone or gristle to cut, only soft flesh.

He considered throwing the severed breasts into the woods, letting the animals dispose of them. Then he had a better idea and decided to keep them.

Breathing hard, he stood up and went back to the car. He wrapped the breasts in an old wadded plastic cleaner's bag tightly, so they wouldn't leak. Then he got a shovel from the trunk.

The earth was soft, and it didn't take long to bury Sherri.

Standing in the middle of the clearing, Rory looked carefully around him. It was as if he and Sherri had never been here. He would get back in his mother's car and drive away, and all of this might never have happened.

It might never have happened, so it didn't happen.

There would be a big fuss over Sherri, but she'd left on the bus and not come back. Not the first girl like her to do that. Things would quiet down after a while. The world would go on. People would forget.

He wouldn't forget Sherri, though. Not ever.

The dead girl.

68

Quinn decided to talk to someone about Dr. Grace Moore's files himself. After all, hadn't her patient Linda called on him for help? Hadn't there been dozens of other women who called Q&A or the NYPD recently maintaining that they were in danger, requesting protection? There simply were too few people to protect them, even if most of their calls weren't legitimate and they weren't in actual danger.

The trouble was, some of them *were* in danger, and it was impossible to know which. It was a small percentage, but they were real. Linda Brooks and Grace Moore had been real, and the danger had been real, and here Quinn was investigating their deaths when he felt he should have known or sensed something that would have prevented them.

That was the problem; he couldn't predict the future, and the killer could forge it.

The building containing Dr. Moore's office was a haven from the heat. Everything seemed to be made of marble other than the occasional potted plant. Quinn found himself wondering what it would feel like to lie down on the cool lobby floor.

Per Quinn's instructions, Pearl and Fedderman were helping Sal and Harold canvass two square blocks of the neighborhood around where Linda Brooks and the doctor had been murdered. Old-fashioned, irreplaceable police legwork. Quinn wasn't sure where Weaver was; she was Renz's special conduit to the commissioner's office, which made her something of an independent operator. Quinn liked it that way. Pearl and Weaver were better kept apart. They could be fuse and explosive.

The elevator in Dr. Moore's building was warm and slow and seemed to stop at every other floor before Quinn got out of the stifling little car. A woman in the elevator had been wearing too much perfume, and he was still trying to fight the urge to sneeze.

When Quinn entered the doctor's office, he found himself in a small anteroom with cream-colored walls and beige furniture. There was a rounded walnut desk with a computer, a printer, and phone on it. He heard nothing but the faint rushing sound of traffic in the street below.

He called hello.

A few seconds later, a door to what he assumed was a larger office opened. A distraught-looking young woman with frizzy dark hair pulled back to make her round face seem even rounder, peered out at him through dark-framed glasses. "Help you?"

Quinn thought she looked like the one who needed help. Maybe with her midterm exams.

He flashed his identification and explained who he was and why he was there.

The young woman, who said her name was Cleo, looked confused and started gnawing her lower lip with large white teeth. "I'm not sure if I should even talk to you about one of Dr. Moore's patients, much less let you see the case file."

Quinn gave her a smile that surprised her with its kindness. "What were you to the deceased, dear?"

"I was Dr. Moore's part-time assistant and receptionist," Cleo said.

"Did you ever meet Linda Brooks?"

"A few times. When she came in for appointments."

"Do you know why she was being treated? Her . . . issue?"

"Not exactly. And like I said, I'm not sure I should be discussing—"

"You don't doubt my identity, do you, dear?"

"Of course not. I've seen you in the papers, on TV news. But don't you need a warrant or something?"

"I can get one, if you want to go on record as being uncooperative."

"Oh, I don't mean to be uncooperative. I just don't know what the patient's rights are, even though . . ."

"The patient is dead," Quinn finished for her. "I suspect that if Linda Brooks could somehow communicate with us, she'd want you to let the people investigating her and Dr. Moore's deaths examine her file."

"Probably," Cleo conceded.

"While you're making up your mind," Quinn said, "can you tell me why Linda Brooks was being treated?"

Cleo fought with her indecision for several seconds, then said, "I guess. She was diagnosed as paranoid schizophrenic."

"Meaning?" He wanted to keep Cleo talking.

"She suspected people of being out to get her. And she had hallucinations. Heard voices." Cleo looked around helplessly. "I don't know the details. Dr. Moore didn't talk much to me about her patients."

"Still, you learned things."

"I learned things," Cleo agreed.

"Had Linda Brooks been getting better?"

"There was no getting better for her. She had to learn to adjust to being . . . disturbed."

"Was she disturbed about anything in particular lately?"

Cleo held on to the back of the desk chair and looked away from Quinn. Then back at him. "She thought someone was following her. A man. She'd thought that before."

"Was he someone she knew?"

"No, but he'd follow her, and sometimes when she'd get home, she'd know he'd been in her apartment."

"How?"

"That I don't know. You'd have to consult the file."

Neither of them spoke for what seemed a long time. Quinn knew when to hold his silence. He made a bet with himself.

"The files are in those brown cabinets behind the doctor's desk," Cleo said.

Quinn smiled slightly but said nothing.

Cleo stood straighter. "I'm going down and around the block for a coffee. Do you mind keeping an eye on things while I'm gone?"

"You can trust me," Quinn said.

Cleo had been clutching a key chain. She laid it on the desk. Without looking at Quinn, she hurried from the office and closed the door behind her, leaving him alone with the ghost of Dr. Moore.

It was easy enough to find the key that unlocked all the drawers of the file cabinet, and it was easy enough to find the file on Linda Brooks.

Quinn had been hoping for some DVDs or cassettes, recordings of the doctor's sessions with Linda. Instead he found copious notes. Pages of them. Apparently Linda had talked, and Dr. Moore listened as a psychoanalyst should, and made notes.

The printer near the computer out in the anteroom was one of those multifunctional ones that also scanned, faxed, and copied. Quinn was glad to see it held plenty of paper.

It took him a few minutes to get onto it; then he got to work making copies of Dr. Moore's notes.

He hoped Cleo would take her time over her coffee.

An hour later, at his desk at Q&A's headquarters, Quinn began to read.

There wasn't much more to learn about Linda Brooks. She did hallucinate. She did hear voices. As Quinn read, he could empathize with the agony the young woman had been enduring, the loneliness. And he got a sense of the courage she must have had in order to adjust as well as she had and build some kind of life despite her persistent illness. He found himself liking this woman he'd let be tortured and murdered.

Jesus! Don't do that to yourself!

There wasn't much in life Quinn hated more than self-pity and its destructiveness. It was an emotion Linda Brooks seemed to have for the most part avoided. She'd been a fighter.

And a fatalist.

That was what this killer knew about his victims—they were fatalists. At a certain point something would break in them and they would give themselves to him. That was the moment the monster in him lived for, the moment they were completely his.

Fedderman came into the office, swiping his forearm across his forehead. He was carrying his suit coat draped over his shoulder and he looked beat. In his right hand was a small brown paper sack.

He nodded a hello to Quinn as he crossed from the door to Quinn's desk. Then he opened the bag and spilled out a dozen or so small plastic tubular objects on the desk top. They looked like cigarette lighters and for an instant Quinn's hand moved toward his shirt pocket where he used to carry his cigars, when he'd smoked them more frequently.

"What are those?" he asked.

"Thumb drives. Or flash drives. I dunno; I can't keep up with tech talk."

Quinn stared up at him.

"You plug them into a USB port in your computer and they hold all kinds of information. Like a disk drive, only they're not."

"What the hell's a USB port?"

"You gotta be kidding." Fedderman pointed to a tiny port on the tower of Quinn's computer.

"Oh, yeah," Quinn said. "I use those all the time." He pushed the plastic cylinders around with his finger. "So where'd you get them?"

"Dr. Grace Moore's apartment. They're videos of the doctor's sessions with some of her patients."

"Including Linda Brooks?"

"Yeah. I watched her latest session on the doctor's computer before I came here. She said she was being fol- lowed by someone who looked like Frank Sinatra."

"Ring-a-ding-ding," Quinn said.

"The doctor was going with Linda to her apartment to prove to her nobody was following her or waiting for her there."

"This was the day of the murder?"

" 'Fraid so."

Quinn bowed his head and let out a long breath.

"Things get on tracks," Fedderman said, "and it's like there's no way to stop the train wreck." He didn't tell Quinn he was actually thinking about Penny and him, where they might be heading.

"Anybody else know you took these thumb drives?"

Fedderman shook his head. "Just the two of us. There are little squares of tape on the bottoms of them, listing the patient's names. You'd be surprised by some of those names."

"I'll make a copy of Linda Brooks's, and we won't watch the others. Then you better wipe them and put them back where you found them."

"You don't think we should hand them over to Renz?"

"Are you kidding?" Quinn asked.

"Actually," Fedderman said, "I am."

That night at the Hamaker Hotel near Times Square, Harley Renz leaned over and kissed Olivia good-bye. She was sleeping deeply, snoring lightly, and didn't notice.

Renz walked lightly even though he was sure he couldn't wake Olivia with a gunshot. She'd taken something, and he hadn't asked what. After dressing carefully, he used a washcloth from the bathroom to wipe the glass he'd used to drink Jack Daniel's; then he slipped the bottle into his briefcase that was propped on a chair. He was sure he hadn't touched anything in the bathroom or the rest of the hotel suite that would leave a legible print. He was always careful to touch almost nothing but Olivia, but especially so since his conversation with Jim Tennyson.

Nothing must go wrong. Women, one of Renz's favorite perks of his office, had brought down more than one hardworking police commissioner. The trouble he went to when he saw Olivia was a precaution, Renz knew, but it allowed him to sleep better.

Or it had before his visit from Jim Tennyson. Weaver was a help in that regard, keeping tabs on Tennyson. But Tennyson was an undercover guy with street smarts. Renz knew he could slip Weaver when it suited him. He had to trust Tennyson, at least until he could get something on him. Mutual damaging information among thieves was almost as effective as honor.

The clock radio by the bed was set for six o'clock, and he knew that Olivia would get up and shower and be gone by seven. Renz stared at her in the dim light. It was hard to imagine something so beautiful being as deceitful as Tennyson had described.

But it wouldn't be the first time Renz had seen it.

He slipped out of the hotel room and locked the door behind him, handling the knob with the dry washcloth, which he stuffed into his pocket as he strode toward the elevator.

No one had seen him exit, he was sure. He began to breathe easier.

Five minutes after Renz had left the room, someone else entered.

69

Penny wasn't quite ready to tell Fedderman about the Shadow Guardians. She wondered if the time would ever be right.

"I saw yesterday how it is when your mind becomes your enemy," Fedderman said.

He and Penny were in the apartment kitchen, drinking coffee and eating a Danish pastry they'd bought last night at the bakery down the street. Penny could do okay on this kind of breakfast. Sugar and caffeine. Fedderman figured he'd be jumpy as a cat until he got some lunch into him.

"Are we talking about insanity?" Penny asked.

"Yeah. Quinn and I listened to a recording of a young woman spilling her guts to her analyst. She was in so much pain I felt it along with her."

"Feds the empathetic cop."

"It made our problems seem small."

Penny laid down her Danish and licked her fingers. "Are you trying to minimize my constant worry that you're going to be seriously wounded or killed?"

"Are you trying to pick a fight?"

"You're the one who implied I was some kind of candy

ass because I worried about you." *You should see me at the pistol range.*

"I didn't say that. Or even imply it."

"Then why bring up this poor woman's misery if not to dwarf mine?"

Fedderman didn't have an answer. He hated arguing with someone smarter than he was.

He stood up and finished his coffee in two long swallows, then went over and put the cup in the sink. He returned to the table not to sit down, but to bend over and kiss Penny's cheek. "I've gotta get to work."

"To practice your religion."

"My job," Fedderman said, still trying to stifle his anger.

"Your obsession."

"Okay, I'll buy that—my obsession."

"It's Quinn. His obsessive behavior rubs off on you and the rest of the people at Q and A."

"Maybe," Fedderman said. "Obsession, persistence, dedication . . . whatever you want to call it, we get results."

"And then?"

"People's lives are saved."

Penny attacked her Danish again. Chewed and swallowed. "So you have the high moral ground again, when both of us know it's nothing more than a dangerous, sick game for all of you."

"It's a game we're trying to end."

"Isn't that true of all games?"

Damn her! Being the intelligent one again.

"Most games," he said.

He picked up his suit coat from where it was draped over the back of a kitchen chair and headed for the door.

"You've got icing all over your fingers," Penny said behind him.

"I don't care."

"Typical."

Chancellor Linden Schueller closed the lid of his laptop computer, then zipped the machine into its soft leather case. He'd been working on a program he'd developed that used GPS, distance, speed, and altitude to calculate metal fatigue on aircraft. The program would soon be working, but he'd probably keep it to himself. Use it to maintain his own private plane.

He sipped his iced tea and settled back in his leather recliner. He appreciated these brief stretches of ennui in his otherwise busy schedule. Where he sat, if he turned his head slightly, he had a wonderful view out the open French doors of Waycliffe's green, manicured grounds.

The preteen lacrosse teams, both male and female, were out on the wide lawn, practicing their moves. They were from the Woodrow Wilson School and the Pierre Laclede Academy, both in towns a few hours' bus ride away. The two schools used Waycliffe College's facilities for practice and to play their games in what was known as the G3 division. The players weren't as developed or skilled as the older Waycliffe athletes, but the chancellor enjoyed watching them. Some of them were future Waycliffe students.

"I see some real possibilities out there," said Professor Wayne Tangler, who taught comparative literature. He was the one who looked like a western gunslinger, with his leanness, bushy mustache, lean build, and gray-eyed stare. He had never sat on a horse or fired a gun.

"Always," Chancellor Schueller said, picking up a pair

of binoculars and watching a tall boy in blue shorts run and weave through the field. "But you never know how much they're going to grow in the next few years."

"Yes, they need size and strength," Tangler said. "Sometimes you can tell their eventual size by looking at their parents."

"If the parents ever bother visiting the campus."

"They'd come more often if they realized it was such a beautiful setting."

Since it was the weekend they weren't in Schueller's office, but in his house on the edge of the campus. It was a large brick two-story with a portico in front. There was a walled-in brick patio in back that turned a corner and ran halfway down the house's west side. The wall was only twenty-four inches high and its purpose was decorative. Ivy grew over some of it, and twined halfway up the side of the house. Two sets of French doors gave access to the patio from the house. There was lawn furniture out there, cushioned chairs, and a round table with an umbrella tilted for shade.

The inside of the house was spacious and eclectically furnished. On display were items acquired by Schueller during his annual journeys overseas. Statuary he'd had shipped from Greece and Italy, a table from Germany. There were circular and square soft leather pads beneath everything that might scratch the expensive wood and its antique patina. The tall mahogany bookcases in the den where they sat sipping iced tea were from France. They were lined up along one wall and half of another. Almost enough books to qualify for a library, arranged every which way in the shelves. The atmosphere was pleasant in here. Overstuffed and scholarly. No doubt exactly what Schueller and his decorator had envisioned. Mounted on one wall was a Manet preliminary sketch of a nude woman reclining on a sofa. Tangler knew the sketch was genuine. On an open French provincial antique secretary with its mottled original finish sat a modern desk computer, a contrast of ages. He knew that Schueller was skillful on the computer, and that he was on Facebook. It was amazing, what you could find on Facebook. Whom you could find. Old friends. New friends. Any kind of woman.

Tangler stood up and walked to the open French doors. He went halfway outside and stared away from the lacrosse players and wide lawn, at the woods behind the house. The stretch of woods, mostly oaks and hard maples, ensured privacy from the direction of the campus. Crickets were chirping back there, making quite a racket. He mused that it wasn't such a good idea to have woods so near a house. For security reasons.

"The cops have come and gone here," he said, "and might come back."

"True," Schueller said. Letting the binoculars dangle on their leather strap around his neck, he produced the briar pipe he usually carried but never smoked. After filling its bowl with aromatic tobacco from a soft leather pouch, he tamped it down with a forefinger. He didn't light the pipe.

"That lie we all told, about meeting in your office the evening of the Macy Collins murder—we still don't know whom we were protecting."

"Better if we don't," Schueller said. "It's fortunate that it worked out that way."

"But there have been more and similar murders. If we were asked questions again by the police, we'd have to lie again. We're accomplices now."

"Only if we're found out. And we can't be, if we simply stick to our guns. And don't forget what else we don't want the police investigating."

"But Jesus, Linden, it looks as if we're protecting a serial killer. We probably *are* protecting a serial killer."

"I seriously doubt that. I do know we're protecting ourselves. Besides, we have no choice. We're in it too deep now, even if we wanted to tell the truth."

"Getting rich through crime is one thing. Murder is something else."

"True," the chancellor said. "Murder doesn't necessarily make you rich."

Tangler stared at Schueller with those cold gray eyes, but Schueller didn't wilt. A tougher guy than he appeared, Tangler thought. There were other, obvious questions he wanted to ask Schueller, but he knew he wouldn't. *Was it planned so we'd have no choice? Does someone control Schueller the way Schueller controls his wayward faculty members?*

Questions left unasked.

We've waited too long and we're stuck. No choice now, other than a conspiracy of silence.

Circumstances had turned a questionable business arrangement into something that had trapped them all.

"That kid in the blue shorts can really run," Schueller said, looking again out the French windows but not in the same direction as Tangler.

"Needs coaching," Tangler said.

"Don't they all?"

"Did you ever consider more sports? Different ones?"

"Yes. But at this level, they cost more than they earn."

"Hm," Tangler said, coming back all the way into the study. "We can only hope Blue Shorts doesn't get hurt and has to study during his college years."

"If he enrolls here," Schueller said, "studying is precisely what he'll have to do."

Through the French doors the chancellor could see one

squirrel chasing another up a large tree, round and round. Neither squirrel was ever in a position to see the other, yet each knew the other was there.

For some reason that reminded the chancellor of that cop, Quinn.

70

Saturday in the summer. Hot, humid, lushly green. Hardly anything or anyone was moving fast in the area of Waycliffe College. Jody figured the campus would be nearly deserted today. That was in her favor.

She parked her rental car at the far end of one of the visitor lots, out of sight from most of the campus, including the administration building. There were a few other cars on the lot, mostly students' vehicles, using the visitors' lot because it was closer to where they were going than student parking. There were quite a few cars in the students' lot.

As she left the cool interior of the car, she glanced around. There were only a few people visible, well off in the distance, and they looked like denim-clad students.

Jody walked hurriedly toward the psych building, but not so fast that she might draw attention, passing only a few students. Once inside, she was pleased to find that the only class being held was on the second floor. No one seemed to be on the main floor. She made her way down the deserted hall to Professor Elaine Pratt's office.

Someone had once advised her that if she was going to do something illegal, she should do it fast.

She approached the door to the complex of offices and tried the knob. It turned and she was inside.

She was now faced with three other doors lined up ahead of her. She chose the one that was Professor Pratt's office and rotated the doorknob.

But only her sweating hand rotated. The door was locked.

Prepared for this, Jody reached into her purse and withdrew an expired credit card with a honed edge. This was something Quinn had told her about. She was grateful for his know-how as she slid the card between latch and doorframe, depressing the latch, and the door opened. She was feeling better now. Her nightmare had been what would happen if the card didn't work and fell down on the other side of the door, where she couldn't reach it.

There was no point in agonizing about something in the past; it was best to move forward. Someone, in one of her classes, had stressed that to her.

She was in. Ready to go forward.

There was enough light streaming through the window that she wouldn't have to switch on a lamp.

She immediately bent to the task of searching through Professor Pratt's desk, and then her file cabinets.

Do it fast. . . .

She was surprised when an hour had passed. And disappointed that she'd been unable to break the encryption code or find any sign of correspondence about her or anything else pertaining to Enders and Coil.

She did find a stock prospectus for Meeding Holding Company, which seemed to be a parent company of Meeding Properties.

So what does this mean? That Elaine Pratt is a shareholder?

So what would that mean? If anything important.

A faint shadow crossed the desk. Someone walking past outside?

She heard a door open and close, not near. Her heart began an accelerated beat and she felt flush, nauseated.

Another door, closer. Leading to the complex of offices. Coming her way.

That was when Jody realized that when she'd entered she hadn't relocked the door to Professor Pratt's office. She backed toward the wall the door was on, with its frosted panes. If anyone peered in, they wouldn't see her. If anyone entered, Jody would . . . *what?*

Brazen it through, pretend I have an appointment and I'm waiting for Elaine Pratt?

No, won't work!

Plan ahead!

When the door opens, run out of here like a scalded rabbit, keep my face hidden, become an unknown intruder who'll eventually be forgotten.

Like that character in Chicago. *Mr. Cellophane.*

A figure appeared in dim silhouette on the frosted glass.

The doorknob slowly rotated.

Jody thought she might faint.

She held her breath, listening to her frightened heart, and pressed motionless against the wall.

The knob turned all the way and the door opened about six inches. A woman's hand explored inside the office like some curious tentacled sea creature, found the knob, and turned the raised ridge that activated the lock. Then she pulled the door closed and tested the knob to make sure it was locked.

Jody got down behind Elaine Pratt's desk and didn't so much as breathe out for fear she'd make some slight noise that would be noticed. Someone had checked and assumed Professor Pratt had forgotten to lock her office door, and locked it for her.

Jody made herself wait ten minutes before moving. Then, since she was behind the desk, she slowly opened and closed its drawers, checking the contents. There was something damned curious there.

In the bottom drawer was a folder with old photos and news articles about Daniel Danielle, how he'd killed a lot of people, been convicted of murder, and then died in a hurricane.

Or maybe it wasn't so curious. After all, Daniel Danielle was a sort of iconic serial killer. And often in the news. Possibly Professor Pratt was researching sociopath behavior for one of her classes. She and her students had analyzed and discussed plenty of grisly subjects, real and fictional. They'd spent almost a week discussing *Silence of the Lambs*.

Jody closed the drawer, then took the time to arrange everything in the office as it was when she'd entered.

She drew a deep breath, told herself to pretend she belonged here in the building, and quickly and silently left the office and made her way back to the hall.

She was safe in the hall. She was sure no one had seen her enter or exit the suite of offices, and the odds were against her encountering someone who knew her before she left the building. She was simply another faceless visitor on campus.

She was walking toward the exit at the far end of the hall when she saw a figure stride past where another hall intersected.

It had all happened too fast and too far away to be sure, but Jody thought the figure might have been Sarah Benham.

* * *

The privacy tag still hung on the doorknob of Olivia's room at the Hamaker Hotel. From outside came the sounds of the city, the honking horns, racing bus or truck engines, occasional muffled shouts. Far away a jackhammer began its muffled chattering.

Inside the room, the only sound was the deep and steady rhythm of Olivia's breathing. Her breasts rose and fell. She was wearing a pink diaphanous nightgown and had one knee raised.

She straightened the knee.

Her breathing became fainter, and was underscored by a soft rattling sound. Flat on her back, her head comfortably resting on a pillow, Olivia raised her right hand and made a flitting motion with it, as if trying to shoo away something bothersome.

Then she lowered her hand and the room was silent.

71

When she entered the offices of Enders and Coil Monday morning, Jody saw through the glass wall of the conference room that something big was going on. Both Enders and Coil were at the long polished table, Enders standing and talking, gesticulating.

Three men and two women, all in business suits, were sitting across from them. Jody recognized the lead attorney for Meeding Properties. She didn't know the other men or the women. As she watched, one of the women raised the water glass before her and took a sip, seemingly only mildly interested in what Enders was saying.

Dollie Baker, forty-five-year-old paralegal and receptionist, looked up from filing a fingernail and saw Jody gazing into the conference room.

"Important stuff," she said.

Jody had within a week pegged Dollie as too loose with her tongue and the facts to be working at a law firm. And she liked to trail gossip bait.

Even knowing this, Jody bit. "Important how?"

"They're deciding whether to go ahead and raze Dash's apartment building while Dash is still in the hospital."

"They've been arguing that for days."

"But Dash has been given a release date. She comes home from the hospital tomorrow, if home is still standing."

That explained the sense of urgency Enders was emitting. He was probably arguing to turn the dinosaur-like wrecking machines loose on the building while it stood empty. That's how Jody had come to think of the destruction of the apartment building, an attack by iron-jawed prehistoric beasts as might be depicted in a high-tech science fiction movie.

"Leaving Mildred Dash an invalid with no home to return to would create such a firestorm of bad press, it wouldn't be worthwhile," Jody said.

"You should be telling that to them in there."

"Hah! Anyway, I thought that was already decided. So what's changed?"

"The development company's position. They'd rather be the bad guys, figuring it would cost less to repair their reputation than it would to delay the project even longer."

"But it isn't a dollars and—"

Dollie grinned and held up her hand in a stop signal. "I hear you, Jody. But the fact is, for them and for us, it *is* a dollars-and-cents issue."

"There's always right and wrong," Jody said.

Dollie smiled. "Notice how odd that sounds in here?"

Jody had noticed. It was as if her words had been absorbed and made meaningless by the deep carpet and thick drapes.

Dollie gave her a reassuring smile. "Remember, kid, this is a law office."

Jody did remember. For a moment she stood watching the silent storm of discussion in the conference room.

"What are you thinking, Jody?"

"Nothing, really."

She was wondering what the development company's

position would be if the Dash apartment building was occupied by someone other than Mildred Dash.

Weaver entered Harley Renz's office and laid a padded yellow envelope on his desk.

Renz reached into it cautiously, as if fearing something might bite him, and pulled out a plastic tube with a metal plug on the end.

"Know what those are?" Weaver asked.

"Thumb drives for a computer," Renz said.

"Right. You plug them into a USB port and you can transfer information to or from them."

"I know all that. I'm not a computer Luddite, whatever that is. Where'd they come from?"

Weaver thought the question a little odd, since it was Renz who'd suggested—indirectly, of course—that Weaver enter Dr. Grace Moore's apartment and search for more information about her patients than her files had provided. Who could tell what kinds of information might be on those drives? Information was Renz's lifeblood, and nobody knew better than Weaver how to scour an apartment.

Weaver also knew enough not to answer the question directly. "They came into my possession last night."

Renz looked at her carefully across his desk. She noticed how red his eyes were and how he appeared more jowly than ever. As if gravity were tugging at his features extra hard this morning.

"Anything about Tennyson?" he asked.

He'd tried to make the question sound casual, but there was a charge in the air that made Weaver's scalp tingle.

She could have said she couldn't know about Tennyson, because Renz had suggested she seek an opportunity to get into Moore's apartment, and she couldn't be two places at once. But she simply said, "Nothing."

Something was very wrong here. It was time to tiptoe.

"Harl—Commissioner, is everything all right?"

He sat back as if the question needed to be mulled over. "Yes. I'd say so." He leaned forward and began shuffling papers on his desk. A caricature of a busy executive. "We got a double homicide in the West Village, an ambulance shot at on Broadway, a foreign dignitary arrested in a bar fight, a professional escort dead from a heroin overdose in a Midtown hotel . . . the usual."

Professional escort?

Weaver's voice was steady. "Got a name on the escort?"

Renz pretended to check for information in his mess of papers. "Olivia something . . ."

Weaver showed no emotion. A game needed to be played here, and she was learning the rules as it went along.

"Any indication of foul play?"

"Not really." He trained sad, angry eyes on her and shrugged. "But who knows for sure?"

"I'm . . . sorry," Weaver said.

Renz suddenly smiled slyly at her. "What for? You want the escort case?"

She couldn't help but smile back. Pretending could have its moments, and once you sold your soul to the devil there was a lot to smile about.

"If it's okay with you, sir, I'll stay on my present assignment with Quinn and his gang."

"Watch those people," Renz said. "All of them. They're slippery as hell."

"Don't I know it," Weaver said.

But it wasn't the slipperiness of Quinn and Q&A that

concerned her. Not right now, anyway. Other questions were tumbling around in her brain. Had street-smart Tennyson figured out what was going on and killed Olivia so the murder might be blamed on Weaver? Did he think it would appear that Weaver had killed Olivia as a favor to Renz?

Sure, Weaver had an alibi; she was illegally searching Dr. Grace Moore's apartment. Try that one on a judge or jury.

Had Harry Primo suspected that Olivia was an informer and killed her because she was a threat to his business? Did Tennyson think Weaver actually had killed Olivia? Did Renz suspect her? Had Olivia simply overdosed on heroin and died on her own, leaving behind the other players to decide what had happened?

There were plenty of questions here that no one wanted asked, much less answered. One thing might lead to another, might lead to total ruin. A balance must be maintained.

It seemed that the three of them, Renz, Tennyson, and Weaver, would forever be locked together in this grotesque dance. That was how it worked—closer than family.

God, corruption could be complicated!

Renz pretended to become preoccupied with the paper storm on his desk, and Weaver left the office.

Wondering what ever happened to closure?

72

They had dinner in the brownstone.

Pearl had outdone herself in the kitchen this evening, stopping at two delis for pre-cooked and heated vegetables that went perfectly with the stuffed pork chops she'd had delivered from a restaurant six blocks away.

"Delicious," Quinn proclaimed, wondering if this was as close as he'd ever again come to a home-cooked meal. He pushed his plate away to signify that he was finished.

"Much better than passable," Jody said.

"It's all in the timing," Pearl said.

"What's that, Mom?"

"Being a good cook is all in the timing, having everything ready and heated at the same time."

Quinn and Jody exchanged glances. Neither knew if Pearl was kidding, so they maintained wooden expressions.

Pearl brought in vanilla ice cream and coffee for dessert. The ice cream was from D'Agostino, some brand Quinn had never heard of, but it was pretty good. The coffee tasted much like the coffee she made at the office. They ate the ice cream with chocolate syrup and a sprinkling of chopped nuts on it.

The ice cream was in fact so good that no one spoke until they were finished eating it. They sipped their coffees contentedly without speaking. A family scene too late for Rockwell. Quinn was reminded of his first marriage, with May, when their daughter Lauri was young and living at home. Somehow the memory didn't make him sad. This was good, what he, Pearl, and Jody had. For Quinn it was like an unexpected bonus. He wondered if the other two felt the same way. He was pretty sure Jody did. Not so sure about Pearl.

Jody dabbed at her lips with a napkin, which she then wadded and put on the table. "Either of you heard of Waycliffe College being involved with Meeding Properties?" she asked.

"Involved how?" Quinn asked.

"I don't know. I've heard mention of the college at the firm, and it's usually in an odd way, as if there's some kind of secret connection."

"Some kind of legal matter," Quinn suggested. "I hear they do that kind of thing there."

Pearl gave him a *be serious* look.

Jody shook her head, not noticing Quinn's sarcasm. "No, I, er, checked and the firm doesn't have anything pending with the school."

"Checked how?" Quinn asked.

"Never mind that."

"Oh. Okay."

Snitch, the cat, appeared and Jody placed her paper deli dish on the floor so the animal could lap up what was left of her ice cream.

"Maybe there's something hush-hush about the way the internship dropped into my lap after Macy Collins was killed."

"You're in an advanced student program," Pearl reminded her. She couldn't help sounding a little proud.

"There's nothing that unusual about you getting the open internship."

"Yeah, so maybe I got the wrong impression. About Meeding Properties, too. They're always whispering about that at the firm."

Quinn sipped his coffee and studied Jody over the cup's plasticized paper rim, which was beginning to break down from the heat. "You're linking the law firm, Meeding Industries, and Waycliffe College together?"

"And Sarah Benham."

"The woman you sometimes go to lunch with?"

"Yeah. We've become pretty good friends. She's also a former Enders and Coil client, but only in a small way. A class action suit against a mutual fund. Diddly-squat for everyone but the lawyers. Anyway, I'm sure I heard her mention my name when she and Jack Enders were talking."

"While you were eavesdropping," Pearl said.

"I was out at Waycliffe today and I think I caught a glimpse of her."

Pearl placed her heated, cooled, and reheated coffee cup where the tablecloth was already stained. "So what were you doing at Waycliffe?"

"I'd gone through all the files at Enders and Coil. Because of the Mildred Dash dilemma."

"Dilemma?" Quinn asked.

"Sure. You must have been reading about it in the papers. How Mildred Dash is in a coma and she's—"

"We know about it," Pearl said. "She was due to go home, but she's staying in the hospital. Which puts Meeding Properties in something of a public relations quandary."

"So I was searching the files for something to use against Enders and Coil."

"Use *against* them?"

"Against their client, actually."

"It amounts to the same thing," Quinn pointed out.

"You were searching for something your own firm did that could be construed as criminal?" Pearl asked.

"Sure."

"Isn't *that* criminal?"

"I could make a case for it being legal. I'm an employee. Why shouldn't I have access to the files? I might have broken some obscure company regulation—though I've never seen anything specific—but that doesn't mean a statute has been violated."

Pearl chewed her lower lip. Quinn tried not to smile,

"I'm not going to argue law with you," Pearl said. "What did you find?"

"Exchanges of encrypted e-mails with somebody at Waycliffe."

"My, my," Quinn said.

"Did you break the encryption?" Pearl asked.

"Enough to see the word *cabal* used more than once. And my business psychology professor at Waycliffe, Elaine Pratt, was the recipient and sender of some of the e-mails. That's why I rented a car and drove up to Waycliffe."

"To do some breaking and entering," Pearl said.

"I'm a student there," Jody reminded her.

"So did you learn something more about Meeding Properties and Mildred Dash?" Quinn asked. "And a cable?"

"Cab*al*," Jody said. "A secret group that has some kind of agenda."

"Did you learn the secret agenda?"

"No. But Meeding is in trouble. Time's running out on the date they have to finish demolition. If they don't make the deadline, they'll lose a humongous amount of money. I could tell even though they were encrypted that the issue with Mildred Dash was what a lot of the e-mails were about."

"So maybe the college is invested in Meeding Properties," Quinn said.

"So why would that be such a big secret?"

"I dunno. PR?"

"Ha! The college portfolio contains cigarette companies, so I don't think they'd be ashamed of Meeding. Unless murder was involved."

"Murder?"

"Maybe. Hard to say for sure, with the encryption. Or Professor Pratt might have been talking about a teaching project. She had a file stuffed with newspaper items about some old murders. We discuss that kind of thing in her class all the time."

"So who was the killer?" Quinn asked.

"Daniel something."

"Daniel Danielle? Last name a female version of the first?"

Jody slapped her forehead so hard her springy red hair jiggled. "Of course! It should have registered. Only this guy died like over a decade ago."

Quinn looked at Pearl. Pearl looked at Quinn and Jody. All of them thinking this could be a coincidence, Professor Pratt researching for her class presentation the same killer who appeared to have returned and taken up where he'd left off when he'd supposedly died ten years ago. After all, Daniel Danielle was a topical subject again. Fair game for a psych teacher.

"Coincidences do happen," Jody said, "or there wouldn't be such a word."

"What are you going to do with your information?" Quinn asked.

"Try to stop demolition somehow on Mildred Dash's apartment."

"You mean calling the shots because you might have something on Enders and Coil?"

"Possibly."

"Leverage?"

"Maybe."

"Extortion?"

"I'm not gaining anything."

"Blackmail?"

"I wouldn't call it that."

"What would you call it?"

"Preventing something criminal. Do either of you know anything about it?"

"I don't," Pearl said.

"We don't," Quinn added.

"Okay."

Quinn and Pearl sat staring at each other. They both felt as if they'd just been spewed from a conversational whirlpool.

Jody smiled and stood up from her chair. "Is it my turn to help with the dishes?"

"It's your turn to *do* the dishes," Pearl said.

"That's right." Jody began collecting the paper plates and plastic utensils supplied by the restaurant and delis.

Off she went into the kitchen, almost tripping over the cat still intent on its ice cream.

Pearl hadn't moved. She was gazing toward the kitchen, looking solemn and concerned.

"Your kid," Quinn said.

73

Pearl shouldn't have followed Jody the next morning, but she did.

Things were accumulating in a way that made her uneasy. Who was this Sarah Benham woman, and what was the basis of her friendship with Jody? What might Jody do to get herself into the kind of trouble that would follow her all her life? Pearl suspected her daughter wasn't far from going to the demolition site of Mildred Dash's apartment and causing a problem. Youth often thought that if enough hell was raised, a solution would be forthcoming.

Why was Jody so discontented? Such a pea under the mattress? Pearl thought about Jody's father. He'd been, if anything, too mellow. It had been as if his music sweetened his life. Even more than Pearl had sweetened it. He had always been too preoccupied to get into the various kinds of trouble that seemed to attract Jody. Where the hell did Jody get—?

Pearl put the question out of her mind so she could concentrate on what she was doing. Following her daughter, as any good mother would.

Ahead of her, Jody paused to look at some junk in a

street vendor's cart. T-shirts, caps, belts, paste jewelry, silver and gold chains, sunglasses, and visors—the gaudy display seemed to sway in the morning breeze. Or maybe that was an illusion.

Pearl moved over to a florist shop doorway, out of the stream of pedestrian traffic. While she watched her daughter absently pick through the street vendor's merchandise, she was thinking *Okay*, or *No, no, don't buy that*.

Mom interfering by telepathy.

Jody did buy something. Apparently some small piece of jewelry. Then she walked on.

As Pearl followed, Jody broke into a jog in order to join a knot of people hurrying across an intersection with the traffic signal.

Uh-oh.

Pearl knew she'd have to jog to keep up, maybe cross over the other way and keep pace on the opposite side of the street. If traffic would cooperate.

All she could see of Jody now was her head of springy red hair. She decided her best bet would be to reach the intersection where Jody had crossed and see if she could catch a break in the traffic.

Pearl thought she might make it and was approaching the curb when a large shadow engulfed her. She slowed, glanced back, and saw that one of those red double-decker sightseeing buses was about to make a right turn in front of her.

She slowed to a walk, giving ground to the behemoth.

When she was almost at a stop, something rammed into the small of her back and shoved her from behind.

She was in front of the turning bus.

Pearl instinctively brought up her hands and slapped at the front of the bus with both palms. She pushed away from the warm wall of metal as the bus came at her. It wasn't moving fast, but fast enough that she couldn't get out of its path. She was in so close she wasn't sure if the driver was even aware of her.

Her palms were stinging, her locked elbows straining, as she backpedaled and tried to hold the bus at bay.

Don't fall, don't fall, don't fall . . . !

Her maneuver worked, but not for long. She found herself falling. There were shouts, the hissing of air brakes.

Someone or something had her left upper arm in a strong grip and yanked her sideways and away, as the bus hissed and squealed to a stop.

Pearl lay limp on the pavement, breathing in the smells of oil and heat and exhaust fumes. She saw that one of the bus's tires was only inches from her twisted right leg. People were gathered around her, trying to help, touching her almost everywhere in order to reassure themselves, and her, that she was alive and not dead or seriously injured.

Pearl brushed them away and managed to get to her feet, leaning against the stopped bus for support.

Standing, squinting, she looked around her. Somebody had given her the extra few inches of pavement she needed in order to survive. Whoever had grabbed her arm and pulled her to the side had saved her life.

She looked at the stunned, silent faces, and knew no one.

Then a hand touched her shoulder and she heard a familiar voice.

"You okay?"

Pearl's savior, Nancy Weaver.

The killer had a way of moving at a near run on a crowded sidewalk without attracting attention. He'd pushed

Pearl slightly harder than he'd intended, and she'd almost been killed. He hadn't wanted her dead; he needed her alive—at least for a while longer.

Fortunately some other woman, very much alert, had kept Pearl from perishing beneath the wheels of the bus. The killer smiled. That wasn't Pearl's fate at all. *He* would decide that.

This was a message to Quinn as well as to Pearl: Anything could happen any time, anywhere, to anyone. But they already knew that. Brakes could hiss, tires screech on concrete, and then *Wham!* And it's a different world.

The message, a simple reminder: *My choice.*

"I had my choice," Weaver said, later at Q&A. "I could save Pearl and make sure she was all right, or I could go after whoever pushed her."

Pearl was sitting in her desk chair, bent forward and holding a damp washcloth on her knee where she'd skinned it. The knee had tiny bits of asphalt in it and stung like hell. Pearl was getting sore all over, the way it was sometimes after an auto accident. She was grateful for what Weaver had done, but anger and humiliation were also in her jumble of emotions.

Weaver must have been tailing her.

Then she thought about what almost happened and her anger paled.

Someone tried to kill me.

The others, Quinn, Fedderman, Sal, and Harold, were listening and watching the two women.

"Didn't you even get a glimpse of whoever shoved you?" Sal asked in his gravelly rasp. It almost hurt Pearl's throat to listen to that voice.

"All too fast," Pearl said, "and from behind."

"It could have been one of two people," Weaver said. "Keep in mind that I was concentrating on Pearl, on what was happening, so the rest was just an impression. Both possibilities were average height and build. They sort of crisscrossed behind Pearl just before she was shoved, so there was no way to know who did what."

"You think they were working together?"

"Naw. Nothing like that."

"How were they dressed?" Quinn asked.

"One guy in a brown suit. The other had on jeans, maybe, and a light blue short-sleeved shirt. Hair color on both of them was brown. Dark, anyway. Neither had a shaved head or a full beard, nothing like that. Average size, maybe on the slender side."

"Not much of a description."

"I was busy saving Pearl's life."

"Tailing her so you could report to Renz."

"Doing my job."

"Question is," Fedderman said, "why did the killer take a run at Pearl?"

"If it *was* Daniel," Quinn said.

"Be too coincidental if it wasn't."

"To Feds's question," Harold Mishkin said, "I think the answer is Quinn. This is a game to Daniel, and Quinn's the dragon he has to slay. He'd see it as a triumph over Quinn if he could get Pearl. Even if he didn't actually kill her. It'd raise the stakes of the game even higher."

"And he's a high-stakes player," Pearl said.

Sal was staring at Mishkin. "Sometimes you surprise me, Harold."

"We'll see what Helen has to say about it when she comes in," Harold said. But they all knew that Helen had more or less weighed in on this one already.

Weaver went over and got a cup of coffee. She sipped

it while she walked back to the group. Her hand holding the cup began to shake, and she held the cup with both hands to steady it.

"This was close," she said. "It wasn't for show." Some of the coffee sloshed onto her hand. "Damn it!" She glared at all of them. "I thought you people were protecting Pearl with your own tail."

"I took it off," Quinn said, "once it became known you were keeping a loose tail on her for Renz."

Weaver smiled miserably. "You weren't supposed to know that."

"Everybody knows everything eventually," Quinn said.

Nobody spoke for a while, everyone thinking it was the who, what, when, and how much that made a difference.

Everyone but Quinn. He was thinking about what happened to Pearl. So close. But was it meant to be *that* close? This wasn't a knife in the dark, slow strangulation in a hog-tie, or artfully applied pain that eventually became shock and death. This wasn't the way the killer took his prey.

This was a message.

"There's nothing more to say on this for now," Quinn said. "Meeting's over."

"One thing," the now perfectly calm Pearl said, looking at Weaver. "Thank you, Nancy."

Rare for Pearl.

The text message Pearl received on her phone fifteen minutes later was succinct and untraceable:

Whew!

74

The next morning, Quinn sat at his desk and called Jerry Lido's cell phone number.

Lido answered on the second ring. Said, "Quinn."

"I know who I am, Jerry. You sober?"

"It's morning, Quinn."

"You sound astonished."

"You woke me up, is why I might sound sort of disoriented. I'm totally unmedicated. I heard about Pearl. How is she?"

"Pearl is . . . Pearl." Quinn knew enough not to ask how Lido had heard about Pearl's close call.

"That's what I wanted to hear."

"I've got a job for you," Quinn said. He told Lido about his and Pearl's conversation with Jody, about Meeding Properties and Mildred Dash and something secretive at Waycliffe College, the professor who had a file on old Daniel Danielle murders, and the mysterious and overfriendly Sarah Benham. And Macy Collins.

"Not to mention Daniel's other, more recent victims," Lido said.

"Not to mention. Daniel is topical again, studied along with Dahmer and Bundy in college courses."

"And you want me to find out everything I can about all of this?"

"That's it," Quinn said. "It's all connected in some way. Or can be connected. Like puzzle pieces that don't quite fit to create a picture."

"Because maybe one is missing."

"Or more than one."

"Waycliffe College," Lido mused. "Don't they have a lacrosse team?"

"One of the best in the country."

"Is that a lie?"

"Might be. Ask Helen the profiler. She's a sports babe and would be happy to talk lacrosse."

Lido emitted a sound like an animal might make while struggling out of deep hibernation. Quinn thought he recognized it as a laugh but couldn't be sure. Why did so many people with genius ability have so many quirks? Pearl was staring at him across the office as if she was wondering the same thing. She could only have picked up a word or two here and there in the conversation, so how could she know what he was thinking? She couldn't know what they were talking about.

He'd tell her after talking with Lido, of course. And tell the others. He was beginning to get the feeling he sometimes experienced when a part of his mind knew an investigation was tracking toward a conclusion. Like radar locking on.

That feeling was seldom wrong.

"Gather round," he told everyone, after breaking off his phone conversation with Lido.

They did, looking curious, oddly eager, with slight forward leans and direct eye contact. Senses were at their peak. These were hunters, picking up vibes from the lead predator.

"This have something to do with lacrosse?" Pearl asked.

75

While she was doing drone work at Enders and Coil, Jody's cell phone played its "I Fought the Law" tune. She flipped it open to see Sarah Benham's number.

That was fine with Jody. Maybe she'd probe and find out what Sarah was doing at Waycliffe while Jody was there.

But Sarah didn't have time to talk now. She'd called to suggest she and Jody have lunch in an hour at their favorite restaurant—Sarah's favorite, anyway—The Happy Noodle.

"We haven't gotten together for a while," Sarah said, "so I thought, why not this afternoon?"

"Why not?" Jody said. "We can catch up with each other."

They agreed on a time, and Sarah called and made a reservation.

It was Sarah who arrived at the restaurant first. Jody saw her standing up and waving among the crowded tables.

Sarah had somehow wrangled a booth, where they could talk with at least some privacy. Jody exchanged air kisses with her and they both sat down.

"I've got two apple martinis coming," Sarah said. "I hope you don't mind."

"No one could mind an apple martini," Jody said. "You've made me a convert."

A waiter arrived with their drinks, and they told him they'd study the menu a while before ordering.

Sarah sipped her drink. She was wearing makeup, but she seemed slightly older today. Thin lines showed when she tilted her head a certain way and changed the cast of the lighting. "So how are things going at Enders and Coil?"

Jody smiled ruefully and sampled her martini.

"Something wrong at the firm?" Sarah asked.

"I'm not sure," Jody said. "Mildred Dash is still hospitalized. She was supposed to come home a few days ago but had a setback, and the situation has become awkward. Her holdout is making bigger news."

"Mildred who? Oh, the woman who was holding out in her apartment. What happened to her?"

"A coma. And now possibly a heart attack. Brought on by the way she was being terrorized."

"Who was terrorizing her?"

"Thugs in the pay of Meeding Properties."

"You know that to be true?"

"No. I only know it to be obvious."

Sarah used both hands to rotate her damp glass on its coaster. "You might well be right, Jody, but if I were you I wouldn't mention that to anyone around the law firm."

"You don't think they know?"

Sarah smiled. "I think they don't want to know."

"What isn't said around that place seems more important than what is said."

Sarah's smile became a laugh. "That's probably accurate. But there are some things that shouldn't be mentioned. Some questions that shouldn't be asked."

Jody wasn't sure if she agreed with that. She was considering asking Sarah what she was doing at Waycliffe College over the weekend, even though that might be one of those questions better left unasked. Like, what kind of secret something was going on at Waycliffe that only certain members of the faculty seemed to know about? She'd parted her lips to speak, when the waiter reappeared.

Both women ordered with only a cursory glance at the menu. A salad and sparkling water for Jody. Penne carbonara and a glass of house wine for Sarah.

As the waiter turned away, Sarah said, "I noticed you at Waycliffe College Saturday."

Jody tried not to look surprised by the fact that Sarah had anticipated and broached the subject. So maybe Sarah hadn't followed her to Waycliffe. Maybe Jody *was* getting a little paranoid. Listening to Quinn and her mother could make someone that way. Cynical at the least.

"I went back there to pick up some of my stuff," Jody said. "How come you didn't let me know you were there? We might have come back together."

"It was from a distance," Sarah said, "and I wasn't sure it was you."

"What were you doing at Waycliffe?" Jody asked directly.

"I have an old friend there. Elaine Pratt. We knew each other in college."

"Professor Pratt?"

"She wasn't a professor then."

"I'm amazed sometimes by the people you know."

Sarah chuckled. "Live a few more years, Jody, and you'll build up a backlog of friends and acquaintances. I'm sure Elaine would be surprised if she knew you and I were friends, but she shouldn't be."

"Six degrees and all that. The Kevin Bacon thing."

Sarah nodded. "Genealogy in the movies. Easier to track in a smaller universe."

"Not to mention help from the credits."

Sarah took a long sip of her martini. Watching her, Jody decided not to mention that she'd found Elaine Pratt's e-mail address, along with encrypted messages, in Enders and Coil files.

"What do you intend to do about it, Jody?"

Jody didn't know what she meant at first.

"Mildred Dash," Sarah explained.

Jody sat back in the booth and folded her hands. "I'm not sure."

"I have a suggestion."

"What's that?"

"Do nothing. Sometimes that's best."

"I'm not sure I'm that kind of person."

Sarah laughed, reached across the table, and touched her arm. "I'm sure you're *not* that kind of person. That's exactly why I'm afraid you might step into something here you won't like. You're still in an unfamiliar environment. There are lots of wheels within wheels at a place like Enders and Coil. Things aren't always as they seem. The obvious isn't always what's important."

"Deliberate misdirection," Jody said. "Subversion of the truth."

Sarah leaned closer. "The truth is a damned slippery item, Jody. Open to a lot of interpretation. Sometimes it's closer to you than you know, but you don't want to see it. Sometimes it's further away than you can imagine, and you're holding on tight to something that only seems like the truth."

"I couldn't argue with that."

"There's reality and there's emotion, and sometimes one's mistaken for the other. It's difficult to understand that at times you must ignore what's in your heart and do what your head tells you. For instance, a small lie might prevent a larger, more damaging lie. That's easy to say, but only a few select people really understand it."

"The end justifying the means."

"Of course. Even if it means going against your own instincts. Or learned behavior that seems like instinct. Look around you, Jody. You see it all the time. But it's the times you don't see it that make the world go round."

"I suppose."

"Then do nothing about Mildred Dash. Be a close observer. A learner. You won't regret it."

"Maybe you're right. It hasn't escaped me that I usually don't regret following your advice."

The waiter arrived with their orders and with practiced efficiency placed plates and glasses on the table, along with a wicker basket of warm rolls that smelled delicious.

Sarah sampled her wine, then raised her glass in a toast. "To the means and the ends."

Jody used her martini to clink glasses. She wasn't quite sure what she was toasting.

You were supposed to grow wiser as you got older, but it seemed to her that the world kept getting more complicated.

"Of course, sometimes you can become trapped in a lie."

"How so?" Jody asked.

Sarah smiled. "I'll let you figure that one out for yourself."

76

Chancellor Schueller stood on the red stone veranda at the back of his house and stared through sunglasses into a cloudless sky. He could see the campus and a distant carpet of green treetops from his vantage point, but he couldn't see the grass airstrip itself. Off in the distance was a windsock on a tall pole, hanging limply in the still and humid summer air. That was the only indication that the strip was there.

The twin prop engines on his small plane sputtered to life, then settled into a soft drone. The chancellor knew the plane would soon be taxiing toward the end of the airstrip.

It was being flown by Hal Kelly, a ferry pilot the chancellor sometimes hired when he was too busy to fly, and carrying a guest speaker on pre-Columbian art back to his home city of Pittsburgh. Schueller thought it would be nice if he was also in the plane, flying away from lies and problems.

The police had never viewed anyone in particular on the Waycliffe faculty as suspicious in the death of Macy Collins, or in the similar deaths that followed, but the chancellor and some of his fellow faculty were no less accomplices in the crime of silence. They had lied to the police about their whereabouts and perhaps those of a killer. Then they had told the police more small lies, knowing they were probably covering for a killer. Nothing could help them now, or prevent them from getting into deeper and deeper potential trouble. Their silences condemned them. Each subsequent murder after that of Macy Collins served to tighten the noose around their necks.

And talking at this late date? Sending the police on a course they knew was wrong? That would serve no one and be a tragedy for many.

Everyone was trapped in the same isolated cabal, whether they liked it or not. No one could discuss the murder without the picture enlarging.

After a few minutes the plane's drone became much louder, then softer again. Schueller saw the small twin-engine craft lift above the trees to the north.

It made a graceful, sweeping turn as it climbed, as if the pilot were considering starting an orbit around the sun. Still climbing, it disappeared in the east. The distant drone of its engines faded.

The chancellor wished again that he was on board.

He removed his sunglasses and turned toward the French doors leading back into the house. As he slipped the glasses into their soft leather case, and then his shirt pocket, he noticed that the lenses were rose-colored. Or maybe they were picking up sunlight reflecting off the bricks.

Rose-colored glasses. God sending a sly message?

The chancellor smiled. *Could happen.*

It didn't occur to him that the message might be from someone else entirely.

* * *

Jerry Lido blew his nose into a white handkerchief, wadded the square of cloth, and stuffed it into his pocket. "Whatever dark secret there is in the little universe of subjects that you gave me to research, I didn't learn it."

He was at his sometimes desk at Q&A, slumped sideways in the chair. His thin body looked as if it might snake down onto the floor any second. His hair was a tangle, his shirt was only half tucked in, and he'd slipped out of his shoes and was in his stocking feet. There was a hole in one sock. There were bags under his eyes. Quinn figured he'd been drinking.

"I worked all night without a break," Lido added.

"You look as if you worked all week," Quinn said. He walked over and poured himself a mug of coffee. "Want some?" he asked Lido, holding up his steaming mug.

"I already had ten or twelve," Lido said. "Stuff's beginning to taste like cow piss."

Quinn went back to where the computer whiz was sitting and stood looking down at him. "So what went wrong, Jerry?"

"Nothing other'n that there's protection at Enders and Coil, and at Waycliffe, like I never saw. Sophisticated stuff, and a lot of it." Lido smiled slightly. "So much protection that there's gotta be something there. We did learn that much. Friggin' something exists. We know by its wake that there's a big ship out there in the night."

"And it's damned important to somebody with the technical expertise to protect it," Quinn said. "Who has that kind of expertise?"

"I can't think of anyone but me," Lido said. "That's what's bothersome."

"I admire your grandiosity."

"I got a right." Lido sniffed and wiped his sleeve across his nose.

Quinn sipped his coffee, even though it was the dregs

left by Lido. The grounds made his teeth feel gritty. "You think these are the same people who hacked into our system?"

"I do," Lido said, "I admit I was bragging, but not by much. Sure there are places like major-league law firms and colleges with high-tech stuff that can stymie me, but the truth is there aren't many people who can put up barriers I can't get around."

"And there aren't many who can get around barriers you put up."

"We both know what that means," Lido said. "Same big ship."

Jody knew she shouldn't be at the hospital, but after giving yesterday's lunch with Sarah a lot of thought, she decided to come anyway. Probably no one would know the difference. Even if Meeding Properties had someone keeping tabs on who came and went to visit Mildred Dash, it wouldn't seem odd to them that a member of Enders and Coil would turn up at the hospital. So Jody told herself.

She was given Mildred's floor and room number at the information desk; then she made her way to the elevators.

The temperature was a few degrees too cool for comfort, as it was in most hospitals. As the crowded elevator's door opened on each floor, the familiar mingled scents of the hospital made their way in. It smelled as if everyone was chewing Juicy Fruit gum, and there was an underlying astringent scent like Lysol. Jody tried to block out this olfactory assault, but without much success. She wasn't crazy about hospitals.

Four people were left in the elevator when it reached the Cardiac floor containing Mildred Dash's room. Jody was the only one who got out on that floor.

She was facing a nurse's center that was a rectangle defined by a wooden counter. Inside the rectangle there was a lot of activity involving people in white coats or pale blue nurses' uniforms. A couple of doctors wearing green scrubs. Half a dozen people were leaning or standing at Jody's side of the counter. There were computers on the counter, facing the interior of the rectangle. There were phones, pens and pencils, and racks with slick and colorful informational brochures.

Jody checked a sign with an arrow on it, indicating room numbers. Mildred Dash's was among them. She nodded a friendly hello to a nurse who was smiling inquiringly at her, then made her way down the tiled hall in the direction the arrow pointed.

There were rooms to her left, most of them with their doors open to reveal patients lying beneath sheets. Sometimes there were pull curtains providing privacy. Several TVs were on, but with muted volume. On her right, Jody was approaching what appeared to be a spacious waiting area with chairs, sofas, and a couple of vending machines. There was a big TV there, too, mounted up near the ceiling and on mute. Somebody was playing a baseball game somewhere, but the uniforms didn't look familiar.

The waiting room contained over a dozen people. About half of them were sitting. The other half were at the vending machines or milling around.

Jody broke stride in surprise.

Among those milling around was a familiar figure in a chalk-stripe gray suit, white shirt, yellow silk tie.

Jack Enders.

And he was looking right at Jody.

"What are *you* doing here?" Enders asked. He seemed not to know whether to smile or frown. Some of the others in the waiting room seemed to have stopped what they were doing and were staring at Jody. Waiting.

"I got this idea I might be able to do the firm some good if I dropped by here and talked to Mildred Dash."

"Do the firm some good?"

Jody shrugged. "I guess it sounds crazy."

Enders looked dumbfounded and tentatively angry, as if someone had unexpectedly punched him on the arm and then run away. He didn't quite have this sorted out yet. "Jesus, does it ever sound crazy! You're an *intern*, Jody."

"I'm trying hard to use my initiative and become something more than that. I thought that was one of the purposes of the internship."

Jody was working intently at this line of bullshit, but it didn't seem to be impressing Enders.

"To begin with," Enders said, "you wouldn't be able to see Mildred Dash anyway because this part of the hospital is the intensive care unit. Almost everything is kept sterile beyond this point. You can't even leave flowers."

"I tried to buy some downstairs," Jody lied.

Enders blew out a long breath and shook his head. What, oh what, were they going to do with Jody?

"It doesn't matter anyway," he said. "Mildred Dash is no longer in Intensive Care."

Jody felt a stirring of cautious hope. "She's been released?"

"She left the hospital two hours ago at the request of her family and under supervision of Hospice. I hadn't known that when, like you, I came here to visit her."

Jody knew her bullshit was now drawing bullshit in return. She cocked her head to the side and fixed Enders with a stare. "And?"

He put on a long face. "I got a call ten minutes ago saying she died shortly after returning home."

77

Renz had his assistant send in Jim Tennyson immediately.

News of Olivia's death weighed heavily on Renz's overworked heart. And alongside it, anger.

Tennyson was in undercover garb and looked like a dope peddler. He had a two-day growth of beard, greasy unkempt hair, and was wearing grimy jeans and a black T-shirt. He also had on one of those vests with a couple of dozen pockets. Everything looked as if it had just been bought at Goodwill. He was wearing a long face that didn't fool Renz.

"I figured you'd want to see me," he said to Renz, "after I heard."

"Where'd you hear?" Renz asked.

"Word gets around on the street. 'Specially about somebody like Olivia. She was one of Harry Primo's stable." Tennyson shrugged in his many-pocketed vest, as if to say, *These things happen*. It made Renz mad, this blasé attitude toward someone he . . . something that had been his.

"Why would you think Primo had her killed?"

"Christ, I didn't say I thought that. Did somebody have her killed, you think?"

"We both know she was killed," Renz said.

"In a legal sense? As in homicide?"

"That's a good question."

Renz had given it some thought. Olivia had been sleeping with the police commissioner, which had been good for Olivia. And in fact good for Tennyson, who was holding the information over Renz's head so he could convince Renz to use his influence to Tennyson's advantage. Olivia—Renz had finally come to accept—had gone deeper and deeper into heroin and had been getting mouthy and untrustworthy. She'd become an increasing danger to the status quo. Tennyson had known that. So had Olivia's employer, Harry Primo. Love being blind, Renz hadn't.

The way Olivia had died made Tennyson's information even more potentially damaging to Renz, who could easily fall into the category of suspect. And of course Primo might have killed her to silence her.

Renz knew he hadn't killed Olivia, so almost surely it was one of the other two men. Or, unlikely as it seemed, her overdose really had been accidental.

So here Renz sat, uncertain.

One thing was for sure. It was in all three men's interest that Olivia's affair with Renz should fade into the past with Olivia.

"It's a damned shame, what happened to her," Tennyson said. Pushing already, as if he was clean and without motive in Olivia's death. He'd catch on soon enough that the game was mutually assured destruction. That's what would tamp down the danger of the dead woman in the hotel room.

Renz understood that Olivia's death would remain a

mystery. Everyone involved had to understand that. Everyone but her killer.

"Her death should go down as accidental," he said, not looking directly at Tennyson.

"Wasn't that what happened? Women like that, sometimes they just get enough of the business, and there's no other way for them to quit. Shit bums like Primo see to that."

"That's God's truth," Renz said. "What's Harry Primo think of all this?"

"Not much one way or the other. Primo loses an Olivia or two every year."

Renz suppressed a surge of grief and anger. "I suppose." It was amazing, he thought, the way the truth could be bent and the past revised.

"I was thinking it'd be nice to work plainclothes." Tennyson smiled. "I'm getting tired of dressing like a bum and not showering. Of course, nobody's ever completely clean."

"Nobody's ever out of danger."

"That's not quite the same thing."

"I'll see about the plainclothes assignment," Renz said. "Over in Queens. Plenty of white-collar investigations there."

"That'd be fine. Maybe you could replace me with Weaver. I been seeing her around lately, out of uniform, almost like she was tailing me. She'd make a great decoy, playing the whore. If you could keep her from actually screwing the suspects."

"It's a thought."

"I was onto her from the beginning and she knows nothing," Tennyson said. "I guarantee that."

"That's reassuring."

"For all of us." Tennyson hitched his thumbs into his

vest and moved toward the door. Before going out, he turned. "Sorry again about Olivia."

Renz didn't move for a while, thinking about Tennyson. His suggestion about Weaver was worth considering. Weaver as a decoy hooker. Like typecasting.

78

In the offices of Enders and Coil was what Jody could only think of as a subdued celebration.

Mildred Dash's death solved a lot of problems.

Jack Enders, holding what looked like a scotch on the rocks, leaned toward Jody in passing and whispered, "*Deus ex machina.*" He grinned. "Know what that means?"

"I think it's Latin for 'We didn't have to kill her,' " Jody said.

Enders moved away, holding the grin for her benefit.

Joseph Coil edged up to Jody and beamed down at her. "You feeling okay? You look a little pale."

"My stomach's a bit upset," Jody said.

"The excitement, maybe." He took a sip of whatever he was drinking. It looked like water. "Listen, Jody, I know this case was of particular interest to you. That you even had a special sympathy for Mildred Dash. You might find it difficult to believe, but we all felt that way about her. At least most of us."

"The law is the law," Jody said.

Coil looked at her seriously. "No, Jody, it isn't."

Dollie the receptionist squeezed past them, bumping Coil's elbow so some of his drink spilled on Jody's arm.

Unaware that she'd caused the problem, Dollie continued on her way.

Coil took the napkin he'd been using to hold his glass and patted Jody's arm dry.

"You do look rather peaked," he said. "Why don't you take the rest of the day off? Rest up. Give it a new start tomorrow."

Jody smiled at him and nodded. There was no way to dislike this man on a personal level, even if he was a highway robber.

"I think I will," she said. "Thank you."

"Take in a show tonight," Coil suggested. "Forget about this."

"Maybe I will. Something with a happy ending."

"It all depends what kind of ticket you buy," Coil said, raising his glass to her and showing her his back.

Meaning my future is my choice.

Everything everybody said in this place seemed to have at least a double meaning. As if life were a courtroom and their words would be reviewed on appeal, and God help them if they were too honest and plainspoken.

Jody was getting tired of that delicate verbal dance and the alertness and dexterity it demanded.

What the hell aren't they telling me?

She didn't go out to a play or swoon into a faint after leaving the firm's ghoulish celebration. Where Jody went after leaving Enders and Coil was to the Meeding Properties demolition site.

Meeding had obviously been prepared and wasted no time. Mildred Dash's possessions had been removed from her apartment and put in storage, in case an heir chose to claim them. Where her apartment had stood was nothing but a cracked concrete slab.

The development company seemed to have sprung to work only moments after Mildred's death. No doubt on the advice of Enders and Coil, they'd made sure the deed was done before any possible sort of stay could be issued.

The block-long wound in the landscape was now unbroken by anything higher than three feet. Yellow bulldozers were scooping up dirt and debris and dropping it into the beds of sturdy-looking trucks. The trucks bounced and shuddered as each mass of weight suddenly crashed down with the metallic clang of the dozer blades. Then they emitted much roaring and clouds of dark exhaust and drove away. Workers in hard hats stood off to the side, leaning on shovels and conferring like wise men witnessing some solemn event.

Well, they were right about that. The end of Mildred Dash's long struggle, everything she'd fought for being devoured by yellow monsters, was indeed somber. Unfair and final and debasing. As far as the eye could see was the mud of defeat.

A short, heavy woman with a round, seamed face like a withered apple approached Jody. She was wearing joggers, jeans, and a T-shirt. At first Jody assumed she was one of the workers and was too careless to wear her hard hat. She looked familiar, but Jody couldn't place her.

"The hospital waiting room this morning," the woman said, seeing that Jody was searching her memory. "We weren't introduced. I'm Iva Dunn, Mildred Dash's niece."

"Jody Jason."

"I know who you are," Iva Dunn said. "And I know of your concern about Mildred losing her apartment."

"I thought she had a legal right to live there. Or at least to slow down the process of eviction so she had some kind of leverage."

"She did slow it down," Iva said, with a glance at open space where the apartment building had stood.

"But not enough." Jody pointed. "Look at them, like voracious monsters eating up the past and the future."

"I just see machinery," Iva said.

Jody shook her head. "I see defeat."

"I thought you might. That's why when I saw you I came over here. Not just to thank you for your efforts, but because you really should believe that Mildred won her battle."

Jody looked at her, confused. Iva Dunn seemed serious. Joseph Coil was so right about the truth being complicated. "How so?" she asked. "The building is gone, along with her apartment. Let's face it; the developer got lucky and Mildred died instead of hanging on for weeks or months. It no longer remains necessary to physically remove her from where she lived for over twenty years, or to stop the demolition."

Iva gave her that knowing smile again. "It was never Mildred's intention to actually stop the demolition. Or even to delay it all that much."

"I understand that. But still and all . . ."

"Mildred knew she'd be gone within weeks. If she had to die soon, she wanted to die here. And she got her wish. Believe me, Jody, she won."

Jody looked again at the yellow dozers scooping up the debris of a life, of so many lives, claimed not by corporate progress but by time. Simple and inexorable time.

"We all fight different battles, Jody. We tell different lies and we know different truths."

Jody thought Iva Dunn sounded a lot like Joseph Coil.

"If that's how Mildred saw it, then I guess it's her victory at that," she said, turning around.

But Iva Dunn was gone.

Jody stayed for a while and watched the demolition.

Malleability.

79

Quinn sat at his Q&A desk and wondered. What was the secret, or secrets, connecting Waycliffe College, Enders and Coil, and the series of young women's deaths? Victims who sometimes bore striking resemblances to Pearl.

If he was a copycat killer, this murderer had done his homework. Macy Collins, interning at Enders and Coil, might have learned something she shouldn't have, and paid with her life. The method of that madness was eerily like that of Daniel Danielle. Perhaps Macy had triggered the other murders, reenergized the bloodlust. Possibly this killer was the real Daniel Danielle, and not a copycat.

It was unlikely, though, that Daniel had survived the hurricane-spawned tornadoes of central Florida.

Most likely his was among the many unrecovered bodies after the deadly hurricane, and the copycat had known the police would at least have to investigate with Daniel Danielle in mind.

Quinn couldn't keep his mind from picking at the subject.

How might Jody fit in? After all, she was a student at Waycliffe.

No doubt she'd asked herself the same question.

What's the thread connecting a victim of Daniel Danielle's—or a copycat's—to Enders and Coil, and to Waycliffe College? Quinn's mood became grim. *And possibly to Pearl's daughter, Jody?*

The phone jangled so abruptly it made his body jerk.

There's such a thing as concentrating too hard.

He reached for the receiver and pressed it to his ear, at the same time glancing at caller ID.

"Whaddya know, Jerry?" he asked Lido.

"Something you should," Lido said. "I was on my computer, giving my browser a workout, when it came up with something interesting. A couple of kids trying to camp out illegally and build a fire pit dug it up."

"Fire pit?"

"Yeah. They dig down a couple of feet so they can build a fire slightly below ground level and it won't be spotted from a distance."

"Smart."

"Not this time. They happened to be on top of a shallow grave and dug up a body."

Quinn had been leaning back in his chair. He let it tilt forward. "When did this happen?"

"Last night. Kids had their cell phones handy and called it in right away. Creeped the hell out of them. That was the end of the camping trip."

"Body identified?"

"Not yet. Woman probably in her twenties, average size, what look like knife nicks on some bones, like she was tortured with a blade. Body bent back and bound. She was buried in an awkward position."

"Sounds familiar."

"Yeah. The ropes hadn't rotted completely away. Neither had the tape that was used as a gag."

"Ropes rotted away? How old is this body?"

"The M.E. there figures at least twenty-five years."

"Where's there?"

"Near Leighton, Wisconsin."

"Long way from here. Long time ago."

"They might know who it is. Girl named Sherri Klinger, disappeared in nineteen eighty-six. Her family's since moved out of the area. Father died five years ago. A mother's all that's left. They've contacted her, but I can't scare up any info on that yet."

Quinn was silent for a while, trying to process this.

"It might mean nothing," he said.

"Yeah, but I got a couple of things I'd like to fax to you. A police artist's drawing of how the dead woman might have looked with flesh on her. Also, there are some old photographs of Sherri Klinger."

Even as Lido was speaking, the fax machine on the other side of the office started to click and buzz.

"Coming through," Quinn said, and the two men sat and waited.

When the buzzing and clicking stopped, and a beeper sounded, Quinn stood up and went over to the fax machine.

He drew four pages from the plastic basket. The first was the police artist's rendition of how the dead woman might have looked when alive, front and profile. The three accompanying pages were copies of old newspaper photos of Sherri Klinger.

All of them looked like Pearl.

Quinn stood staring for several seconds then, carrying the faxes, returned to his desk.

"Pearl," he said.

"Not exactly," Lido said, "but it could be her sister. Anyway, that was the first body."

"What?"

"A cadaver dog found another body, buried about twenty feet from Sherri's Klinger's grave. Young woman, killed the same way as Sherri. Haven't identified that one yet."

"She'll resemble Pearl," Quinn said.

And then said something else, under his breath:

"Daniel Danielle."

80

Quinn phoned Chancellor Schueller at Waycliffe and posed the same questions.

The chancellor's voice got higher, as if he were experiencing sudden gravitational pull. He said, absently, "I'm not aware of any of these so-called connections. As for Professor Pratt gathering material for a topical subject . . . why, that's easy enough to understand."

Yet you seemed troubled when I asked you about it.

"I suppose," Quinn said.

Schueller absently repeated it. "An eminent domain case in the city . . . does it have something to do with Waycliffe?"

"It might." Quinn could picture Schueller, youthful and dynamic, as university chancellors went, seated at his desk, sucking his unlit pipe, wearing his blazer with the leather elbow patches, lying his ass off.

What's wrong with this picture?

"Ah! Yes!" Schueller said. Was he snapping his fingers, up there at Waycliffe? He was trying to sell what he was saying; Quinn could easily sense that, even over the phone. For a guy like Schueller, who was used to lying and was practiced and smooth at it, the slight upward pitch of his voice told Quinn he was hearing bullshit.

Quinn waited.

"I remember now," Schueller said. "If I'm not mistaken, some of Waycliffe's money is invested in Meeding Properties stock. But then so are the funds of a number of investment firms."

"I'm thinking of a law firm that recently celebrated a woman's death so they could advise their clients to move in on her property."

"You're speaking of Enders and Coil, I assume. We and that firm have a long history. They employ several Waycliffe alumni. Two associates and an intern, if memory serves."

"I think it does."

"Even students bright enough to matriculate at Waycliffe like to party," Schueller said.

Quinn couldn't argue with that.

"Law firms aside, why do you suddenly inquire about a serial killer in connection with Waycliffe?" Schueller asked.

"He isn't nearly finished."

"Good Lord! How can you know that?"

"There were two similar murders in Wisconsin," Quinn said.

"Recently?"

"About twenty-five years ago. Two young women, buried not far apart."

"Surely that has nothing to do with what's happening in New York now."

"*Surely* is a word I use carefully."

"I understand that. But what have murders that happened long ago in Leighton, Wisconsin, have to do with—"

"Did I mention Leighton?"

For a fraction of a second, Schueller was silent. When he did speak, there was no uncertainty in his voice. "I'm pretty sure you did. Or maybe I saw or heard it on the news without realizing it and it stuck in my mind."

"That word *sure* again," Quinn said.

"Perhaps, like many people, I use it too much," Schueller said.

"I think we all do," Quinn said. "I overheard some detectives talking about the Wisconsin cases and was sure somebody mentioned Waycliffe. He might not even have said that, but something that rhymes with it. Or maybe somebody named Waycliffe. Turns out it had nothing to do with the college. You've satisfied my curiosity, Chancellor."

"Good. That's more or less our business."

"I appreciate you taking the time."

"Those deaths in Wisconsin," Schueller said, "is there some suspicion that they somehow, in some manner, involved Waycliffe College?"

"Why would you ask that?"

"I'm interested in anything that involves our young people. Or our grand tradition. I'm proud to say there aren't many historical black marks on this institution. I'd appreciate it if you'd confirm my belief that no one at Waycliffe was involved."

Quinn considered lying to him, then decided that if Schueller knew more than he was telling, it wouldn't be a bad idea to let him sweat.

"We always try to look at every possibility," he said. "Thanks again for your time, Chancellor."

He hung up before Schueller had a chance to reply.

The chancellor sat silently for a long while, trying to think of something that rhymed with *Waycliffe*.

* * *

The sun sent angled rays of gold through the tall windows of the Albert A. Aal Memorial Library, illuminating the Crime Fiction section of the Literary Department. The rays were also heating the glue of the book spines so that they emitted the certain smell that could be found only in repositories of old books. Ms. Culver loved that smell.

The morning should have been conducive to her happiness, but it wasn't.

"Amazon announced again that it's selling more e-books than conventional paper and text books," Ms. Culver said. She was woefully reading the news online while seated at one of the library's computers, but Penny thought it would be wise not to point that out.

Instead, she said, "Someone told me that at one time people thought the gramophone would destroy the book market. That people would be making celebrities of professional narrators rather than writers. Folks would be no more interested in whoever wrote what was being read than they're interested in screenplay writers today."

"It makes a kind of sense," Ms. Culver said.

"Yet books continued to thrive."

Ms. Culver didn't bother looking over at her. She didn't see how you could make the comparison. "Apples and bicycles."

"Those are still thriving, too," Penny pointed out.

One of the library doors opened and closed. Not time yet for the mail, so it should be a reader. Both Penny and Ms. Culver turned to peer toward the front of the library.

A tall, thin but potbellied man in a wrinkled Armani suit appeared around the corner of nonfiction. Larry Fedderman, showing the effects of the heat outside the comparatively cool and quiet library.

"Your husband," Ms. Culver said in a neutral voice.

Penny brightened. "Feds!"

Then she remembered she was annoyed with him. Despondent over the fact that he kept pursuing a job that might abruptly end his life and their happiness. Pursuing a killer. With effort, she changed her expression to one of grim tolerance.

What Penny felt like doing was dropping by the shooting range and blasting away at the anonymous male figure on the target sheets.

Fedderman grinned as he came toward them.

"Apples and bicycles," Ms. Culver said.

"Nooners are out already," Mimms, the vice cop, said, where he sat with Nancy Weaver in a battered, unlettered white van. He was a veteran cop with tiny dark eyes that were set too close together and almost nonexistent lips.

Another cop, known by Weaver only as Chick, probably because of his blond cowlick that looked like a rooster comb, sat in the seat behind her. Behind Chick, the van was caged and equipped to serve as a temporary holding cell and a paddy wagon.

Chick was wearing earphones that were plugged into a receiver bolted to the bottom of the van's dash board. Also mounted in the van was a small video recorder, the camera of which was concealed in the van's grille and aimed at a moderately busy corner in South Manhattan. There was a second camera on a nearby streetlight, aimed at the same area as the first but at a different angle. Both cameras' feeds were to the digital video recorder inside the van. The corner where the van was parked had a reputation something like Weaver's.

All three cops were in plainclothes, though Weaver's short red skirt, fishnet stockings, tight black T-shirt, and black calf-length boots didn't quite fit the description.

"It's not even eleven-thirty," Weaver said, trying to tuck in the flimsy T-shirt. It was made out of some kind of stretch material that kept working back up from beneath her thick black leather belt.

"That's okay," Mimms said. "We can nail the johns out for early nooners." He pointed out the van's windshield. "Go stand on the corner over there and say something, so Chick knows your wire's working okay. We'll flash the headlights if you're coming through loud and clear."

"And remember," Chick said. "Get them to give you the money. Then you say something to let us know the exchange has been made, and we'll be over there and reading them their rights in no time."

"You won't be in any danger," Mimms assured her for about the twentieth time.

Weaver didn't see why not.

She waited until there was a slowdown in traffic, so a minimum of people would notice her exit the van. Then she opened the door and lowered herself onto the street, trying to do it modestly and almost falling in her five-inch heels. When she found her balance and stood up straight she felt tall in the boots. Hell, she *was* tall.

The embarrassment she'd felt climbing down out of the van left her. She tucked in the T-shirt again, felt it pop up above her belt, and decided to leave it there. Bare midriff would be a turn-on for these jokers.

Walking in the boots was kind of a hoot. She could feel people's eyes on her, and Chick and Mimms had to be watching from inside the van.

She brought her elbows back so her breasts protruded, then gave her ass a lot of swing as she crossed the street and took up position on the corner in front of a closed tavern.

There was a NO PARKING TO CORNER sign there that made it possible for cars to pull to the curb. Weaver stuck out a hip.

"Everything seem to be working okay?" she asked the air.

The van's headlights blinked on and off enthusiastically.

No sooner had that happened than a blue Lexus SUV pulled toward the curb near her. The driver-side tinted window dropped.

At first Weaver just stood there, then she sashayed around the car and peered in through the window. A guy in his fifties leaned toward her. He had a buzz haircut to disguise the fact that he had little hair anyway, and was wearing a jacket and tie. Mr. Executive. Maybe he was only going to ask for directions.

"You got a permit for those dangerous weapons?" he asked, nodding toward her boobs.

Weaver grinned. "Awww, how sweet."

She realized that for some reason she'd laid on a Southern accent. She could imagine Mimms and Chick laughing back in the van.

"You working?" the man in the Lexus asked.

Weaver gave him her biggest smile. "Ah surely am. Ah cain't just give it away."

The man reached for his wallet, all the while unable to take his eyes off her. Mimms and Chick had told her the going rate on this corner was fifty. But what the hell, the guy was driving a Lexus. "Ah don't come cheap."

"A hunert dollars do it?"

"A hunert'll get you somethin' real special," she said.

He held out a single bill. "You gotta earn it, sweetheart. Fifty up front, the rest afterward."

"Ah do thank you for this," Weaver said. She stood up straight, tucking the bill beneath her belt for the benefit of the camera and for Mimms and Chick.

She had the view from the SUV blocked, but she saw the van's doors open and her two fellow cops emerge and start striding across the street. They were both grinning like hyenas, but they had on their deadpan expressions by the time they were flashing their shields and asking the Lexus driver to step out of his vehicle.

Mr. Executive began cursing Weaver as soon as his rights had been read. She ignored him and lit a cigarette. Smoked it in a long ivory-colored holder. For all she knew it was illegal to smoke here, but so what? It went with the outfit.

Mimms looked at her and rolled his eyes. Chick loved it.

They were right about the nooner business. It was brisk until almost two o'clock.

Weaver started having fun well before then.

81

It was approaching midnight, and Jerry Lido was out-and-out drunk.

Sober, he was an expert on the computer. Inebriated past a certain point, he was an Internet genius.

Tonight he'd sacrificed his sobriety in order to solve at least part of the nagging problem Quinn had laid in his lap.

As usual, he wrote everything down so he'd remember it when he recovered from his alcohol-saturated state the morning after. He wrote very carefully with a rollerball pen on a single sheet of lined paper. From time to time he would sit back and marvel at the fullness and clarity of his handwriting. The written English language could be so elegant! Such a beautiful thing in and of itself! It was poetry without poetry—insightful and inspiring.

He wondered just how drunk he was. He knew that a certain part of his mind was functioning very well indeed. Staring at the cursive glory of his thoughts on paper, he stifled a sob of joy. And yet . . .

A quill! He wished he had a quill to do his thoughts true justice.

Might there be a pigeon about?

He stood up unsteadily and stumbled to the window, threw it open and felt a bracing wall of cool air engulf him.

What?

What on earth would I want with a pigeon? And don't they sleep at night?

He staggered away from the open window, toward the sagging sofa. He fell forward on the sofa so that he was lying on his stomach, one arm dragging on the carpet.

Where do pigeons go at night? What do they do?

Gotta find out. Make a note to find out . . .

He drifted off to sleep, comfortable enough to coo.

When he awoke and focused a bleary eye on his clock radio, Lido was pleased to see that it was only 5:15. He could sleep a while longer, if he could contain himself and not jump up and hurry to Q&A.

He punched up his pillow and settled back into the bed's lumpy mattress. Tossed. Turned.

Maybe he should call Quinn. He could be an early riser. Sometimes.

But when Lido heard a pigeon and glanced toward the window, he saw that there was something different about the light.

It seemed to be getting darker outside.

Must be something wrong with the sun.

Then he realized the sun was okay; it usually knew what time it was. Five-fifteen was the right time, only it was not morning but evening.

No wonder Lido's head felt ready to explode. He snatched up the papers from the bedside table. His vision swam and he was having difficulty reading his wobbly handwriting. He did not even attempt to climb out of bed yet, but lay on his back, head propped on his pillow, and reviewed his notes.

The very fact that he had to decipher his own writing jolted his memory of what he'd accomplished last night. He'd managed to hack into and decipher encrypted e-mails that had been sent and received by the second Wisconsin victim, Sherri Klinger, and her teenage boyfriend, a kid named Rory. Sherri was distraught over the death of her dog, Duffy. The e-mail correspondence mentioned where Duffy had been buried by someone and then found and moved. It was very near where the two dead women were found buried. Rory hinted at having seen something horrible (his word) at that site. Lido assumed he was referring to the earliest victim being tortured.

Christ! What effect would that have on a teenage boy?

A hacking expedition into County Sheriff's Department files indicated something that would surely interest Quinn. The panties on the earlier, unidentified victim didn't fit her. Sherri's panties, the later victim's, were her usual label and their remnants suggested they'd been her size.

But the most intriguing thing about the other murder was that dates of several e-mails indicated that the teenage Rory not only knew about it, but knew about it *before* the police. He almost *had to* have witnessed it.

The Waycliffe college faculty e-mails, bearing more recent dates, were also curious. They referred vaguely to a secret agreement (called a compact) that they had no choice but to embrace. It seemed to be about something more important than money and possible jail time, which were pretty damned important. Some critical deadline had passed, and the truth now would bring ruination (Armageddon) to them and to an institution that was never named but was undoubtedly Waycliffe College.

It was also revealed that Waycliffe College's investment account (hacking banks and brokerage firms was easy for Lido) was top-heavy with ownership in Meeding Properties. Lido recalled that Pearl's daughter, Jody, was interested in that company. Something about eminent domain. Amazing how, when you followed the strings, they all led to the same ball of twine.

Quinn would surely now want to take in some of the faculty at Waycliffe, put them under the lights, sweat the truth from them, and find out about this secret they shared and that had come to possess them.

It seemed as if someone at Waycliffe might know something about whether Daniel Danielle was alive and on another murder rampage, or whether he had an imitator. The puzzle pieces that might fit and complete the image were out there, waiting to be picked up and tried. The fruit was ripe and ready to pluck.

Lido smiled. It seemed that the more metaphors a case suggested, the closer they were to a solution.

He was feeling better. What might have been a developing pile-driver of a headache had faded away. He felt . . . *proud*.

For an instant the image of a pigeon flashed in his mind. He had no idea why.

Lido knew he had to get up out of bed. And now.

Things to do.

He stubbed his toe and bumped his head almost simultaneously while getting into the shower. He didn't want to waste time before making himself presentable and plausible at Q&A.

A shave might have put him over the top, but Lido was afraid his hand wasn't steady enough to achieve that without nicking himself. Unshaven, he wore an unstained tie with a blue short-sleeved shirt and an unstructured linen sport coat that was incredibly wrinkled. His feet were unsocked. His theory was that everything went okay with jeans and scuffed brown Sperry Top-Siders.

Quinn and Pearl were still in the office. Fedderman had just come in. Sal and Harold were out in the field, checking probably meaningless inconsistencies in witness statements.

Lido nodded a shaky hello.

"We've got leftover sandwiches and coffee," Quinn said, thinking it was mostly the coffee Lido needed. Either that or he'd already had ten cups.

Lido simply shook his head no, and then pulled a desk chair out so he could sit on it facing the other three.

"Obviously," Pearl said, "you have something to tell us."

Lido sat there side-shadowed by a desk lamp, looking smug.

"Whaddya got?" Quinn asked, getting tired of this game, and increasingly curious. Lido, undoubtedly coming off a drunk, seemed uncharacteristically satisfied with himself.

"First off, I deciphered some of the encrypted e-mails between faculty at Waycliffe and employees of Enders and Coil," Lido said. "It was a clever code, but I figured out that each letter after the second letter—those two were meaningless—was the third letter after the preceding letter that—"

"Never mind all that," Quinn said. "What did you learn?"

"I'm still digging on Waycliffe and the law firm. Mostly I learned about a couple of kids in Leighton, Wisconsin, Rory and Sherri, who used pretty much the same encryption. Sherri was one of the two 1986 murder victims."

Quinn waved a hand. "Whoa. This code thing makes a connection between the dead girl in Wisconsin and Waycliffe College?"

"Gotta be," Lido said. "Rory's full and legal name is Linden Riordon Schueller."

Quinn felt the air go out of him. His mind wrestled with what he'd just heard. "Waycliffe College Chancellor Linden R. Schueller?"

"Unless there's two of them," Lido said.

He pulled a wrinkled sheet of lined paper out of a pocket so he could check it now and then as he spoke. The handwriting on it was incredibly sloppy and almost itself in code.

Lido read what he'd learned so far about Waycliffe College, Enders and Coil, and Meeding Properties. It was a maze of financial payoffs, kickbacks, and insider trading. The development that had contained Mildred Dash's apartment was going to be business and residential space, used to wash dirty money from even more nefarious activities.

Apparently Macy Collins discovered what was going on while an intern at Enders and Coil, and, like Jody, put together what she'd learned at Waycliffe with what was said and done at the law firm.

"She had to be killed," Pearl said, thinking about Jody.

The part about the college, the law firm, and the development company was a tangled mess that bore thinking about. Right now, it was the links between them, and two dead women in Wisconsin, that most interested Quinn and his detectives.

"They've got secrets," Lido said. "That we know for sure. And those Wisconsin murder victims were teenagers."

"We talking child molestation?" Fedderman asked.

"Could be something even worse," Pearl said. "And more recent. It sounds like some of the faculty at Waycliffe know about the latest Daniel Danielle murders. For whatever reason, they chose to look the other way the first time, and then they were sunk. If they dummied up about one murder, they had to do it with the others."

"They were in deeper and deeper with each murder," Quinn said. "Once they let themselves become accessories, the crime they were committing grew more and more serious. They knew—and still know—something they're not saying about those murders."

"Like whether we've got an older, savvier Daniel Danielle on the loose, or if it's some sicko committing copycat crimes."

"Some people out at Waycliffe have been sitting on their asses," Quinn said. "On information we could have been using to stop a killer."

"Accessories to murder," Lido said.

"Friggin' right," Pearl said. "Guilty like those jerks who sit on child molestation information. They look the other way and become part of the crime."

"There might be something besides the murders," Lido said. "Enders and Coil, and Waycliffe College, look like majority shareholders in Meeding Properties Development, the corporate entity that's developing the area Jody's concerned about. Illegal insider trading seems to have gone on, and money was shifted around. Other investors' money might have gone from Meeding stock to Waycliffe, and back to Meeding. Then to something called Meeding W. Investments, a private company that isn't listed on any exchanges. Its principals seem to be Linden R. Schueller, Elaine K. Pratt, and Wayne G. Tangler."

"Uh-oh," Quinn said.

Fedderman said, "Fraud, insider training, stock manipulation. Wow."

"Don't forget murder," Pearl said. She looked at Quinn. He was wearing an expression she'd seen before, and that scared her. "What are you considering?" she asked.

"Leverage."

Lido made an unsuccessful attempt to fold the wrinkled paper he'd been reading from, then gave up and stuffed it back in his pocket.

He then pulled another, folded, sheet of paper out of the pocket and laid it on the desk.

"What's that?" Quinn asked.

"High school yearbook photo of Linden Riordon Schueller."

They all huddled over the photo of a young, dark-haired man with what could only be described as a devilish smile. He did resemble Chancellor Schueller.

"Could be," Quinn said.

"Is," Fedderman said.

Pearl said, "I'm not so sure."

"Look at the ears," Fedderman said. "The ears don't lie."

"Where and how on the Internet did you obtain this information?" Quinn asked Lido.

"You don't want to know."

"You're right. I probably wouldn't understand if I did know, so I choose not to ask."

"Maybe like those folks out at Waycliffe," Pearl said.

"There's a big difference," Fedderman said.

"Oh, I dunno," Lido said. "Fire with fire."

"We're looking for a serial killer," Quinn said. "We need answers, and we know where to find them. If there's a conspiracy of silence at Waycliffe, it's about to end."

"What makes you think they'll talk now?" Pearl asked. "We don't have any substantial evidence that was legally obtained."

"Yet," Quinn said, picking up the phone.

"Be careful," Pearl said. "We might be wrong about this."

"I'm calling to make sure."

* * *

Chancellor Schueller took Quinn's call, and Quinn explained what one of his investigators had learned. He decided, for the time being, to keep the focus on murder.

Schueller listened quietly and didn't once interrupt. Quinn figured the chancellor had to be wondering just how this information was compiled.

"My question," Quinn said, "is why did you lie to us?"

"I didn't lie."

"There are lies of omission."

"I don't believe that's a legal term."

" 'Accessory after the fact' is. So is 'accomplice.' "

"We both know we're not nearly at that point, Detective. I was afraid you'd misinterpret information any of us volunteered. As it turns out, I was right."

"I won't mind putting that to the test."

"You really had no reason to question anyone here, so let's hypothesize that we made an agreement simply as a precaution. In case you suspected anyone at Waycliffe we *knew* was innocent. We were actually facilitating your investigation without you knowing it."

Hoo, boy! Quinn thought. "Who are these people you trust so implicitly?"

"Those whom I and the others know well enough to be sure they aren't torturers and killers."

"You don't think you might misjudge people?"

"Not the faculty I know at Waycliffe. Anyway, the odds of the killer having anything to do with this institution are so long that all of us are aware that by covering for each other, we're not taking any substantial risk. That's *if* we had such a pact, *if* we were covering each other—which we're not doing. I'm simply working with your hypothesis."

"I thought it was yours."

"Let's say it's ours."

Quinn sighed and stood up behind his desk. "Information feeds on itself and creates a larger and more dangerous beast. That's the phase of the investigation we're in now. When the beast grows large enough, I'm going to turn it loose on you. It goes for the throat."

"You certainly make a colorful case for citizen cooperation," Schueller said. "But it's only an ominously phrased excuse for harassment that you regard as admirable conduct. I'll contact our legal counsel and see what they think about illegally obtained information and witness intimidation." He was lying with practiced ease. "That unfettered beast you refer to might leap in any direction."

"That's true," Quinn said. "The only sure thing is that it will draw blood."

"You do have a way with words, Detective."

"If you think I'm good, you should read the *New York Times*."

"Another thinly veiled threat?" Schueller asked.

"Not so thin," Quinn said. "We'll see what you think in another few days."

He hung up.

The office was quiet for about ten seconds. Then Quinn related the other end of his conversation with Chancellor Schueller.

He looked at his detectives. "Schueller was waiting to be contacted. He had his response rehearsed."

Everyone agreed with him.

"He's gonna get in his airplane and fly away," Pearl said.

"Maybe," Quinn said. "He's assessing the situation."

"Think we should call Renz on this?" Fedderman asked.

"We don't want to spook them with a light show,"

Quinn said. "We want to get what we need so we can roll them up tight."

That was when Jody entered the office. She stopped cold, sensing that something was going on.

Quinn looked at Pearl. This was going to be her call.

"I want her with us," Pearl said.

Quinn nodded.

"Now what?" Fedderman asked.

Quinn looked at his watch. Said, "We ride."

82

Quinn's phone conversation with Schueller had convinced Quinn that the chancellor must be the killer. Pieces had to be found and fitted to the picture before the entire image became clear, but Schueller knew too much—and not enough.

Sal and Harold drove to Waycliffe College in the NYPD unmarked, while Quinn, Pearl, Fedderman, and Jody went in Quinn's Lincoln. Jody had strict orders to observe only.

Sal and Harold were assigned to watch Schueller's office, and to contact Quinn if Schueller or anyone else involved in the investigation might come or go.

It would be best if they could nail the suspects at the same time in the same place, preferably the same room, to tie them together in the collective mind of a future jury. Co-conspirators. Accessories after the fact. The entire nest of snakes.

Quinn, thinking like a cop.

They parked the Lincoln well off campus property and told Jody to stay locked in it, then entered the woods. Quinn knew they'd soon be clear of the trees. There would be a wide stretch of ground, then more woods, then Schueller's house, facing away from the main campus. It was on the edge of campus property, but still secluded and a long way from the road where the Lincoln was parked.

Darkness was closing in fast, and cicadas were screaming their grating, shrill mating call. Quinn was glad for the continuous racket; it would help to cover any noise he and the others might make.

As they broke from the first stretch of woods into the wide clearing, Fedderman squeezed Quinn's shoulder and pointed.

There near the trees was Schueller's small twin-engine plane, staked down with cable, and with a blue tarpaulin lashed over the glass of its cockpit.

"Makes you think the feds should be in on this," Pearl said.

"*They'd* think so, anyway," Quinn said. "But it's not so unusual for a college to own an airplane." He had no idea whether that was true, but it sounded logical.

"I see those Harvard jetliners at LaGuardia all the time," Fedderman said.

They were into the woods again, but not for long. Ahead of them in the moonlight was Schueller's home, a decorator's brick and ivy dream. Beyond the low stone wall around the veranda were padded lounge chairs and a round table with an umbrella. Though it was almost completely dark, the house showed no lights.

Fedderman worked his way around front and returned five minutes later.

"Lights on in two of the windows in front," he said. "But there's no sign of anyone moving around in there."

Someone *was* moving through the brush.

Before anyone had a chance to react, Jody approached.

"It was damned creepy alone in that car," she said. She looked at Quinn. "You pissed off because I'm here?"

"What I am is damned—"

Quinn's cell phone vibrated in his pocket. He pulled it out and saw Sal Vitali's number.

As soon as Quinn pressed TALK, he heard Vitali's raspy whisper. "Schueller left his office. He's coming in your direction, driving some kind of customized golf cart. He's alone."

Jody couldn't possibly hear Sal's voice or follow the conversation, but she had her head cocked to the side as if listening. A mosquito droned close to Quinn's ear. He slapped at it and missed.

"You and Harold stay put for a while," he said to Vitali. "See if anyone turns up at his office."

Quinn stuffed his phone back in his pocket. "Schueller's on his way, alone and driving a converted golf cart."

"He drives that thing around all the time," Jody said. "It's got a special parking space near the administration building."

They didn't hear Schueller arrive, but saw light play over the trees up front. Within a few minutes more lights came on inside the house. The den or library on the other side of the French doors was illuminated, making it all the more difficult for anyone inside to see out.

Quinn signaled everyone to move closer.

Suddenly Jody whispered, "*There's Sarah!*"

Everyone stood still and watched a woman walk across the veranda to one of the French doors. She rapped once lightly on the glass, pushed the door open, and entered.

"I thought she might be dead," Jody said in a relieved voice, still somewhat under the woman's spell.

Quinn had other ideas about Sarah Benham.

He saw that the French doors farther down the veranda were dark. He suspected they'd be unlocked, like the doors Sarah Benham had used to gain entrance to the house.

He handed Pearl something in the darkness. It was a

small plastic box with a coiled wire and what felt like an ear plug.

"What the hell is this?" she asked.

"It's a receiver. I was going to plant bugs in the house so we could listen in after Schueller made bail. But things are moving too fast so there's been a change of plans. I'm going in with the microphone end of that thing and see if I can get something useful on tape. So we'll not only have arrest warrants, we'll be able to make them stick."

"With tapes obtained after an illegal entry?" Jody the attorney asked in a dubious tone. She decided not to point out to Quinn that the recordings would be digital, not on tape. Let the technosaur have his old-fashioned terminology.

"The judge who granted the arrest warrants also gave permission to bug the premises," Quinn said. He was pretty sure the permission didn't say exactly when.

"But—" Jody began.

Pearl gave Jody a hard look and made a twisting motion with her hand as if rotating a key between her locked lips. Jody pursed her lips in unconscious imitation of her mother.

Pearl turned her attention to Quinn.

"The three of us are going in," she said, with a glance at Fedderman.

He nodded.

Pearl handed the receiver to Jody. "Jody stays here and listens through the earbud, calls the state cops if the situation goes all to hell."

Jody opened her mouth to protest.

"It's recording when the green light is on," Quinn said, giving her a look that caused her to bite off her words. "Shield the light with your hand so it can't be seen."

"I don't want—"

"Be a grown-up!" Pearl snapped. "This is no time for a smart-mouthed kid to pitch a hissy fit!"

"So when's a good time?"

"When nobody has a gun."

Watching her mother check a nine-millimeter Glock and hold it pressed against her thigh, Jody reluctantly settled back in the bushes and set about learning how to work the recorder.

"An idiot could do this," she said, fitting the plug in her ear. "It's wireless and automatic, so why don't we just leave it hidden here and I'll go with you?"

But the others were gone.

83

The second set of French doors was unlocked. Its hinges squealed slightly as Quinn pushed one of the heavy doors open.

He led the way inside.

The air was cooler and the room was darker than outside. As his eyes adjusted to the dimness, he could make out a sofa and chairs, a credenza or desk on one wall, framed paintings suspended on thin cord or wire that was hooked on crown molding, so the walls needn't bear scars from nails or screws. This would be the living room, more formal than the book-lined den where Schueller and Sarah Benham were meeting.

Quinn could hear their voices but couldn't make out what they were saying. He led the way silently across plush carpet toward tall louvered doors that were standing open, folded against the living room walls. Light spilled from the doorway, and Quinn knew it must lead directly to the den.

He edged closer, holding the tiny microphone before him so it would pick up voices. He knew it was sensitive—he hoped sensitive enough.

Pearl and Fedderman hung back silently as Quinn moved to within inches of the doorway to the den.

". . . had to be done," Sarah Benham was saying. "But what about the others, who served a recreational purpose? Or the appeasement of a hunger?"

"The first one, Collins, was absolutely necessary. She learned too much," the chancellor said. He drew his briar pipe from a pocket of his blazer.

"And she talked in her sleep," Sarah Benham said. "I can attest to that."

"I'll bet." Schueller got a leather tobacco pouch with a drawstring from another pocket and began filling the briar's bowl.

Suddenly Quinn realized where he'd seen such a pouch before. One had been sent to him as a gift. He stared at it, and at Schueller's leather elbow patches.

He felt his stomach churn.

Schueller replaced the soft leather pouch in his pocket and made no move to light the pipe. "You want a glass of wine? Red, like blood."

The bastard! Quinn actually felt a chill and had to fight against yelling, *Got you!* If Jody was picking this up back in the garden, tonight was working out beyond anything he'd expected.

"Why not?" Sarah said.

"I'll have a glass, too," a male voice said. Quinn stole a glance and saw that a tall, lean man with alert gray eyes had entered the room. Tangler, the literature professor.

"There was seldom anyone there to listen to Macy," Sarah said. "Thanks."

The "thanks" must have been for the glass of wine. Quinn had to restrain himself from peeking into the room again and watching Sarah Benham take a sip.

"Um," she said. "Good."

After a pause, she spoke again: "The problem turned out to be that one of our prize students, Macy Collins, was too smart. She figured out what was going on."

"The police should have concluded that at its worst, our alibi about Macy was a simple and harmless lie," the chancellor said. "Or was intended as such at the time."

"Possibly they weren't smart enough to grasp the nuances and go for the feint."

"They were soon on top of it," Tangler, said. "They suspected the lie concealed a larger lie."

"Maybe you can't lie about murder," Sarah Benham said.

"The police would agree with that," Schueller said. "Fortunately all they seem to be investigating now is murder, and not our exercise in extreme capitalism."

"Selling stock that doesn't exist," Tangler said, "is that wrong?"

"To the uninitiated," Sarah said.

"And unlucky."

A moment passed as they all toasted their good fortune.

Schueller's voice: "The irony is that everything might have come tumbling down with those two ancient murders discovered in Wisconsin."

"You think Daniel Danielle committed them?" Tangler asked.

"That's for the police to find out."

"The police are incompetent," Sarah said. "It's good that we found it out sooner rather than later. This wine French?"

"California."

"Amazing. You wouldn't think the soil—"

Sarah was suddenly silent. Quinn felt his heart pick up a beat. Had they been heard? Seen?

Schueller's voice: "Somebody's at the front door. It's Elaine. She has a key, and she'll find her own way back here."

Silence now, while the missing piece to the puzzle made her way through the dimly lit house. Quinn's phone call had worked perfectly, creating enough anxiety to cause concern and prompt a meeting, but not so much that any of the prey would bolt.

The front of the house was to the left of where they stood. Quinn knew it was unlikely that "Elaine"—undoubtedly Elaine Pratt—would pass through the darkened living room. And he was sure that Sarah, Tangler, and Schueller would be waiting, standing holding their wineglasses and looking away from him and his detectives, toward the opposite door into the den.

Quinn moved silently forward and craned his neck.

There were Sarah and Schueller, just as he'd imagined. Only Schueller wasn't holding a wineglass. Both were facing away from Quinn, waiting for the visitor to appear. Tangler was off to the side, his thumbs hitched in his belt, also focused on Elaine's entrance. Quinn could hear Pearl breathing close behind him. She'd moved closer. He didn't know where Fedderman was. Watching their tails, he hoped.

Quinn moved nothing other than his right hand, sliding his police special revolver out of its belt holster.

A figure appeared in the doorway.

Elaine Pratt.

The vipers were all in the pit. Now the conversation could get even more interesting, And incriminating.

The problem was that everyone in the room was facing away from Quinn other than Elaine Pratt. He shifted position only slightly, and she did a double take and stared directly at him.

Quinn drew a deep breath and stepped into the room.

Chancellor Schueller and the others were momentarily frozen by surprise. They were in that slight lurch of time that provided opportunity.

Quinn knew this had to be fast.

It was something everyone knew.

There was a rush toward the door. The flustered academicians bumped into each other. In the confusion, from somewhere near his desk Schueller produced a sawed-off shotgun.

He swung the shotgun around and fired it before it had completed its arc.

Leading the charge into the den, Quinn was aware of Fedderman making a grunting sound behind him.

Quinn had only a few seconds. He took a shot at Rory Schueller, grazing his leg, as Schueller slipped through the French doors out into the night. Behind him there were blood spatters on the threshold, and on the paving bricks beyond the door.

Yelling for Pearl and Fedderman to stay in the house and secure the others, Quinn stepped out onto the veranda and followed the blood of the thing Daniel Danielle had spawned.

The monster wouldn't escape this time.

The tornado moving in the night was Quinn.

84

Beyond the low stone wall bordering the veranda, Quinn stopped and looked quickly in all directions. There was enough moonlight for him to see the large stretch of ground that sloped gradually toward the campus, and off to his left more mown lawn leading toward the woods bordering the county road. The only cover other than the trees was a small storage shed, probably where a riding mower and gardening equipment were kept.

The shed. It was much closer than the trees. Schueller might be in it or behind it.

The way he was running, his wound must be slight. He might even have doubled back and be in or near the house, behind Quinn.

Perspiration like ice water trickled down Quinn's spine.

He was turning back to glance at the house when motion in the corner of his vision caught his eye. His head snapped around in time for him to see Schueller break from the cover of the storage shed and bolt for the woods. He was carrying the shotgun in his right hand.

Schueller was beyond range of Quinn's handgun, and

he knew it. Even if Quinn stood still and fired a perfectly aimed round, it would dig into the ground well behind the fleeing killer.

Quinn began to run. He was like a mountain gaining momentum, slow off the mark, but picking up speed.

Schueller had a good lead, and he was running fast despite his wounded leg. Certainly faster than the older and heavier Quinn.

But could he keep running?

He stopped suddenly and whirled. The shotgun he was carrying interfered with his running rhythm and slowed him down, and he had a better use for it. He fired it toward Quinn, who paid it no attention. The shotgun didn't have nearly the range of his pistol.

Quinn watched Schueller toss the gun aside. He recalled that it was a double-barreled model, good for only two shots without a reload.

A mistake, not waiting for me to come within range. You're rattled.

Schueller settled into a swift pace toward the trees. Quinn took an angle that would cause them to meet a hundred feet or so before the trees, and tried to breathe evenly so he wouldn't get winded so fast. He knew that behind him someone had surely called in the state police, but they wouldn't get here soon enough. All Schueller had to do was reach the county road and flag down a motorist, or make his way to some unsuspecting homeowner who had a car, and that would be the end of the chase.

And maybe the homeowner.

Quinn felt pain creeping into his thighs, and a burning in his lungs. A slight ache began in his right side that he knew would soon become a stitch and double him over.

He swallowed the pain and lengthened his stride.

Gradually, inexorably, he began to gain ground.

Schueller glanced over his shoulder and saw that Quinn

was getting closer. He spun momentarily so he was running backward, grinned, and waved at Quinn. Then he turned back around and picked up speed.

Quinn matched him stride for stride, and then some.

When the trees loomed ahead of them, Schueller was within pistol range, but still too far away for accuracy. He would soon be lost in the cover of the woods.

Every step was agony for Quinn. He cocked the hammer of his revolver, then stopped running and planted his feet. Unable to steady himself, he didn't hold out much hope for what he was about to try. Gripping the gun with both hands, he laid out a pattern of shots in the direction of Schueller just before Schueller was swallowed by the sheltering darkness of the trees. Quickly Quinn reloaded and fired another pattern of shots into the shadows.

His chest heaving, he trudged toward the woods.

In the shadowed silence of the trees, Quinn glanced around and saw what looked like blood on some of the undergrowth. Felt it and found it damp.

Schueller's blood.

But he couldn't determine direction.

Within a few minutes Quinn heard an engine whine and turn over. Then another. He recognized the sound immediately and remembered the small twin-engine plane parked on the edge of the airstrip.

He charged into the undergrowth and dry leaves, toward the sound of the aircraft engines.

Now the engines were roaring. Quinn could imagine the small plane taxiing, bumping across the grass. It wouldn't need much speed or distance to become airborne.

He broke from the trees just in time to see the plane picking up speed down the airstrip, moving away from him. He stopped and stood still, sighted in on the small aircraft, and fired the remaining two shots in his revolver.

They seemed to have no effect on the plane.

And then they did.

Something was preventing the plane from taking off. It slowed, sat still for a moment, and then the left motor roared louder and it turned around near the far end of the grass runway to return the way it had come.

Both engines howled, and the aircraft came at Quinn, earthbound but picking up speed at an alarming rate. He fumbled to reload his revolver as he side-shuffled toward the woods.

He barely made it into the safety of the trees. He was safe.

But Schueller wouldn't or couldn't stop or veer the plane. The aircraft made the edge of the woods, slammed a wing into a tree, spun, and rocked to a halt, facing away from Quinn. One engine was mangled, its three-bladed propeller twisted and stopped. The other engine was still roaring, its propeller whirling. Quinn found himself in a hurricane of littered wind.

He squinted into the gale of the prop wash and saw Schueller half climb, half fall out of the cockpit. The plane's left wing was sheared off at the engine nacelle. Schueller staggered as if drunk, stopped, and stood between Quinn and the whirling propeller, leaning back slightly and letting the prop wash help support him. He was injured from the crash, or one of Quinn's bullets had found him. Blood flowed from a wound in the side of his head, black in the dappled moonlight. More blood ran down his arms, which were hanging limply at his sides, raised slightly and tremulously in the rush of air.

Both men knew that the game was up.

Quinn pointed his revolver at Schueller and with his free hand motioned for him to come forward.

Schueller smiled. Shrugged.

Instead of moving forward, he backpedaled, and the propeller had him.

Quinn heard the engine's roar momentarily change pitch, saw Schueller suddenly become parts rather than a whole human being. Quinn felt wetness on the backs of his hands, on his cheeks and forehead.

He turned around and sat down on the ground, hearing the engine cough and become silent.

He bowed his head in the throbbing stillness of the woods.

He didn't look behind him.

85

Penny had a difficult time conversing with Fedderman, the way he was lying on his stomach, with half his face mashed into his hospital pillow. The nurses, with cunning expertise and Velcro restraining material, had made it impossible for him to turn over.

"Thish p'low mush have a thread count about three," he said.

It struck Penny as odd that Feds would complain about the pillowcase's roughness on his face rather than the holes left by the pellets that had penetrated his right back and shoulder when he'd instinctively turned away from Schueller's shotgun. One of the pellets had almost lodged in his spine, and possibly would have paralyzed him. As it was, he should completely recover but for a peppering of scars on his back.

"I guesh you were right about the rishk factor," Fedderman said.

Penny had been crying intermittently since hearing from Quinn that her husband had been shot. Shock had become relief, then anger, then . . . something else. The crying she did now was for relief if not actual joy.

She leaned close to Fedderman. "You're an idiot, Feds."

He knew that tone of voice. He smiled.

"No," she said, "*I'm* the idiot. You don't marry someone intending to change him. And now you've made me realize how much I'd miss you, and I'm trapped."

"But you don't mind?"

She kissed him. "The question doesn't apply," she said. "I've got you. We have each other. As close to forever as we can make it."

He smiled into his pillow. "Shwell," he said.

"I'm not going to buy a gun," she said.

"Shwell."

Huh?

While Enders and Coil sometimes served as legal consultants to Waycliffe College and its faculty, there wasn't enough evidence to indict the law firm. The Waycliffe conspirators, along with mid-level Meeding Properties executives, received guilty verdicts on counts of fraud, insider trading, and impeding an investigation. They were found not guilty as accessories in all six homicides; Chancellor Schueller, in death, bore all the guilt.

Enders and Coil knew how to sweep up after their clients, and themselves.

Sarah Benham, a decorated former Marine who was in the employ of Meeding Properties to help facilitate the eminent domain case and eviction of Mildred Dash, was also convicted.

Though Sarah was a troubleshooter in Meeding Properties Security, she did in addition insure art, which was the basis for her relationship with Waycliffe College. It had led to her acting on behalf of the co-conspirators in the Meeding Properties–Mildred Dash dilemma, and to sharing in their mutually supportive lie.

While free on bail and awaiting sentencing, she was found in her bathtub with six empty martini glasses nearby and her wrists sliced.

Not only was the defendants' legal team supremely skilled at speaking untruths without lying, they knew how to deflect. They had managed to have the recording made at Chancellor Schueller's house declared illegally obtained and inadmissible in court.

And inaccessible to the public.

Waycliffe College would survive the storm of damaging truth and innuendo, so the respected institution could sever itself from its past.

For everyone involved, nothing was cheap

Jody was terminated at Enders and Coil before Mildred Dash's family filed suit claiming Mildred's death was premature and caused by Meeding Properties and the law firm harassing her in a campaign of terror to try forcing her illegal eviction.

Jody became a friend of the plaintiffs, and in her room above Quinn and Pearl in the brownstone prepared herself to testify for Mildred Dash's family in court.

Quinn and Pearl would sit on the sofa with after-dinner drinks and listen to her, though they couldn't quite understand what she was saying.

"It sounds as if she's talking to herself and answering," Pearl said.

"She is," Quinn told her.

"Is that healthy?"

"Not for anyone who gets crossways with her."

"Should we be worried?"

"No," Quinn said. "She's asking the right questions, and I suspect her answers are good ones."

EPILOGUE

Rio de Janeiro, the present

On Corcovado Mountain, half a mile above Rio, stood a statue of Christ the Redeemer, arms spread wide as if blessing the sprawling city below. Also beneath the beneficent figure of Jesus, Daniel Danielle reclined on a padded lounger on his sun-washed fifth-floor balcony, facing the city's edge and the beach near Grande Tijuca. Daniel preferred these beaches near the *favelas*, where many of Rio's thousands of homeless street kids swarmed.

Street children were a problem in Rio, but not for Daniel Danielle. They were a savvy, hard-bitten lot, but they were also made vulnerable by lack of time on earth. Prey for predators. Hundreds, perhaps thousands, of these children join the disappeared each year. No one seemed to notice. No one seemed to care. No one searched for them. The poor greatly outnumbered the rich in Rio, and there was little to spend on the welfare of wild children.

Daniel placed his espresso on the round tiled table next to his lounger and put on his sunglasses. They had prescription lenses, and he enjoyed sitting in the late morning sun and reading the latest edition of the *New York*

Times. The paper had certainly been interesting lately, but now that was over and he knew the news would be more mundane.

At least for a while.

Occasionally Daniel felt the urge to travel, to return to the U.S. and take up his old hobby. But he knew that truthfully it was safer to indulge in it elsewhere. Perhaps, ideally, where he was.

A warm breeze played over his bare legs. He removed his prescription glasses and put on plain tinted ones, the better to observe the beach. He smiled, as he did most mornings. He knew he had much to smile about. Life was going smoothly. His investments using stolen money had performed admirably. The problems of the common man were for others. What he needed he had in abundance.

He stretched languidly, closed his eyes, and decided on a short nap. Afterward, perhaps he'd make plans for tonight.

Before him, like a bestowal from God, were the children of Rio.

ACKNOWLEDGMENTS

The author very much appreciates the invaluable assistance of Marilyn Davis, Sharon Huston, and Barbara Bradley.

And of course, the savvy Michaela Hamilton.

Don't miss the next exciting thriller
featuring Frank Quinn

TWIST

Coming from Pinnacle in 2013